The Mourning Breaks

The Mourning Breaks

101 "PROACTIVE" TREATMENT STRATEGIES
BREAKING THE TRAUMA BONDS
OF SEXUAL ABUSE

A Creative Companion to Publication
JUST BEFORE DAWN
by
Jan Hindman

Published by:
AlexAndria Associates
911 S.W. 3rd Street
Ontario, Oregon 97914
(503) 889-8938

Printed in the United States of America
Northwest Printing
Boise, Idaho
ISBN # 0-9611034-5-0
Library of Congress # 91-073696

Dedication

to Hannah and her friends

Tom and Tuna, R.W., M.K., Clyde and King; Harriet and Humphrey; Charlie, Ramsey and Marion; Buster and Betty Lou; Dick and, yes, Alex.

— we miss you all!

The Mourning Breaks is about suffering and healing. The trauma, the pain, the "mourning" symbolizes grieving the loss or death of childhood. The treatment, the healing process, the breaking of trauma bonds, symbolizes a path, moving sexual victims toward a new day, and a new beginning.

Contents

Chapter Five — Page 177

Mourning Maps to Recovery

. . . portraying six general treatment goals that allow unique respect for the intricacies of trauma bonding and each child's special needs for recovery.

Chapter Six — Page 221

The Mourning After

. . . portraying innovative, proactive organizational plans for design of the ultimate in successful treatment guarantees — the resolution scrapbook.

Chapter Seven — Page 283

Making the Mourning Break

. . . presenting 101 proactive treatment strategies for breaking the bonds of trauma.

Acknowledgements

A special acknowledgement to the State of Oregon's Children's Services Division and Ginger Peterson. This agency, as well as other Child Protection organizations throughout this nation, often face criticism, controversy and conflict. Even though America would like to pretend that children are important, that they are a priority, those agencies with the impossible task of protecting children are often understaffed, overworked, limited in resources and facing tremendous **scrutiny,** for demands of a perfect performance, with less-than-perfect opportunities and options.

The state of Oregon has taken a courageous step in adapting a general acceptance of these innovative, "proactive" treatment philosophies for victims of sexual abuse. A less sophisticated, more traditional approach would have been so much easier. With the reality of limited budgets, litigation burdens and over-extended sexual victim therapists, a generic, curriculum-based approach was more predictable for another state less inclined as the State of Oregon to strive for perfection.

From children in the arid, cool breezes of the Eastern and Central Oregon Blue Mountains, from children in the warm winds of the Columbia Gorge, from children in the plush green of the Willamette Valley, the beautiful Oregon Coast and the vast forests of Southern Oregon — "Thank You."

Introduction

Introduction

The publication, <u>Just Before Dawn</u>, was a significant success in 1990, providing professionals with new reflections in understanding the trauma suffered by victims of sexual abuse. With these new strategies, the tragedy of tradition was abandoned and Sexual Victim Trauma Assessments paved the way to more personalized, and more effective treatment plans for breaking the bonds of suffering. Finally, sexual victims had the opportunity to be evaluated according to their own special circumstances and trauma intricacies, which resulted in "tailor-made" treatment plans. Rather than considering all victims traumatized the same, (which results in generic, ongoing, directionless treatment), each sexual victim had an opportunity for recovery based on unique, individual needs.

An ideal world would allow each precious child who has been sexually abused to receive a comprehensive Sexual Victim Trauma Assessment. Each child would have a carefully prepared treatment plan emerge from the assessment, with a professional "team" guided by each word and each suggestion. Every victim, male, female, infant, adolescent, short, tall, big, little, rich or poor would receive individual therapy, carefully designed and strategized for complete rehabilitation. Each therapeutic step would be systematically evaluated by staff review. No time factor or cost would restrict efforts. This is not too much to ask in a perfect world that places a high priority on the needs of children.

Unfortunately, the real world does not exist. In practicality, sexual victims receive far less attention than their counterparts — those who offend them. Sexual victims rarely have the benefit of a Sexual Victim Trauma Assessment and some do not have the fortune of any therapeutic intervention. Children who do have the opportunity to receive "treatment" are often placed in therapy that is conducted in a group setting with limited resources and opportunities. Many therapists are forced into less-than-perfect situations and do not always have the luxury of conducting treatment activities that are uniquely tailored to children's treatment plans that were never actually designed in the first place. Children commonly participate in groups where the quality of therapy depends upon time restrictions, available resources, or other factors such as transportation, supplies, or space, rather than being based on the needs of traumatized children.

With these sad realities, therapists are often forced to develop "curriculum-based" therapy plans. Within these unfortunate modalities, each victim will complete the same tasks on the same day, within the same time frame, which does not nurture uniqueness or attend to special needs. Curriculum-based treatment typically pays "lip-service" to the intricacies of trauma and treats each victim the same.

But, the <u>Just Before Dawn</u> research begs for uniqueness, and requires respect for each victim's special needs. But, reality often prohibits the approaches and modalities which are best. So, what can be done in this conflict of reality and "hope?" The "marriage" of the conflict can be found in this creative companion to <u>Just Before Dawn</u>. <u>The Mourning Breaks</u> is a cookbook, generic collection of treatment activities that can be tailored to each victim's individual needs. Rather than providing a "curriculum-based" treatment modality in isolation, which is disrespectful to children's needs, <u>The Mourning Breaks</u> presents treatment activities that can tailor "curriculum" to individual suffering.

Recognizing the reality of limited resources, but also recognizing the importance of each child's individual needs for recovery, <u>The Mourning Breaks</u> attempts to find the balance between rejecting curriculum-based treatment and using available and realistic treatment tools. This book is a practical, cookbook presentation of 101 treatment activities that can be designed to show respect for children's individual needs. The modified Sexual Victim Trauma Assessment allows for a "less than comprehensive" Trauma Assessment to pinpoint unique therapeutic requirements for each victim. The modified version of the Sexual Victim Trauma Assessment allows the most frustrated, "least endowed with resources" therapist, to assess trauma, create an individual treatment plan, and then use general "curriculum-based" treatment activities for all victims. Special, unique tailoring of these treatment activities can demonstrate respect for the intricacies of each unique child, and, at the same time, respect budgets, time constraints and such things as melted crayons and thoroughly dried Play Doh.

Chapters One through Five of The Mourning Breaks provide a simple review and reorganization of the extensive research outlined in Just Before Dawn. Specifically, myths and misconceptions regarding trauma are dispelled in Chapter One and an overview, "easy-to-reference" description of realistic trauma indicators are described in Chapter Two. A synopsis of Trauma Assessment philosophy and organization is described in Chapter Three, as well as a modified, easy-to-administer Sexual Victim Trauma Assessment which mirrors the comprehensive Sexual Victim Trauma Assessment. Chapter Four and Five present the "tools" for conducting therapy that is tailored to each victims' outlined treatment plan.

As the Just Before Dawn research, the Sexual Victim Trauma Assessment, and the individual needs of victims dictate, suffering and recovery from suffering is not consistent or generic. The best methodality for bringing uniqueness to general treatment activities is the resolution scrapbook. Chapter Six of The Mourning Breaks presents several organizational plans and strategies for victim scrapbook preparation allowing each "limited," but creative therapist to provide a final touch of healing to each sexual victim.

Chapter seven is the major content of this practical publication. The "cookbook" presentation of treatment suggestions first provides a preamble of therapeutic "do's and don'ts" for implementing treatment plans. This "preamble" or introduction presents additional methodalities for use of general treatment activities tailored for each victim's needs. Finally, 101 treatment activities are presented, some of which are comprehensive and will take months to complete, while others may be simplistic and basic. These "proactive" treatment activities provide creative therapists with a process and structure to balance the world of reality with limited resources and opportunities, but to also respect victims unique needs. The Mourning, the pain, the suffering, can be alleviated, "broken" with the marriage of these proactive strategies and the real world.

Chapter 1

MOURNING MADNESS — CONFLICT, CONTROVERSY AND CONTEMPLATIONS REGARDING TRAUMA AND TREATMENT

. . . discouraging acceptance of archaic ideations and beliefs concerning victim's pain, and moving toward new reflections in breaking the bonds of trauma.

Chapter 1

MOURNING MADNESS — CONFLICT, CONTROVERSY AND CONTEMPLATIONS REGARDING TRAUMA AND TREATMENT

In order to effectively treat the trauma of sexual abuse, traditional thinking must be contemplated and sometimes abandoned. Dispelling myths and misconceptions regarding sexual abuse trauma and treatment, and moving toward a more competent and research-based approach is necessary. Child sexual abuse has emerged as an epidemic problem for this nation in the recent decade and many erroneous, although perhaps well intentioned, ideas about solutions to the problem have surfaced. At times, these unfounded perspectives have caused conflict and confusion, but most importantly, these ideations contribute to poorly designed treatment plans for desperate victims. Few emerging philosophies that guide many treatment programs have been founded on research and data. What has been accepted in the field and what is rejected as erroneous, is often based on nothing more than clinical impression.

Among professionals, responses and reactions to sexual abuse vary between horror and disbelief. Efforts are often exerted to avoid the problem or discount the reality of sexual abuse. Because of intense emotional reactions to sexual exploitation, ignorance and misinformation often pervade. Since it is often difficult for those individuals who do not molest children to understand reasons or etiology for those who do molest children, it is likely that erroneous ideas emerge as not only acceptable, but as accurate and factual information. Before responsible intervention can occur for victims of sexual abuse, misinformation must be dispelled and discarded. Inappropriate information must be discarded so that adherence to proper treatment protocols can be accepted without interference from old and archaic ideas. And most important, objective research and data should be used to determine which ideations must be dismissed and which should become the tools for healing.

The Mourning Breaks is a "cookbook" approach to treatment. It is practical, skill-based and designed as a work horse for therapists. However, understanding the intricacies of trauma is a prerequisite to effective treatment planning and for implementing these treatment activities. Controversial conflicts and mythologies regarding how children suffer must be resolved in order to successfully manage treatment and break the bonds (mourning) of trauma.

MYTH #1

*Sexual victims are traumatized
in similar ways, therefore, treatment
can be generic and similar*

Delicate Differences

Many myths and misconceptions regarding how children are traumatized through sexual abuse pervade the field of victimology. One of the most "destructive" ideations involves the misunderstanding of the intricacies and differences in how children suffer. If professionals believe that children are traumatized in similar ways, the treatment of sexual victims will repetitious, time-based, and "generic" for all children. Traditional ideas concerning how children are traumatized often results in "curriculum" — subject modules of treatment, for all children, under the same conditions, with the same time frame and the same outcome.

In the vast array of accepted human differences in nearly every other perspective, it seems unusual that a common belief of therapists is that children will be traumatized from sexual exploitations in nice, tidy packages. In other areas, it is clear that some children are more prone to trauma just as some adults seem to be more likely to be energetic or resilient to tragedies that would devastate others. From a physiological perspective, some immune systems of individuals seem to be more resilient to bacteria while other humans seem to perpetuate a lifetime of illness or disease. Psychologically and emotionally, it is clear that some individuals face crisis with tenacity, while others crumble and strain under the burden of what appears to be insignificant impact.

Children, like adults, have different coping skills, different physiological defenses and different psychological perspectives. Even children who are sexually abused by the same offender, at the same developmental time period and with the same sexual activities may respond in very different ways. As an example, it is not uncommon for a rape victim of five years to excel in school and perhaps become a Rhodes Scholar. Another victim who may have been "just fondled" on "just one occasion" may appear to be traumatized for life. Clinical impressions from professionals treating sexually abused children generally perceive victims responding differently. Unfortunately, treatment plans seem to abandon those accurate clinical impressions and children are often placed in generic, time based treatment, which would seem to be a direct conflict with observable knowledge.

MYTH #2

Violence and penetration are significant indicators of trauma

Violence, Penetration and Trauma

Two major mythological perceptions regarding trauma to children can be found in the thoughts involving the factors of violence and the type of sexual activity (i.e., penetration). Extensive research conducted and described in the publication, <u>Just Before Dawn</u>, indicated that professionals, especially therapists, viewed these two factors as significant in predicting which children would seem to be minimally traumatized as compared to those children who would be likely to suffer for many years. Treatment plans from these same professionals tended to intensify treatment for children who were abused through intercourse or victims who were "violently" abused. Unfortunately, those children who were "just fondled" or who were sexually abused with tenderness and love were often abandoned or minimal therapeutic intervention was exerted.

Like most factors concerning ideology surrounding the trauma of sexual abuse, the issues of penetration and violence seem to be borrowed from the legal system that uses these criteria to determine the dangerousness of criminals. Sexual offenders who penetrate children, or sexual offenders who use violence in the commission of their sexual acts are punished more severely and are regarded, by the legal system as more dangerous. The research suggested, however, that these two issues were **never** intended to pertain to how children suffer, although treatment plans reflected an acceptance of that theory.

When those victims who seem to be severely traumatized were categorized, assessed and researched, the element of violence and penetration did **not** correlate with severe trauma. Some victims who were evaluated as having minimal trauma had participated in intercourse or other kinds of penetration, and some had been abused in situations where violence was a pervading theme. How did these individuals escape trauma if two of the most significant factors in determining trauma were present in their sexual abuse experiences?

Additionally, more individuals in the severely traumatized group did not have a high correlation with violence or intercourse in their sexual abuse situations. With both factors of violence and penetration in consideration, no correlation with severe trauma appeared to exist. Also, individuals in the severely traumatized group had other issues they shared in common much more often than they shared a connection with violence and penetration.

It can be speculated that the elements of violence and penetration (especially when pain is experienced) provide sexual victims with knowledge that is important to the recovery process. Psychological identification of the "victim and the offender" is an important issue in determining how some children will be resilient to trauma and why others will seem to be damaged forever. Violence and the imposition of pain seems to provide the victim with information about innocence, about lack of responsibility, and about the clear status of the offender, which is quite different than psychological responses from victims involved in different abusive scenarios.

MYTH #3

Frequency of sexual abuse incidents has a significant correlation with trauma, minimizing or maximizing victims' pain

The Frequency Factor

"I know he's not telling me about all the incidents, he's too traumatized for the sexual abuse to have only occurred once."

The number of incidents, or frequency of abuse, is traditionally believed by professionals, to correlate with minimal and maximum trauma. Those children who are abused over a long period of time or who experience multiple incidents are often evaluated as more traumatized and their treatment plans tend to be more complicated and comprehensive. On the other hand, children who report a single incident are commonly viewed as less traumatized and may be excused from the therapeutic intervention, especially if the sexual behavior, during this single incident, is also evaluated as insignificant.

Research from the Just Before Dawn publication, in comparing minimal trauma to maximum trauma, reveals that the number of incidents does not correlate with trauma, but correlation does exist in trauma and time. The time frame in the child's development where sexual abuse issues remain unresolved and contribute to the "collection" of destructive perceptions, seems to damage the victims' normal sexual development. In other words, five incidents over a five year period could be more traumatic considering a time factor than 50 incidents occurring in a five week period.

Appreciation of children's developing process suggests that trauma is an issue that is "cultivated" in the child's sexual development. At each opportunity and with each new piece of information, perceptions of the sexual abuse change. Each time the child is forced to re-evaluate the sexual contact, new trauma emerges through the continuation of distorted views and confusion. Trauma is a logistical or "time" issue rather than a component of frequency of incidents.

MYTH #4

Age is a determining factor in trauma since younger children are more traumatized than adolescents

Ages and Stages

The factor of "age of onset" in determining maximum from minimal trauma emerges as a paradox for professionals. Quite clearly, therapists developing treatment plans demonstrated through survey, the belief that younger children tend to be more traumatized than those victims who are abused in adolescence. In all likelihood, this information was also obtained or borrowed from the legal system which places a much more severe penalty on sexual offenders who sexually engage three-year-olds, as compared to those individuals who sexually abuse 13-year-olds. Again, it would seem that the more severe the penalty for sexual offenders, the more likely therapists are to relate that same issue to children's suffering.

The connection between the seriousness of sexual offenses from offenders and trauma to children, has never been founded and the connection was never intended to correlate. An additional paradox occurs, however, since treatment specialists associate severe trauma to the abuse of younger children, but rarely provide therapy for those younger victims. Even though a three-year-old child will be viewed as "severely traumatized" because of age, it will be rare that a comprehensive treatment plan will be adapted for this same three-year-old victim.

Beyond a paradox, however, is the sad reality that perhaps three-year-old children are viewed in this society as more valuable than 13-year-old children and perhaps for this reason, laws are established concerning the seriousness of crimes relating to the age of the child. It may be even more unfortunate that therapists may use those guidelines for establishing treatment plans for children suggesting that children's value relates to their age.

MYTH #5

*Young victims will forget and,
therefore treatment is not needed*

Memories, Memories, Memories

A common belief or "hope" for professionals and parents is that the younger victim will forget the sexual abuse and, therefore, treatment is not only unnecessary, but may traumatize children by fixating on memories that would normally fade away. Additionally, the asymptomatic child is often viewed as having even more capacity to forget or disregard the sexual abuse that occurred during the child's early developing years. Adults often cite a lack of symptoms as evidence supporting the contention and belief (or hope) that memory will fade or become blurred as with many other childhood experiences. Both of these ideations (that memory will fade and treatment is harmful) are erroneous and may contribute to unnecessary trauma for victims in the future.

The lack of symptoms for sexually abused children simply attests to the absence of "developed" symptoms. Unfortunately, the lack of symptomology is the foundation for the belief that children will forget about the abuse. A careful understanding of memory will refute these ideations that can cause irresponsible treatment planning for sexual victims.

Only a small portion of memory of past experiences seems to be cognitive or within the "thinking realm." Skin memories, emotional memories, phobic reactions, or distorted cognitions are common foundations in memory for adults who were abused in childhood. Many compulsive behaviors or out of control responses occur for adult victims, and when cognitive memory is absent, victims seem to be more traumatized. For those adult victims who have a cognitive awareness of their past abuse, many obsessive and phobic responses seem more understandable and manageable. In fact, victims who have no cognitive awareness and do not understand their bizarre behaviors, appear to be more traumatized since they feel tremendous shame and anxiety for being "out of control" without a reason or history. The **lack of memory** then, seems to enhance trauma rather than reduce pain.

Unfortunately, when the cognitive memory is erased or encouraged to fade, more traumatization for children may occur in adulthood. Proactive therapeutic interventions, therefore, require a recreation of the sexual abuse in a positive and safe memory so that victims are not plagued with confusing or disconnected memory in adulthood. Even if parents are correct in assuming children "forget" some things in their cognitive memory, many destructive, affective memories remain. The choice is not if the victim will remember, but how, and under what circumstances. A positive, "corrected" memory can be created in the safety of therapy **or** the memory will be left to chance with the same predictability as Russian Roulette.

MYTH #6

Sexual victims always exhibit symptoms and therefore treatment plans can be implemented according to "presenting problems"

Symptoms — Maps or Madness?

An erroneous assumption causing conflict and controversy in not only sexual abuse investigations, but in treatment planning, is the belief that children who are sexually abused will exhibit symptoms that can be used to determine valid from invalid complaints, as well as determine the direction, or "map" for treatment plans. Both of these views are naive and have a tremendous potential to hamper professional interventions.

Clearly, sexual contact between children and adults is prohibited since children do not have the cognitive capabilities for consent. Our society has determined that sex without consent is inappropriate, and since children are unequal to adults, their consent is impossible. Children do not have the developmental capabilities for recognizing the significance of making a sexual decision. Even though children may acquiesce, may cooperate, may even initiate sexual contact with the perpetrator, they cannot consent because they are children. They lack the cognitive development to make sexual decisions.

Logically, then, if children cannot consent to sexual contact due to their developmental limitations, it would also seem reasonable that children may not have the cognitive ability to understand what has happened to them and therefore, they may not be **able** to exhibit symptoms. An asymptomatic child may simply be a child who has no ability to understand the sexually abusive situation. Without understanding the inappropriateness of sexual abuse, trauma may not yet exist. The fact that the child does not demonstrate symptoms may be quite consistent with the child's inability to sexually consent. Unfortunately, professionals often evaluate an asymptomatic child and make critical decisions that do not respect the ongoing process of child development.

Additionally, the lack of symptoms for sexual victims is often viewed as evidence that sexual abuse has not occurred. A victim, as an example, who may openly describe a sexual abuse scenario with competency (demonstrating no symptoms) may simply be a child who does not understand the significance of sodomy or performing cunnilingus on his mother. This evaluation of "no trauma equals no validation" is absurd and insensitive to the developmental limitations of children.

In actuality, the lack of symptomology in children who have been sexually abused may simply mean the lack of "**developed**" trauma. As children become older and become more cognizant of sexual issues, trauma often emerges. The lack of symptoms in a sexual victim may simply mean the child has not yet developed the trauma because trauma occurs through a "cultivation" period as the child becomes more knowledgeable and culpable.

Finally, treatment planning may be disastrous if therapeutic decisions are made through interpreting the lack of symptoms or the presence of symptoms. Therapists developing treatment plans for sexual victims have a tendency to discount the severity of the abuse when a child appears to have minimal symptoms. Children who seem to be asymptomatic or who demonstrate few problems may be released from treatment or may be ignored. This assumption suggests that children are capable of demonstrating symptoms and that the current situation of "no symptoms" will not change in the future. Actually, the asymptomatic child may simply indicate that the child has not yet developed trauma and, therefore, a treatment plan designed to deal with only those symptoms which are currently presented will be drastically lacking in competency.

Effective treatment plans must consider symptomology, but "proactive" treatment plans must also **predict** trauma that is likely to emerge in the future. Based upon research and the study of adult victims, it is clear that treatment plans need to respect the child's potential for developing trauma in the future. Recognizing that the child cannot consent to sexual contact, competent treatment planning will appreciate that the child cannot "consent" to demonstrating trauma.

MYTH #7

Children's feelings about the perpetrator are consistent and provide a good foundation for treatment planning

Perpetrators, Are Perpetrators, Are Perpetrators?

Perhaps one of the most significant misconceptions concerning trauma to sexual victims is the confusion regarding how children feel toward their abusers. Primary to the foundation of confusion regarding the offender/victim relationship is the belief that all victims have negative feelings for sexual offenders and that treatment is less necessary if victims seem to hate their offenders. Recognizing that children don't always have negative feelings for the abuser demonstrates respect for victim's multiplicity of feelings for the offender but this recognition is not always accepted.

Unfortunately, even though some professionals do not believe that children have a single feeling toward those who abuse them, those treatment providers often fail to recognize that victim's feelings are in a constant process of developing. Children's lack of cognitive competence is important to recognize. Even if children have **a** specific attitude toward the perpetrator at age 5, that attitude will likely change as the child moves through normal developmental changes.

Most often, children are sexually abused by someone known to them, usually someone with whom the victim has a relationship. The relationship that exists between the perpetrator and the victim is often positive and may contain many elements of attachment and support. The mythology that suggests sexual victims hate their perpetrators and will benefit from punitive actions toward the perpetrator, can create tremendous difficulty in treatment planning and may further traumatize sexual victims.

When children are sexually abused by a stranger or by someone with whom they do not have a positive relationship, rehabilitation is often easier and less difficult. The "identification" (the psychological identification) of the victim and the perpetrator is an extremely important issue in the rehabilitation of sexual victims. When the identity of the **guilty person** and the **innocent victim** is blurred, rehabilitation is impaired. When children are sexually abused by someone who is clearly seen as the perpetrator (i.e., a stranger or an individual with many liabilities), rehabilitation of the child is enhanced and treatment may be expeditious. When a positive relationship exists between the perpetrator and the victim, the psychological identification of the "guilty and innocent" is unclear and treatment is much more difficult.

An additional problem regarding this issue is the underlying implication given to children that positive feelings toward either the perpetrator or the sexual contact will be viewed by professionals with criticism and repulsion. If these subjective views are held by professionals and children are asked about feeling negative toward the sexual contact or toward the perpetrator, conflict may arise for the child. If neither negative feeling exists, victims may feel as though they will be rejected for not being consistent with the therapist's attitude. The subtle implication may be that the child SHOULD have felt badly about the sexual contact and SHOULD have negative feelings toward the perpetrator. Feelings of shame and rejection may emerge for children who feel they have disappointed adults.

Many therapists also believe that when children voice outrageous expressions of anger toward their offenders, automatic indicators of growth and progress occur. Children who can express overt anger and hatred toward offenders are evaluated as "healing." Unfortunately, this may not be true. Children who are forced to express anger toward the perpetrator may be following the suggestions of the therapist and may be discounting their own personal feelings.

Certainly, some children feel antagonistic and hateful toward the individuals who have sexually abused them in the past. These feelings should not be discarded nor ignored. The general view that all children respond in the same manner, however, can be detrimental to those children who may be ambivalent or confused about their feelings. If victims are forced to feel or respond in a single, generic modality, children's personal needs or feelings seem unimportant. Children may feel the need to "please" the professional, since uniformity of attitudes about the perpetrator exists in the therapeutic arena. Even though the initial reaction may seem to elicit a positive response as children attack bean bags or loudly vocalize their discontent toward offenders, many children may eventually withdraw and withhold more personal expressions of feelings since the pervading ideation in the therapeutic environment is to value consistent, negative feelings toward the perpetrator.

Proper therapy allows children to express a variety of feelings, attitudes, and responses. Objective approaches, encouraging expressions from many perspectives, allow children the best opportunity for recovery. Additionally, appropriate treatment planning respects children's changing developmental status.

In evaluating the maturational process of not only children, but of adults, it is clear that attitudes, feelings, wants, needs and expectations change through time. As an example, A seven year old boy may easily profess acceptance toward the perpetrator because of clear memories that focus on the child's present needs and expectations. A new bike, more privileges or a trip to Disneyland pervade the seven year old's primary thinking process. At thirteen, however, when he realizes that most mommies don't masturbate their sons, this preteen now has a new perspective. Things that were not important at seven, such as trust, peer sexual contact or hormonal body changes, force this young man to re-examine his attitude.

Treatment planning that encourages children to express **any** and/or many feelings toward the perpetrator will be enhanced by recognizing that children not only have a right to change their feelings but that they may need to re-evaluate their feelings toward the perpetrator in the future. Objectivity, encouraging expression and support for individuality and developmental changes experienced by children, are the cornerstones for effective treatment.

MYTH #8

*Trauma is a constant factor and treatment
should be clearly defined and differentiated for
young children, as compared to adolescents*

Little, Middle, Big? or One Size Fits All?

Treatment planning often takes on a well intentioned, but sometimes ill-fated, approach designating curriculum based upon the age of victims. Treatment activities for adolescents are typically separated from therapeutic plans for young children. Likewise and perhaps most in error, treatment activities for children under the age of seven or eight are never included in therapeutic recovery plans for adolescents. This differentiation between the needs of younger children and adolescents may be insensitive for the future development of children and, therefore, is not "proactive."

Sexual abuse trauma is a cultivation process, just as children are in the process of developing. Believing that children's trauma is consistent with symptoms, believing that the presenting problems are only those needed for consideration of healing, are mistakes commonly made in the development of therapeutic programs. However, seven-year-olds will become 17-year-olds. A proactive approach to treatment will evaluate the 7-year-olds symptoms and provide therapy for current crisis and traumatization. The proactive approach, however, will also recognize that impending trauma lurks in the child's future as the child's perceptions change and the child moves toward the 17-year-old developmental phase.

Additionally, the 17-year-old victim needs to become more connected and grounded to the 7-year-old's perspective if the proactive treatment philosophy appreciates the 17-year-old's future. Adolescents who participate in treatment activities that are designed for younger children, but are "framed" with an emphasis on the 17-year-old becoming a 27-year-old parent, are most effective. Proactive therapy moves adolescents backward toward younger children's treatment issues, in teaching how to become better parents and how to break the cycle of sexual abuse. Additionally, therapeutic interventions need to appreciate the 7-year-old's developing process of becoming a 17-year-old so the younger victim will have a more productive and skill-based future.

MYTH #9

*Primary modalities for successful treatment
are introspection, analysis and
expression of feeling*

"And How Do You Feel About That?!!?"

Traditional views of productive therapeutic components generally emerge from the psychoanalytical approach which initiates introspection, analysis and expression of feelings. "How do you feel about that?" is a common treatment methodology used for recovering sexual victims. This treatment approach is an adult modality that is unfortunately, and sometimes without forethought, applied to children. Adults have often expressed psychological and physical relief from tension through the expression of feelings and verbal interchanges with therapists. This modality may be helpful to adults, but several problems occur when these modalities are applied to children.

First, sexual victims have usually been conditioned to verbal secrecy. Treatment plans that concentrate on verbal expressions, declarations and explanations may be accentuating a modality which is difficult and painful for victims of abuse. Although it may be productive for victims to verbally express feelings, sensitive treatment planning should recognize that verbalizing traumatic issues may be particularly uncomfortable and therefore, many other options should be initiated and encouraged.

In addition, children are in the process of developing and changing their thinking patterns. When therapy is based upon a verbal expression of feelings, and the development of conflicting, contemplating and confusing thinking is not appreciated, problems may emerge. Children cannot remain consistent in their impressions because they are constantly changing and re-evaluating as they develop. Therapeutic interventions that are primarily verbal may be lost in the ever changing process of maturation.

Proactive treatment plans are directed toward the future, eradicating problems that do not currently exist, and having the potential to impact the child's development. "Doing," processing, demonstrating, acting, etc., are much more productive methodologies for treatment than traditional introspection and analysis. Certainly, the expression of feelings is an important component, but only if those expressions are captured in a tangible form to remain constant with the child's ever-changing, erratic process of child development. However, verbalization may be a very insignificant treatment modality as compared to those proactive techniques that involve body movement, physical competency, kinesthetic, auditory and visual memory. These treatment modalities create competency, capture the ''corrected'' memory and go far beyond introspection and analysis.

MYTH #10

*Treatment for sexual victims can have
pre-post testing for
guaranteed success indicators*

Now and Then

Just as it may be inappropriate to assess the presenting symptoms of children and design treatment plans accordingly, it may be just as improper to believe that a "time-capsule" exists for children and, therefore, therapeutic plans can be assessed for success and failure with such tools as pre and post testing. This belief suggests that trauma is a constant factor and, therefore, treatment plans and treatment measures can be constant, as well.

A proactive therapeutic approach is appreciative of trauma bonding. Trauma bonding can occur toward a human being such as the individual who abused the child or toward another person who was in a significant relationship with either the victim or the perpetrator. Additionally, trauma bonds can occur toward phobic reactions or cognitive distortions in the future. Breaking trauma bonds requires a proactive treatment approach, one that recognizes that traumatization "moves" and is not constant and that trauma has the potential to develop in the future. Trauma bonding suggests that pain vacillates and is not constant.

If a patient has a multiplicity of feelings toward the perpetrator, (which is common) trauma bonding will occur in direct proportion to the force with which the victim vacillates. "I really, really love my daddy, but I wish he were dead for doing this to me.", is an example of trauma bonding perceptions that creates perpetual motion. Traditional therapy, based on myths and misconceptions, may suggest that the victim will rehabilitate if both feelings are expressed. The conflict cannot be resolved, however, unless the victim is able to participate in a process where both feelings are not only expressed, but both feelings are viewed as productive and helpful toward the future (proactive!).

Additional proactive perceptions in appreciation of trauma bonding indicates that what may appear to be a reasonable resolution when a child is six may, in fact, merge into a trauma bond when the victim is 26. If a non-offending parent, as an example, does not believe a six-year-old child, but the six-year-old doesn't seem to understand the significance of the rejection, trauma appears non-existent. Trauma bonding may occur in the child's future, however, when she becomes more cognizant of denial systems surrounding sexual abuse, of the reality of sexual exploitation from adults to children, and when she experiences her own feelings as a 26-year-old mother.

Trauma bonding requires a tangible representation of treatment in order to break the bonds of trauma (mourning) and to move toward a future with adapted coping skills. Proactive therapy looks toward the child's future and anticipates trauma bonding. Pre and post test treatment, that is based upon presenting symptoms or that suggests the trauma has been revealed in a constant form is not sensitive to the victim's future. Even though presenting problems, as evaluated in a post test appear to indicate therapeutic success, potentially destructive trauma bonds lurk in the child's future.

Chapter 2

MORE ABOUT MOURNING —
HOW CHILDREN SUFFER

. . . presenting a review and easily accessible synopsis of Just Before Dawn research concerning the intricacies of victim's suffering.

Chapter 2

MORE ABOUT MOURNING —
HOW CHILDREN SUFFER

In organizing an effective methodology and approach to treatment, sensitivity for new information regarding traumatization must be generated. The single most important ingredient in establishing effective treatment is in completing a Sexual Victim Trauma Assessment. Trauma to children is not generic and, therefore, treatment must be sensitive to the intricacies of trauma. Research in <u>Just Before Dawn</u> not only dispelled myths regarding erroneous and traditional ideas about trauma, but found significant issues that either reduce or maximize trauma.

More About Mourning —
RESEARCH OVERVIEW REGARDING A
TRADITIONAL VIEW OF TRAUMA CORRELATION

The difficulties in research regarding the trauma suffered by sexual victims is profound. Statistics would suggest that one-quarter of our children will be sexually abused before age eighteen. Sexual abuse occurs at different ages, at different times, and in different families, with different sexual behaviors and different frequencies. Children are not traumatized the same. Sexual abuse of children is an overwhelming problem with intricacies that stagger the mind.

It is not unusual for therapists to see four children sexually abused in the same family, in the same community, by the same offender, with the same sexual behavior. It is also not uncommon for these same four children to manifest completely different symptoms in responses to similar sexual abuse situations. And most importantly, it is not unusual for these same four children to rehabilitate or recover at different rates, with the same therapeutic intervention.

Rather than looking at the sexually abusive scenario, the offender, or the sexual behavior, a sample of sexual victims needed to be categorized, researched, diagnosed, and understood. Although individual therapists may not be in a position to conduct research, understanding data concerning the issues that minimize or maximize trauma is important for therapists to understand. The following list of guidelines, summarizes research relating to the intricacies of how children are traumatized:

In the Future

The <u>Just Before Dawn</u> research demonstrated that there are victims of sexual abuse who endure horrible experiences but who also may have an opportunity to have minimal trauma if treatment planning "predicts" trauma in the future and treats symptoms that do not necessarily exist. Time was a significant research finding. Professionals must look to the future and the issue of "developing" trauma in order for treatment plans to be effective.

Violence

Although violence is traditionally viewed as an issue that creates increased trauma, survey and evaluation of victims suggested that violence does not seem to correlate with damage. Research contained in the publication, <u>Just Before Dawn</u>, demonstrated that there does not appear to be a significant correlation between individuals who were severely traumatized when violence occurred during their abuse. In fact, significant research results suggested violence can act as a rehabilitating factor if violence helps children recognize themselves as victims. When children are smashed, bruised or hurt during the abuse, they seem more able to accept their status as a "victim." However, when sexual abuse involves tenderness, caring and pleasure, the "offender/victim" status is vague.

Penetration

The issue of penetration was also believed to be a significant indicator of trauma. Surveyed professionals overwhelmingly rated the behavior of penetration or intercourse as a predictor of severe trauma. The Just Before Dawn research, however, found no correlation between the behavior of sexual contact and those individuals who seem to be extremely traumatized compared to those individuals who seemed better able to survive their abuse. Severely traumatized victims did **not** experience penetration at a higher rate. It would seem that the behavior of intercourse is significant to professionals and perhaps parents, but it does not seem to correlate with degrees of trauma for victims. The research demonstrated that there are many issues in the sexual abuse scenario that are more traumatizing than the actual sexual behavior committed upon the child.

Age at Onset

The age at which children are abused was also viewed as a primary factor in determining trauma. The perceived "innocence" of children perhaps may be the focus or etiology for this idea. Children are traditionally viewed as being more traumatized if they are offended when they are young, yet these young, asymptomatic children are often ignored for treatment considerations. It is common for parents, caretakers, and even professionals to view a happy four-year-old who has been sodomized at the daycare center, as not in need of treatment because he is asymptomatic, young and apparently not traumatized.

A Matter of Time

The research suggests that it is not the age at which the abuse occurs, but it is the number of years spent in sexual development without assistance from others, that seems to maximize damage. Those victims who proceed through development without assistance, intervention, or rehabilitative efforts seem to be severely traumatized regardless of their age at the time of the abuse. Victims who were "left to drown" regarding their perceptions of the abuse and society's influence on the subject of sex, tend to be more traumatized. Children who have an opportunity to resolve their abuse, to create a **correct** memory, who make a tangible representation of the abuse, will develop in healthy ways without connecting the sexual abuse to normal development. It is the changing, the moving, the re-evaluating of the abuse experience that creates a trauma bond for the future.

Frequency of Abuse

The issue of frequency suggests that ongoing abuse, occurring many times, is more traumatizing than a single incident. New reflections in research indicate this is not true. In fact, a significant number of individuals, who had a single incident, manifested extremely high levels of traumatization. It is important for treatment specialists to understand that it is not the number of incidents, but, the victims time frame that forces the child to struggle without resolution. In order to establish an effective treatment program, the philosophy of treatment must recognize that "time is of the essence" and that the time period spent without assistance or intervention, has a direct correlation to traumatization.

OVERVIEW OF SIGNIFICANT ISSUES CORRELATING WITH TRAUMA

Sexual Responsiveness

A significant number of individuals who were severely traumatized reported sexual responsiveness during the abuse. Sexual stimulation and/or sexual responses included clitoral or penile erection, vaginal lubrication, ejaculation, or any other kind of genital stimulation causing pleasure. The stimulation or pleasure received from the experience seemed to be a tremendous source of pain for the victim at a later time because of guilt associated with pleasure. Bruised and beaten children knew their status as a victim, orgasmic children felt like sexual partners.

Terror

A second factor that correlates with trauma is the issue of terror. The majority of severely traumatized victims participated in terror-building activities which required prolonged periods of abuse and/or ritualistic activities. There seems to be a strong correlation with children who either had to "wait" for their abuse or who were involved in behaviors that seemed to create terrorizing and fearful "anticipation." The amount of time between when the abuse was anticipated by the victim and when the abuse occurred, has a correlation with traumatization. Contrarily, children who are quickly abused, even smashed or slashed do not experience the elements of terror or agonizing anticipation.

Offender Status Confused

The majority of victims who seem to be severely traumatized, emerged in the research with particular consistency regarding their relationship with the offender. When the sexual offender was someone who the child could not identify as the guilty criminal, more traumatization occurred. In other words, traumatization is enhanced if in the victim's mind, the offender has positive characteristics. Confusion about the offender/victim role is extremely important in understanding the depth and potential for trauma.

Victim Status Confused

Likewise, research indicated children who seem to have low self-esteem or who were already struggling with negative attitudes about themselves were more traumatized than their counterparts. Strong, assertive, competent children did not seem to be as acquiescent to sexual abuse and seemed to view themselves as "victims," — indignant and complaining. This issue suggests that the "baggage" children take into the sexual abuse scenario is extremely important in understanding trauma. Competent, confident children can be severely sexually abused and respond with relatively low levels of trauma, in spite of what happens to them during the abuse. Additionally and quite unfortunately, insignificant sexual behaviors committed on children who are already struggling with self-esteem can have tremendous impact.

More Time for Trauma

A high prevalence of children within the research sample of severely traumatized victims were under the age of twelve. The correlation may not be age, however, but what happened in these children's development in the years following the abuse. Although the majority of severely traumatized children were sexually abused under the age of 12, the most significant factor was that these children proceeded through childhood without assistance or rescue. They did not tell or report. They were left to move through development alone. The younger age of children, added to the fact that no reports were made, again makes trauma relate to time spent "developing trauma" since the research also showed that younger children who reported immediately, and who received a positive system response, rehabilitated very quickly. Sadly, their colleagues who kept the secret, spent entire childhoods alone and abandoned.

Coping Skills

The "situation" of the sexual abuse scenario seems to shed light on some important factors in understanding severe as compared to minimal trauma. Children cope with sexual abuse in a variety of ways in order to survive. In childhood, these coping skills, or "footprints," assist the victim in avoiding the reality of pain. It is often these footprints that set lifelong patterns for trauma in the victim's future.

Research suggests that two kinds of coping skills appear to be most common in the severely traumatized group. Children who use amnesia, dissociation, or self-abuse appear to have a high probability of elevated trauma. For this reason, the treatment specialist needs to be particularly sensitive to those parents who hope "she'll forget about it" or "he won't remember if we just leave it alone." Amnesia, or FORGETTING, may contribute to an extremely destructive coping-skill-pattern for the child's future.

"Forgetting" usually means the absence of cognitive memory, but affective memory will likely exist in the form of phobias, unfounded obsessions, out-of-control feelings or other struggles of unknown etiology. In adulthood, "actual" cognitive memory seemed to relieve trauma to some degree, giving the victim some sense of understanding and connection. Those victims with symptoms, but who used the coping skill of amnesia or dissociation seemed more vulnerable and more damaged because they lacked a foundation of memory.

If victims did not use amnesia or dissociation as a footprint, there appeared to be a high correlation with trauma and those children who, in early years, developed a coping skill by "being bad." Matching badness with badness is a common solution adapted by children to help them avoid feeling the reality of their abuse. As an example, if a child is being sexually abused by his mother, but his mother is a church leader, school teacher, and positive community member, the sexual abuse situation is completely incongruent. "Bad feelings" about touching does not match with "Good Mommie." However, if this contemplating boy decides that the badness lies within himself rather than with his mother, a "solution" occurs.

> "What's happening to me is bad. If I am bad, it matches,
> and I can still have a good mommy."

Obviously, this little boy is likely to develop a lifelong pattern of traumatization through self-abusive cycles. This tendency of adapting self-abusive solutions to problems may protect the child from pain but may have disastrous results through his lifetime in the form of alcoholism, failed relationships, self-mutilation or other destructive patterns.

Secrecy

In the <u>Just Before Dawn</u> research, a high correlation existed between sexual abuse secrecy in childhood and severe traumatization. The most severely traumatized children never reported their abuse in childhood. The longer children keep the secret of abuse, the more traumatizing the event will be in adulthood. The damage to children seems to be cultivated by "building upon" the sexually abusive perceptions and making deviancy the foundation of sexual development. Research found that the majority of severely traumatized victims never told anyone about their abuse — sealed to secrecy until adulthood.

System Response

The research also indicated that for the small number of severely traumatized patients who did report their sexual abuse in childhood, they met with such disastrous and severe responses that they would have been less traumatized if a report had never been made. Some responses were so disastrous that post-disclosure seems to be as traumatizing as the sexual abuse itself.

These post disclosure traumatizations can be as insignificant as what may occur in the therapist's waiting room. Other examples of traumatizing post-disclosure responses were such things as harsh or punitive treatment of family members following disclosure. Finally, it is clear that secrecy traumatizes. However, responses from the system to those children who give up the secret can also make significant contributions to the elevated level of suffering.

Trauma Bond

Finally, new research suggests that a high correlation exists with trauma bonding to the perpetrator and increased trauma. TRAUMA BONDING can take place in three different categories. Trauma bonding can occur between the victim and the perpetrator, between the victim and another individual who is significant to both the victim and the offender, or trauma bonding can occur toward things such as phobic reactions and cognitive distortions.

The research suggested that trauma bonding toward the perpetrator seemed to be most traumatic. Victims who remain psychologically attached to their offenders through fear, hope, love, pain, etc., seemed to be much more traumatized. It seems that the lack of resolution, the lack of knowledge or understanding, the continued conflict, kept the abuse ''alive'' and kept the trauma bond in motion.

It is for this reason that the best philosophy of treatment usually suggests a commitment to coordinate victim and sex offender therapists. Using the sexual offender to repair the damage to the victims appears to be an effective treatment modality. Believing that a child who has been sexually abused in an incestuous family will automatically benefit from a divorce or a severed relationship with the offender, may produce treatment plans that are doomed to failure. Not only does the entire family appear to be traumatized by incest, but typically all family members have a contribution to make in breaking the victim's trauma bond.

Minimal Trauma

Before designing an effective treatment program, examination of those factors which cause minimal traumatization should occur. Although it may be controversial to contemplate, it is important to recognize that there are a significant number of individuals who are sexually abused and seem to be minimally traumatized. Some believe that efforts to document minimal or "no trauma," will eventually exonerate offenders. Actually, recognizing minimal trauma does not excuse offenders but provides hope for reducing trauma to more children.

Four issues appear in the research to suggest why some children will escape sexual abuse with minor trauma while others will be traumatized for life. It is also interesting that these four factors seem to be the direct opposite of the factors that predict severe trauma. And, what may be most promising, is that there is a potential for parents, teachers or other caring adults to control these issues and, therefore, reduce children's suffering.

Victim/Offender Identity Clarity

The first issue relating to minimal traumatization indicates that children who survive abuse, perceived themselves as the victim and recognized the criminal aspect of the sexual offender's behavior, while the abuse was occurring. Even though some of these victims were forced to endure brutal, violent, and degrading sexual activities, the cognitive processes were different among these minimally traumatized children that other children who suffered extensively. These victims had the tools to think "escape," or "outrage" during their abuse rather than formulate thoughts of humiliation or embarrassment. The fact that the identification of the victim and the offender was clear to the child at the time of the abuse seemed to allow the victim the best opportunity to take a step toward the second factor, which also appeared at a high correlation rate with those children who were not traumatized.

Immediate Report

The response or the child's action following the sexual abuse also made an important contribution to rehabilitation, according to the research. Obviously, an immediate report will occur if Factor #1, the "offender/victim identification" was clear. Children who believe themselves to be victimized will report immediately and the secrecy, shame, and damage to sexual development will have the **potential** to be eliminated. However, if the next issue "positive system response" does not occur, the potential for recovery will be significantly diminished.

Positive System Response

Reporting the abuse, however, did not seem to be enough. The difference between those children who were more traumatized and those children who were less traumatized, (but also reported immediately), seemed to be correlated to the post-disclosure response from family and professionals. Although immediate reports occurred for many children in the research sample, some seemed to **become** traumatized because the response following the report was not positive and did not reinforce Factor #1, which defined the victim's initial and healthy identity of the "guilty and the innocent." Not only did **children** need to identify themselves as an innocent victim, but the person to whom the child reported needed to continue the same identification process. Children who were met with disbelieving adults, resistive parents, or an unfriendly "system," became traumatized even though the elements for minimal traumatization initially existed with factors #1 and #2.

Respect for the Future

Regrouping of the first three factors for minimal trauma suggests that the identification of the victim must be clear, a report must follow, and the response to the child's report must be positive, reinforcing the child's status as an innocent victim. However, many traumatized children who had all three of these ingredients, became traumatized because the fourth factor did not occur. The fourth issue that seems to have a tremendous contribution to traumatization relates to how the child proceeds through sexual development "remembering" the sexual abuse.

Even though the initial response to sexual abuse may have been positive for children, if victims were not given a tangible, constructive representation of what had happened to them, they proceeded through developing years re-evaluating and reassessing their abuse. Sexual abuse became entangled in their normal sexual development even though the ingredients for total rehabilitation existed in childhood. The memory moved. It changed as the child changed. Distortions, confusion and vagueness became the result of the victim's re-evaluation process. Traumatization was created because of the ever-changing movement of trauma bonding.

Effective treatment must recognize that sexual abuse needs to be captured and represented in something tangible, something that will not change. As an example, performing fellatio on a father creates one perception at age three. That perception will change for the victim at age six, at age twelve, in teenage years, and perhaps on the victim's wedding night. For the ultimate opportunity in this three-year-old child's rehabilitation, performing fellatio on her father must be captured in a tangible representation and must never change throughout her developing years. For this reason the resolution scrapbook will become an important part of effective treatment.

RESEARCH REORGANIZATION — THE SEXUAL VICTIM TRAUMA ASSESSMENT

Research clearly indicates what causes and what tends to alleviate trauma to victims. If the healing process is to occur then, an assessment of the victim, based on the **new** research must take place. The Sexual Victim Trauma Assessment was designed from this new research. It is a formulated method of evaluating each victim within areas that are known to correlate with trauma. It is a process designed to discover the unique nature of the child's pain and it is necessary for treatment to be effective. Just as it would be improper for a physician to attempt to treat cancer without knowing the type of cancer and the location of the affliction, it is improper to treat victims without carefully assessing the nature of their trauma.

Some treatment specialists may be placed in a position where conducting an extensive, formal, Sexual Victim Trauma Assessment may not always be possible. Even in consideration of these limitations, understanding the Sexual Victim Trauma Assessment, adjusting treatment activities with respect to the results of the Trauma Assessment will provide the best treatment possible for sexual victims. Knowledge of the Trauma Assessment then, is a prerequisite to developing effective treatment plans.

The Sexual Victim Trauma Assessment not only becomes a road map toward the victim's future recovery and rehabilitation, but it also provides information concerning the design of treatment. The Sexual Victim Trauma Assessment takes into account the present level of feelings, attitudes, and capabilities for victims, but it also takes a proactive step toward examining what may lie ahead in the child's future. Phobic reactions and cognitive distortions lurk in the child's development. The potential for proceeding to the future and building upon sexual deviancy, as a foundation for sexual development, is tremendous. The Trauma Assessment for children evaluates what has occurred, but, most importantly, it evaluates what may emerge if treatment for these potential problems is not effective.

THE RELATIONSHIP PERSPECTIVE OF THE SEXUAL VICTIM TRAUMA ASSESSMENT

Looking Around

The Relationship Perspective of the Sexual Victim Trauma Assessment is the first of three components comprising the evaluation process. In this portion of the Trauma Assessment, the treatment specialist needs to examine relationships within a triangular approach. At the corners of the triangle are:

The Sexual Victim

The Perpetrator

And Others who are Important to the Sexual Victim and Perpetrator.

Table I

RELATIONSHIP PERSPECTIVE

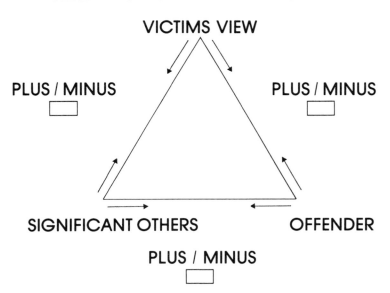

In the Relationship Perspective, the treatment specialist must assign pluses and minuses on varying sides of the triangle in order to determine the child's perceptions in identifying the "victim" and the "perpetrator." As the child, at the top of the triangle, examines relationships, decisions are made regarding such issues as guilt, responsibility, and blame. As indicated in the research, children who clearly see themselves as being innocent and who view the perpetrator as being responsible, have the greatest chance for rehabilitation. Those children who were confused about the victim/offender identity because the perpetrator had positive attributes and the victim had low self-esteem, struggled with recovery.

Offender and Victim

The first step in the relationship triangle assessment involves the right hand side, evaluating the offender/victim relationship. Children who seem to feel positive about the perpetrator will perpetuate a "plus" suggesting it is impossible for the child to give the perpetrator the psychological identification of "the criminal." Positive feelings from the offender to the child make it even more difficult for the child to see the offender as responsible.

Table II

RIGHT SIDE TRIANGLE
VICTIM / OFFENDER
RELATIONSHIP

VICTIM

PLUS / MINUS

OFFENDER

Offender and Others

The bottom of the triangle assesses the victim's perception of how the perpetrator is evaluated by others who are important to the victim. The bottom of the triangle is the connection between the perpetrator and significant others (the non-offending parent, the siblings in the family, the community, the church, extended family members, etc.). As the victim evaluates these connections to the offender, decisions are made regarding how this group of "significant others" examines the perpetrator concerning his/her guilt or innocence. If the victim evaluates the bottom of the triangle with a minus, it would appear to the victim that the group of significant others, collectively, views the perpetrator as responsible. If a plus emerges on the bottom side of the triangle, from the victim's perceptions, the victim believes that others cannot identify the perpetrator as being a criminal and responsible for the crime.

Table III

BOTTOM SIDE RELATIONSHIP TRIANGLE
SIGNIFICANT OTHERS / OFFENDER
RELATIONSHIP

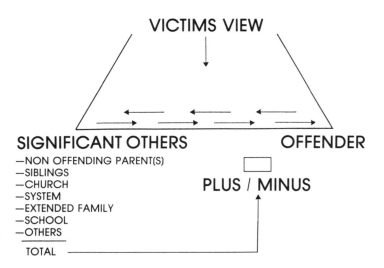

The Victim and Others

Finally, the left side of the triangle evaluates the victim's perceptions of how the "significant others" group, accepts or rejects the victim's status as innocent. Even if the group of significant others views the perpetrator as being guilty, (bottom of triangle), but this group does not support the victim as being an innocent child who was robbed of sexual safety and security, trauma may exist.

Differences between children's self-esteem determines how much the victim **needs** from significant others. Research indicated that strong, assertive children need less support from others. However, if the victim is struggling from low self-esteem, and the support from significant others is marginal, trauma could emerge. On the other hand, if marginal support existed for another victim, but the child had fewer needs because of a positive self image, trauma could be minimized. The most rehabilitating scenario would occur when the victim feels psychologically and emotionally "rescued" by significant others. The victim was identified as an innocent child, the victim of a crime, and therefore rehabilitation has already begun.

Table IV

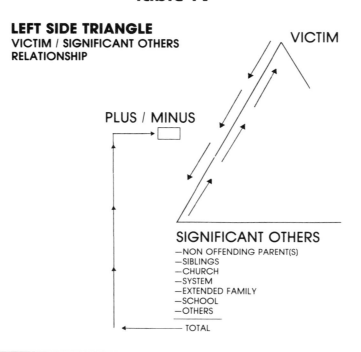

LEFT SIDE TRIANGLE
VICTIM / SIGNIFICANT OTHERS
RELATIONSHIP

VICTIM

PLUS / MINUS

SIGNIFICANT OTHERS
—NON OFFENDING PARENT(S)
—SIBLINGS
—CHURCH
—SYSTEM
—EXTENDED FAMILY
—SCHOOL
—OTHERS

TOTAL

The Victim's View

It is important to realize that in this portion of the Sexual Victim Trauma Assessment, the professional is evaluating the victim's attitude and "scoring" the identity of the victim and the perpetrator, from the victim's view. The treatment specialist's views are not important, rather it is the child's perceptions or how others who are important to the child, perceive the triangulation. Even the most dangerous or disgusting perpetrators can be, in the victim's mind, an important person who may not be able to take on the role of the offender according to the child's perceptions. Additionally, the treatment specialist's view of the child may be extremely positive, but if cultivation of negative feelings toward the victim has occurred from others, these positive messages to the child may be unclear or distorted. In spite of the treatment specialist's view, victims may not see themselves as innocent and free of guilt. It is the child's perceptions that are significant.

QUESTIONS FOR CONSIDERATION IN THE RELATIONSHIP PERSPECTIVE

"What are the victim's perceptions of support or lack of support from the perpetrator?"

"Does the victim have ambivalent feelings about the perpetrator or is it clear that the victim has either negative or positive views?"

"Can the victim separate the sexual abuse behavior from the perpetrator or is the sexual offender's personality, entangled with other issues?"

"What does the victim perceive as support from the non-offending parent(s)?"

"What does the victim know about the perpetrator's support or lack of support in the community?"

"Is there a list of individuals known to the victim who have either positive or negative views toward the perpetrator?"

"Does the victim feel supported by siblings in the family?"

"What is the perpetrator's role with the non-abused children in the family?"

"What can be said about the victim's self-esteem or how much does the victim need from significant others?"

DEVELOPMENTAL PERSPECTIVE

Looking Backwards

The Developmental Perspective of the Sexual Victim Trauma Assessment is the second component comprising the evaluation process. In this portion of the Trauma Assessment, the treatment specialist needs to examine three areas:

The Victim's Stage of Sexual Development at the Time of the Abuse.

The Sexual Environmental Contributors to the Victim's Perceptions.

The Losses of Trauma to the Victim's Sexual Development.

The Developmental Perspective of the Sexual Victim Trauma Assessment addresses perhaps one of the most neglected areas in the treatment of sexual victims. As research indicated, severely traumatized children appear to be those who were sexually abused when they were under the age of twelve. Additionally, research shows that the majority of children who were asymptomatic or who had very little trauma, were also younger children. This paradox indicates that it is not necessarily the age at which the child is abused that is significant. It is what happens to the child's **sexual development** in the process of building upon sexually deviant impressions, that seems to be of primary importance.

As an example, if children are sexually abused in preteens or in adolescence, there is some hope that sexual development has been partially normal, previous to the sexual abuse. A potential for positive sexual development exists. For younger children, when the sexual abuse was discovered and separated from normal sexual development, they seemed to have a much better chance for rehabilitation than their counterparts who were sexually abused and proceeded through sexual development without assistance.

A positive consideration is that smaller children seem to be much more accepting of intervention and may be better treatment candidates than an older child who has spent time cultivating distorted cognitions and phobic reactions. The younger child who reports sexual abuse may have the greatest chance for rehabilitation if the sexual abuse can be separated from normal development. Developmental concerns then, are extremely important to assessing trauma.

Looking Backward

If the Relationship Perspective of the Sexual Victim Trauma Assessment involved the victim "looking around," putting forth effort to identify the roles of the perpetrator and the victim, the developmental perspective of the Sexual Victim Trauma Assessment examines the victim proceeding through development, but constantly "looking backward" toward the abusive scenario "for reference." The backward, constant, examination of the abuse builds sexual development upon those negative memories and ideations.

Generally, children anticipate "moving forward" in sexual development. They begin to wonder about their bodies and about the bodies of their opposite-sex friends. They see kissing on television and they anticipate kissing. Normal sexual development is futuristic, in an ongoing, building process. For the sexual victim, sexual abuse provides a foundation of deviancy which exists as sexual victims travel through sexual development "looking backward" at their own guilt, shame, responsibility, and horror.

One, Two, Three

The Developmental Perspective of the Sexual Victim Trauma Assessment first evaluates how the child has perceived what has happened, according to stages of development at the time of the abuse, and secondly examines what information was available to the victim during this period of contemplation. As an example, extraneous issues such as parent's attitudes toward sex, exposure to pornography or family codes of modesty, will impact the child's sexual perceptions and add to, the chronological consideration of age.

Thirdly, the Developmental Perspective examines what has been lost in normal sexual development due to the fact that children continue to "look backwards" on their perceptions of the sexually abusive scenario from the past. Damage to normal sexual development is a critical issue in the Trauma Assessment. Research indicates that those victims who had access to information separating their abuse from normal sexual development had the best chance for rehabilitation. Research also indicates that those children who continued to build sexual learning upon sexually deviant ideations, had little chance to rehabilitate and establish normal, positive, sexual futures.

The Developmental Perspective of the Sexual Victim Trauma Assessment will consider many questions and answers regarding not only what has occurred in the child's sexual development, but this portion of the Trauma Assessment also examines perceptions of children based on the sexual environment influences, and what will happen in the future, if these negative perceptions are not re-evaluated and interrupted. There seems to be a neglect for child sexual development issues in most treatment programs. The proactive approach redirects negative learning and more positively contributes to future sexual development.

General questions for the Developmental Perspective of the Trauma Assessment should include;

"What were the victim's perceptions at the time of the abuse according to age and the victim's stage of sexual development?"

"What sexual information was available to the child in the household environment?"

"What negative or positive feelings does the victim have about such things as body functions?"

"Are there religious overtones in the family that provide sexual information to the victim?"

"Does the sexual relationship of the parents provide information to the victim that is detrimental or helpful?"

"What are the codes of modesty in the family?"

"Does this victim have positive ideations toward human sexuality?"

"What are the specific negative perceptions that seem to pervade the victim's understanding of sexuality?"

SITUATIONAL PERSPECTIVE

The Situational Perspective of the Sexual Victim Trauma Assessment is the third component comprising the evaluation process. In this portion of the Trauma Assessment, the treatment specialist needs to examine three areas in order to determine the potential for phobic reactions and distorted cognitions.

The Sensory Activation during the Sexual Abuse (Minus Cognitions)

The Sexually Abusive "Scene" (Sensory Activation Plus Cognitions)

The Sexual Victim's Entire World (Environmental Influences)

Table V

SITUATIONAL PERSPECTIVE
HABITS OF THE HURTS
LOOKING FOREWARD

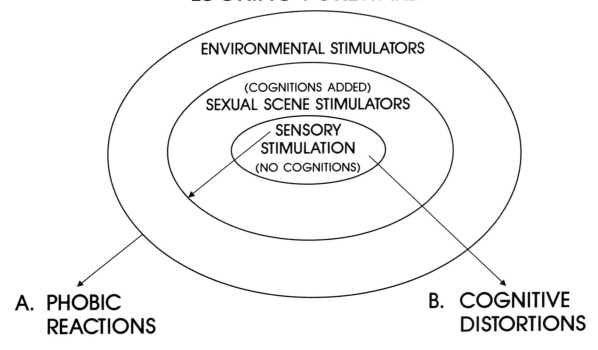

ENVIRONMENTAL STIMULATORS

(COGNITIONS ADDED)
SEXUAL SCENE STIMULATORS

SENSORY
STIMULATION
(NO COGNITIONS)

A. PHOBIC
REACTIONS

B. COGNITIVE
DISTORTIONS

Stumbling Forward

The situational perspective of the Sexual Victim Trauma Assessment considers the sexually abusive "scene" and examines the victim's potential for establishing deadly patterns of coping that will accompany victims into the future. As the Relationship Perspective requires the victim to "look around" and the Developmental Perspective requires the victim to "look backwards," the Situational Perspective of the Sexual Victim Trauma Assessment predicts how the victim will "look toward" the future, establishing distorted cognitions and phobic reactions. These "footprints" for the future will be conceived within the "situation" of the abuse according to how, and under what circumstances the sexual abuse occurred. The Situational Perspective of the Trauma Assessment concentrates on the future, and considers preventing trauma in the child's adulthood.

If the issue of consent and why sexual abuse is a crime is re-examined, the incapability or inequality of children surfaces. Victims are unable to understand the significance of sexual contact when they are children, implying the reason why sexual contact with children is a forbidden taboo. When exploitation occurs in the sexually abusive scenario, the victim must establish coping mechanisms in order to manage since the abuse is incomprehensible to non-sexual children. They must rearrange reality in order to manage the pain.

It is from the sexually abusive "scene" (smells, sounds, tastes, conversations, visual perceptions, etc.), that the victim attempts to order or to rearrange. The details of the efforts to manage the situation of the abusive scenario become the foundation for establishing coping skills or "footprints." Destructive coping skills are developed as victims perceive the sexual abuse as being beyond their capability to understand, so "solutions" are developed. If the victim is terrorized, as an example, beyond endurance, the victim may simply say:

"This is bad. I will not survive unless someone else survives for me." (The child is beginning the process of dissociation.) "This is bad, so I won't be here," allows the child to substitute "someone else" to endure the pain.

As another example, children who use amnesia to cope with their abuse, survived the sexually abusive scene by saying, "This is bad, so I won't remember." This "footprint" provides the foundation for using amnesia to survive. Unfortunately, skin memories or affective responses will occur even though cognitive memory remains a secret. Often, the Situational Perspective of the Trauma Assessment discovers the keys to unlocking the memory. Since the victim could not survive with a cognitive memory, amnesia is used. Unfortunately, the affective responses will remain and be stumbling blocks in the victim's future.

One, Two, Three

The coping skills or the "footprints" can be discovered in the Situational Perspective of the Trauma Assessment. The senses that are activated for the child's computer are the first level of examination in the sexually abusive scene. These sensory activators must be examined without cognitions. They are a pure form of triggers. Secondly, the "scene" of abuse beyond the senses is examined as cognitions are added to sensory perception. Conversations, extraneous items, sexual behaviors, etc., must be evaluated in order to understand the victim's choice of coping. Finally, the entire world of the victim, including post-disclosure issues, or contemplation of disclosure, will provide information regarding how the victim will "pack the baggage" to be carried into the future.

QUESTIONS FOR CONSIDERATION IN THE SITUATIONAL PERSPECTIVE

"What senses were activated during the abuse which will 'trigger' the victim back to the same feelings of pain."

"What conversations occurred in the sexually abusive scene and how did the victim respond to, or feel about, those conversations?"

"What was happening immediately before the sexual abuse took place and what effect did that event have on the victim's understanding of the abuse?"

"What occurred in the victim's perceptions thirty minutes after the sexual abuse took place? How did the victim perceive this event?"

"What methods were used by the perpetrator before, during or after the abuse, to coerce secrecy?"

Caution!

Each sexual victim should participate in an evaluation that will assess the specific nature of trauma. It is strongly recommended that the publication, <u>Just Before Dawn</u>, be an important part of the treatment specialist's training. Understanding the complete and comprehensive Sexual Victim Trauma Assessment is important for successful treatment planning. The chapter's previous overview of the trauma assessment will assist therapists who are in the process of expeditious treatment planning due to time restraints and limited resources. The foundation of knowledge from <u>Just Before Dawn</u>, regarding the intricacies of trauma assessment administration and interpretation is recommended, however, in order to provide therapists with the ability to administer a modified or shorted version of the Sexual Victim Trauma Assessment.

USES FOR THE TRAUMA ASSESSMENT

The Trauma Assessment has many purposes beyond the planning of treatment, however, and could be extremely effective in a variety of ways. Uses for the Sexual Victim Trauma Assessment are varied and expansive.

Effective Treatment

Treatment cannot be as effective unless the treatment specialist understands specific issues relating to each unique victim's trauma. As an example, if a treatment activity regarding the relationship between the victim and his mother is implemented, a generic approach will not be as beneficial to victims with individual struggles. In planning this generic treatment activity concerning resolution of the mother/son relationship, specific attention needs to be given to the information gleaned from the Relationship Perspective of each trauma assessment for each group member. Assuming that all children will feel the same about a mother's rejection is insensitive. Time constraints, budgets, or lack of resources may prohibit the formal writing of a comprehensive Trauma Assessment, or the use of individual therapy to deal with this specific issues. If more general group work is to occur, however, all victims in the group process should have their individual trauma assessments be considered when plans are made to conduct the group activity. The Sexual Victim Trauma Assessment then allows the opportunity to use a generic activitity "tailored" to individual victim's needs.

Reality Check

Many conflicts arise in the treatment of the incestuous family due to the lack of support from the non-offending parent(s). Some parents may wish to deny, blame, rationalize, or abandon children, either because of their own abuse in childhood or because of the residual effects of family dysfunction. Presenting a formal Trauma Assessment to the non-offending parent(s) can be an effective way of pinpointing exactly what trauma has occurred and what trauma will emerge in the future if noncompliance and nonsupport from the non-offending parent continues.

Treatment specialists cannot assume that parents are able to understand the intricacies of trauma. Many professionals are only now learning these new concepts. The Sexual Victim Trauma Assessment becomes an educational tool, assisting parents in understanding not only what has happened to their child, but what will happen in the future if treatment does not occur. Being presented with a comprehensive, formal evaluation can bring a reality to the trauma, which will be very effective and helpful in soliciting support from parents. As long as trauma can be mystified, unclear, rationalized, or misunderstood, non-offending parents will remain in denial. The trauma assessment provides realistic knowledge that can be helpful in gaining support for victims.

For Offenders

The third purpose for the Sexual Victim Trauma Assessment, pertains to sex offender therapy coordination. It is often difficult to align support between those professionals who treat the sex offender and those professionals who treat victims. The victim's treatment specialist may have a clear understanding of the pain the child has suffered in the months following disclosure. The victim's therapist may be providing a therapeutic environment where the child demonstrates symptomology and trauma on a weekly basis. The sex offender therapist, on the other hand, may not have any contact with the child and may have differing views about the offender's progress based on the offender's needs rather than the pain of the child. The sex offender therapist may not understand the intricacies of trauma in the same light as the victim's treatment specialist.

The Sexual Victim Trauma Assessment becomes the cornerstone of coordination and communication between victim and sex offender therapists. It is usually through a lack of understanding that communication deteriorates between these therapists rather than a lack of compassion for sexual victims. If victim treatment specialist can conduct a Sexual Victim Trauma Assessment and present the evaluation to the sex offender therapist, coordination will be enhanced and the victim will have the best opportunity for effective clarification and resolution.

It is also important to note that understanding the trauma that has been inflicted upon a child is extremely effective in sex offenders therapy. What seems to separate those men and women who sexually offend children, from those who do not, may be some understanding about the trauma that is caused through sexual abuse. Presenting the Sexual Victim Trauma Assessment to those therapists who work with offenders may not only enhance coordination of treatment, but it may also provide an extremely important component for offender rehabilitation. Offenders who prepare generic, nonspecific clarifications or apology letters may be missing an important opportunity to change distorted thinking and avoid recidivism in the future. When sex offenders are required to prepare their own Victim Trauma Assessment, that mirrors the professional Trauma Assessment, significant impact may be made in the sexual offender's recovery progress.

Interagency Decision Making

Another effective use of the Sexual Victim Trauma Assessment is a contribution interagency coordination. As an example, in many situations, the prosecutor may be perplexed in attempting to decide the best course of action in child abuse cases. Likewise, defense attorneys may be unclear about what advise would be most appropriate for the client. When the "system" is unclear about how to proceed in a case of sexual abuse, the Sexual Victim Trauma Assessment can outline information that may be helpful in the decision making process.

Some argue that when victims participate in a criminal trial, the process may be more devastating that the sexual abuse itself. Others may suggest that proceeding through legal channels may be the most appropriate response for the sexual offender, but those same professionals may be unclear about how the court requirement may affect the child who must confront the offender in court. When a Sexual Victim Trauma Assessment is conducted and presented to professionals involved in interagency coordination, the decision making process can be enhanced. This is especially true in systems where the needs of the victim are of primary importance.

A case example indicates that the system intervention is at a stalemate due to confusion about how to proceed. A 16-year-old boy is raped at gunpoint in a small, rural community. This young man is devastated by his participation in a "rape kit" at a local hospital. Eventually, the young man is hospitalized for three weeks due to emotional trauma as the result of headlines on the front page of the local newspaper describing lurid details of the sexual assault. The offender confesses to the rape, but refuses to admit to the use of the gun. The offender's attorney alleges that the gun was present, but had nothing to do with an effort of coercion. Obviously, the use of a weapon in a sexual crime creates a much stiffer penalty for the perpetrator. The interagency system is perplexed regarding the decision of whether to proceed through a criminal trial requesting a stiffer penalty against the perpetrator or whether the current guilty pleas should be accepted as the offender has described, which would, in essence, protect the child from testifying, but lessen the penalty for the rapist.

The Sexual Victim Trauma Assessment provided information to those professionals involved in the intervention of this case, and the decision making process was made easier. Law Enforcement officers who may have been particularly interested in stiffer penalties against the offender were assisted in changing their views through exposure to the Trauma Assessment. The prosecutor was better prepared to make charging decisions based on the needs of the adolescent. Without the Trauma Assessment, a potential for making inappropriate decisions existed which may have enhanced the adolescent's trauma.

Expert Witness Testimony

The final purpose for the Sexual Victim Trauma Assessment is to outline court testimony. Many situations may arise where the treatment specialist is required to present either evidence and facts about sexual abuse or an "expert opinion" about the sexual victim. What seems to be difficult in criminal cases of sexual abuse, is the myths and misconceptions regarding the trauma suffered by children. Juries are often perplexed when as an example, they are presented with a child who seems to have strong attachment toward the alleged perpetrator. Jurors may ask, "How could this child wave to the defendant and appear to care for the defendant if sexual abuse has occurred?" Other jury questions may emerge such as, "Why does this child describe horrible sexual contact with such a comfortable demeanor?" These questions will be answered in the Sexual Victim Trauma Assessment. Understanding the intricacies of developmental issues, as an example, can provide the jury with important information to assist in making the best decision possible regarding the questions. The Trauma Assessment can become the outline for the treatment specialist's testimony and can provide extremely important information to the court and to the jury.

In Chapter 3, a shortened form of the Sexual Victim Trauma Assessment is presented so that treatment planning can be effective under a variety of situations. Caution should always be exerted, however, that to short-circuit the Trauma Assessment will greatly impair the possibility that children in a treatment program can fully recover. Initiating treatment, without understanding special considerations for each victim, may be disastrous, although initially, the victim may appear to recover faster, if treatment is immediately expedited. Finally, it should be recognized that the Trauma Assessment is an ongoing process. Treatment specialists need to continually contemplate the victim's functioning in terms of the three Assessment categories and their implications for creating different treatment strategies.

CHAPTER 3

MODIFICATIONS IN
ASSESSING MOURNING

. . . explaining strategies, philosophies, and organization of the modified, easy-to-use Sexual Victim Trauma Assessment.

CHAPTER 3

MODIFICATIONS IN ASSESSING MOURNING

Ideally. . .

An ideal world would allow each precious child who has been sexually abused to receive a comprehensive Sexual Victim Trauma Assessment. Each child would have a carefully prepared treatment plan emerge from the assessment, with a professional "team" guided by each word and each suggestion. Every victim, male, female, infant, adolescent, short, tall, big, little, rich or poor would receive individual therapy, carefully designed and strategized for the child's complete rehabilitation. Each therapeutic step would be systematically evaluated by staff review. No time factor or cost would be a restriction. This is not too much to ask in a perfect world that places a high priority on children.

Unfortunately, it is not a perfect world and victims receive much less attention than their counterparts — those who abuse them. Reality dictates that treatment specialists strive for perfection but use whatever tools available for breaking the bonds of trauma. These are important points to remember for proactive therapists, with perfect intentions, but living in a less-than-perfect world.

A) A formal Trauma Assessment is always the preferred methodology for effective assessment of present and future trauma bonds.

B) The Trauma Assessment process **is** treatment, and can be a very therapeutic endeavor.

C) Treatment should not be generic, but through generic activities, special Trauma Assessment information can guide the treatment "emphasis" to accomplish specific goals for victim's unique needs.

D) Information pertinent to the Trauma Assessment can be gathered indirectly in an ongoing group process.

E) The Trauma Assessment should provide the outline for family resolution and clarification sessions.

F) If a complete trauma assessment is impossible to administer, a modified assessment should be conducted.

G) Specific Trauma Assessments should always be reviewed prior to preparation of each treatment activity.

THE MODIFIED TRAUMA ASSESSMENT

If a complete Trauma Assessment cannot be administered, knowledge and awareness of comprehensive trauma assessment outcomes must be a prerequisite to enhance therapists' ability to complete a shorter form evaluation. The modified version of the Trauma Assessment can only summarize and encapsulate trauma issues. The foundation of the Just Before Dawn research, the philosophy of trauma assessment organization and the significance of trauma bonding can provide a foundation of knowledge that will allow this modified Trauma Assessment form to be productive. Without the foundation of knowledge as outlined in Just Before Dawn, the modified version of the sexual Victim Trauma Assessment will not be effective.

MODIFICATIONS OF MOURNING ASSESSMENT

Modified Sexual Victim Trauma Assessment

The modified Trauma Assessment will concentrate on six areas of organization:

I.   BACKGROUND INFORMATION

II. SYMPTOMOLOGICAL PERSPECTIVE

III. RELATIONSHIP PERSPECTIVE

IV. DEVELOPMENTAL PERSPECTIVE

V.   SITUATIONAL PERSPECTIVE

VI. SUMMARY AND TREATMENT GOALS

An explanation statement at the beginning of each of these sections provides an overview of purpose. Modified Sexual Victim Trauma Assessment forms are included in this chapter to use for the collection of information. The forms themselves can be removed and/or copied, as needed.

BACKGROUND INFORMATION EXPLANATION

The first task in outlining background information is to create a family diagram, beginning in the middle of the family tree with the child's natural parents at the time of birth. Siblings from the natural family should be recorded, as well as siblings' ages. "Family Tree" geneology must be understood in order to conduct the Relationship Perspective of the Sexual Victim Trauma Assessment.

It is also important to obtain information regarding the victim's parents' previous relationships and children. If the victim's parents have been divorced, remarried, and produced children, those events should be recorded.

To further expand on background, a chronological description of the preschool, grade school, and adolescent time period should be prepared. Within each of these time frames, the following issues should be considered:

Geography and Family Mobility
Family Structure
Living Situation
Caretaker
Employment
Academic Issues
Medical Concerns
Mental Health Problems
Religious and Moral Issues
Substance Abuse
Financial Concerns
Self-Esteem Issues
Family Discipline
Significant Events

A background sketch of the child's life during each of the chronological periods should include some information about each of these significant issues. Obviously, some items will not be applicable or some information may not be available. These categories should stimulate discovery. Background information relating to sexual abuse or relating to trauma should be excluded. This section should be a **background information** portrayal, withholding information about sexual victim traumatization. Information should provide a picture, a perspective, a feeling for the child's life during these chronological periods.

Examples of questioning strategies to secure this information are:

"Tell me what it was like in your family before you started the first grade."

"Who lived with you and your family while you were in grade school?"

"Did you live in one house or lots of houses before you went to school?"

"Where did your father work?"

"Was anyone ever sick in your family?"

"What did you learn about church or about God when you were growing up?"

"Tell me about Christmas time when you were five."

"Did anyone in your family drink alcohol?"

"What were your favorite things to do when you were six?"

"During recess time at school, what did you like to do most?"

"Who took care of the pets in your family?"

"When you got into trouble, who took care of you?"

BACKGROUND INFORMATION
Family Constellation

Name of Child _____

Date of Birth _____

Location _____

Parents at Birth _____

Mother's Previous Marriage to		Father's Previous Marriage to	
_____		_____	
Children	Age	Children	Age
_____	_____	_____	_____
_____	_____	_____	_____
_____	_____	_____	_____
_____	_____	_____	_____

Patient's Natural Mother		Patient's Natural Father	
_____		_____	

Children	Age
_____	_____
_____	_____
_____	_____
_____	_____
_____	_____
_____	_____

Divorced

Mother Remarried to		Father Remarried to	
_____		_____	
Children	Age	Children	Age
_____	_____	_____	_____
_____	_____	_____	_____
_____	_____	_____	_____
_____	_____	_____	_____

CHRONOLOGICAL DESIGNATION
(Consider Described Issues)

Preschool _____
_____
_____
_____
_____
_____
_____
_____
_____
_____

Grade School _____
_____
_____
_____
_____
_____
_____
_____
_____
_____
_____

Adolescence _____
_____
_____
_____
_____
_____
_____
_____
_____
_____
_____

SYMPTOMOLOGICAL PERSPECTIVE EXPLANATION

The Symptomological Perspective of the Sexual Victim Trauma Assessment occurs in two separate stages. The first process inquires **about** the symptoms and the second step requires evaluation of the victim's or caretaker's ability to understand or accurately portray symptoms. As an example, inquiring of victims about their ability to get along with others may provide an answer that, on the surface, seems positive. However, a second step consideration may reveal conflicting information.

"Tell me about your very best friend in school."

The answer from a child who has no idea about healthy relationships may initially seem positive. The child may report that "Michael" is her best friend. Taking the second step and inquiring about Carrie's understanding of "a best friend" will provide very different information.

Treatment Specialist: "What do you like best about your friend, Michael?"

Carrie: "Michael's my best friend because he only hits me hard on the bus. The rest of the kids hit me hard all day long."

By taking two steps, important information emerges concerning this child's ability to understand positive and negative relationships. Initially, Michael appears to be a valuable friend. In actuality, Michael is simply "less cruel" to Carrie. This information suggests that Carrie has many dysfunctions in the area of self-defense and treatment needs to change her tendencies toward abusability.

When parents provide information, the second step must also be completed. Some parents wish to discount the symptoms of children, while other naive parents have distorted views, but are nonetheless well-intentioned.

Sonia's mother, as an example, is very motivated to assist her daughter in therapy. She reports during the symptomological portion of the Sexual Victim Trauma Assessment that she is concerned because Sonia does not seem to be able to have positive relationships with men. Sonia is removed from classes where male teachers are present. Sonia's mother is honestly fearful that her daughter will never marry and may eventually live a life of loneliness.

Recording Sonia's mother's concerns accomplishes the first step. However, re-examination of this information at the completion of the Symptomological Perspective provides a different view. Actually, Sonia is not fearful of adult men. She has developed a coping skill of believing that her sense of self-worth is related to her sexuality. If Sonia receives a poor grade in school, she runs her hand up the inner thigh of the male teachers' legs. It is true she is being removed from classes where males teach; however, the reason for this symptom is very different than the mother's perception and certainly requires a different treatment approach.

Treatment specialists will need to evaluate symptomology in three specific areas. Examination must occur concerning how the child functions with people, (RELATIONSHIP DYSFUNCTION), what is the potential for psychological problems (PSYCHOLOGICAL DYSFUNCTION), as well as determining how the child is maintaining on a day-to-day basis (LIVING SKILL DYSFUNCTION). In the assessment of younger victims, it is important to remember that many symptoms must be "predicted." A proactive approach must emerge. The lack of symptomology may simply suggest the lack of **developed** trauma.

The following list suggests samples of questioning strategies that can be used when evaluating symptoms. These examples also demonstrate the importance of informality in inquiries.

"When you were little, what were the jobs you had to do around the house? Did your parents need you or did you need them?" (symbiosis)

"When do you feel the very best and when do you feel just rotten?" (depression)

"When you close your eyes at night, what do you see in your dreams?" (sleep disorders)

"When you get really, really mad, what do you think about doing and what would you like to do?" (anger management)

"Do you ever have time periods that you can't remember what happened?" (dissociation tendencies)

"Do you ever have dreams in the daytime?" (sleep disorder/dissociative disorder)

SYMPTOMOLOGICAL PERSPECTIVE

Step One:
Relationship Dysfunction

Record the child's symptoms within the relationship realm. Consider such things as abnormal attachments, passive-aggressive behavior, superficiality, dishonesty, secrecy, sexual acting out, communication problems, or discipline problems.

_____

_____

_____

_____

_____

_____

_____

_____

_____

_____

_____

_____

_____

_____

_____

_____

_____

_____

_____

_____

_____

_____

_____

_____

_____

_____

_____

_____

_____

_____

SYMPTOMOLOGICAL PERSPECTIVE

Step Two:
Psychological Dysfunction

Record any psychological problems that the child appears to have or mental concerns that have been described or documented. Discuss previous mental health involvement or diagnosis, tendencies toward schizophrenia, delusions, psychosis, mood or anxiety problems, etc. Problems with impulse control, eating disorders, depression, or tendencies toward personality disorders should also be described.

_____

_____

_____

_____

_____

_____

_____

_____

_____

_____

_____

_____

_____

_____

_____

_____

_____

_____

_____

_____

_____

_____

_____

_____

_____

_____

_____

_____

_____

_____

SYMPTOMOLOGICAL PERSPECTIVE

Step Three:
Living Skill Dysfunction

Describe the child's ability to function within the living skill arena. Consider such things as the child's problem solving abilities, struggles in school, criminal behavior, runaway tendencies, substance abuse problems, anger mismanagement, previous residential placements, self-abusive behavior, sleep disorders, or family mobility conflicts.

_____

_____

_____

_____

_____

_____

_____

_____

_____

_____

_____

_____

_____

_____

_____

_____

_____

_____

_____

_____

_____

_____

_____

_____

_____

_____

_____

RELATIONSHIP PERSPECTIVE EXPLANATION

The Relationship Perspective of the modified trauma assessment will be divided into three sections, evaluating three sides of the relationship triangle. Tabulation should occur as the victim's perceptions designate the ''offender/victim'' identity. The **victim's** perceptions rather than reality is the most important issue. ''Reality'' or the treatment specialist's view is insignificant compared to the child's perceptions of the victim/offender identity. (See Chapter 2 for Reference)

RELATIONSHIP PERSPECTIVE

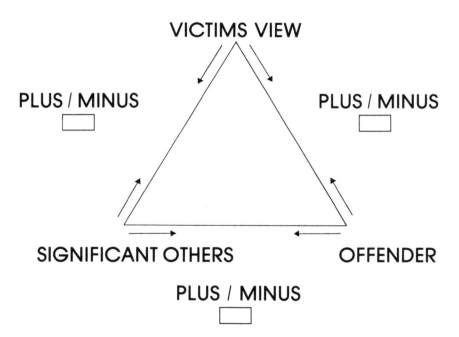

Triangle-Right Side

The first step of the Relationship Perspective is to evaluate how the child views the perpetrator. Questions must first examine how the child evaluates the perpetrator's feelings in reciprocity. Children who feel negative responses emerging from the perpetrator will have an easier task in attaching the identity of the "criminal" to the offender. Children who feel support and love from the perpetrator will have a more difficult time.

A plus on the right hand side of the triangle indicates there are many treatment issues to resolve since the child views the perpetrator in an extremely positive light, and therefore unable to take on the status of "perpetrator." A minus indicates that the treatment plan needs to **reinforce** the already existing criminal status. Even though the triangle may have healthy indicators at the time of the assessment, proactive treatment considers potential trauma and requires a reinforcement of those ideations, since they initially seem to be healthy. Reactive therapy accepts "no current problems" as indicators of success while proactive therapy looks to the future.

Triangle-Bottom

The bottom of the triangle evaluates the offender's identification or lack of identification of "criminal status" from a group of "significant others." This side of the triangle is most precarious, but, on the other hand, holds tremendous possibilities for rehabilitation. If a minus emerges, the victim believes that the collective group of "significant others" view the offender in a criminal light. This understanding must be reinforced in treatment and affirmed in the resolution scrapbook.

If in reality, support of the "significant others" exists, but the child is not aware of the support, treatment modalities must be designed to make the support that currently exists, known to the victim. As an example, the treatment specialist may learn that extended family members are outraged at the perpetrator within the family. The child, however, may be confused about the extended family's attitude and may not be aware of family member's support. Even though the child's perceptions may indicate a plus on the bottom of the triangle, the treatment specialist becomes aware that affirmation of the unknown support is an important treatment goal. Soliciting letters from those extended family members will not only be an easy task, but extremely important.

Triangle-Left

Finally, the left side of the triangle requires an evaluation of the child's sense of self-esteem and the child's view of support from the same group of "significant others." A plus on this side of the triangle indicates that the child believes he/she is viewed by others as an innocent child and truly a "victim." The victim's self-esteem will be very important in this assessment perspective since children who are assertive and competent previous to the abuse, have less need for support from this group of individuals. In some situations, the support may be present, but the child has such low self-esteem and such tremendous need, support from "significant others" cannot possibly provide an adequate reassurance.

RELATIONSHIP PERSPECTIVE

Step One:
Evaluating the Relationship Between the Victim and the Offender

How does the victim describe the offender's attitude toward him/her?

_____
_____
_____
_____
_____
_____
_____
_____
_____
_____

What assets or liabilities does the victim believe the perpetrator would use to describe the child?

_____
_____
_____
_____
_____
_____
_____
_____
_____
_____
_____

What is the victim's view of the perpetrator's attitude toward disclosure?

_____
_____
_____
_____
_____
_____
_____
_____
_____

What assets and liabilities can the victim describe about the perpetrator?

_____
_____
_____
_____
_____
_____
_____
_____
_____
_____
_____

What does the victim wish would happen to the perpetrator?

_____
_____
_____
_____
_____
_____
_____
_____
_____
_____
_____
_____
_____

What changes in the victim's relationship with the perpetrator have occurred since disclosure?

_____
_____
_____
_____
_____
_____
_____
_____
_____
_____
_____
_____
_____

Final Tabulation: Plus _____   Minus _____

RELATIONSHIP PERSPECTIVE

Step Two:
Evaluating Offender's Relationship With Significant Others

Who does the victim list as being in a positive support system with the perpetrator?

_____
_____
_____
_____
_____
_____
_____
_____
_____
_____

Who does the victim describe as identifying the perpetrator as being guilty of a crime?

_____
_____
_____
_____
_____
_____
_____
_____
_____
_____

What is the victim's view of the non-offending parents support or lack of support with the perpetrator?

_____
_____
_____
_____
_____
_____
_____
_____
_____
_____

How does the victim view the system's response to the perpetrator?

_____

_____

_____

_____

_____

_____

_____

What is the victim's view of extended family's support of the perpetrator?

_____

_____

_____

_____

_____

_____

_____

_____

What is the victim's view of the sibling's view of the perpetrator?

_____

_____

_____

_____

_____

_____

_____

What is the victim's view of the community's support or rejection of the perpetrator?

_____

_____

_____

_____

_____

_____

_____

_____

Final Tabulation: Plus _____   Minus _____

RELATIONSHIP PERSPECTIVE

Step Three:
Evaluating Victim's Relationship With Significant Others

What is the assessment of the victim's sense of self-esteem?

_____
_____
_____
_____
_____
_____
_____
_____
_____
_____

How does the victim describe personal assets and liabilities?

_____
_____
_____
_____
_____
_____
_____
_____
_____
_____

What special problems, handicaps, struggles, has the victim had in the past that would affect self-esteem?

_____
_____
_____
_____
_____
_____
_____
_____
_____
_____

What is the victim's perception of the non-offending spouse's support?

_____
_____
_____
_____
_____
_____
_____
_____
_____
_____
_____

What is the victim's perception of the non-abused sibling's support?

_____
_____
_____
_____
_____
_____
_____
_____
_____
_____
_____

What is the victim's view of the community's support?

_____
_____
_____
_____
_____
_____
_____
_____
_____
_____
_____

What is the victim's view of the system (legal, child protection, mental health, etc.)

_____
_____
_____
_____
_____
_____
_____
_____
_____
_____
_____

What is the victim's view of extended family?

_____
_____
_____
_____
_____
_____
_____
_____
_____
_____
_____
_____
_____

What is the victim's view of miscellaneous group (school, friends, church, etc.)?

_____
_____
_____
_____
_____
_____
_____
_____
_____
_____
_____
_____

Final Tabulation: Plus _____   Minus _____

DEVELOPMENTAL PERSPECTIVE EXPLANATION

The Developmental Perspective of the Sexual Victim Trauma Assessment evaluates three components, with the first concerning the victim's chronological development at the time of the sexual abuse. How victims perceive, evaluate, or understand the sexual abuse depends on the victim's stage of development at the onset of abuse. The stages of sexual development outlined in <u>Just Before Dawn</u> can be described in the time frames relating to:

Unaware (preschool)

Unfortunate (early puberty development)

Uncomfortable (adolescent victim)

These stages of development need to be understood in order to understand the child's perceptions. Memories, beliefs, ideations and perceptions from this perspective will traumatize or rehabilitate. These perceptions provide the foundation for many treatment goals.

Secondly, the treatment specialist needs to evaluate sexual information that was available to the child at the time of the abuse in order to effectively plan treatment. No conclusions can be made based on the developmental stage of the victim, in isolation. The second step of the Developmental Perspective examines environmental influences which, in turn, influence the victim's perspective and which often need readjustment in a proactive treatment plan.

Finally, it is important to evaluate what has been lost in normal sexual development for the victim. Understanding how the child views such things as body functions, body image, or "sexual play" as compared to sexual abuse, will be important to use for outlining the treatment plan. It is important to recognize that "normal" sexual development tends to be rather negative. Treatment planning therefore should be proactive! As an example, it may be normal for children to be uncomfortable with body functions. However, a sexually abused child may expand this normal problem to extremes with enuresis or encopresis because of sexual abuse. Treatment should not take children simply back to a normal stage of development where children are uncomfortable with body functions. With a proactive approach children need to discover positive feelings about normal body functions.

DEVELOPMENTAL PERSPECTIVE

Step One:
Stage of Sexual Development

Describe developmental stages pertaining to the time of abuse including liabilities and limitations within each category of sexual development. Describe what children typically perceive during the stage of development corresponding with this specific victim at the onset of abuse. If children have been abused during different sexual stages, describe each of those stages with corresponding developmental perceptions.

_____

_____

_____

_____

_____

_____

_____

_____

_____

_____

_____

_____

_____

_____

_____

_____

_____

_____

_____

_____

_____

_____

_____

_____

_____

_____

_____

_____

DEVELOPMENTAL PERSPECTIVE

Step Two:
Examine Environmental Influence

Describe sexual environmental influences within the child's environment. Discuss such issues as: morals, values, religious views of sexuality, available sexual information, sexual relationship of parents, male/female sexual role training, formal sexual education in school, sexual activities with peers, body development, and perceptions of sexual body image.

_____

_____

_____

_____

_____

_____

_____

_____

_____

_____

_____

_____

_____

_____

_____

_____

_____

_____

_____

_____

_____

_____

_____

_____

DEVELOPMENTAL PERSPECTIVE

Step Three:
Losses to Normal Development

Carefully consider damage to normal sexual development that seems to have occurred or will occur in the future. Answer the following questions.

Does the victim appear to have, or does it appear that in the future the child will have, a sexual "appetite?"

_____
_____
_____
_____
_____
_____
_____
_____
_____

Does the body image of the victim appear to have a destructive quality or does the victim's body image appear to be reasonably positive?

_____
_____
_____
_____
_____
_____
_____
_____
_____

What are the attitudes or trauma that emerge concerning the issue of body functions?

_____
_____
_____
_____
_____
_____
_____
_____
_____

What does the victim seem to have learned about male/female sexual roles?

_____
_____
_____
_____
_____
_____
_____

What sexual phobias appear to be developing or appear to have the potential to develop?

_____
_____
_____
_____
_____
_____
_____

What is the victim's general attitude about normal arousal (as compared to the sexual abuse)?

_____
_____
_____
_____
_____
_____
_____

What problems seem to appear for the victim in the area of sexual identity or sexual preference dysfunction?

_____
_____
_____
_____
_____
_____
_____

SITUATIONAL PERSPECTIVE EXPLANATION

The Situational Perspective of the Sexual Victim Trauma Assessment evaluates the environment where the sexual abuse occurred in order to determine the child's potential for developing phobic reactions and cognitive distortions. Issues from sensory input in the sexual abuse scene and from subsequent environmental influences provide information to the victim's "computer." Those pieces of information allow the child to develop lifelong patterns of coping. For review, this section of the Trauma Assessment evaluates three levels:

1) Sensory Activation (minus cognitions)
2) The Sexually Abusive Scene (sensory activation plus cognitions)
3) The Victim's General Living Situation or Environment (distorted cognitions)

Before examining the sensory and cognitive input that creates phobias or distorted thinking processes, evaluation must be made concerning what sexual contact occurred. Desensitization must be managed in the treatment plan and accurate information about sexual abuse behaviors must be obtained in this portion of the Trauma Assessment.

The Modified Data Collection Form allows consideration of a "checklist" of sexual behaviors that could have occurred during the sexual abuse. Treatment specialists should record all sexual behaviors. It is important to desensitize children by inquiring about a wide variety of possible sexual activities. Processing through a checklist should only occur if sexual abuse has already been validated. The "checklist process" would be an inappropriate way to conduct an investigation into allegations of sexual abuse.

Secondly, sensory activation that occurred during the abuse must be discovered. It will be these triggers (without a cognitive connection) that will be the basis for many phobic reactions in the child's future. Often, misbehavior in group therapy, in the home, or other areas is related to sensory activation that may have been discounted or misunderstood. Finding these triggers or potential phobias will be a very important part of treatment planning.

Next, examination of the sexually abusive scene needs to occur. **HOW** the sexual abuse took place has a tremendous ability to impact children's trauma. Rather than concentrating on the sexual behaviors that occurred, the "scene" of sexual abuse needs to be revisited. Many children, as an example, perceive connections between things that are erroneous but those things will later influence the victim. Without understanding the child's perceptions of the scene, treatment may be directionless and less effective.

Evaluation of the child's entire environment needs to occur in the final step of the situational perspective in order to determine the coping skills that are likely to develop. Issues such as domestic violence, alcoholism, or arbitrary discipline in the family will effect the child's traumatization. Looking at the child from a "holistic" perspective will be very important in understanding the victim's development or future development of destructive coping skills.

Predictions or evaluation of distorted cognitions/coping skills completes the last phase of the trauma assessment. Direct reference to <u>Just Before Dawn</u>, will be very helpful. As an example, if the child appears to be adapting the coping skill of amnesia, tremendous effort must be exerted to capture the memory in a very structured way so that this coping skill can be discouraged. If another victim seems to be adapting a "helpless" coping skill, the treatment plan must encourage a strong sense of empowerment for this child, perhaps different from another child who may be adapting a coping skill of becoming abusive to others.

SITUATIONAL PERSPECTIVE

Step One:
Checklist of Sexual Behaviors

Examine and document all sexual behaviors that occurred during the abusive scenario. Use this space to describe a "typical" abusive situation for this specific child.

Fondling

__Vulva   __Buttocks   __Breast   Other_____

__Legs   __Penis   __Testicles   Other _____

Penetration (Digital/Penile/Object)

__Anal   __Vaginal

Oral Contact

__Fellatio   __Cunnilingus   __Anal   __Other

Additional

__Ejaculation   __Photography   __Sexual Apparatus   __Fetishism

__Orgasmic Response   __Bestiality   __Pornography   __Masturbation

__Cross Dressing   __Group Sex   __Voyeurism   __ Vulvar Coitus

__Exhibitionism   __Weapons   __Bondage/Restraints

__Obscene Phone Calls   __Rituals   __Urination/Defecation

Describe A "Typical" Abuse Situation

_____
_____
_____
_____
_____
_____
_____
_____
_____
_____
_____
_____
_____
_____
_____
_____
_____
_____

SITUATIONAL PERSPECTIVE

Step Two:
Describe Sensory Activation That Occurred During The Abuse.

Tactile Responses

_____
_____
_____
_____
_____
_____

Olfactory Responses

_____
_____
_____
_____
_____
_____

Visual Perceptions

_____
_____
_____
_____
_____
_____

Audio Perceptions

_____
_____
_____
_____
_____
_____

Taste Perceptions

_____
_____
_____
_____
_____
_____

SITUATIONAL PERSPECTIVE

Step Three:
Describe The Sexually Abusive "Scene" For Discovery Of Phobias Or Distorted Cognitions.

What was the typical environment for the sexual abuse, and what contributions were made to the victim's perceptions?

_____
_____
_____
_____
_____
_____
_____
_____
_____
_____
_____

What seemed to occur 30 minutes before and 30 minutes after the abuse, and what effect do these events have on the victim's perceptions?

_____
_____
_____
_____
_____
_____
_____
_____
_____
_____
_____

What conversations took place during the abusive scenario, and what is the effect of those conversations?

_____
_____
_____
_____
_____
_____
_____
_____
_____
_____
_____

What is the position of locality of others during the abuse, and what effect do the periphery individuals have on the victim's perceptions?

_____
_____
_____
_____
_____
_____
_____
_____
_____
_____
_____
_____
_____
_____
_____
_____
_____
_____

What occurred in the abusive scenario concerning the issue of coercion? Consider such issues as violence, terror, force, as well as bribery, seduction, or the victim's cooperation?

_____
_____
_____
_____
_____
_____
_____
_____
_____
_____
_____
_____
_____
_____
_____
_____
_____

What is known about the victim's sexual responsiveness or sexual arousal, and what impact does this issue seem to have?

_____
_____
_____
_____
_____
_____
_____
_____
_____
_____
_____
_____
_____
_____
_____
_____
_____
_____
_____
_____
_____

What extraneous issues or items in the sexually abusive scene seem to have the potential for phobic reactions? (Also, use this section to list phobic reactions that will occur from a sensory activation standpoint as indicated from the previous sections).

_____
_____
_____
_____
_____
_____
_____
_____
_____
_____
_____
_____
_____
_____
_____
_____
_____
_____
_____

SITUATIONAL PERSPECTIVE

Step Four:
Evaluate The "Holistic" Environment Of The Victim For Discovery Of Distorted Cognitions Or Future Coping Skills. Examine The World Of The Family And The Effect Those Perceptions Have On The Child.

How does the family constellation, in consideration of adoption, divorce, birth of children, birth order, etc., impact the victim's trauma?

_____
_____
_____
_____
_____
_____
_____
_____
_____
_____
_____

What contributions do family finances or vocational issues make to the victim's trauma?

_____
_____
_____
_____
_____
_____
_____
_____
_____
_____
_____

What issues concerning family health, impact the elements of trauma for the victim?

_____
_____
_____
_____
_____
_____
_____
_____
_____
_____
_____

What morality issues within the entire family environment provide messages to the victim and create trauma?

_____
_____
_____
_____
_____
_____
_____
_____

How does the family situation in the community influence trauma?

_____
_____
_____
_____
_____
_____
_____
_____

What influence does family discipline have on trauma?

_____
_____
_____
_____
_____
_____
_____
_____

What post-disclosure issues have effected the victim's traumatization?

_____
_____
_____
_____
_____
_____
_____
_____

Diagnose the victim's development of coping skills. Consider such things as outlined in <u>Just Before Dawn</u>, such as amnesia, dissociation, self-abuse, abusive cycles, guilt, responsibility avoidance, secrecy, obsessive behavior, aggressive behavior, helplessness, symbiosis, perfection, failure, etc. If coping skills do not appear to have been manifested at this time, predict what may occur.

_____
_____
_____
_____
_____
_____
_____
_____
_____
_____
_____
_____
_____
_____
_____
_____
_____
_____
_____
_____
_____
_____
_____
_____
_____
_____
_____
_____
_____
_____
_____
_____
_____
_____
_____

SUMMARY AND TREATMENT GOALS
RELATIONSHIP PERSPECTIVE GENERAL GOALS "Identification of the Offender and Victim"

_____
_____
_____
_____
_____
_____
_____
_____
_____
_____
_____
_____
_____
_____
_____
_____
_____
_____
_____

DEVELOPMENTAL PERSPECTIVE GENERAL GOALS "Damage to Normal Sexual Development"

_____
_____
_____
_____
_____
_____
_____
_____
_____
_____
_____
_____
_____
_____
_____
_____
_____
_____
_____

SITUATIONAL PERSPECTIVE GENERAL GOALS "Adaptation of Phobic Responses and Destructive Coping Skills (Distorted Cognitions)"

_____
_____
_____
_____
_____
_____
_____
_____
_____
_____
_____
_____
_____
_____
_____
_____
_____

Additional comments:

_____
_____
_____
_____
_____
_____
_____
_____
_____
_____
_____
_____
_____
_____
_____
_____

MODIFIED
DATA COLLECTION FORM

for

SEXUAL VICTIM
TRAUMA ASSESSMENT

May be reprinted.

BACKGROUND INFORMATION
Family Constellation

Name of Child _____

Date of Birth _____

Location _____

Parents at Birth _____

Mother's Previous Marriage to

_____

Children	Age
_____	_____
_____	_____
_____	_____
_____	_____

Father's Previous Marriage to

_____

Children	Age
_____	_____
_____	_____
_____	_____
_____	_____

Patient's Natural Mother

_____

Patient's Natural Father

_____

Children	Age
_____	_____
_____	_____
_____	_____
_____	_____
_____	_____
_____	_____

Divorced

Mother Remarried to

_____

Children	Age
_____	_____
_____	_____
_____	_____
_____	_____

Father Remarried to

_____

Children	Age
_____	_____
_____	_____
_____	_____
_____	_____

CHRONOLOGICAL DESIGNATION
(Consider Described Issues)

Preschool _____
_____
_____
_____
_____
_____
_____
_____
_____
_____

Grade School _____
_____
_____
_____
_____
_____
_____
_____
_____
_____
_____
_____

Adolescence _____
_____
_____
_____
_____
_____
_____
_____
_____
_____
_____
_____

SYMPTOMOLOGICAL PERSPECTIVE

Step One:
Relationship Dysfunction

Record the child's symptoms within the relationship realm. Consider such things as abnormal attachments, passive-aggressive behavior, superficiality, dishonesty, secrecy, sexual acting out, communication problems, or discipline problems.

_____

_____

_____

_____

_____

_____

_____

_____

_____

_____

_____

_____

_____

_____

_____

_____

_____

_____

_____

_____

_____

_____

_____

_____

_____

_____

_____

_____

_____

SYMPTOMOLOGICAL PERSPECTIVE

Step Two:
Psychological Dysfunction

Record any psychological problems that the child appears to have or mental concerns that have been described or documented. Discuss previous mental health involvement or diagnosis, tendencies toward schizophrenia, delusions, psychosis, mood or anxiety problems, etc. Problems with impulse control, eating disorders, depression, or tendencies toward personality disorders should also be described.

_____
_____
_____
_____
_____
_____
_____
_____
_____
_____
_____
_____
_____
_____
_____
_____
_____
_____
_____
_____
_____
_____
_____
_____
_____
_____
_____
_____

SYMPTOMOLOGICAL PERSPECTIVE

Step Three:
Living Skill Dysfunction

Describe the child's ability to function within the living skill arena. Consider such things as the child's problem solving abilities, struggles in school, criminal behavior, runaway tendencies, substance abuse problems, anger mismanagement, previous residential placements, self-abusive behavior, sleep disorders, or family mobility conflicts.

_____

_____

_____

_____

_____

_____

_____

_____

_____

_____

_____

_____

_____

_____

_____

_____

_____

_____

_____

_____

_____

_____

_____

_____

_____

_____

_____

_____

_____

_____

RELATIONSHIP PERSPECTIVE

Step One:
Evaluating the Relationship Between the Victim and the Offender

How does the victim describe the offender's attitude toward him/her?

_____

_____

_____

_____

_____

_____

_____

_____

_____

What assets or liabilities does the victim believe the perpetrator would use to describe the child?

_____

_____

_____

_____

_____

_____

_____

_____

_____

_____

What is the victim's view of the perpetrator's attitude toward disclosure?

_____

_____

_____

_____

_____

_____

_____

_____

_____

What assets and liabilities can the victim describe about the perpetrator?

_____

_____

_____

_____

_____

_____

_____

_____

_____

_____

What does the victim wish would happen to the perpetrator?

_____

_____

_____

_____

_____

_____

_____

_____

_____

_____

_____

_____

What changes in the victim's relationship with the perpetrator have occurred since disclosure?

_____

_____

_____

_____

_____

_____

_____

_____

_____

_____

_____

_____

Final Tabulation: Plus _____   Minus _____

RELATIONSHIP PERSPECTIVE

Step Two:
Evaluating Offender's Relationship With Significant Others

Who does the victim list as being in a positive support system with the perpetrator?

_____

_____

_____

_____

_____

_____

_____

_____

_____

_____

Who does the victim describe as identifying the perpetrator as being guilty of a crime?

_____

_____

_____

_____

_____

_____

_____

_____

_____

_____

What is the victim's view of the non-offending parents support or lack of support with the perpetrator?

_____

_____

_____

_____

_____

_____

_____

_____

_____

How does the victim view the system's response to the perpetrator?

_____
_____
_____
_____
_____
_____
_____

What is the victim's view of extended family's support of the perpetrator?

_____
_____
_____
_____
_____
_____
_____

What is the victim's view of the sibling's view of the perpetrator?

_____
_____
_____
_____
_____
_____
_____

What is the victim's view of the community's support or rejection of the perpetrator?

_____
_____
_____
_____
_____
_____
_____

Final Tabulation: Plus _____   Minus _____

RELATIONSHIP PERSPECTIVE

Step Three:
Evaluating Victim's Relationship With Significant Others

What is the assessment of the victim's sense of self-esteem?

_____
_____
_____
_____
_____
_____
_____
_____
_____
_____

How does the victim describe personal assets and liabilities?

_____
_____
_____
_____
_____
_____
_____
_____
_____
_____

What special problems, handicaps, struggles, has the victim had in the past that would affect self-esteem?

_____
_____
_____
_____
_____
_____
_____
_____
_____
_____

What is the victim's perception of the non-offending spouse's support?

_____
_____
_____
_____
_____
_____
_____
_____
_____
_____
_____

What is the victim's perception of the non-abused sibling's support?

_____
_____
_____
_____
_____
_____
_____
_____
_____
_____
_____

What is the victim's view of the community's support?

_____
_____
_____
_____
_____
_____
_____
_____
_____
_____
_____

What is the victim's view of the system (legal, child protection, mental health, etc.)

_____
_____
_____
_____
_____
_____
_____
_____
_____
_____
_____

What is the victim's view of extended family?

_____
_____
_____
_____
_____
_____
_____
_____
_____
_____
_____

What is the victim's view of miscellaneous group (school, friends, church, etc.)?

_____
_____
_____
_____
_____
_____
_____
_____
_____
_____
_____

Final Tabulation: Plus _____   Minus _____

DEVELOPMENTAL PERSPECTIVE

Step One:
Stage of Sexual Development

Describe developmental stages pertaining to the time of abuse including liabilities and limitations within each category of sexual development. Describe what children typically perceive during the stage of development corresponding with this specific victim at the onset of abuse. If children have been abused during different sexual stages, describe each of those stages with corresponding developmental perceptions.

_____

_____

_____

_____

_____

_____

_____

_____

_____

_____

_____

_____

_____

_____

_____

_____

_____

_____

_____

_____

_____

_____

_____

_____

_____

_____

_____

_____

DEVELOPMENTAL PERSPECTIVE

Step Two:
Examine Environmental Influence

Describe sexual environmental influences within the child's environment. Discuss such issues as: morals, values, religious views of sexuality, available sexual information, sexual relationship of parents, male/female sexual role training, formal sexual education in school, sexual activities with peers, body development, and perceptions of sexual body image.

_____

_____

_____

_____

_____

_____

_____

_____

_____

_____

_____

_____

_____

_____

_____

_____

_____

_____

_____

_____

_____

_____

_____

_____

_____

_____

_____

_____

_____

_____

DEVELOPMENTAL PERSPECTIVE

Step Three:
Losses to Normal Development

Carefully consider damage to normal sexual development that seems to have occurred or will occur in the future. Answer the following questions.

Does the victim appear to have, or does it appear that in the future the child will have, a sexual "appetite?"

_____
_____
_____
_____
_____
_____
_____
_____
_____
_____

Does the body image of the victim appear to have a destructive quality or does the victim's body image appear to be reasonably positive?

_____
_____
_____
_____
_____
_____
_____
_____
_____

What are the attitudes or trauma that emerge concerning the issue of body functions?

_____
_____
_____
_____
_____
_____
_____
_____
_____
_____

What does the victim seem to have learned about male/female sexual roles?

_____

_____

_____

_____

_____

_____

_____

What sexual phobias appear to be developing or appear to have the potential to develop?

_____

_____

_____

_____

_____

_____

_____

What is the victim's general attitude about normal arousal (as compared to the sexual abuse)?

_____

_____

_____

_____

_____

_____

_____

What problems seem to appear for the victim in the area of sexual identity or sexual preference dysfunction?

_____

_____

_____

_____

_____

_____

SITUATIONAL PERSPECTIVE

Step One:
Checklist of Sexual Behaviors

Examine and document all sexual behaviors that occurred during the abusive scenario. Use this space to describe a "typical" abusive situation for this specific child.

Fondling

___Vulva   __Buttocks   __Breast   Other_____

___Legs   __Penis   __Testicles   Other _____

Penetration (Digital/Penile/Object)

___Anal   __Vaginal

Oral Contact

___Fellatio   __Cunnilingus   __Anal   __Other

Additional

___Ejaculation   __Photography   __Sexual Apparatus   __Fetishism

___Orgasmic Response   __Bestiality   __Pornography   __Masturbation

___Cross Dressing   __Group Sex   __Voyeurism   __ Vulvar Coitus

___Exhibitionism   __Weapons   __Bondage/Restraints

___Obscene Phone Calls   __Rituals   __Urination/Defecation

Describe A "Typical" Abuse Situation

_____
_____
_____
_____
_____
_____
_____
_____
_____
_____
_____
_____
_____
_____
_____
_____
_____

SITUATIONAL PERSPECTIVE

Step Two:
Describe Sensory Activation That Occurred During The Abuse.

Tactile Responses

_____
_____
_____
_____
_____
_____

Olfactory Responses

_____
_____
_____
_____
_____
_____
_____

Visual Perceptions

_____
_____
_____
_____
_____
_____

Audio Perceptions

_____
_____
_____
_____
_____
_____

Taste Perceptions

_____
_____
_____
_____
_____
_____

SITUATIONAL PERSPECTIVE

Step Three:
Describe The Sexually Abusive "Scene" For Discovery Of Phobias Or Distorted Cognitions.

What was the typical environment for the sexual abuse, and what contributions were made to the victim's perceptions?

_____
_____
_____
_____
_____
_____
_____
_____
_____
_____
_____

What seemed to occur 30 minutes before and 30 minutes after the abuse, and what effect do these events have on the victim's perceptions?

_____
_____
_____
_____
_____
_____
_____
_____
_____
_____
_____

What conversations took place during the abusive scenario, and what is the effect of those conversations?

_____
_____
_____
_____
_____
_____
_____
_____
_____
_____
_____

What is the position of locality of others during the abuse, and what effect do the periphery individuals have on the victim's perceptions?

_____

_____

_____

_____

_____

_____

_____

_____

_____

_____

_____

_____

_____

_____

_____

_____

_____

_____

_____

What occurred in the abusive scenario concerning the issue of coercion? Consider such issues as violence, terror, force, as well as bribery, seduction, or the victim's cooperation?

_____

_____

_____

_____

_____

_____

_____

_____

_____

_____

_____

_____

_____

_____

_____

_____

_____

_____

What is known about the victim's sexual responsiveness or sexual arousal, and what impact does this issue seem to have?

_____
_____
_____
_____
_____
_____
_____
_____
_____
_____
_____
_____
_____
_____
_____
_____
_____
_____
_____
_____
_____

What extraneous issues or items in the sexually abusive scene seem to have the potential for phobic reactions? (Also, use this section to list phobic reactions that will occur from a sensory activation standpoint as indicated from the previous sections).

_____
_____
_____
_____
_____
_____
_____
_____
_____
_____
_____
_____
_____
_____
_____
_____
_____

SITUATIONAL PERSPECTIVE

Step Four:
Evaluate The "Holistic" Environment Of The Victim For Discovery Of Distorted Cognitions Or Future Coping Skills. Examine The World Of The Family And The Effect Those Perceptions Have On The Child.

How does the family constellation, in consideration of adoption, divorce, birth of children, birth order, etc., impact the victim's trauma?

_____
_____
_____
_____
_____
_____
_____
_____
_____
_____

What contributions do family finances or vocational issues make to the victim's trauma?

_____
_____
_____
_____
_____
_____
_____
_____
_____
_____

What issues concerning family health, impact the elements of trauma for the victim?

_____
_____
_____
_____
_____
_____
_____
_____
_____
_____

What morality issues within the entire family environment provide messages to the victim and create trauma?

_____
_____
_____
_____
_____
_____
_____
_____
_____

How does the family situation in the community influence trauma?

_____
_____
_____
_____
_____
_____
_____
_____
_____

What influence does family discipline have on trauma?

_____
_____
_____
_____
_____
_____
_____
_____

What post-disclosure issues have effected the victim's traumatization?

_____
_____
_____
_____
_____
_____
_____
_____

Diagnose the victim's development of coping skills. Consider such things as outlined in <u>Just Before Dawn</u>, such as amnesia, dissociation, self-abuse, abusive cycles, guilt, responsibility avoidance, secrecy, obsessive behavior, aggressive behavior, helplessness, symbiosis, perfection, failure, etc. If coping skills do not appear to have been manifested at this time, predict what may occur.

_____
_____
_____
_____
_____
_____
_____
_____
_____
_____
_____
_____
_____
_____
_____
_____
_____
_____
_____
_____
_____
_____
_____
_____
_____
_____
_____
_____
_____
_____
_____
_____
_____

SUMMARY AND TREATMENT GOALS

RELATIONSHIP PERSPECTIVE GENERAL GOALS "Identification of the Offender and Victim"

_____
_____
_____
_____
_____
_____
_____
_____
_____
_____
_____
_____
_____
_____
_____
_____
_____
_____
_____

DEVELOPMENTAL PERSPECTIVE GENERAL GOALS "Damage to Normal Sexual Development"

_____
_____
_____
_____
_____
_____
_____
_____
_____
_____
_____
_____
_____
_____
_____
_____
_____
_____

SITUATIONAL PERSPECTIVE GENERAL GOALS "Adaptation of Phobic Responses and Destructive Coping Skills (Distorted Cognitions)"

_____
_____
_____
_____
_____
_____
_____
_____
_____
_____
_____
_____
_____
_____
_____
_____
_____
_____
_____

Additional comments:

_____
_____
_____
_____
_____
_____
_____
_____
_____
_____
_____
_____
_____
_____
_____
_____
_____
_____

Chapter 4

MOURNING MENDING MODALITIES

. . . presenting creative, effective, proactive treatment methodologies and modalities respectful of new reflections in breaking the bonds of trauma.

Chapter 4

MOURNING MENDING MODALITIES

With trauma of sexual victims understood, and an individual treatment plan developed, therapy begins. With tradition abandoned for assessing trauma to victims, methodologies must emerge creative and innovative. Proactive methods of treatment require new thinking and new approaches.

Six modalities or methodologies should be used for effective treatment with sexual victims. These modalities are not traditional and they require "new reflections" as outlined in Just Before Dawn. In appreciation of distorted cognitions, damage to developmental sexual systems, and confusion about the offender/victim identity, these modalities have been designed with respect for traditional purposes but with a new direction and philosophy.

Modality #1
DOING

Methods of one-to-one, clinical interchanges regarding expression of "feelings" can be found in the traditional psychoanalytical model approach. Unfortunately, inquiring about how children "feel" or requiring victims to introspect on a surface level may be asking an impossible task. Internal pain needs to be externalized, which is a process within itself. The traditional method of inquiring about inner feelings and expecting appropriate responses may need to be questioned.

Rather than requiring the child to externally project confused and distorted internal feelings, the methodology of "doing" allows this same process to occur in nonverbal terms. Additionally, there is an inherent process of "possession" in activities that require victims to "**DO!**" The methodology of "doing" smacks of capability and ownership. Eventually, this process becomes a much more effective way of learning. Externalization signifies the ultimate in the process toward rehabilitation for children. "Doing" is a more effective method in allowing the internal pain to become externalized rather than simply asking victims to introspect and project.

Because of the trauma suffered, sexual victims tend to feel out of control, incapable, and vulnerable. Any activities or exercises that allow the child to bring the pain outside, but under control, is effective in breaking the bonds of trauma. "DOING" fits into this process.

Art work, letter writing, journal preparation, body exercises, role playing, flash cards, list preparations, etc. are all specific examples of activities, skills, and techniques that allow children to have a sense of capability in the process of healing. If therapists only rely on discussions through group participation, the process of rehabilitation may not be as effective. Because of their sexual abuse, victims are typically forced to distort, confuse, and entangle the reality of their pain in order to survive. The process of completing small increments of successes or activities, enhanced by the process of DOING, has a much greater chance for breaking the bonds of trauma.

If, as an example, a group activity focuses on the non-offending parent's rejection, a traditional approach may bring failure to victims. Many behavior problems and management issues emerge since victims are, in essence, being asked to discuss their pain. It is understandable why adolescents or even younger children act in outrage and demonstrate behavioral problems each time they are asked to "process" feelings about their parents rejection. If, however, the same activity is broken down into steps that require art work, tangible activity, body movements, accomplishment and control, more comfort will emerge.

A specific example in the treatment activity section can be used to illustrate this point. If the objective is to have children discuss feelings of abandonment by their mothers, that is obviously an important treatment issue. Discussion requires internalization and verbalization which are both painful. If, however, under a "doing approach" children are allowed to prepare Mother's Day cards and if they are exposed to 25 or 30 salutation possibilities regarding the different ways mothers may respond, the DOING exercise of preparing the generic salutations, as well as choosing which salutation will be used for each child's card, will provide a much better way of attaining control and discovery. The steps are physical, more external and more management.

Many professionals are concerned about behavior management and control of children during therapy. More than likely, these problems are associated with the implementation of an adult modality of verbalization (psychoanalytical) for use with children. Group discussion alone, may be less effective than an activity of doing, doing, doing; cutting, pasting, moving, talking, presenting, dialoguing. This approach tends to keep children under control and will obviously contribute to a healthier therapeutic environment and more successful treatment outcomes.

Modality #2
TRUSTING, UNFOLDING, AND RELEASING

Raging conflict exists regarding the therapeutic relationship with sexually abused children and the treatment specialist. Some advocate that only those professionals who have been sexually victimized themselves should be providing therapy to sexual victims. This idea suggests that empathy is impossible unless trauma is personally experienced. On the other end of the spectrum are those who suggest that professional objectivity only occurs with therapists who were not sexually abused as children and therefore only those therapists who were **not** victimized are effective. As the debate rages, common sense may dictate the most appropriate treatment modality.

The ideal relationship between therapists and sexual victims should be one in which children find a SANCTUARY. Trust is very important. Victims need unconditional safety. They need therapists who are accepting of their feelings, attitudes, responses, and ideations regardless of the therapist's past. Victims should be free of any obligation to the professional. Children should be able to express feelings and, most importantly, they should be able to change feelings as the road to recovery is taken. When an intimate or personal relationship occurs between the therapists and the patient, the sanctuary is lost, therapy may be retarded, and, most importantly, victims may have unfair obligations.

The destructive results of an intimate or subjective relationship between children and therapists occurs in three stages, with the first stage relating to the issue of reciprocity. Even though the therapist may not overtly demand something from victims, a subtle or underlying obligation to return positive support is clear. The "I care for you" has an indirect demand of "will you care back?"

Sexual victims are usually responsible for many things in the incestuous family as a result of sexual abuse. The demand for reciprocity in the therapeutic relationship seems unfair as victims may become responsible for the therapist's needs. If children have a sanctuary within the therapeutic environment, void of obligations, and if the victim is to rehabilitate, the effort should be directed toward recovery of the victim, not directed toward taking care of the treatment specialist. Children who have been sexually abused often are obligated to care for the perpetrator, to keep the family together, or to fulfill the sexual needs of family members. In the past, the victim may have been responsible for keeping the perpetrator out of jail or for keeping the perpetrator employed. Whether the child is 3 or 13, obligation or responsibility should discontinue as the therapeutic relationship unfolds.

Give Me Your Secret

Initially, treatment specialists may feel as though sharing personal issues or trauma in childhood may be effective for victims. Children may, at first, respond with empathy, understanding, and with positive affirmation. The initial therapeutic relationship may seem closer and enhanced as victims learn personal information about their therapist. Victims may feel they will be understood because intimate details of the therapist's life have been divulged. Unfortunately, sharing of intimate details creates a situation where the victim may become responsible for the professional as therapy progresses.

Regardless of what the therapists believe is, or is not, demanded from the child, sharing intimate details suggests a need for reciprocity and a sense that equal status has been attained between patient and therapist. Equality may appear to be a democratic term, enhancing the therapeutic relationship. Unfortunately, equality subtly demands that the child "take care of" the therapist on the basis of equality. This is exactly what victims have often commonly experienced in their own incestuous family.

As an example in therapy, the victim may be discussing intimate details of abhorrent abuse and may see the treatment specialist respond emotionally. Tears form and lips tremble. Although is a natural response for any therapist, regardless of a personal abuse, the victim may see the therapist as needing compensation and sensitivity because the therapist is a victim or has other personal frailties. The observing child may withhold discussing more intimate details or may, very similar to their own incestuous situation, put forth effort to protect the therapist from further distress. This creates an even more unequal scenario, but obviously one similar to the victim's past.

Run From Intimacy

A second potential of difficulty in an improper therapist/victim relationship is the deadly result from attempts to become personal with individuals who have been traumatized by "intimacy" in the past. If therapists reach out on a personal level to a child who has been offended and traumatized by personal relationships, the victim may cope by RUNNING. The "I care for you" may be interpreted by the child as another opportunity to be exploited. As therapists reach for the child on a personal level, especially the adolescent, the victim may reach for the door.

Running from intimacy or from those who seem to care is a common pattern for many sexual victims. Children who have spent much of their childhood associating tenderness, intimacy and caring with exploitation and abuse, are likely to reject the personal approach from a therapist. Again, good intentions may exist, but a common reaction may be similar to one from the victim's childhood. Intimacy or personal commitment may elicit feelings of impending exploitation, since intimacy has been painful in the past and the victim may need to avoid intimacy to stay SAFE.

Release??

A final issue concerning the professional's personal relationships with victims involves a definition of "recovery." The ultimate objective in the therapeutic relationship should be one in which the child can be rehabilitated and released into situations where survival will continue. The child must be freed, into a world where day-to-day coping occurs **without** the therapist. If, in therapy, an intimate relationship is established, one with personal connotations, it may be difficult for the victim to be released since "getting better" or recovery, means losing the valuable commodity of the therapist's personal relationship. Survivorship, therefore, is attached to the personal relationship rather than to the victim's ability to make progress.

The victim may need to "stay sick" in order to maintain the relationship with the therapist. Recovery may be retarded since being released, leaving therapy, may seem lonely and cold to victims, especially those who are positively attached to their therapist. Remaining traumatized may be more comfortable than losing the personal therapeutic relationship.

The debate regarding whether therapists should disclose information about their childhoods is one that emerges frequently. Regardless of the answer to the victim who asks "were you a sexual victim in childhood?" a "no win" situation occurs if the question is contemplated and answered. If the professional is a victim and that information is disclosed, the underlying message is that the issue **is** important. Initially, the victim may feel protected, understood, and contented with a sense of "comraderie" with the therapist's pain.

Unfortunately, by answering the question, acknowledgement has been made that the therapist's personal life is important. If therapy is productive, the paradox is that the victim can only be understood, nurtured, and protected by someone who is also a sexual victim. Vulnerability for children in contact with individuals who are not victims is an automatic assumption. The answer to the question suggests that releasing victims into a world of "nonvictims" will not be safe or productive.

If the therapist denies sexual abuse as a child, the message may be that therapy will be unimportant and ineffective. It is as though the therapist is saying, "I have limitations." The victim who may be looking for reasons to avoid pain may leave the therapeutic environment or remain in therapy with denial heavily entrenched with, "I will stay with this therapist who will probably never understand me anyway."

The most significant issue in answering this question is the connected suggestion that **IT MATTERS**. Ultimate success for therapists allows a "sanctuary" and safety of feelings in an environment where survivorship will emerge. Power and control over the victim's destiny should be internal and not based on the professional's personal past. The victim must be encouraged to "own" each step of progress and recover with internal growth rather than be influenced by the professional's personal life.

> "My victimization or lack of victimization as a child does not matter. I am going to help you, help yourself, heal. You have the power to get better. I am just going to guide you. When you are finished, you will be able to look back and say, 'I did it because of me, regardless of my therapist's childhood, my family's childhood, or anyone else's childhood.'
>
> There will always be people who will help you and there will always be people who will not help you. Your success or failure does not depend on people outside of you, it depends on you. Let us not look outside for where we should go, but look inside and find the road map to recovery."

Modality #3
PROCESSING TO A PRODUCT

Because of victims' distorted thinking, compartmentalized tendencies, confusing and disastrous coping skills, **processing** must occur in order for treatment to be successful. However, the traditional "process" group needs more direction and focus for victims. Children who participate in open-ended, nonspecific treatment programs, often remain disconnected and prone to distortion. For some children, even the smallest tasks seem overwhelming. Small increments or steps to success lead the victim toward the therapeutic "product." Each one of those steps is as important as the product itself.

Step By Step

Some children may not have benefit of a comprehensive Sexual Victim Trauma Assessment. Limitations may exist in state budgets or time constraints will not allow individual therapy or individual Trauma Assessments. Generic, ongoing groups with similar curriculum and protocol will seem to be easy and most desirable. Treatment modalities must be respectful toward realistic limitations, but nonetheless support the idea that children recover at a more rapid rate if they understand the direction or the product they are working toward. Competency occurs when victims achieve success in **steps** that provide increments of productivity. This is especially true when children feel safety in understanding the steps previous to implementation.

Past, Present, Future

As an example, not only does a proactive therapeutic program need to be directed for the future, but reminders of the past can make the future even more appealing. The healing process should always emphasize impressions about the past and about a future. Each successful step toward the victim's recovery can be enhanced through therapeutic "reminders." Demonstrating to the victim clear explanations of each step of success, directs more hope toward the future. Understanding of past successes also enhances future successes.

An important process issue for this non-traditional approach is the genesis of the Trauma Assessment, working toward treatment planning and eventually evolving toward the resolution scrapbook. Recognizing that a victim's scrapbook could actually be completed within one week will point out the inappropriateness of "product" thinking. Participating in a "process" of extensive evaluation in the Sexual Victim Trauma Assessment must suggest to the child that what happened is significant and that healing is not haphazard. Having children participate in developing a treatment plan also suggests that recovery is not only important, but it is specific, complicated and personal. Establishing specific treatment goals that fit the individual victim implies uniqueness and creates a sense of importance, but most importantly a sense of direction.

Scrapbook . . . The Ultimate Doing

Finally, the scrapbook emerges as a representation of all that has been completed over the **process of treatment**. As an example, many therapists are accomplishing effective treatment goals in therapeutic sessions. Without pointing out progress and comparing where the victim has been in the past to where the victim is going in the future, a potentially effective activity may be limited in value. Recapturing treatment accomplishments in the scrapbook is the ultimate example of process treatment activity enhancement. Children who see a list, who evaluate possible outcomes, who choose an objective, will feel much more accomplished when that goal is attained. Children who attain the same goal but were not aware of the complicated process toward the goal may view the progress as less significant and their recovery will be limited.

Modality #4
EDUCATION

An important modality for sexual abuse treatment is to educate, educate, educate! The simple value to education is often overlooked in victims' treatment. Education is not the only treatment methodology, but education is important for proactive treatment, especially in consideration of victims' distorted cognitions and the damage to their normal sexual development. The education modality of prevention, for example, is important for children who have been sexually abused. Proactive education efforts should go beyond preventing sexual abuse, however, and should be more profound than "just say no." Effective prevention is a process of internalizing a reason for protection, which results in a much more comprehensive educational program than simply teaching children how to verbalize resistance. Reactive therapy stops abuse, proactive therapy emphasizes future sexuality and teaches "why."

Stud Horse Theories

An example of an important component for the educational modality of treatment involves teaching how human beings are different from animals. Although sexual arousal may not be controllable, sexual activity **is** under the control of adults. Society's messages from the media, however, often teach that it may be possible to render adults out of control through presentation of certain sexual stimulus material and, therefore, victims may be responsible for sexual abuse. Teaching the difference between animals and human beings is an important example of the educational modality, which may stop the guilt that occurs for some children. Without the educational discussion of human body functions and the human sexual response, as an example, the trauma associated with guilt will be difficult to rectify.

Another example of the important use for the educational modality is found in the discussion of "orgasms" or human sexual activities. Sexual responsiveness and sexual stimulation on the part of victims tends to be particularly traumatizing since they may feel confused or guilty about causing sexual arousal in the perpetrator. A "CLINICALIZATION" of orgasms through a comprehensive education modality, may be required to resolve feelings of guilt for the victim. Teaching the "demystification" of orgasms or the human sexual response, may assist victims understanding that their sexual responses were normal. A simple educational definition may be helpful.

"An orgasm is an explosive discharge of accumulated neuromuscular tensions."

The guilt inducing idea of orgasm, when demystified, "clinicalized," understood, calculated, graphed, charted, and observed becomes less powerful. The educational model will be extremely important since the traditional therapeutic model may be more emotional and psychoanalytical. Children may have spent years feeling degraded and repulsive about their body responses. Through the educational modality, the insignificance of the orgasmic response is a valuable contribution to resolving guilt.

Positive Sexual Futures

It is also important to recognize that sexual functioning is often taboo, or at least not viewed as positive in American culture. Sexual intimacy is certainly more traditionally taught in negative terms. Proactive treatment teaches victims about the positive aspect of sexuality. Unless educational modalities are used, this task will be difficult. Body functions, sexual stimulation, and the human sexual response must be taught in a positive way in order for children to understand that sexual arousal and sexual responsiveness are normal and natural. Only processing feelings about sex, without educating on "what should be," traps victims into stagnation.

Finally, an educational model must be used in order to teach a sense of innocence and identification of the victim status. Unfortunately, this learning does not emerge automatically or through indirect processes of discussing feelings. Many therapeutic programs suggest that victims will somehow "know" that by defending themselves from future abuse, they will recognize the positive aspects of human sexuality and intimacy. Unfortunately, this is not true for children who have not yet proceeded through developmental stages where this information would be clear.

Children need to go through an educational process which, through a step-by-step protocol, "proactively" teaches about the value, or positive commodity associated with genitalia and sexual decision making. The publication A VERY TOUCHING BOOK is one of the few prevention programs that takes this proactive approach, teaching children something positive about their sexuality and about their rights to make sexual decisions, as adults, in the future. Therapists must recognize that this learning does not come automatically and that it must be an intricate part of the educational modality for sexual victim therapy.

Bicycle Robberies

Vulnerable children need to learn about their bodies and they need to learn that their bodies and genitalia feel different to touch than other parts of their bodies. They must be taught to feel positive and excited about sexuality. Too often treatment plans focus on the damage and pain and fail to recognize what lies ahead for a victim who continues to cultivate these negative ideas. Children who recognize that their sexuality and their genitalia is as important as their bicycles will rehabilitate at a much greater rate. "Bicycle Robberies" are an excellent way to prove why the "proactive" educational modality is so important for victims of sexual abuse.

Children protect their bicycles because their bicycles are wonderful. Children become excited about their bicycles long before their legs can reach the pedals. The reason they protect their bicycles lies in a positive attitude toward bicycles. There is very little opportunity or reason to protect something that is smelly, dirty, awful, nasty, and certainly unmentionable, such as sexual body parts. Educational modalities must be emphasized and implemented in the effective treatment program so that victims of sexual abuse can learn to appreciate their sexuality with the same vigor as they appreciate their bicycles.

Modality #5
TOUCHING

The touching of children in the therapeutic process is a tremendous source of controversy among professionals. Some suggest that victims should never be touched since touching has previously caused trauma. Others advocate that touching should occur and be forced upon children. "Middle of the road" advocates suggest that children should only be touched if they give consent.

Children who have been abused through sexual touching are usually traumatized. Although some sexual behaviors of a non-touching nature may occur, TOUCHING is the primary vehicle for trauma in sexual abuse. Therefore, it is an important treatment process to incorporate non-sexual touching into treatment protocols in order to continue implementing the sanctuary or safe environment in the healing process. Touching is a wonderful behavior between human beings and certainly there is a professional obligation to provide safe, non-sexual touching when absolutely no commitment is involved. Learning to touch in the safety of the therapeutic environment may be one of the most important components in therapy for victims. In fact, touching is an excellent behavior control technique.

Touching, Touching, Touching

It is rare that sexual abuse between a child and a perpetrator involves only genital touching. In many instances, entire bodies of children are involved in hugging, holding, caressing, and kissing. There is tremendous potential for the victim to incorporate reactions to these normally wonderful human behaviors as a response to sexual abuse. Therefore, victims benefit from re-enacting many nonsexual kinds of touching that occurred in the sexual abuse experience, but with therapeutic safety. The desensitization of inappropriate touching will occur as safe touching is a common factor in the therapeutic environment.

Memories Are Made of This

Skins memories are some of the most significant memories in adulthood and they often connect the adult victim back to the pain of childhood sexual abuse. Often, cognitive awareness may be unavailable (as in cases of amnesia), but tactile, as well as affective responses remain. Approaching skin memories and diffusing the potential for phobic reactions is extremely important for children in therapy. This effort is proactive and respectful for the victim's future.

Touching techniques go far beyond providing noncommittal affection and attention to children. Touching activities are not limited to hugs and handholding, but they actually require design of activities concerning "body work." Often, memories will be rekindled from touching areas of the body that hold secrets. Without the modality of touching, skin memories will remain powerful and recovery will be limited.

Touching Tools

In accepting the commitment to touch children in teaching noncommittal affection, several guidelines and recommendations exist. "Talking and touching" is an important requirement for safe touching in therapy. A verbal response should initially occur before touching and, when touching does occur, it is not, therefore a secret. Hugs in the waiting room, next to the secretary's desk, or in a situation with other family members, are examples of nonsecretive, safe touching. Talking and touching is very important to prohibit "secrets" about touching.

> ''It feels so good to have good touching. How about if you give this hug that I am giving to you, to your cat when you get home?''

When words explain that, first, touching will occur, and when talking about touching occurs simultaneously, secrecy subsides. Talking and touching and desensitizing touching eventually occurs.

And what about the resistive child who seems to not want to be touched? Can children decide competently? It may be unfair to openly ask victims to consent to touching since they may resist and miss an important opportunity for recovery. An appropriate comment to make may be,

> ''We need some good touching here in the waiting room next to your mom.''

If the victim seems to resist, either verbally or through body language, a follow-up statement may be,

> ''Well, how about if we start with giving some good touching to the cats? Would that be all right this time, and maybe next time we can give big hugs to each other?''

Giving children choices, such as, ''Do you think your mom should get some good touching, or do you think I should get some, or do you think we should give our hugs to the cats?,'' is another important way to establish touching ''consent.'' If extreme resistance occurs, a final technique allows inquiry of the child, ''When do you think you will be ready for some good touching?''

Victims should never be forced into touching, but all children need guidance and encouragement from adults who are better equipped than children to make decisions regarding therapeutic goals. Touching has traumatized children and victims' consent has been ignored through sexual abuse. To ask children if they want something that is good for them is the same as asking children if they would like braces or if they would like to eat their vegetables. On the other hand, it seems improper to force children into situations that are similar to their own abuse. Working with children to obtain their consent, but still recognizing that they are unable to give fully informed consent is the best method for accomplishing this modality.

Modality #6
EXTERNALIZATION

An important treatment modality concerns the EXTERNALIZATION of issues surrounding sexual abuse. Sadly, therapy is sometimes presented as simply "talking about the abuse." It is not uncommon for victims groups to be focused on a discussion or expression of feelings or simply a process of describing stories of "what has happened." Certainly, if all children were able to externalize their feelings, therapy would be much easier. The problem remains that in the internalization or stifling of feelings through abuse, victims often don't have the ability to externalize and, therefore, other methods must be implemented.

Inside Out

This important treatment modality requires therapy to be focused around a process of externalization. Returning to the abusive scene, dissecting what happened, putting the abuse in a scrapbook, making pictures, talking, and contemplating is far different from simply encouraging victims to report how they **FEEL** about their abuse.

Clarification and resolution of sexual abuse is an extremely important component or modality under the externalization process. The resolution scrapbook is an example of how this modality is implemented. Sexual abuse trauma is internalized and sexual abuse rehabilitation requires the opposite "externalization." Trauma bonding allows a perpetual pain in motion. The victim moves from one view to another, re-evaluating, contemplating, and ruminating over a variety of ideations. Through the externalization process, sexual abuse feelings become clearly under the control of the victim. The treatment modality of creating a scrapbook can be particularly helpful for a child who is extremely young, perhaps preverbal, or a child who may be in the late teens. Professionals working with the preverbal child may contemplate such issues as,

> "She'll probably forget," or "He'll be able to go on without bringing this up."

These rationalizations are "hopeful" that children will forget what has happened to them and that they will move toward a life free of trauma. Nothing could be further from the truth. In fact, nothing will more clearly guarantee the child pain and traumatization in the future than leaving the memory to internal "chance."

Only a small part of memory is cognitive. Many memories take place in the skin, emotions, phobic reactions, and sensory stimuli. Through the externalization process, memory of sexual abuse can be under the control of the victim. The identification of the perpetrator and the victim can emerge clear, even for young children who have no capability to understand in childhood, but who will understand in adulthood as they peruse their scrapbooks.

A positive sense of sexual esteem can be encouraged through tangible recreations of what did, and did not happen in the abuse experience. The trauma bond and phobic reactions can be dissolved, in actuality, before they have been experienced, by externalizing trauma bond tendencies in therapy. The cycle of sexual abuse can be prevented from occurring and survivorship can be implemented for children before any other traumatization has been initiated. Corrected, controlled, externalized, and strategized memory can not only avoid traumatization, but can provide rehabilitation.

For each step in the treatment process, effort must be made to provide an externalization process that brings the sexual abuse under control. As the famous muffler commercial indicates, "We can pay now or we can pay later." The memory will reoccur as will the traumatization. Some memory will be cognitive, some will not, but memory will reoccur. Treatment specialists can choose to control the memory through the process of externalization, or victims can be left to memory that emerges, uncontrollable and sporadically over the child's sexual development, causing traumatization for many years.

Chapter 5
MOURNING MAPS TO RECOVERY

. . . portraying six general treatment goals that allow unique respect for the intricacies of trauma bonding and each child's special needs for recovery.

Chapter 5
MOURNING MAPS TO RECOVERY

Even though each victim of sexual abuse is traumatized differently, and even though treatment plans must be unique, there are basic treatment modalities and treatment goals for victims who are either two or ninety-two. These general goals provide a direction or a "road map" to recovery. Each victims' special needs create individual plans within these general goals that tailor recovery to unique paths.

The Trauma Assessment lends itself to specific issues, individual for each victim, just as trauma is unique. Each special therapeutic goal, within each victim's treatment plan, however, is found in general objectives pertinent to all victims. Specific methodologies to accomplish goals will always remain unique for each child. As the treatment plan is organized, general modalities and goals can become part of the foundation for treatment planning, while special consideration must be made for specific issues raised in each child's Trauma Assessment.

Goal #1

IDENTIFY THE VICTIM
AND THE PERPETRATOR

GOAL #1

IDENTIFY THE VICTIM AND THE PERPETRATOR

The identification of the perpetrator and the victim is one of the most important components in rehabilitation for sexually abused children. Victims who view themselves as innocent and not responsible, rehabilitate faster. Confusion about the offender/victim identity indicates potential for continued trauma. For most victims, some confusion regarding the offender/victim role will emerge. The status of the victim and the offender may also change over time. The Sexual Victim Trauma Assessment reveals how distorted or how clear the victim perceives the "innocent robbery victim" and the "robbery criminal."

Does this goal indicate that the victim should absolutely hate and abhor the perpetrator? The answer is "no." Separating the perpetrator from the perpetrator's sexual acts may be important in order to accomplish this goal. Positive attributes of the perpetrator may prevent the "offender identification" which relates to victim recovery. Separation of the offender's positive attributes from the crime of sexual abuse may need to occur before proper identification of the victim and offender can be made. This separation may need to occur in order to stop the motion of trauma bonding. "I hate her, I love her" bounces the victim in perpetual motion of pain.

The "status of the victim" also needs to be examined as far as its' potential to change over time. For younger children, predictions of changes in perceptions in developing years must be understood. The psychological identification is precarious and upcoming changes in perceptions are pending.

As an example, a 7-year-old male victim may learn in therapy that he was innocent and acts committed upon him were unacceptable. He may appear to have accomplished the first treatment goal. However, this young man's attitude may change as he later learns of the possibility for homophobic responses from society. Additionally, this male victim's erectile responses during the sexual abuse may predict a need for ongoing identification of his victim status as he proceeds through sexual development. This goal must not only identify the victim and the offender at the current intervention and treatment stage, but children have needs to review this idea to protect from the development of trauma in the future as the victim's attitudes change over time.

Victim or Survivor?

Concerns have always been raised about the word "survivor" being in conflict with the word "victim." The first treatment goal is to identify the victim and the perpetrator, but respect must be given to the sixth treatment goal, which is to "become a survivor." Some victim treatment programs are offended by the word "victim" and choose to adopt the semantic term of "survivor" at the onset of therapy. There seems to be a pervading sense of accomplishment and control in the word "survivor." However, becoming a survivor is a process — something to work toward, and only if it is logistically managed and planned can survivorship be appreciated.

Being a "victim" requires recognition of the innocence of the child's status when the abuse was taking place. Unfortunately, unless the internal process moving toward survivorship occurs where the child is first a victim, an innocent child; survivorship may be superficial and only a word. The automatic "survivorship" status may abandon the small child "within" the victim who needs to go through the **process** of being identified as hurt and traumatized before becoming a survivor.

Victims who had accomplished the first treatment goal of "becoming a victim" would be able to say:

> "I am an innocent child. I did not have the option to say 'no' to adults. My cooperation in the sexual act only indicated I was manipulated into cooperation in order to survive. I reported a crime."

> "I am not responsible for family upheaval, or lack of money in the family, or for breaking up the family. I am not responsible for 'no contact' between my brothers and sisters and the offender. I am also not responsible for the expense of treatment. I am not responsible for the fact that the family has been embarrassed. I did not cause this to happen. These problems happened because someone sexually abused me."

> "I reported a crime. I did not let anyone down or 'rat' on anyone. Children are protected by the law and a crime was committed against me — a precious child."

C.R.I.M.E.

The most important word in accomplishing this treatment goal is C.R.I.M.E. Victims need to recognize that a crime was committed upon them. In the physical and emotional sense, our system can assist in accomplishing this goal by charging the perpetrator with a crime. However, if the system cannot respond because prosecution is impossible, the issue of C.R.I.M.E. still needs to be implemented into the treatment plan. Understanding the elements of the crime, understanding the punishment that could have been given to the perpetrator, understanding the basis for protection of children under the law, will be extremely important in accomplishing this goal.

Goal #2

CREATE POSITIVE
SEXUAL SELF-ESTEEM

GOAL #2

CREATE POSITIVE
SEXUAL SELF-ESTEEM

If the first treatment goal is accomplished and the "victim status" was clear to the child, a sense of innocence or lack of responsibility should emerge. The second goal of improving sexual self-esteem goes beyond the first treatment goal, however. Previous to the onset of sexual abuse, children who have healthy self-concepts have a greater chance to avoid trauma as they seem resilient to pain. Sex offenders, unfortunately, seem capable of choosing children who are struggling and who feel inadequate. With these struggling children, secrecy is insured. Even though intellectually, the victim's status may be clear as indicated in the first treatment goal, effort on the part of the offender may continue to attack the victim's self-esteem. Being intellectually innocent is not the same as believing in an innocent body image.

The second goal of improving sexual self-esteem is much more internal and affective. As the first treatment goal accomplishes an intellectual and cognitive process of recognizing the child's innocence, the second goal travels much further, strengthening attitudes about the victim in the arena of sexuality. This second goal nurtures the first goal and expands the victim identity to a body image perspective.

Body Work

This treatment goal requires such issues as body image, sexual self-esteem, and positive personal impressions to be created. Feelings such as body contamination and devaluation may emerge as trauma issues from the Sexual Victim Trauma Assessment, especially in the Developmental Perspective. These trauma areas need to specifically address those elements of trauma found in the Developmental Perspective in order to rehabilitate the victim's sexual self-esteem.

> "I am/was a precious, beautiful child. I have a sexual body that has been misused, not used. Since as a child I could not consent, that means my future sexual decisions will be wonderful, private, and special. My sexuality is something of value."

This victim voice affirms a renewal and a rebirth of positive attitudes. This second goal goes beyond the crime itself and points the victim toward an improved interpersonal ideation of positive sexuality.

"Proactive" approaches must be used even when educating very young children about the human sexual response and the "beauty of consent." Many treatment programs fail as efforts are reactive, simply "preventing sexual abuse." **"JUST SAY NO"** will fall drastically short of accomplishing this second treatment goal.

Ignorance Equals Innocence

Since the sexual victim has already been exposed to sexual behavior, the choice must be made whether children should be presented with sexual information in the "proactive" method, or whether realistic sexual information should be avoided. Some parents may resist this goal, wanting to secure "innocence" in their children. Teaching the positive aspects of sexuality may be resisted as parents still hope that "ignorance equals innocence." This attitude is counter-productive since sexual victims have already been exposed to sexually **deviant** contact. Through avoidance of sexual information, victims will have only one foundation of knowledge — that of exploitation. The choice is not whether the victim should be exposed to sexuality, but how, and under what conditions will the victim develop a sexual awareness.

The proactive approach to this treatment goal will actively teach children about the beauty of consent, the acceptance of their bodies in their natural form, and it will encourage enthusiasm about a future of appropriate sexuality. Rather than simply teaching children to avoid further sexual contact, this treatment goal must lay the foundation for encouraging children to develop a positive future in intimacy.

Goal #3

BREAKING THE TRAUMA BOND

Goal #3

BREAKING THE TRAUMA BOND

Sexual victims may be suffering from trauma bonds with the perpetrator, with significant others, or with phobic reactions and cognitive distortions. However, for some children the trauma bonds may not yet be developed. The Trauma Assessment reveals a potential for that difficulty in the child's future. The third treatment goal first requires analysis of the nature of the trauma bond the child is likely to suffer or how the child is currently being traumatized from the perpetual motion of trauma bonds.

The Conflicting "Children"

Looking into the child's future will provide the best approach in accomplishing this goal. In adult victims, vacillation between the "raging child" and the "pleading child" causes the trauma bond to exist. The outraged child is out of control and often abusive to others or self-abusive. If the outraged child takes vicious action against the perpetrator (either emotionally or in reality) or against other significant family members, the outraged child often BECOMES THE PERPETRATOR in the opinions of others. The rage turns to a perceived badness and the actual perpetrator becomes exonerated in comparison to the "obnoxious" victim.

On the other end of the spectrum is the disheveled, beaten, bewildered, depressed, "pleading child," begging for acceptance and love. The pleading child's response is often the result of the aftermath from the outraged child. The outraged child acts inappropriately and then retreats to feelings of guilt and remorse. The pleading, begging child must often apologize for the behavior of the raging child, figuratively or in actuality.

Trauma bonds exist because the victim remains an uncontrollable "child," either raging or pleading. Accomplishing the third goal for children requires an analysis of the potential trauma bond in the future and it requires establishing therapeutic measures to help the victim avoid being controlled by the "battling children within."

Table A

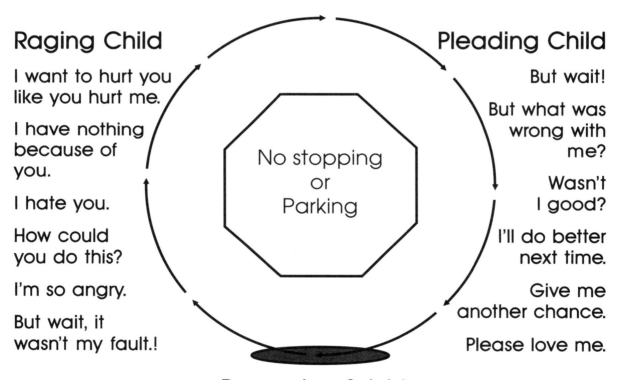

TRAUMA BONDING PERPETUAL PAIN

Raging Child

I want to hurt you like you hurt me.

I have nothing because of you.

I hate you.

How could you do this?

I'm so angry.

But wait, it wasn't my fault.!

No stopping or Parking

Pleading Child

But wait!

But what was wrong with me?

Wasn't I good?

I'll do better next time.

Give me another chance.

Please love me.

Depression, Suicide,
Self-Mutilation, Hopelessness, Etc.

Save the Child

Accomplishing this goal is difficult for therapists. It is easy to take on feelings of outrage toward someone who has sexually abused a child. The raging child is easy to applaud. Confronting the pleading, begging child is much more difficult. Some raging children are viewed as "resolved" or healthy, while the pleading child within most victims is a source of puzzlement for therapists. It is not that either "child" is more or less resolved. It is the battle between the two forces that causes the motion in trauma bonds. Recovery requires a solidification of feelings. Both "children" (raging and pleading) must mature and co-exist.

Anger or rage can be a healthy emotion as long as it is controlled, properly vented and purposeful. Mourning the rejection and abandonment suffered in childhood is also a legitimate emotion provided it does not become self-destructive, depressive or life threatening. These opposing forces must co-exist for balance rather than causing "movement" which is manifested in perpetual pain.

Listen to the balance in these victim voices

"I have the right to feel any or many feelings about the person who did secret touching to me."

"I do not necessarily have to forgive my offender. If I choose, I can re-evaluate the person who did this to me."

"I have the right to change my feelings about the person who sexually abused me."

"People should have protected me and they let me down. That doesn't necessarily mean I wasn't worth protecting."

"I have the right to withhold my feelings about the sexual abuse."

"I have the right to separate my feelings for my offender and for the criminal who did this."

"The perfect world of families does not exist. I must say good-bye to the one I never had and accept the one I have."

Significant Others Trauma Bonding

Although it is typical to concentrate on the power of the offender, individuals who are significant to the offender and victim can also cause severe trauma bonding. Often, the victim/offender relationship may have a reasonable resolution but relationships with people who were connected to the offender may be the subject of trauma bonding.

As an example, trauma bonding may occur with non-abused siblings in cases of family incest. The victim may feel tremendous rejection and scorn from brothers and sisters in the family who were not abused. This often occurs in incestuous families where the perpetrator put forth effort to drive "wedges" between siblings. Children who have not been sexually abused may have been excluded from special favors or from punishment. Often the dynamics of the incestuous family suggest inequitable and arbitrary discipline among children. Non-abused siblings may be resentful toward the victim due to special compensations given to the victim by the perpetrator. The abused sibling may be resentful toward the non-abused siblings since sexual abuse did not happen to others and the victim feels indignant about safety of the other children in the family.

Regardless of the specific situation, the lack of resolution in relationships may be profound and trauma bonding may occur between incest victims and their siblings. Since all of the "players" in this scenario are children, treatment plans should benefit all children within the incest family.

Perhaps the most significant example of trauma bonding that does not involve the perpetrator, pertains to the rejection, abandonment or coldness of the non-offending parent. The sexual offender may either solicit support from the parent and encourage rejection of the victim, or in some cases the offender is neutral and the non-offending parent acts independently.

At times the trauma bond is the result of overt anger and hostility. The non-offending parent does not doubt the abuse happened or neglect the victim's needs, but overtly blames the victim. Some parents may be jealous, may compete with the victim while other parents' coldness or lack of feeling creates a chilling atmosphere for the child who needs warmth and support.

Other "significant other" trauma bonding can occur between the victim and the system which does not protect or which blames the child. Extended family members, the church, or school, etc. all have the potential to traumatize victims by creating trauma bonds through unresolved issues. Without a clarification or an understanding of issues related to Goal #1, the victim can be enmeshed in a trauma bond with a variety of people or entities.

Table B

TRAUMA BONDING TO SIGNIFICANT OTHERS

The Victim Reaches Out

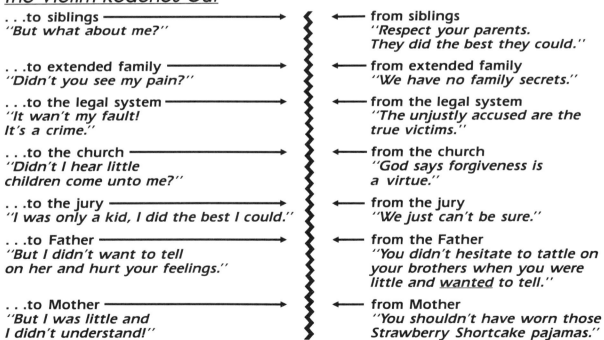

...to siblings
"But what about me?"

← from siblings
"Respect your parents. They did the best they could."

...to extended family
"Didn't you see my pain?"

← from extended family
"We have no family secrets."

...to the legal system
"It wan't my fault! It's a crime."

← from the legal system
"The unjustly accused are the true victims."

...to the church
"Didn't I hear little children come unto me?"

← from the church
"God says forgiveness is a virtue."

...to the jury
"I was only a kid, I did the best I could."

← from the jury
"We just can't be sure."

...to Father
"But I didn't want to tell on her and hurt your feelings."

← from the Father
"You didn't hesitate to tattle on your brothers when you were little and <u>wanted</u> to tell."

...to Mother
"But I was little and I didn't understand!"

← from Mother
"You shouldn't have worn those Strawberry Shortcake pajamas."

Trauma Bonding to Things

Some trauma bonding has the potential to connect the victim to phobic reactions as a result of sensory activation during the sexual abuse. Phobic reactions or cognitive distortions may be profound for a child and may cause devastation in the future. Touch, taste, smell, sight, and sound may elicit stimulation that will return the child to the same affective responses of the abuse, resulting in a lifetime of trauma bonding to "things." Often, the trauma bond is toward these "triggers" and therapy must extinguish the potential for phobias and distorted cognitions. These potentially traumatizing stimuli must be brought under control, desensitized, and framed in a perspective of safety, in order for children to rehabilitate.

Table C
TRAMA BONDING TO THINGS

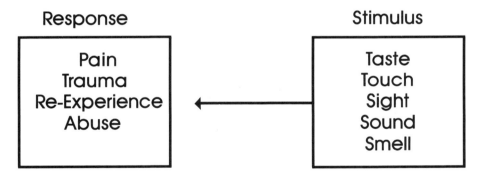

Response	Stimulus
Pain Trauma Re-Experience Abuse	Taste Touch Sight Sound Smell

This is a particular challenge for any professional working with small children. Phobic reactions often do not emerge for younger children or, due to victims' lack of verbal skills, these potential phobias are not commonly discovered. Proactive treatment approaches will be respectful toward victim's future development of these phobic reactions and cognitive distortions.

Trauma Bonds to Thinking

Finally, trauma bonding occurs as victims develop coping skills of distorted thinking such as:

"I'm helpless"

"I'll abuse others to relieve my pain"

"I won't remember"

"I will avoid privacy at all costs"

Table D

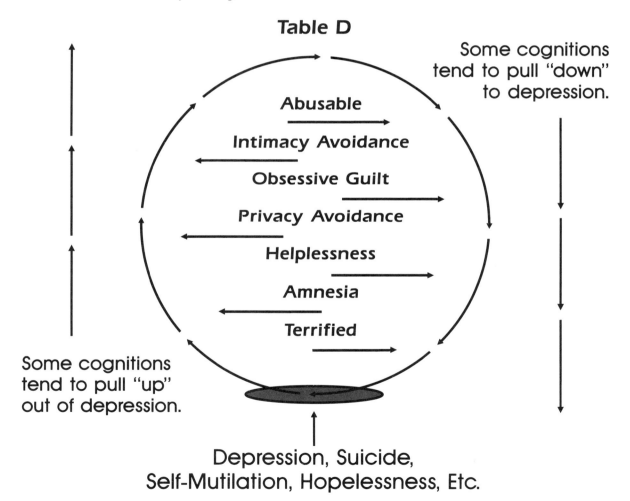

Some cognitions tend to pull "down" to depression.

Abusable

Intimacy Avoidance

Obsessive Guilt

Privacy Avoidance

Helplessness

Amnesia

Terrified

Some cognitions tend to pull "up" out of depression.

Depression, Suicide, Self-Mutilation, Hopelessness, Etc.

These thinking patterns developed by victims to avoid trauma in childhood are common forms of trauma bonding. These thinking patterns keep the victim away from pain, but keep the victim in "motion." Breaking trauma bonds to distorted thinking require analysis, acceptance, desensitization and "reframing" to learn new skills in arranging the reality of the abuse experience.

Goal #4

SETTING GOALS

Goal #4

SETTING GOALS

It may seem absurd to designate a goal of "setting goals" for sexual victim treatment yet this is a very important part of proactive therapy. Not only is trauma specific and unique to each child, but rehabilitation and treatment planning is also unique. Therapy needs to process toward specific rehabilitating directions, recognizing that each family will be different and each "potential for goal achievement" will be different. Automatic or generic plans assume to know what is best for all victims, but that attitude may be destructive and ineffective. If specific goals are not set, and all victims strive for the same objective, some children will be doomed for failure while other treatment outcomes may be retarded or unable to reach full potential. The best treatment approach will assess what is **potentially** attainable and what may not be attainable for each victim, under each unique set of circumstances.

Reality, Reality, Reality

Unfortunately, sexual victims do not live in a Utopian world. Many children are the product of dysfunctional incestuous families. As an example, the therapeutic intervention may discover a doubting but perhaps minimally accepting non-offending parent or spouse. The parent may, therefore, be negatively judged by professionals. Personal views of the professional regarding what should and shouldn't emerge from this marginal parent (based on a Utopian situation) may contribute to increased trauma suffered by this victim. Since the parent does not meet the ultimate standard, the parent is rejected. The victim is prohibited from feeling **any** support from the parent and therefore, suffers more deeply. Setting appropriate goals within the range of what is attainable and securing whatever support possible, maximizes victim's chance for healing.

A doubting, cool and perhaps, offensive parent may be resistive to intervention in some situations. If a generic criteria for positive family relationships is applied, unnecessary effort may be exerted toward encouraging goals that are not attainable. Failure seems imminent as the victim reaches for the impossible. Effective treatment planning requires assessment of the family, setting attainable goals, and processing within the perspective of the family's assets and liabilities. Certainly, encouragement and education in the direction of perfection is needed for resistive parents. This treatment goal does not suggest sacrificing what may be best for the child. This goal simply requires an assessment of that which is possible so that some support, no matter how small can be experienced for each victim.

A clear example of this dilemma emerges when a non-offending, but perhaps offensive spouse seems unwilling to believe the child who made the report. For professionals, this dilemma is a tragedy, resulting in traumatization of the child perhaps more severe than the original sexual abuse. The non-offending parent may have been so supportive of the perpetrator that prosecution was impossible and the inevitable outcome forces the child to be removed from the home and placed in a permanent planning situation. Although this is a devastating situation for a victim, the most appropriate response is to organize a treatment plan that is guaranteed for success in spite of these traumas.

Taking What We Can Get

In spite of this victim's desperate situation, some treatment goals are attainable, such as breaking the cycle of abuse so that the child does not become the same kind of parent, expressing outrage and anger toward the victim's situation, or creating scenarios where the child is extremely supported by a variety of individuals outside the immediate family. This child may have an opportunity for success because of the "adjusted" treatment plan. If the only respectable treatment goal was to gain acceptance from the rejecting parent, then the treatment plan was doomed for failure.

This is not to suggest that recovery plans should not be exerted toward a high standard of care. Setting goals requires working toward the "ideal situation," but moving in directions that are realistic and where some guarantee of success exists. Giving children the ultimate opportunity for support in their families requires realistic goal setting. If the perfect situation is not attainable or possible, it is important to avoid "throwing the baby out with the bath." Many treatment plans develop into a stalemate because the "ideal" goals were not attained. Having the ability to readjust the goals throughout the treatment program in order to set goals that are attainable is the art of effective therapy.

Messiah Complex

Finally, the "messiah" complex can influence treatment planning, encouraging a belief that "we can be all things to all people." Pressure exists for professionals who care about children, to adapt goals that will be perfect. Many situations emerge for victims that are out of the control of professionals and if the "messiah complex" pervades, depression and burn-out may result. Being able to recognize the reality of the victim's situation, to set goals that are attainable, and to work toward those goals, may ensure success for not only the child, but for the professional as well.

GOAL #5

BREAKING THE CYCLE

GOAL #5

BREAKING THE CYCLE

Breaking the cycle of sexual abuse has two important components for children. First, it is important to work toward stopping sexual abuse. But in addition, a commitment should be made to discontinue the cycle of sexual abuse being repeated from one generation to another. The ability to "break the cycle" for victims is proactive therapy. Victims tend to feel abusable and they tend to attract abusive people in their futures, creating significant potential for destructive futures.

As an example, reactive therapeutic efforts assist children who are rejected by their parents, to process and describe the pain. Proactive approaches go further and teach the victim to avoid continuing the same cycle as the destructive parents. Children who are sexually abused have tremendous potential for becoming like their abusers or like the individuals in their family who did not protect them from abuse. Stopping further abuse is not enough. Preventing these children from becoming abusers, or from becoming parents like the parents who neglected them, is accomplished in this proactive treatment goal.

And, to the Future

More specifically, treatment programs often deal with the pain suffered by children who are not supported by their mothers. Poems, songs, letters, and other treatment activities can be implemented, dealing with the pain of abandonment. A proactive addition must occur, however, in order to effectively accomplish this goal. Children must not only be affirmed in their feelings of abandonment, but children must "proactively" learn how to become better parents. Children cannot be expected to proceed into adulthood being different from their own parents unless treatment plans teach "the way it should be."

This goal is especially true in situations where futility abounds. The offender may not have been prosecuted, the offending parent may not believe the child and the victim is abandoned. Rather than a simple affirmation of these feelings, a proactive approach teaches how to be different. This goal should not suggest a rejection of the parents since children tend to be psychologically attached to their parents forever. The victim may need to process feelings of affirmation and anger toward both parents. Accepting some status of these individuals into the victim's life may be accomplished with Goal #4 as the trauma bond is broken. It is important, however, that the victim process these feelings in a therapeutic environment that actively encourages departure from becoming a similar kind of parent.

Cycle Races

It is also important to recognize that the cycle of sexual abuse does not necessarily follow the offender as previously believed. Research suggests that sex offenders may not have been sexually abused as children any more often than the population at large. This issue is important for children to understand who are sexually offended so that a self-fulfilling prophecy does not occur as the child feels destined to become abusive.

Actually, it seems that the cycle of sexual abuse tends to follow the non-offending female parent. Females who have been sexually abused in childhood seem to have a tendency toward marrying individuals who will perpetrate their children. Although a self-fulfilling prophecy of "becoming an offender" must be avoided for males, it is important for female victims to understand the "cycle" issue as well. Proactively teaching the potential for repeating the cycle in female children is an important treatment issue, as well as teaching any child who has been abused, that they are not predestined to become offenders.

GOAL #6

BECOMING A SURVIVOR

GOAL #6

BECOMING A SURVIVOR

A common cry from those individuals who have survived sexual abuse is "I am a survivor." The word "survivorship" often suggests the absence or management of pain and the recovery from trauma. The word "survivor" may be initially rehabilitating due to the sense of empowerment, courage, and assertiveness. Survivorship, however, should not be given immediately to victims but something that is attained — a goal and a process that has been completed. Survivorship for children in therapy should be the final stage of treatment with a grandiose celebration of accomplishment. Children who have accomplished survivorship should have completed treatment goals and should have learned the skills to maintain those goals. If the word "survivor" is used initially, the first goal of identifying the perpetrator and the victim is forgotten.

Significantly, younger children are in the process of developing and their initial survivorship status may be a hope on the part of therapists that is founded in a naive understanding of child development. As indicated earlier, asymptomatic children may be children who have not proceeded through the **opportunity** to be traumatized. Announcing survivorship for younger children may encourage a sense of secrecy at a later time if trauma emerges but the victim has already "survived." Working through the process of 1) first becoming a victim, 2) attaining sexual self-esteem 3) breaking the trauma bond, 4) setting goals and 5) breaking the cycle are important in the process toward survivorship. Sexual victims must not be forced to "survive" before they have worked through the **process** of rehabilitation. Survivorship will impart a sense of maintenance of the first five treatment goals, which will give the child the best opportunity for recovery.

The Balance

The sexual victim scrapbook must attest to survivorship, but, most importantly, contents of the scrapbook must be **in companionship** with the symbols of the "victim status." If only the victim status is developed in the scrapbook, children will remain victims, living a life of either self-abuse or continued abuse by others. If victims only create survivorship scrapbooks, the tender, abused, innocent child will be overlooked, thus creating a "time bomb" for eruption and trauma in the future. The balance of "victimization" and "survivorship" can provide the ultimate opportunity to break the bonds of trauma and stop the "Mourning."

Chapter 6

THE MOURNING AFTER

. . . portraying innovative, proactive organizational plans for design of the ultimate in successful treatment guarantees — the resolution scrapbook.

Chapter 6

THE MOURNING AFTER

The Just Before Dawn research clearly indicates that "victims who had ongoing access to information separating sexual abuse from normal sexual development, had the best opportunity for complete rehabilitation." A record, a permanent tangible record, becomes the vehicle for insuring that victims involved in sexual abuse treatment have a way to make this important separation. These victims' voices emphasize not only pain from a lost childhood, but they exemplify the pain of incomplete treatment. Some of these victims healed wounds in childhood, but they did not have an opportunity to capture the success of treatment in a tangible record that would provide a safe journey through adulthood.

"Where is my childhood . . .Is any piece of me remaining that was innocent, precious, or good?"

"I have such confusion and 'smearing'. I don't know what really happened or what I have dreamed."

"Why didn't I do something about it? Why didn't I stop it? How could I have been so stupid?"

"I feel so creepy now. There is nothing upon which to focus. I just feel dirty. If only I could find it and wash it."

"Where were my mother and father when this happened? Did they allow it? Did they care?"

"All I can remember is smiling faces when I told. Where was everyone? Didn't anybody care that a crime had been committed against me?"

These voices scream for a need of permanency, something recorded, something tangible, and eventually something controllable. The resolution scrapbook becomes the mechanism or the vehicle, taking victims safely through upcoming developing years. The resolution scrapbook also enhances treatment providing an immediate physical reinforcement of each therapeutic success by "scrapbooking" after each session.

Capture the Moment

As an example, the treatment specialist may accomplish an important goal in treatment, such as teaching a sense of empowerment or celebrating the victim's disclosure. Words such as "courage" and "bravery," written on brightly colored paper, may be presented to a specific child as a lively group of eight-year-olds applaude in support. The group process may take one and one-half hours and, during this 90 minute time frame, positive reinforcements and treatment successes occur. Unfortunately, children's lives are constantly bombarded with new information. Following the session, this particular victim may return to a home that is less than positive about the disclosure. Applause may be replaced by rejection, anger or silence. It will not take long for the "90 minutes of success" to fade or to at least dim as the victim is exposed to new situations and new information that is not as safe as the therapeutic environment. Recognizing the potential to lose the impact of treatment success, efforts need to capture positive accomplishments in each victim's scrapbook **after** the therapeputic experience.

Children have a variety of modalities for remembering and for believing. As an example, victims may hear, see and experience group participation regarding the celebration of disclosure. The process of taking pictures of the activity, having other children write letters of congratulations, and putting those items in each victim's scrapbook, doubles the impact of success. In the months following the treatment activity, the value of the 90 minute group can be re-emphasized by returning to the scrapbook and spending 9 minutes glancing through representations of the positive, tangible, supportive appluase for disclosure.

Desensitization

Another important component or use of the resolution scrapbook is through the desensitization process. Children need to be protected from triggered memories or "knee jerk" reactions. As an example, the Sexual Victim Trauma Assessment may pinpoint certain items in the abusive scene that will, likely "trigger" the six-year-old victim in the future. Perhaps, the child may have been sexually abused in conjunction with animal abuse or torture. Avoiding contact with animals will do nothing but postpone traumatizing phobias from developing. Specific therapeutic tasks, where children collect pictures of animals, poems about animals, stories about animals, or artwork about animals can be placed in the scrapbook, to prohibit the potential for triggers regarding animal pain. As representations of animals are cut, pasted, stapled, touched, and manipulated, the desensitization process occurs. Without the process of the scrapbook, the treatment goal of controlling triggers will be more difficult, if not impossible, to accomplish.

Corrected Memory

As indicated throughout this publication, sexual victims are usually in the process of developing, and their cognitive processes will change. Additionally, coping skills or footprints used by the sexual victim to avoid pain are readily available for more distortion and re-evaluation. It is as though the sexual victim has many more tools to distort, to forget, to confuse and to be in conflict with the reality of the experience, rather than having helpful tools for recovery. A well-designed and comprehensive treatment plan may be initially effective, but in need of the final touch or the "after" thought of capturing successes in a tangible representation. This final step in treatment must occur to ensure that success is not lost to distorted cognitions and ever changing developmental thinking patterns.

Finally, the most important purpose of the scrapbook is to keep the sexual abuse from changing as children proceed through their development. Each day or each developmental step allows or forces children to re-evaluate their sexual abuse. As perceptions change, the once accepted innocence of the victim may fade, only to be replaced by guilt. The innocence of the child must be captured in the pages of the scrapbook before negative feelings of responsibility emerge. The identity of the victim and the offender must never change. Support from professionals or from family members must always remain encased in the pages of the scrapbook. If victims are given the chance to change their perceptions of the abuse as they proceed through development, they will be traumatized with each movement in the vicious cycle of trauma bonding.

If victims are allowed to capture their "correct" memory in the tangible representation of the scrapbook, the movement stops, the "mourning breaks." With myths and misconceptions abandoned, with the Trauma Assessment completed, with productive modalities and treatment goals in mind, the Trauma Assessment guides the clinician or therapist toward comprehensive and successful treatment planning and implementation. The proactive therapeutic approach requires that the future of sexual victims be considered, especially in respect for distorted cognitions and changes in developmental thinking patterns. The aftermath or the final treatment consideration (the mourning after) is completion of and respect for the sexual victim scrapbook.

Interception

Victims then, live in a constant traumatic movement as each stimulus exposure situation takes the victim back to the original pain. The scrapbook intercepts this process and each time the victim is triggered through exposure to stimulus, the victim is triggered back to the safety of the scrapbook and the corrected memory. Victims will always be triggered. The scrapbook process triggers victims back to the safety of each treatment success so that the "stimulus-response" chain reaction becomes a "soft place to land."

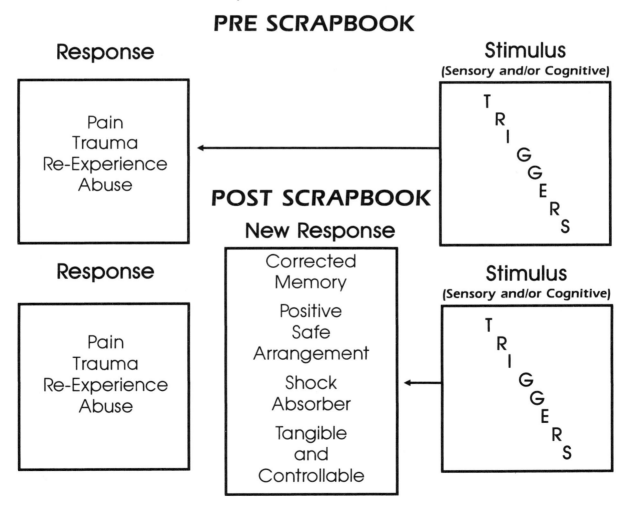

PRE SCRAPBOOK

Response

Stimulus
(Sensory and/or Cognitive)

Pain
Trauma
Re-Experience
Abuse

TRIGGERS

POST SCRAPBOOK

New Response

Response

Corrected Memory

Positive Safe Arrangement

Shock Absorber

Tangible and Controllable

Stimulus
(Sensory and/or Cognitive)

Pain
Trauma
Re-Experience
Abuse

TRIGGERS

Scrapbook Cookbook

Since each victim is traumatized differently and since the proactive approach to therapy recognizes that the Trauma Assessment and the treatment plan will be specific and individual, each victim's scrapbook organizational plan should follow the same structure, which respects the uniqueness of children. Each victim may choose to have different perspectives, goals and accentuation in their scrapbook. Therapists may choose to formulate a generic structure, but victims and their treatment needs should dictate specific decisions about scrapbook preparation and organization.

SCRAPBOOK ORGANIZATIONAL

PLAN #1

This scrapbook structure encourages separation of trauma assessment issues in clear sections. The recapturing of childhood will be in oppositional format with the "competent child" and the "innocent child" balanced. All three sections of the trauma assessment will be represented in successive sections with the final portion of the scrapbook representing support from the system which attests to the dual status of "innocent" victim and accomplished "survivor."

PLAN #1

STEP #1:
HANDLE WITH CARE

The first item in this resolution scrapbook organizational plan is a preface, separating the victim's scrapbook from other books, such as <u>Jack and the Beanstalk</u> or <u>Peter Pan</u>. For the victim or for a caretaker of the victim, the importance and sensitive nature of the scrapbook must be understood. Trauma, because of inappropriate use or exposure of the scrapbook must be avoided. Exhibiting a child's scrapbook at a slumber party or a family reunion would obviously have the potential to traumatize the victim. Children may not be developmentally capable of recognizing that the scrapbook will have extremely intimate and ''precarious'' information and, that it must be handled carefully. The first section of the scrapbook simply states to the child that this book should be handled with care.

Sample:

Dear Kyle:

This book belongs to you. Lots of people wrote in this book so you would be able to remember, in a very special way, what happened to you. As you learned in the treatment program, SECRETS HURT!

All of the people that have written in this book wanted no more secrets for you because they care about you. These people wanted you to remember not only what happened, but, they wanted you to remember how important you were. Most important, these people wanted you to remember the good things that happened.

This is a very special book — not like the other books you may have in your room or at school. This is a special book and it should be kept in a special place. It is for you, but you should always make sure you read it with someone who can help you understand it. It is best to read this book with one of the people who helped write it. If you read this book one time, or 101 times, always remember how many people cared for you and how many people were proud of you for giving up your secret.

STEP #2:
REKINDLING AND REVISITING CHILDHOOD

Secondly, the scrapbook should accentuate those elements of the victim's life that will constantly exemplify the innocence of childhood. Helplessness (not because of incompetencies, but because of the precious nature of children) should be clear. A variety of items could be used to recapture and revisit childhood. Photographs provided by a parent are an excellent example. Children's drawings of their house where they lived "when the touching trouble happened" could also accomplish this goal. Representations of children's dogs, schools, report cards, could also be captured in this portion of the scrapbook. The more childlike, the more innocent, the more incapable the victim can be portrayed in this section of the scrapbook, the more successful the efforts will be to rescue childhood.

An important part of the non-offending parent's treatment may be to write stories or make representations of "childhood" for the victim's scrapbook. Parents may have forgotten the special nature of children and may need encouragement to assist in this goal. Writing stories about unique childlike behaviors or events can be an excellent way to not only capture childhood for the victim, but to encourage support and a belief of the child's innocence on the part of the non-offending parent.

STEP #3:
SELF-ESTEEM OR THE COMPETENT CHILD

The Third Step in the resolution scrapbook should resolve the potential for poor self-esteem and a lack of confidence. This need is especially evident for children who seem to be asymptomatic in treatment, but who are not demonstrating trauma because they do not have the ability to understand what has happened to them. The competent, assertive six-year-old may not be competent and assertive as the child becomes more "aware" and reaches adolescence. Just as the second section in this scrapbook plan focuses on the innocent and perhaps naturally incompetent child, the third section of the scrapbook should "glorify" and emphasize the child's positive self-esteem and accomplishments. Each treatment activity that centers around empowerment or assertiveness could be included in this section of the scrapbook. **Collecting** the child's accomplishments in treatment that emphasize a sense of success is just as important as conducting those exercises in the therapeutic process.

Step Three of this organizational plan may seem to be in conflict with Step Two. In actuality, representing the child's competency without emphasizing the child's innocence and inadequacies may cause the child to miss out on an important comparison. Both sides need to be presented for balance and for breaking the trauma bond. The victim who over-emphasizes personal competencies, may feel guilty that the abuse was not prevented and that, in acceptance of the child's competencies, the abuse should not have occurred. Thoughts from the competent child may say, "If I was so powerful, why was I abused?" On the other hand, if in Step Two, the innocence of the child and the child's incompetencies are over-emphasized, and Step Three, (describing the child's competencies), does not occur, the victim may have a tendency to gravitate toward a victim's cycle of depression and helplessness. One section should not be over-emphasized so that an effective balance can emerge. Balancing both Step Two and Step Three are extremely important in breaking the bonds of trauma "movement."

STEP #4:
PEOPLE POWER

The Fourth Step of this scrapbook organizational plan should pertain to the Relationship Perspective of the Sexual Victim Trauma Assessment. The Trauma Assessment will reveal potential problem areas within the relationship triangle. Seeking responses from these individuals within the relationship scenario will elicit important rehabilitating contributions to the victim's scrapbook.

Those treatment activities that emphasize the Relationship Perspective should, in most situations, be included in this section of the scrapbook. Those assignments or treatment activities that pertain to readjusting the identification of the victim and the perpetrator are important for inclusion in this section. Returning to the Trauma Assessment and finding areas of relationship traumatization, pinpoints the direction of effort that will assist the child in recovery.

If, as an example, the victim felt rejected or disbelieved by the church, contact with that same church needs to occur as the scrapbook is completed. Most churches would be pleased to provide support to a sexual victim, especially the church that may have initially doubted but eventually changed that stance. Solicitation of letters from the church needs to occur. In appreciation of confidentiality, this task may be best suited for the non-offending parent or another supportive, "non-professional" person. Often, the sex offender involved in a cooperative therapeutic program could also solicit support from the church. Therapists need to be the "coordinator" of these efforts to repair the damage in the relationship perspective.

Many churches, schools, extended family members, etc., care about children who have been sexually abused, but they are uncomfortable discussing the issue or they lack skills in understanding. These individuals who would like to make a contribution, but feel overwhelmed or inadequate, need assistance. Providing a sample scrapbook letter and/or limiting the requirements for the letter will usually provide these individuals with the best opportunity to make a valuable contribution.

The Two Step

Basically, letters of support in the relationship section of the scrapbook should be solicited from individuals other than those involved in the professional "system." These non-professional letters should complete two steps, with the first step acknowledging the child's status as a victim and celebrating the disclosure. The second step should encourage the child to feel competent in completing treatment. Basically, these two steps suggest: "First, you were a victim and I'm glad you told," but second, "you were a survivor." Some individuals may be reluctant to make specific statements about the sexual abuse, but they nonetheless have the potential to make an important contribution to the victim by taking these simple steps. Even a letter with official letterhead, and a positive greeting, wishing "good luck" to the victim, could be helpful.

As an example, the minister of the church may feel uncomfortable writing a letter to a child if the allegations of sexual abuse remain as a conflicted issue within the congregation. The minister may, however, choose to write a letter of support to the child and the "officialness" of the support (included in the child's scrapbook) will allow the victim to feel signficant support.

Dear Ryan,

I am so glad I had a chance to write you a letter. I understand you are finishing treatment and that is just great. I am very proud of you.

Ryan, I want you to know that God loves you and you are welcome at church. God will always love you and you will always have a place in our hearts.

Yours truly,

Reverend Lindsey
United Methodist Church

Obviously, some letters within the Relationship Perspective should be more complicated than simply giving the child support. A detailed letter from the non-offending parent will be extremely important. The non-offending parent group may spend valuable group time preparing letters for victims scrapbooks. Additionally, if a parent remains extremely unsupportive, some documentation of love and attachments (even though separate from specifics of the abuse) may be the only contribution that can be salvaged. Some mothers, as an example, may be so angry at their children for reporting that even after many months of therapy, resentment for the child's disclosure may remain. A "moratorium" may be the preferred choice of response since the mother chooses, in this example, to not support the child's allegatons, but will agree to avoid criticism of the child. A letter of love, even though the sexual abuse is not mentioned, could be included in this section, which would provide some consolation to the child.

Dear Candi,

I remember when you were born and we all laughed at your tiny little toes. Our cat "Ralph" didn't know what to think of you, but we did. We loved you and thought you were beautiful. You didn't have much hair, but I used scotch tape and made you a ribbon. You giggled and we took a picture of you in your yellow dress with a yellow ribbon taped to your forehead. You smiled and smiled.

Sometimes, I smile when I think about you now. I especially smile now that you're big and have a long pony tail with a yellow ribbon that's not taped.

Love,

Mother

Likewise, extended family members may also have difficulty contributing to victim's recovery if alliances have split the family or if the subject matter is so painful that specific mention of sexual abuse is unbearable. Letters suggesting the child is competent and supported may be the extent of some family members contributions. The ideal is the two step letter, but some supportive letters without structure, may be powerful on their own.

Dear Tommy,

We're sorry about the trouble you've had with touching. It made us really upset, but we were never upset with you. We're glad you told. You were very brave.

Your mom tells us that you have just done terrific in your treatment program. She said you were going to graduate, and we could write a letter. We know you will do just great and we are very proud of you.

Love,

Grandma and Grandpa

P.S. Grandpa doesn't write very good, but he sends his love, too.

Dear Andrea,

You're a great kid. I miss you out on the farm. I especially used to like it when you would go irrigating with me and catch polliwogs in the pond. I've missed you, and I think the frogs have, too. You can go irrigating with me anytime.

Love,

Uncle Raymond

STEP #5:
INTIMATE IMAGES

Issues concerning trauma to the sexual development of the victim will be resolved throughout many portions of the scrapbook. Recapturing childhood in Step #Two of this scrapbook organizational plan is a developmental issue. Much of what the sex offender may write in clarification (Step #Six) also makes contribution to re-establishing positive sexual development. Step #Five, however, specifically requires consideration of any sexual development trauma that has not already been resolved or portrayed. Contamination in the victim's sexual development is preditable unless this portion of the scrapbook is enhanced and accentuated.

Additional components of this section of the resolution scrapbook should focus on body image, sexual abuse prevention activities, and the creation of a positive, sexual self-esteem. Physical body perceptions, pictures of the child, or descriptions of the child's body image are all examples of items that could be contained in this part of the scrapbook. If medical examinations of children are conducted as an example, documentation should occur to enhance positive body image and avoid future fear about body contamination.

Holy Mother Hospital
Pediatric Division
1108 S.E. 10th
Elliotsville, CT 03201

Dear Rachel,

My name is Dr. John Randolph, and I am the doctor who examined you after you had your touching trouble. I don't know if I will ever get to see you again, so I wanted to write this letter. I know you didn't feel too good when you came to see me because touching trouble is not fun. I do want you to know that I checked your body and you are just fine. There is nothing wrong with you. Everything is terrific. If you ever have any questions, come and see me.

Sincerely,

Dr. Randolph, M.D.

STEP #6:
THE SITUATIONAL PERSPECTIVE

The Sixth Step in this resolution scrapbook organizational plan is often a clarification from the sexual offender or this section contains the clarification from a therapist's work. The offender ideally prepares a comprehensive clarification for the victim and verbally presents that information to the victim and the victim's family. In addition to the verbal statements of the sexual offender, a written document should be prepared for the resolution scrapbook. If the perpetrator is not available, therapists or other individuals must create these components as outlined in specific treatment activities. Each clarification component should be represented in the scrapbook, whether it is written by the sexual offender, by a non-offending parent, or by another family member. Ideally, the offender will make these contributions, but whenever that is not possible, creative efforts must take place.

A second component of Step #Six in this scrapbook organizational plan is to desensitize the tendencies toward phobic reactions and cognitive distortions. Information in the Situational Perspective should outline the tendencies the child may have in the future toward phobias or deadly coping skills. Desensitization of these potentials or the undoing of distorted cognitions must occur in these pages of the scrapbook.

STEP #7:
VICTIMS AND SURVIVORS

The final portion of this organizational plan of the resolution scrapbook should combine the first and last goals of treatment using the Trauma Assessment as a guideline. The identification of the child as a "victim" of a crime must occur in Goal #1. However, a sense of "survivorship" must close the scrapbook. The final portion of this seventh step of scrapbook planning emphasizes the victim's status, but also creates a sense of survivorship, "coordinating treatment goals 1 through 6."

Some professionals, such as those involved with Law Enforcement, the Corrections Division, or the court system rarely have an opportunity to make direct contributions to victim rehabilitation. Interagency coordination often breaks down because it is easy to discount or disregard children who are not seen or heard. Bringing professionals together in the final portion of the scrapbook plan helps both the victim and interagency cooperation.

As an example, an investigating officer may write a congratulatory letter to the victim upon graduation. The probation officer who supervised the perpetrator may also make an important letter contribution. Any professional directly or indirectly involved in the victim's situation may affirm the child's status of innocence and competence. It is important that each of these letters not only attest to the victim's status, but also have a positive overtone of survivorship.

The following letters are not grammatically perfect or proper. They are in the language of children from people who care about children, but who may not be professional writers. These letters may also be insignificant as far as time, costs, and fiscal budgets are concerned. These letters, however, have a priceless contribution to the victim's rehabilitation and the victim's future.

Central Counseling Clinic
1432 Washington St.
Vale, CT 98332

Dear Hannah:

I wanted to write this letter to you and tell you what a good job you have done in treatment. A long time from now you might forget about me but I wanted you to remember what a good time we had when you came to visit. Usually, on Tuesday, your mom would bring you in and we would visit and talk about lots of things. Sometimes we talked about your touching trouble. You were so brave and you did such a good job of giving up the secret. One day you even helped me fill up the candy jar with Valentine candy so that the other kids would have a treat. If I remember, you and I slipped a couple of pieces in our pockets for ourselves and for our office kittens, Clyde and Claude.

Thanks for your help, and thanks for bringing some sunshine into our office. You did such a good job and we will always remember your smile.

Tracy Martin
Secretary/Bookkeeper

Lane Treatment Center
1125 Elm Lane
Elmhurst, CT 04211

Dear Hannah:

My name is Douglas Elliott, and I am the man that usually gave you a big smile when you came in to visit Jan Hindman. If you remember, we had a big dog named, *Alex*, who usually sat in my office. Every now and then when you were finished with Jan, you would come into my office and give Alex a big hug. Sometimes she gave you a slurpy kiss. One day Alex even gave you a ride out to your car. She is really big!

Someday you will be big and you might have a hard time remembering all of the good things that happened to you here. I hope this letter will help you think of us and think about how important you were. You had touching trouble, but you also did a great job. Everyone will remember you.

Great Job!

Douglas Elliott

Department of Human Resources
Corrections Division
45678 Ventura Park
DrapeVille, CT O8765

Dear Hannah:

My name is Russell Barnes. I am the probation officer that has supervised Greg Powell. He has been on probation and I have been keeping track of him.

It makes me happy to hear what a good job you have done in treatment. You should be proud of yourself. I never got to see you, but I was thinking about you. I wish you the best in the future.

Yours truly,

Russell Barnes
Juvenile Probation

Newton A. Smith
District Attorney for Elliottsville County
Elliottsville County Courthouse
Kingtree, CT O9845

Dear Hannah:

I don't know if you remember me, but you came to talk to me in my office about the touching trouble with Greg Powell. You didn't like what happened to you, but you did a very good job of telling. What Greg did to you was a CRIME and that's a very important word for you to remember. It is not okay to do secret touching to kids.

You told me about it and we even talked in the courthouse. Like a very brave six-year-old, you told the judge what happened. Everybody believed you.

I want you to know that it took a lot of courage to tell about the secret touching and to go to court with me. You did a great job. Don't ever forget two things. First, don't forget that what happened to you was not okay, but, secondly, don't forget what a great job you did.

Sincerely,

Newton A. Smith

SCRAPBOOK ORGANIZATIONAL

PLAN #2

This scrapbook format is one of structure with therapeutic steps and process. This is a logistical organization. This simple, but effective procedure allows each treatment activity to close with a scrapbook "capturing" of each step of therapeutic success.

PLAN #2

Another example of scrapbook preparation and organization is a plan that focuses on actual treatment activities. Not only do some children need extensive structure, but some children feel more comfortable if each treatment session is closed or terminated with a predictable activity. Spending the last 30 minutes of each treatment session creating a tangible representation of therapeutic success, can not only provide a vehicle whereby children accentuate progress, but can also provide a sense of comfort for the therapeutic structure.

It is important to recognize that children proceed through schedule, structure and daily routines in many areas of their life, especially within the academic realm. This structure can create a sense of safety. When children feel a structure to treatment, the same as they may feel a structure to school, (which involves recess, math, or spelling,) many apprehensions about attending therapy may be relieved. Allowing the scrapbook preparation to be a continuation of each treatment activity may be very helpful to children and may be an easily aadaptable modality for treatment processes with limited resources.

The ideal scrapbook may not always be possible, especially within treatment centers involving group therapy without the opportunity for comprehensive Trauma Assessments. If the comprehensive representation of the scrapbook (as outlined in Plan #1) cannot be made, the most adaptive and perhaps and the most facilitating organization of the scrapbook could be simply arranged according to treatment activities.

Special Ingredients

As with all scrapbook organizational processes, inclusion of some components of the comprehensive scrapbook plan should also be included. Special consideration should indicate a need for information about a "special book" for children in appreciation of confidentiality as outlined in Step One of organization Plan #1. Additionally, treatment activities may not automatically include letters from professional individuals indicating the important balance between "the victim's status and survivorship." Hopefully, treatment activities would encompass all phases of the Sexual Victim Trauma Assessment and would intermittently reflect treatment successes within those areas. All organizational plans would need documentation protecting confidentiality, as well as letters from professionals. Steps One and Six of the Scrapbook Organization Plan #1 should be added to all scrapbook models.

SCRAPBOOK ORGANIZATION

PLAN #3

This organizational plan provides a focus for the scrapbook by emphasizing the three sections of each sexual victim's Trauma Assessment. This structure allows treatment planning and resulting scrapbook organization to follow the Sexual Victim Trauma Assessment of each victim.

PLAN #3

The Innocent and Competent Child

Another example of scrapbook organization adheres to the outline of the Sexual Victim Trauma Assessment and these five sections serve as a guideline for structure. Beginning with Background Information from the assessment, the death of childhood can be recaptured and significant effort can be exerted with pages in the scrapbook revealing the precious childhood of the victim. This section would mirror Steps #Two and #Three in scrapbook organizational Plan #1.

Bleeding Business

Secondly, from the Symptomological Perspective, information from the Sexual Victim Trauma Assessment describing the pain and trauma victims feel as manifested in their symptoms can be emphasized. This section of the scrapbook would be significant in the **desensitization** process. It may also be important for proactive therapists to predict future symptoms that may arise and not only document, but desensitize these symptoms. The symptomological portion of the scrapbook would be characterized as a "bleeding" or a cleansing process, bringing pain to the surface in this scrapbook section.

Relationship Resolutions

The Relationship Perspective of the Sexual Victim Trauma Assessment could be portrayed in the next section of this scrapbook organizational format. In actuality, triangles could be drawn for older victims creating many representations of how abandonment or support has occurred within these significant relationships. There are many treatment activities connected to the Relationship Perspective as indicated in Chapter 7. Those specific activities could be collected in this section of the scrapbook if this organizational plan is chosen.

Developmental Dilemmas

The Developmental Perspective of the Sexual Victim Trauma Assessment should pinpoint losses or trauma to normal sexual development. If this format for organizing the scrapbook is chosen, the next section would include those treatment activities which specifically pertained to the Developmental Perspective. The issues for inclusion relate to body image work, positive sexuality learning, as well as such issues surrounding sexual functioning and sexual consent.

Situational Steps One, Two, Three

The final perspective of the Sexual Victim Trauma Assessment should be portrayed in the last section of the scrapbook if this organizational format is used. The Situational Perspective of the Sexual Victim Trauma Assessment predicts phobic reactions and distorted cognitions based upon "**how**" the sexual abuse occurred. Taking the three step process of: 1) discovering potentials for cognitive distortions or phobic reactions; 2) desensitizing those issues; and 3) making a positive reframe, would provide an organization to this section of the resolution scrapbook. This process could be extremely effective in helping victims to recognize pitfalls that lie ahead with phobic reactions and in understanding how distorted coping skills will prohibit healing and recovery.

Post-Disclosure

Finally, if this organizational format is used, a natural closure to the scrapbook is post-disclosure issues. The Situational Perspective of the Sexual Victim Trauma Assessment deals primarily with either what happened to the victim following disclosure or what the victim contemplated would occur if the secret was reported. Post-disclosure issues are a final consideration in the Trauma Assessment and would be the last focus using this organization of the scrapbook. Letters (taking the two step process of celebrating both the child's "victim status" as well as the child's accomplished survivorship) from professional people involved in post-disclosure would be an effective way to finalize this scrapbook plan.

SCRAPBOOK ORGANIZATIONAL

PLAN #4

This scrapbook organization focuses on the step by step accomplishment of the six general treatment goals designed for victim rehabilitation (Chapter Five). This process is another rearrangement of trauma issues found in the Sexual Victim Trauma Assessment.

PLAN #4

Another example of scrapbook organization occurs through treatment goal understanding, outcome and representation. Each of the six treatment goals (as outlined in Chapter Five) could be a separate section for a victim's scrapbook using this organizational plan.

Goal #1

Identify the Victim and the Perpetrator

There are many treatment activities pertaining to the acceptance of the victim's status and the perpetrator's identification as a criminal. Treatment activities that pertain directly to the innocence of children, and the criminal aspects of the perpetrator could be included in the first section of this scrapbook organization.

Goal #2

Build Sexual Self-Esteem

Those treatment activities which primarily pertain to human sexuality, intimacy issues or repairing the damage to traumatized sexual development could be organized into this section of the scrapbook. Body image work, picture taking, or documentation of physical issues and successes as examples of items recommended for inclusion.

Goal #3

Breaking the Trauma Bond

The next section of this scrapbook organization plan contains tangible representations of the type of trauma bonding found with each individual victim. Some issues pertaining to trauma bonds that are toward the perpetrator or significant others may already be included in Goal #1, which requires "Identification of the Perpetrator and the Victim." In order to enhance victim's sense of control and organization, those issues should perhaps be reframed in an appropriate manner to accentuate the type of trauma bonding that has occurred.

If trauma bonding has emerged for victims in the area of phobic reactions or cognitive distortions, this section of the scrapbook could be particularly profound. Using the three step process of 1) Identifying the phobic reactions; 2) desensitizing; and 3) making positive reframes, could provide an important focus of safety for each victim.

Proactive contributions to this section of the scrapbook would not only evaluate and describe trauma bonding issues or the potential for trauma bonding, but it would also indicate a proactive, or future emphasis. If, as an example, a young man has a phobic reaction to ejaculation, he may be in a trauma bond with sexual functioning. Proactive therapy would not only document the trauma bond, but would allow pages in the scrapbook to indicate positive feelings toward ejaculation and normal body functions.

Goal #4

Setting Goals

The next portion of this organizational scrapbook plan requires revisiting and emphasizing specific treatment goals for each victim. This effort needs to be proactive and look toward the future. Victims should be able to document in their scrapbooks first, what they would like to have happen (according to specific goals), but, most importantly, what is possible. Emphasis for this section should be placed upon each victim's future. If, as an example, the victim hoped for her father to admit to the sexual abuse and to be reunited with her family, those aspirations should be documented. If, however, the reality of her situation was that her mother supported the offender and the victim was emotionally abandoned, the approach should assist this child in accepting her situation, but to also look toward the future and vow to prohibit these tendencies in the future. Sexual victims tend to become like their parents. This section of the scrapbook should indicate not only what the victim would have liked to have happened, but should also give each victim skills in knowing how to respond in the future, should these same parenting dilemmas or family dysfunctions emerge.

Goal #5

Breaking the Cycle

This treatment goal is intermixed and woven in nearly all treatment activities. As indicated above, victims commonly have a tendency to become like their parents. This section of this scrapbook plan should carefully document a variety of treatment activities that break the cycle and teach victims ways to avoid old patterns and tendencies. This is an important "future" or proactive consideration, especially important for incest victims.

Goal #6

Becoming a Survivor

If this scrapbook organizational plan is used, an appreciative and congenial closure of the scrapbook will naturally occur. Survivorship is not an issue that is automatically attained, but something that is needed at the final stage of recovery for all sexual victims. As the scrapbook closes, victims using this organizational process should peruse all other treatment accomplishments and make representations of how those goals will be maintained in the future. This section of the scrapbook should be a summary, a recapture and a re-emphasis of what has been accomplished with other goals. This is a proactive section that should not only recreate success that has occurred in treatment, but should positively project toward the future.

Plan #5?????

Scrapbook Organizational Plan...?????

Scrapbook organizational plans provide therapists with many varieties and choices for scrapbook implementation. Some decisions will be made according to available resources or time factors. Other decisions may be made according to specific interests, talents or obligations of either the victim or therapist. Most importantly, creativity, flexibility and uniqueness should always be considered in choosing a scrapbook organizational plan.

Some victims may have special needs requiring, as an example, as an "equally divided" scrapbook. If a unique situation emerged where the victim's major trauma was found in confusion about the offender/victim role, a special scrapbook design may be necessary. Half of the victim's scrapbook may need to emphasize the child's status and innocence. Many issues and treatment goals could be incorporated into this half of the scrapbook section. For balance, the second half of the scrapbook could exemplify the offender's status as a criminal. Again, many treatment goals, objectives and individual trauma issues could be incorporated under the general subject of the offender's criminal status and the victim's innocence.

Other situations may suggest a need for a single issue scrapbook while another creative scrapbook organizational plan may indicate a need for a collection of oppositional issues.

"These are the things that I will appreciate and respect in my mother forever."

"These are the things that will always remind me of the purposeful pain my mother gave me."

The list of possible scrapbook organizational plans is endless. A general philosophy and understanding of the scrapbook purpose, coupled with appreciation for individual trauma needs and realistic opportunities will allow flexibility and effective treatment outcomes.

The Mourning After

A final and perplexing consideration is handling of the resolution scrapbook. In actuality, through the scrapbook creation process, confidential information has been projected from a case file into a manageable document prepared by the child. Much of this material is sensitive and confidential. If children cannot consent to sexual abuse, they certainly cannot consent to how the information in their scrapbook could be or might be disseminated. Important choices and decisions need to be made as part of the therapeutic plan.

Some children may choose to have their scrapbooks taken home and become part of the incest family resolution and clarification process. For incestuous families, it is important to have a positive way to remember what has occurred, but to also avoid having the sexual abuse as the primary issue within the family. The scrapbook can provide a modality for which families can avoid being secretive about the sexual abuse that occurred, but also avoid being "permeated" with discussions about sexual abuse, which would negatively impact the family's recovery and regrowth.

For other victims, taking the scrapbook home may be an impossible task. For children in foster care, for children who do not have supportive families, appropriate decision making is important in order to assure emotional safety and yet nonetheless comply with important therapeutic needs of each victim.

Benefits of the resolution scrapbook are many. The scrapbook can be opened and closed under the control of the victim. The scrapbook becomes the way in which the victim has the abuse under control and in a tangible form. Resolution scrapbooks may remain in the therapist's office and may be examined by the victim upon request. Some families place the scrapbook in a safety deposit box in a bank, while other families have the scrapbook carefully secured at home. Finally, some victims may choose to destroy their scrapbooks as an ultimate representation of empowerment.

Whatever organizational plan is chosen and implemented, whatever decision is made for disposition of the scrapbook, the "process" of choice, preparation and productivity makes a profound contribution for breaking the bonds of trauma.

PREAMBLE TO CHAPTER 7

Preamble to Chapter 7

Caution

The danger of presenting specific "cookbook" treatment strategies lies in the potential that special therapeutic skills, sensitivity to individual trauma or inherent creativity may be abandoned, allowing children to be "warehoused" through a process of completing "x" number of treatment activities. Contained in this chapter are 101 "proactive" treatment activities for use in treating victims of sexual abuse. These treatment activities should be a "guide" to therapy, but will not substitute for innovative therapeutic process and procedure. Hopefully, through dispelling myths and misconceptions (Chapter 1), through understanding and conducting trauma assessments (Chapter 2 and 3), as well as through adapting creative modalities and goals for treatment (Chapter 4 and 5), adequate preparation for to use of these treatment activities will occur. These treatment activities have the **potential** to support and augment sensitive treatment plans that appreciate both the uniqueness of trauma and victim's special needs. If these activities are not used correctly, the potential to stagnant creative treatment efforts also exists.

In summary of issues and answers raised in previous chapters, in respect for children's needs and with careful consideration of the specific treatment suggestions, therapeutic plans can be designed for success. Before implementation or choice of these 101 treatment activities, the following issues should be contemplated.

One Size Fits All

Some treatment activities are designated specifically for certain age groups, while the majority of activities are pertinent for "all ages."

Only in unusual situations will a treatment activity be limited to a specific age group since the proactive approach to treatment accepts children at their present stage of development, but always looks toward the future. As an example, a treatment activity designed for very young children, such as reading <u>A Very Touching Book</u>, could also be very effective for adolescents within the proactive framework. With respect to the treatment goal of "breaking the cycle", it is important that adolescents prepare to be future parents who will be protective of their children. Creative therapists will tailor treatment activities to fit all ages. Rather than presenting <u>A Very Touching Book</u> to younger children for content alone, this treatment activity should also be used "proactively" for teaching adolescents to become future protective parents.

Indirect Directness

Treatment activities that are clearly directed by therapists in an overt manner will usually be less effective than those treatment steps where children teach each other. Treatment specialists need to be very direct in treatment **preparation** by examining the Trauma Assessment of each victim and by preparing specific treatment tools. A proactive treatment approach, however, encourages victims to learn and then teach each other, allowing therapists to appear indirect. This effective treatment process will not only make each treatment goal and objective more likely to be accomplished, this "direct directness" also increases victims' ability to cooperate, to be empathic and to feel ownership of therapeutic success.

Be Patient!

One of the dangers in providing therapists with treatment activity lists, is that **production** often becomes more important than process. With patience and respect for process, a single treatment activity could, in some cases, develop over several months and have the capability of being divided into several valuable steps. These 101 treatment activities are not automatically designed for a two hour group meeting or a one hour individual session. Some of the best treatment is accomplished through such indirect processes as anticipating a treatment activity, contemplating objectives, and speculating about the treatment outcome.

In the past, victims lives have been out of control through sexual abuse allowing their cognitions and thinking patterns to be interrupted and distorted. Presenting process "steps" that are manageable and understandable, allows victims to feel in control as they work toward not only resolving their pain, but feeling their pain. Quick, "product" directed activities may be less effective than those which carefully take victims through small steps of success, working toward a predicted and expected outcome.

New Sensory Steps

Appreciation of sensory memory and the sensory triggers that cause pain is important for successful victim recovery. With this understanding, treatment activities should always respect the need to recreate "new sensory activation" that is reframed in a positive way. As an example, a helpful treatment activity occurs if a victim role-plays a scenario where feelings are expressed to an individual representing the perpetrator. Expressing feelings to a victim's perpetrator is a productive externalizing process. Expression of feelings, however, is not enough. Proactive therapists will capture the role-playing activity on video and create a process where the visual perceptions of the child's sense of empowerment (through expression of feelings) will occur when the victim views the video. New sensory memory is created. This second sensory step makes this treatment activity even more powerful. Remembering that children's senses were traumatically activated during sexual abuse makes it clear why different, more positive sensory activity is important for treatment to be successful.

Gender Issues

The ideal treatment program would not divide groups according to gender. The ideal adolescent group, as an example, would involve both males and females, discussing their plan and resolving conflict together, without sexist role influence. A perfect world does not always exist, however, and some therapists may be uncomfortable or unwilling to mix genders. This is unfortunate since both males and females benefit from learning about the opposite sex roles, conflicts and resolutions. Sexual exploitation has a significant element of sexism and, therefore, separation of males and females in therapy may enhance sexual role trauma and may limit efforts to eradicate the problem.

If groups must be segregated according to gender, it is important to integrate the opposite sex perspective in all treatment activities. Language should be structured to create sensitivity to both males and females. Case examples should be nongender specific or with mixed emphasis. Whenever possible, opposite sex groups should be joined for special activities or events so that both the male and female victims elicit empathy. It is also important to emphasize that both male and female offenders abuse children. Believing that only males can treat males or that females will always benefit more from female therapists is unfortunate and usually will limit the therapeutic recovery process.

Positive Sexuality??

These proactive treatment activities cannot be completed without a general attitude and philosophy, on the part of therapists, concerning positive sexuality. Proactive therapeutic approaches not only consider victims's future relating to trauma, but proactive therapy teaches positive sexuality in the future. It will be difficult to complete these activities if professionals do not have a positive feeling toward sexuality and a comfort level in discussing sexuality. The "beauty of intimacy" and other positive issues concerning human sexuality must be emphasized with treating victims. Without these internal positive feelings for therapists, these proactive activities will be difficult, if not impossible.

Group or Individual?

The common modality for use of these treatment activities is the group process. Victims traditionally seem to gain a sense of comraderie in groups since peer influence is extremely important. These treatment activities, however, could be used in individual therapy, as well. Sexual victims need to have personally tailored treatment plans so that their specific needs can be met. Proactive therapy, in appreciation with the Sexual Victim Trauma Assessment, however, can allow individual needs to be accentuated in the group process, in individual therapy or even in family counseling.

Scrapbooking

The scrapbook is the tangible representation of each child's therapy successes and should always be a consideration for each treatment activity. As goals and objectives are accomplished, successful treatment steps need to be captured in some form for the scrapbook to enhance success and new sensory learning. Just as it is inappropriate to teach children mathematics through lecture only, it is also inappropriate to assist children in recovering from sexual abuse without making visual, tactile and auditory representations of treatment issues. Some treatment activities have an obvious methodology for inclusion in the scrapbook while others will require more creativity. Sensitivity toward children's representational systems should occur so that scrapbooks can be designed with respect for those victims who tend to be more visual, more kinesthetic, or more auditory.

Have Big, Movable Fun!

Treatment of sexually abused children should be fun, it should be demonstrative, and it should have body movement. Sitting in chairs and verbalizing issues is not enough for therapeutic success. Children need to move to act, to demonstrate, to enjoy, and to participate in many modalities of success beyond verbalization. Therapists who are demonstrative and find physical ways to express ideas and issues will have a much greater chance of therapeutic success.

Trauma Assessment Guide

The Sexual Victim Trauma Assessment, either in the comprehensive form or the modified form, should be the guide for treatment preparation. These 101 Proactive treatment strategies have the potential to be used in a generic, non-specific form, which may not traumatize children, but may inhibit their possibilities for complete recovery. However, these treatment activities can have a direct relationship to specific trauma that is revealed in each child's Trauma Assessment. These treatment activities have the **potential** to be tailored to specific issues of trauma. Even though the treatment activity may be the same for all group members, special emphasis and individual needs should be addressed, especially as the treatment success is captured for the scrapbook.

Order Please?

These treatment activities are not presented in a specific order and not **all** steps for **each** activity are presented. Additionally, supplies other than what may be listed can be used and implemented into the therapeutic activity. These omissions and lack of order are purposeful, hoping that therapists will be creative and make adjustments according to the needs of victims rather than according to the exact order of treatment activities or to the specificity of lists and supplies. Some treatment activities, as an example, could be expanded into a three to four month period, while other treatment activities may be accomplished in one session. Different subjects can be formatted into a variety of activities. Time frames are purposely avoided so that victims needs will dictate time, emphasis and involvement rather than following a "recipe" type of structure and order.

Parent Participation

Whenever possible, parents should take an active role in the treatment of sexually abused children. Sharing with parents treatment activities' specific goals and objectives is an excellent way to enhance communication and gain parents' trust. In some instances, having parents attend certain portions of the treatment process can also be helpful. For younger children, the "stumbling, bumbling parent" who needs assistance and direction can be helpful to the therapeutic process, as children need to teach their "incompetent" parents.

For preteens or adolescents, parental involvement may be less specific, but nonetheless effective when it occurs. Parents who believe that they will become their child's therapist in the future may take a more active role in treatment objectives. Parent groups for preteen and adolescents can be effective if scheduled monthly and orchestrated so older victims make presentations, conduct role-plays, or demonstrate treatment successes through sharing of their scrapbooks. Treatment specialists who put forth effort to engage parents, even parents who initially seem resistive, will always increase the therapeutic value for victims.

"Children" — Our Most Precious Resource

Finally, the term "children" is used throughout the explanation of the 101 proactive treatment activities. The use of this term is in respect for the childhood which has been robbed from victims. Some may find the term "children" offensive for older victims, but adolescents **are** children and a 17-year-old needs to be recognized as a child as far as recovery is concerned. Proactive therapy is not only reaching toward the future, but is always respectful to the past and the loss of innocence in childhood. Children are our most precious resource and the seventeen-year-old's lost childhood is as important as the losses suffered by the seven-year-old.

101 TREATMENT ACTIVITIES

PP	=	Pre Pubescent
L	=	Latency Age
Ad	=	Adolescent

Chapter 7

Making the Mourning Break

. . . presenting 101 proactive treatment strategies for breaking the bonds of trauma

1

SETTING THE TONE FOR TREATMENT

OBJECTIVES:

1) Children will be able to establish rules and protocol to enhance emotional safety and sensitivity in the group process.

2) Children will be able to avoid conflicts or typical resistance to sexual victim therapy.

3) Children will be able to express feelings and eventually prevent the development of negative cognitions regarding therapy.

4) Children will be able to learn empathy and understanding for others.

5) Children will be able to "reframe" the perception of treatment requirements, from mandated obligations to enthusiastic participation.

AGE GROUP:

Age 6 through adolescence (some younger children below the age of 6 will be able to benefit with reasonable success.)

SUPPLIES:

1) 3 x 5 cards

2) Butcher paper for writing group "Pledge" or chalk board

3) Construction paper

4) Magic markers or colored pens

PROCESS:

The process of this group activity should take place when a new victim group has been formed, or when new group members are joining an existing group. If this activity has not occurred in the past, an already functioning group will also benefit from implementing this process.

Why Am I Here?

The activity should begin with a discussion about each group member's feelings concerning group attendance and participation. As an example, many adolescents feel as though they are being forced to attend treatment as a result of disclosure. "Telling" seems to equal a "punishment." These feelings should be addressed or groups are doomed to fail.

For younger children, less discussion and more "process" will need to occur to establish group protocol. Encourage children to discuss and record their feelings on lists or cards. Do not complete this step quickly. Externalize these feelings toward group participation regardless of positive or negative overtones and make tangible representations of these affective responses.

Right to Recovery

The focus of this process should move toward the understanding that sexual victims need care, nurturing, support, and they need to learn ways of recovery. Clarity should be given to the fact that attendance in group for preteens or adolescents should not be interpreted as an obligation or a punishment. These attitudes should be reframed to statements suggesting the victim's "Right to Recovery." A list of victim's rights to recovery may be created for display or copying for scrapbooks.

Protocol Please

Eventually, the group process should move toward establishing a group protocol or process that is rewarding, fulfilling and guarantees victim's rights, not one that suggests an obligation. The discussion should focus upon confusing and negative feelings group members tend to have when they enter the group or when they are contemplating attending group. Group members could prepare 3 x 5 cards and time should be taken to have group members write personal thoughts or feelings that reflect their feelings when attending their first group. Examples of these statements may include:

"I felt angry because they told me I HAD to come."

"If I didn't do anything wrong, why do I have to go to treatment?"

"I feel so frightened and exposed — almost like when I was abused."

"Sometimes I'm so angry that I get mad at people who didn't cause this to happen."

"Sometimes when I'm hurt, I hurt others and then its even worse."

"I feel embarrassed when I have to come here. I don't think anyone will ever really understand."

(For younger children, these statements will need to be made more simple, such as:)

 "When I come here, I feel afraid."

"I worry when I come here."

"I am afraid I don't have the right answer."

"I need help from my friends here."

After group members have expressed feelings about attendance, (either on 3 x 5 cards or through group discussion), a visual representation of these personal "group worries" and frustrations should be made. If each group member has been able to write their feelings on a 3 x 5 card, each group member should be able to verbally express those feelings. It would also be beneficial for each group member to write their expression of feelings on large pieces of butcher paper or on a chalk board for perusal. This step in the process encourages sharing a personalization of trauma as compared to the more generic concerns of the whole group at the beginning of the activity. These feelings may need to be captured in a letter or a list for new group members, to prevent these negative ideations from emerging.

In order to enhance confidence and group comraderie, each victim should be able to move from experiencing internal feelings that are negative to sharing those feelings with group members. If 3 x 5 cards have been used, then each group member should be able to read their "feelings" to the group and then hopefully work toward writing those words or feelings on a chalk board or butcher paper. A visual representation should be made of all group members' fears and frustrations so that observation and contemplations of all ideas can be made.

A Soft Place to Land

From that step, ground rules should be set and empathy needs to be taught. Group leaders should have prepared written statements that will encourage sensitivity, empathy, and support among group members. For younger children, these statements should be written on larger pieces of paper, allowing each child to hold a poster and read from the poster. For older victims, reading from 3 x 5 cards should suffice. Previously prepared statements should prevent group difficulties and conflict in the future. A positive tone should be set to lend support, before the lack of support and frustrations become destructive for the group process. Prepared statements should be made using the following kind of examples:

"It's really hard for me to talk — please help me."

"If sometimes I look mad, it's just that I'm mad at what happened — not at all of you."

"If I look like I don't care — it's because people forgot to care about me."

"If I talk too much, help me listen — I know when I talk that I don't have to feel my pain. Help me listen and help me feel my pain with safety."

"If I don't talk in group, it's not that I don't care about all of you. It's just that I've kept secrets so long. I may need help."

"I may look like I don't want to be here. That's just because sometimes I feel punished for something that was out of my control."

"If I giggle, it's not that I think this group is silly. I just have had so little laughter in my life that I want to laugh whenever I get a chance."

"If I'm quiet, don't be mad. Help me feel comfortable enough to talk."

For younger children, these ideas need to be tailored to a more simple level of understanding. The recorded statements should predict what traditionally occurs in the group process that is destructive so that the problem is "solutionized" before it happens (proactive). Each statement should also describe some kind of solution so that group members can recognize these behaviors as typical, but will also have solutions to combat these destructive tendencies.

Establish group protocol from the cards and "capture" in some official form for constant group reference. Next, engage the group in a trouble shooting process. Ask "what should we do when someone cries?" or "How can we help if someone talks too much or never talks at all?" Assist the group in establishing solutions for these events that tend to deteriorate the group therapy process.

Even younger children can respond to directions for trouble shooting if solutions are simple rather than complex. For younger children, some "solution" examples may be:

> "In group, we need to listen."

> "In group, we need to help each other because we all might be afraid."

> "In group, we need to not get mad at each other, we should be angry at touching troubles."

> "In group, we need help so that we can learn about good touching."

TRAUMA ASSESSMENT PERSPECTIVE:

This activity pertains primarily to the Situational Perspective of the Trauma Assessment dealing with the family environment. Children who have been sexually abused within a family tend to become very much like their parents. In many instances, the incestuous family lacks the ability to provide support and to communicate openly. This group activity will help group members become empathic and hopefully break the cycles that are likely to be repeated within victims future families.

This group activity is also appropriate for preventing distorted cognitions that typically develop for incest victims as indicated in victims becoming abusive to others, helpless, secretive, self-abusive, etc. Therapists should contemplate the trauma assessments of each victim and discuss group members tendencies toward distorted cognitions, making sure those issues are represented as the group rules are established.

2

CHANGES UPON CHANGES

OBJECTIVES:

1) Children will gain skills in being able to understand and accept "upheaval" as a result of disclosure of sexual abuse.

2) Children will be able to understand and rectify problems as a result of changes that have occurred since disclosure of sexual abuse.

3) Children will be able to understand relationships that have been damaged following disclosure of sexual abuse within the incestuous family.

4) Children will gain support from other group members who are experiencing similar feelings of devastation regarding post-disclosure trauma.

AGE GROUP:

Age six through adolescence.

SUPPLIES:

1) Construction paper for creating pages in the scrapbook.

2) Magic markers

3) Writing pens

4) Magazines for cutting pictures

5) Scissors

6) Paste, glue, scotch tape

7) Tape Recorder

8) Video Recorder

9) Writing Paper

10) Poster Paper

PROCESS:

Safety of Secrets

The process of this group activity first focuses on each victim's description and feelings about disclosure of sexual abuse within their family. Secrecy is an important issue. Victims should be able to discuss the "status quo" that took place previous to the sexual abuse disclosure even though the abuse was occurring. Some victims may choose to draw a picture of their house, to write a poem, or to make a tape recording of their "pre-disclosure situation." Treatment specialists who are cognizant of disclosure issues may need to elicit certain responses from some children since avoiding pain of disclosure may be a tendency for victims. It is important to recognize that even though victim's previous situation of secrecy was familiar and perhaps predictable, it was nonetheless in need of "change."

Changes with No Secrets

The next step in the process evaluates the "changes" that have occurred since disclosure. Victims should discuss changes from a positive **and** a negative viewpoint. In some instances, small children may be able to make posters with a "happy face" and "frowning face" representing positive and negative changes that have taken place since the sexual abuse was reported. Therapists should be aware of each child's post disclosure situation and encourage both discussion and revelation of these issues. For older children, more sensitive frameworks should be made regarding feelings about changes, such as abandonment, embarrassment, disbelief, or safety. Many representations could be made for scrapbooks regarding pre and post disclosure feelings, worries and responses.

Good Changes

The next step in the treatment process is to abandon discussions about personal issues relating to sexual abuse. This part of the treatment activity should concentrate upon more generic changes that seem to be easy to accept. These "changes" should elicit discussions concerning changing clothes, changing hair styles, changing friends or changing houses. All group members should be able to recognize how changes can be made, but that changes also can become positive. Therapists should encourage attitudes toward discovery of the positive aspect of "changing," such as moving toward more "safe" friends, changing homework habits, or changing from dirty to clean socks.

This treatment activity should encourage a positive attitude about changes in victims that may be meaningful and supportive. For some victims who feel degraded and worthless, they may need to recognize that positive changes can occur in their lives since the disclosure of sexual abuse has been made. These positive changes should be the focus as the group activity closes. All group members should finish the treatment activity with resolving negative feelings about changes and to look toward further changes with encouragement.

TRAUMA ASSESSMENT PERSPECTIVE

This treatment activity primarily pertains to the Situational Perspective of the Sexual Victim Trauma Assessment. Post-disclosure issues are of great concern to the process of developing distorted cognitions, which can be described and discovered in the Situational Perspective of the Trauma Assessment.

#3

PROGRESS NOTES FOR KIDS

OBJECTIVES:

1) Children will gain skills in evaluating progress in treatment.

2) Children will gain a positive attitude about treatment intervention successes.

3) Children will gain skills in expressing their feelings.

4) Children will gain skills in introspection

SUPPLIES:

1) Xeroxed Copies of Progress Notes (as designed by treatment specialists)

2) Stickers for attachment to Progress Notes

3) Colorful Marking Pens

PROCESS:

Sexually abused children usually struggle with self-image and often have difficulty expressing their feelings and evaluating their feelings. Additionally, it is common for sexually abused children to feel punished by being required to attend treatment. With these issues in mind, it is important that children participate in a process of evaluating their progress in therapy. By children participating in self-evaluation, their progress is personally assessed, they are able to describe their feelings, and they will hopefully have a more positive attitude about the therapeutic process.

Making a List, Checking it Twice

A variety of progress notes and approaches can be used. For younger children, a check-off list may be most appropriate. The items on the check-off list should be those kinds of activities that will create a helpful group process and which will be effective in creating a sense of comfort and safety in the group. The list for smaller children's check-off list should be tailored so that it would be almost impossible to fail. Suggested items are:

"I smiled."

"I gave good touching."

"I got good touching."

"I listened."

"I shared."

For older children, a somewhat more complicated process may be added. A three-pronged approach may be effective for adolescents who find it easy to write, such as:

"Today, I did."

"Today, I felt."

"Today, I accomplished."

If, however, older children will be using this more complicated format, it is nonetheless important to have a check-off list, as well. Even though older children have more competency, they also have needs to remember those components of positive group interaction and positive communication. For adolescents, a check-off list attached to the progress note is effective allowing them to express themselves about items such as:

"Today I listened carefully."

"Today I gave constructive criticism."

"Today I shared my thoughts."

"Today I helped another group member."

"Today I gave up more of my secrets."

Progress notes could be dated and collected in a very positive fashion for the scrapbook. Children will benefit from seeing their progress unfold.

TRAUMA ASSESSMENT PERSPECTIVE:

This treatment activity pertains to the Situational Perspective of the Sexual Victim Trauma Assessment where distorted cognitions and feelings of self-worth are inadequate. Post-disclosure issues found in the Situational Perspective may also be emphasized if victims feel that treatment is a punishment for reporting.

4

BECOMING A PEER COUNSELOR

OBJECTIVES:

1) Children will discuss post-disclosure trauma and express appropriate feelings to those experiences.

2) Children will gain skills in becoming more empathic and understanding to others who are sexually abused.

3) Children will gain skills in breaking the cycle of incest for the future.

AGE GROUP:

All ages — (Primarily 10 and Older)

SUPPLIES:

1) 3 x 5 cards

2) Colored felt pens

3) Printed Certificates for "Certification of Counselors"

4) Blackboard or easel

5) Construction Paper

6) Video to record role playing (if possible)

7) Formal document or paper for "Code of Ethics"

PROCESS:

I Need Your Help

This activity may take four to eight group sessions. It is a complicated process, but very valuable to victims in treatment and to children entering treatment. The first step is to arrange for a law enforcement officer to visit a therapy group and request registration of volunteers who would be willing to "counsel" new victims. Encourage feelings of support for other victims, but also register a concern for confidentiality. After the law enforcement officer has departed, a plan should be made for interested group members to become "volunteers."

Begin by preparing a list of "do's and don'ts" for counseling new victims. Have each group member write on 3 x 5 cards, the most painful things that occurred during his/her disclosure period. Also, prepare cards for positive things that either happened or that the victim would have appreciated during disclosure. Pass the cards in group, share and discuss feelings. Eventually, make two lists from cards, giving direction on "what to do," and "what not to do" as a volunteer counselor.

Role play scenarios while creating situations where one child takes on the role of a victim with an opposing feeling, will be helpful to address individual victim needs. (Example: If an adolescent was extremely saddened during disclosure, provide a scenario where a different feeling is required such as anger.) Group members may role play being inappropriate **and** appropriate counselors. Other group members critique and support.

Code of Ethics

Create a Code of Ethics through the group process. Eventually, each new "counselor" should pledge to follow the group Code of Ethics for counseling new victims. Include such items as:

"I pledge to allow any feelings to be expressed."

"I pledge to respect privacy and confidentiality."

"I pledge to always be truthful."

"I pledge to remember that people feel differently about sexual abuse."

"I pledge to respect the right to have different feelings."

Using volunteer counselors, or "sponsors" is an excellent component of any treatment program. Children of all ages benefit from individual contact with a supportive peer. Even though counselor preparation may be somewhat limited for younger children, creative therapists can adapt this treatment activity for younger victims. The "process" of preparing to be a volunteer counselor or sponsor is as valuable to victims in treatment as the services provide for newly disclosing victims.

TRAUMA ASSESSMENT PERSPECTIVE:

This activity will primarily pertain to the Situational Perspective of the Sexual Victim Trauma Assessment in dealing with post-disclosure trauma. Additionally, this activity will have tremendous contribution to teaching adolescents to respond appropriately to disclosure of sexual abuse should the cycle of incest continue in their families in the future.

5

IT'S ME AT LEAST FOR TODAY

OBJECTIVES:

1) Children will be able to express feelings concerning post-disclosure issues.

2) Children will be able to express and understand a multitude of responses to traumatization because of secrecy.

3) Children will be able to gain skills in being empathic and supportive of other group members.

AGE GROUP:

All Ages

SUPPLIES:

1) 3 x 5 Cards (adolescents)

2) 5 x 7 Cards (preteens)

3) Construction Paper (younger children)

4) Glue/Tape/Staples

5) Construction Paper or Other Paper for Inclusion in Scrapbook

PROCESS:

Finish the Thought

This treatment process is a simple technique often used for assessment and evaluation. The Sentence Completion Inventory provides the beginning of a sentence and "subjects" are required to finish the thought. Using this same modality, a variety of feelings can be expressed in the group process, but, most importantly, this activity completed intermittently in the treatment process suggests to children that change in feelings, attitudes and beliefs is not only acceptable, but may be important to recovery.

This treatment process encourages victims to recognize that they will often be asked the same kind of questions at specific intervals, and that they will be given the opportunity to change feelings or to express different feelings. This treatment activity also enhances group comraderie since children will be choosing partners, eliciting responses, and providing support.

Previous to initiating this treatment activity, therapists should be cognizant of specific trauma issues relating to specific victims as indicated in the Sexual Victim Trauma Assessment. Some generic presentations may be made in the treatment activity, but the process is always enhanced if victims are allowed to discuss or relate to specific concerns as relating to their own suffering.

Cards should be prepared by therapists with the first part of sentences, designed to encourage group members to finish the thought. Sentence Completion Inventories commonly used would provide effective strategies, such as the following issues:

"Sometimes I think I feel like . . ."

"People like me when I . . ."

"The best thing about me is . . ."

"When I'm alone, I . . ."

"I am sad because . . ."

"Being me is nice because . . ."

"What I hate most about what happened to me is . . ."

Creative therapists, however, will prepare presentations or cards relating to specific issues found in each victim's Sexual Victim Trauma Assessment. Examples of these issues would be:

"Today, I feel most happy because my mother . . ."

"Today, I think the person who did secret touching at school should . . ."

"Today, if I could say one thing to my father about secret touching . . ."

"If I had a Fairy God Mother about secret touching, I would . . ."

Changing Times

It may be effective to prepare these "contemplation cards" and have them displayed in the group room on a continued basis. The idea "hangs" in the air for victims, suggesting changes or reaffirmation. The purpose of this activity is not simply to express feelings, but to allow victims to understand that a change in feelings or a multiplicity of feelings is important.

Varying pages in children's scrapbooks must be represented. Most importantly, this activity should be revisited so that children feel a confidence in expressing feelings and feel exonerated if those feelings change over a period of time.

TRAUMA ASSESSMENT PERSPECTIVE:

There seems to be no limits for this treatment activity pertaining to all three sections of the Sexual Victim Trauma Assessment. Relationship conflicts can be expressed and captured for the scrapbook. Contemplation cards could be prepared pertaining to feelings of poor body image and sexual self-esteem, commonly found in the Developmental Perspective. Post-disclosure issues and cognitive distortions, which emerge in the Situational Perspective of the Trauma Assessment should also be pertinent to the development of contemplation cards and to the success of this treatment activity.

6

WHERE DID I COME FROM?

OBJECTIVES:

1) Children will gain skills in understanding human sexuality.

2) Children will gain skills in learning positive attitudes about the human body.

3) Children will gain skills in learning about body functions and human reproduction.

AGE GROUPS:

All ages

SUPPLIES:

1) Where Did I Come From? by Peter Mayle

2) Construction paper

3) Pencils

4) Paper

5) Camera

6) Video/VCR (optional)

7) Chalkboard

PROCESS:

This treatment activity can be very brief, but nonetheless helpful to children in understanding human sexuality. Peter Mayle's book is a very positive portrayal of sexuality, which includes reproduction issues. Children who are under the age of eight or nine find the book delightful, sensitive and positive. To enhance the treatment process for younger children, the book should be read and discussed.

Victims in therapy should then complete the task of capturing the learning experience in their scrapbooks in some reasonable and positive (proactive) form. This process could occur, as an example, through videotaping the reading of the story by a therapist to the group. Children may watch the video at a later time. This therapeutic "replay" enhances the treatment activity through repetition, but additionally, children may not suffer boredom while listening to the book for a second time if the book was first read on a video and then children watch not only the therapist, but their group members enjoying the video. If video is not available, then victims should go through the process of making posters or papers with several things they learned about the book, Where Did I Come From?

Older children can be more specific in discussions and talk about their birth (dates, the weather, current events, etc.) if information was elicited from parents concerning each child's birth. Parents who are also involved in the treatment program may enhance this treatment activity with writing letters about the specialness of their child's birth. This process can have a tremendous impact on self-esteem in conjunction with teaching positive sexuality.

A Future Parent

For the older child, the book, Where Did I Come From? should be presented as a tool to use in the future when the adolescent is a parent. The activity should be presented as an educational process, whereby adolescents will learn how not to have a "purple face" and how to educate their future children regarding sexual issues. This process could be broken down into several steps with the first step encouraging adolescents to talk about "As a child, what I would have like to have known about sex."

Using a chalkboard or pieces of construction paper, therapists can elicit from adolescents statements or ideas about information that would have been helpful to them concerning sex education. The therapist may need to encourage these statements to emerge, but the **context** of the activity should be in teaching adolescents to become appropriate sex educators, not necessarily for the purpose of educating the adolescent, although this is an obvious, but covert treatment outcome.

The next step in working with adolescents on this treatment activity is to provide trouble shooting responses that are likely to happen from curious children. Using 3 x 5 cards, each adolescent could write on a card what they imagine their future children may ask, that might be embarrassing, uncomfortable or silly. Sharing examples of "purple faces" or discomfort may create a sense of positive humor. More than likely, these issues will be questions that the adolescent wanted to ask or may have asked in the past, but from which the child may have received a negative consequence.

Parenting Paradiums

Finally, one adolescent should be chosen as the "parent," role playing an activity by reading several pages of the book, <u>Where Did I Come From?</u>. Other group members should sit at the feet of the "reader" and interrupt by asking embarrassing questions that appeared in the previously prepared 3 x 5 cards. Discussion should take place concerning how to answer the questions and how to present the material. To enhance this treatment activity, video tapes could also be made to be viewed at a later time. A final enhancement of the treatment process may be to show the videos to the parent group for affirmation, communication and quite possibly for humor and comraderie.

Finally, adolescents should make some tangible representation of what they learned from this treatment activity for their scrapbooks. Some adolescents may wish to write poems or prepare papers with such titles as:

> These are the things I would like to have known about sex when I was little.

> These are the things I promise to teach to my own children.

TRAUMA ASSESSMENT PERSPECTIVE:

This treatment activity pertains primarily to the Developmental Perspective relating to damage to normal sexual development. This is a very pro-active assignment, which not only will create positive attitudes toward sexuality, but may also break the cycle of abuse by teaching children to become better parents in the future.

#7

WHAT'S HAPPENING TO ME?

OBJECTIVES:

1) Children will gain a positive understanding toward body development and puberty.

2) Children will be able to erradicate damage to sexual development in the form of phobias and negative ideations about sexuality.

3) Children will be able to gain comfort in body changes.

4) Children will be able to have a positive attitude toward the onset of puberty.

5) Children will be able to break the cycle of sexual abuse by gaining skills in parenting for the future.

AGE GROUP:

All ages

SUPPLIES:

1) What's Happening to Me? by Peter Mayle

2) Construction paper

3) Pencils

4) Paper

5) Camera (for capturing positive body celebrations)

6) Video/VCR (optional)

7) Chalkboard

8) Any artwork certificates or other items for "celebrations"

PROCESS:

To the Future

Peter Mayle's book, <u>What's Happening to Me?</u>, is a portrayal of puberty in a very positive and humorous manner. Ideally, for younger children, steps should be taken to prepare them for puberty long before the onset of this developmental stage. Although <u>What's Happening to Me?</u> is a positive portrayal, therapists of smaller children will be productive by reading the publication and encourage grand anticipation for each body change or development for sexual victims.

As an example, it is common for children to feel embarrassed and uncomfortable with the onset of breast development. For younger children who have not gone through this process, they need to understand a positive and demonstrative presentation of the "excitement" for upcoming breast development. A sign may be made and group members may talk about the "celebration" that will occur as girls' bodies begin to mature. The same positive, proactive approach is required for males in the example of a "wet dream." If groups are not mixed, boys should nonetheless be aware of the onset of breast development and menstruation for girls, just as girls should become aware of the positive aspects of male development.

Celebrations for body changes that have occurred or will occur in the future should occur under a variety of modalities.

Celebrations

Before reading, <u>What's Happening To Me?</u>, these significant stages in development should be portrayed to children and positive celebrations should be anticipated and discussed. Using construction paper, children may make a list of the kinds of things they would like to have happen when these developmental stages occur. This is particularly helpful for younger children to share these hopes with their parents. Examples include:

When my breasts begin to development, it means I am growing up to be a woman. This will be a great thing and here is what I hope happens.

1) My mom and dad will be excited, too.

2) We will go shopping for my first bra.

3) Everyone in my family will be proud of me for changing.

4) I will work very hard to feel happy about the changes in my wonderful, special body.

Once the anticipation of body changes have been made, children could then proceed through the process of reading Peter Mayle's book as a group. Some representation of the group process should be captured for the scrapbook on pages of paper listing what children have learned from the activity. A video may be made of the children listening to the story <u>What's Happening to Me?</u> and played later to enhance the learning process.

Step One, Two

For older children who have already begun their development, this treatment activity will need to be slanted toward two steps, with the first step encouraging discussion of their discomfort or anxiety about body development. Older children need to take the opportunity to express their fears and trauma regarding body changes. This can be done privately on 5 x 7 cards and passed to group members so that each victim reads another group member's fears or pain. For group members who have reached a level of sophistication, they may be able to discuss their own difficulties. Connected to this process is the issue of "what I would have liked to have heard or known before my body began to change." Lists could be made for scrapbooks to complete this step in the process.

Finally, some activity of reading <u>What's Happening to Me?</u> should occur for adolescents. For sophisticated or advanced patients, the process may include learning how to educate their future children. For preteens, it may be marginal whether they can benefit in a treatment activity designed for future parenting. Therefore, pre-teens may be able to complete the same goal by discussing how they might teach a younger brother or sister about body changes and body functions. Much the same as with younger children, adolescents and preteens need to have a positive grandiose presentation about the onset of puberty. "Celebrations" could occur for reaching these landmarks in body development. The entire activity, whether for adolescents or younger children, should celebrate body development and change as well as encourage positive attitudes for each victim's future.

TRAUMA ASSESSMENT PERSPECTIVE

This treatment activity pertains primarily to the Developmental Perspective of the Sexual Victim Trauma Assessment. Damage to normal sexual development may occur as victims develop phobic reactions to their own body development or as they become involved in self-abusive behaviors as a response to feelings of contamination and discomfort about body functions. This entire process should be one of celebration for human sexuality.

8

WHY, WHY, WHY?

OBJECTIVES:

1) Children will recognize the logic behind preventing sexual abuse.

2) Children will gain skills in learning a positive attitude toward human sexuality.

3) Children will understand rights to privacy.

4) Children will gain skills in understanding the beauty of consent.

5) Children will gain skills in becoming a protective parent in the future.

AGE GROUPS:

All ages

SUPPLIES:

1) <u>A Very Touching Book</u> by Jan Hindman

2) Other sexual abuse resources, such as:

<u>Alice Doesn't Babysit Anymore</u>, by Kevin McGovern

<u>Feelings</u>, by Marcia Morgan

<u>No More Secrets</u>, by Adams and Fay

<u>No Is Not Enough</u>, by Adams, Fay, Loreen-Martin

3) Construction paper for signs or chalkboard

4) Role playing tools

5) Christmas artwork (optional)

6) Paper for Charts

7) Writing materials

PROCESS:

Why?

This treatment activity is important for all ages of children due to victim's confusion about resisting sexual abuse. Traditionally, treatment activities focus primarily on avoiding sexual contact and expressing feelings. Unfortunately, a logic or an understanding as to **WHY** children should have rights to privacy in childhood is generally omitted. Many sexual abuse prevention materials provide a scenario where the child is abused and then rescued, but the understanding of why sexual contact between children and adults is inappropriate, is rarely emphasized.

The "logic" of sexual abuse is particularly important to not only prevent future abuse, but to create a positive attitude about sexual consent in the future. If children do not understand why sexual contact should be avoided, they are at risk to be abused again, but most seriously, without a "logic," the assumption will be made that all sexual contact is bad. Therefore, this treatment activity implies and explains a logistical framework for consent, as well as encouraging prevention.

It should be noted that the logic behind sexual abuse prevention is often confusing even to adults. Victims, therefore, need to proceed carefully through this complicated learning process. This treatment activity will appear to be designed for younger children, although this treatment activity can also be tailored to adolescents under the guise of teaching older children how to protect their children in the future. Adolescents often feel offended if treatment activities appear to be too simple unless these treatment processes are encased in the framework of teaching them how to be appropriate parents in the future. This treatment activity also enhances discussions for adolescents about their own lack of protection as children, which will be an important treatment modality for desensitizing memories and resolving internal conflicts.

How It Is

The first step in this process is to enhance the general and educational perspective of sexual abuse. A variety of resources could be used explaining about how sexual abuse occurs. Books, such as <u>My Feelings</u> or <u>Alice Doesn't Babysit Anymore</u> explain a sexual abuse scenario. Many other resources can also be used to explain how abuse occurs and how children respond. For preteens, other books such as, <u>No More Secrets</u>, can be used. <u>A Very Touching Book</u> should not be used during this treatment step. It will be saved for later when the "logic" of prevention is emphasized. This first step does not provide a logic, but, like most prevention materials, provides scenarios where it is clear sexual contact between children and adults is inappropriate.

Why It Is

The second step in the treatment process is to pose the question of "why." Therapists may pretend to be ignorant and make statements, such as, "Why not let secret touching happen?" Paying particular attention to the fact that some children may have enjoyed the sexual contact, statements could be prepared emphasizing these issues indirectly, but not pertaining to specific victims. Therapists may prepare large cards with statements such as,

"Well, why not? Older people give us good touching. Why not secret touching? Sometimes it may feel good."

Other therapists may initiate information, such as, "Maybe you liked the person who did the secret touching, so maybe it's okay." This step in the process should create a question for children as to why the sexual behavior between children and adults is unacceptable and special attention should be made to specific issues elicited in each victim's Trauma Assessment that pertain to these confusions.

The next step in the process should be to teach that the logic of preventing sexual contact between children and adults begins with understanding that genitalia is treated differently than other body parts. Using <u>A Very Touching Book</u> as a guide, children need to recognize that sexual body parts are treated differently than perhaps ELBOWS AND EARS. Discussions should center around how people keep these parts of bodies private and different than other body parts using an example of avoiding sharing of sexual parts of the body on the school bus, in the shopping mall or at the movies. This activity should be done with laughter and, of course, for adolescents, it should be framed under the concept of being a future parent. As an example, for adolescents, the question could be asked,

"What if your own children want to share the private parts of their body at your tupperware party? What will you do as a father?"

It is important to enhance victim's ideas that:

"These parts of our body are kept private, not because they are dirty or smelly or nasty, they are kept private because of what happens to these body parts when children grow up."

The issue of future sexual consent should be emphasized in the next step of therapy.

> "Sharing the private parts of our bodies when we grow up is a wonderful thing for grown-ups. It's even more wonderful when we keep our body parts private, as kids. Keeping our body parts private when we are children makes sharing them with someone when you grow up, a wonderful thing."

The idea of Christmas occurring each day could be presented to children as another example demonstrating that some things are special because "they don't happen often." Using A Very Touching Book as a guide, children can learn that part of the excitement and special nature of Christmas is related to the fact that it only occurs once a year. Children should take this example and learn that, by keeping their body parts private and special, their decisions to share those body parts at a later date can be exciting and wonderful, as well. Any activities or discussions relating to Christmas could occur to enhance this process.

Big "D" for Decisions

The next step in the treatment activity teaches children that choosing someone with whom they will share their body is a very important decision. DECISIONS should be the focus of this step in the treatment process. Charts or other paper should represent the kinds of things children should decide, such as choosing puppies, the color of their socks, or a special flavor of ice cream. It should be made clear that children's decisions are important while they are children, but children should not be making decisions about sharing the private parts of their bodies. The decision-making process for the future should appear to be exciting, wonderful, but entirely out of the realm of possibility for children. Appropriate decisions for children need to be accentuated to enhance self-esteem and a sense of power, but the treatment activity needs to emphasize that making sexual decisions is not only impossible as children, but inappropriate.

Pages in children's scrapbooks should be made concerning decisions they are allowed to make and decisions they should not have to make. There should also be positive representations in children's scrapbooks for becoming an adult and making sexual decisions. It is extremely important for children participating in this process to recognize that regardless of their apparent participation in the sexual contact, regardless of the level of secrecy, regardless of their feelings during the abuse, they did not give CONSENT. Many children will reveal in the Trauma Assessment that they entered into the room, they initiated the sexual contact, or through secrecy, they gave a nonverbal affirmation. Therapists should be aware of these issues in each victim's Trauma Assessment and discuss these tendencies in the treatment process, pointing out that regardless of those behaviors, **children cannot consent.**

TRAUMA ASSESSMENT PERSPECTIVE

This activity pertains primarily to the Developmental Perspective of the Trauma Assessment enhancing positive ideas about human sexuality and hopefully dispelling trauma that may impact normal sexual development. Additionally, the Situational portion of the Trauma Assessment where children have adapted coping skills or distorted cognitions concerned with guilt and responsibility will be important for this treatment activity.

#9

I REPORTED A CRIME

OBJECTIVES:

1) Children will gain understanding of their status as a sexual victim.

2) Children will gain an understanding of the "criminal" status of the perpetrator.

3) Children's guilt and anxiety because of participation in the sexual abuse will be relieved.

4) Children will gain skills in understanding society's attitude about sexual abuse of children.

5) Children will gain positive ideations and identification of individuals who can be protective in the future.

6) Children will gain a positive attitude toward mental health intervention.

AGE GROUP:

All ages

SUPPLIES:

1) Badges

2) Autographed pictures of legal representatives

3) Blackboard

4) Construction paper

5) Markers or other writing materials

6) Travel modalities

7) A local police person

8) Camera

PROCESS:

Crime

The psychological identification of the victim and the offender is an important issue in the trauma suffered by children and in victim's ability to recover. Many treatment activities will deal with this issue, but this treatment approach primarily pertains to the word — "CRIME." It is assumed that this treatment activity cannot necessarily take place unless treatment activities have occurred previously presenting the logic for rules against sexual contact between children and adults (for example, the treatment activity, WHY, WHY, WHY?), as well as treatment processes relating to the rights of children (KIDSRIGHTS). This treatment activity will collect tangible representations of the criminal aspects of sexual behavior between children and adults but the psychological foundation of this activity will have previously occurred.

The treatment process should begin with recognitions, (according to different developmental and intellectual abilities) regarding the definition of the word — "CRIME." Words such as:

"against the law"

"criminal"

"prosecutor"

"jury"

"judge"

"legislator"

should all be used for definition. Older children may want to prepare these definitions for their scrapbooks, while younger children may need these words printed on large cards. Before discussion of sexual abuse, "crimes and criminals" and society's responses should be understood. Some crimes, such as bank robbing, running a stop sign, or stealing will be excellent representations for discussion. This should not be done haphazardly and the process should not move into the realm of sexual abuse, too quickly.

It's a crime to litter.

It's a crime to eat an apple in the store without paying for it.

It's the Law

The next step in the process encourages recognition of the legal elements of the crime of sexual abuse against children. For older victims, a trip to the law library may be appropriate or the public library may have some representations of the law. "Children's Rights and the Law" (Lexington Press) would be an example of a book that could be used to demonstrate the legalities of sexual abuse of children. For smaller children, a visit from a local policeman in uniform may be helpful. It is important in this treatment activity to collect many representations of the legal aspect of the crime of sexual abuse. Examples of these representations are as follows:

1) Take children to the local police station and have their picture taken individually or as a group. The caption under this picture

in the scrapbook could simply read, "Policemen at the Salem Police Department help kids when criminals do secret touching."

2) Children could be taken to the courthouse and have their picture taken in front of the courthouse or on a witness stand even without an official court procedure. If transportation is impossible, therapists will benefit from having pictures of the courthouse readily available and having individual captions under each picture for children's scrapbook.

3) Play badges from a Sheriff's Department can often be obtained with either a picture of a smiling sheriff or some reasonable facsimile of the Sheriff's Department for each victim's scrapbook.

4) Autographs from people involved in the legal system will be most helpful, such as the Prosecuting Attorney, Corrections Department employees, or even a judge. Although it is most valuable if these autographs can be personal, a generic response from a Senator, the Governor, or any other person in a position of "legality" could be collected for victims to help them feel legally appreciated.

Protection Not Punishment

In this treatment activity, it is important to emphasize the protection issue concerning the laws rather than being negative and criminally critical toward the perpetrator or instilling a fear of what will happen to the perpetrator. As an example, taking children to a jail may elicit feelings of guilt about making a report rather than teaching children they are protected under the law. If individuals in the legal system make contributions to children's scrapbooks, it is important that they make a positive contribution to the protection of children and avoid statements about the legal system's negative and punitive response toward people who commit crimes against children. All of these items or accomplishments should be collected and presented for the scrapbook.

TRAUMA ASSESSMENT PERSPECTIVE:

This treatment activity primarily pertains to issues within the Relationship Perspective where the identification of the victim and the perpetrator is unclear. This treatment modality is especially effective in the triangle relating to the category of "significant others" and their view of the perpetrator as being "guilty" and their view of the victim as being "innocent."

#10

WHAT TADOO?

OBJECTIVES:

1) Children will gain skills in being able to understand appropriate and inappropriate touching.

2) Children will be able to recognize their feelings about sexual abuse.

3) Children will be able to gain skills in protection of future sexual abuse.

SUPPLIES:

1) Video entitled, "What Tadoo"

2) Construction paper

3) Markers

4) Camera (optional)

PROCESS:

This is a simple treatment modality that allows children to view the video, "What Tadoo." This is a very positive video with a study guide and a reasonably effective portrayal of sexual abuse. Children should be encouraged to watch the video, which eventually leads children toward recognizing their options if inappropriate touching occurs. This video describes different kinds of "crisis" situations for children, in addition to sexual abuse and it can also be very effective for general problem solving.

This resource, like many other resources, should be p.r.o.c.e.s.s.e.d. Begin by discussing the title and asking children to speculate about the meaning of the words. Have children brain storm about other situations where they contemplate "what tadoo." Create anticipation. Watch the video and then find ways to emphasize the concepts.

Process the Product

The treatment activity should close with children preparing a list of "what tadoo" if they have situations in the future that need assistance. Some of these problem solving techniques can be related specifically to children's situations, especially those who may be living in foster care or other residences other than their own family. These tangible representations of the learning process should be placed in each child's scrapbook.

TRAUMA ASSESSMENT PERSPECTIVE:

This treatment modality deals primarily with the Situational Perspective of the Sexual Victim Trauma Assessment where tendencies develop toward helplessness and misunderstanding. Distorted cognitions that are negative can be prevented if children learn a sense of empowerment and control in their futures.

#11

ISSUE OF FORGIVENESS

OBJECTIVES:

1) Children will gain skills in recognizing conflicts regarding the issue of forgiveness and sexual offending.

2) Children will gain skills in understanding the impact of the issue of forgiveness on sexual trauma.

3) Children will be able to gain skills in making personal, informed and appropriate decisions about forgiveness of the offender.

4) Children will be able to understand the concept of "clarification" as it pertains to the issue of forgiveness.

AGE GROUP:

13 and older.

SUPPLIES:

1) Forgiveness Letter (attached)

2) Pens/Pencils

3) Writing Materials

4) Video Camera/Player (optional)

5) Cassette Recorder and Tape (optional)

6) Construction Paper

7) Role Playing Facilities

8) Envelopes (optional)

PROCESS:

This treatment activity involves a complicated trauma issue for sexual victims, which is the issue of forgiveness. The concept of forgiveness seems to be a potentially traumatizing issue, especially in cases of family incest. There is often pressure placed on the victim to "forgive" the offender. Since forgiveness is sometimes viewed as a virtue of the victim, this issue may be a conflict for many older victims, however, the "potential" conflict regarding this issue exists for younger children who may be faced with decisions about forgiveness, decades into their futures.

Pressure!

The first step in resolving the conflict relating to forgiveness is to understand the potential trauma to the victim if possible traditional views of this concept are implemented. Forgiveness is often viewed a "quick fix" unless the concept is discussed and handled appropriately. Many victims may be in conflict with parents who are encouraging them to act quickly and resolve the sexual abuse situation through the act of forgiveness. The first step then, is to process all possible feelings relating to the pressure to forgive.

Pieces of construction paper could be used by adolescents as they verbalize their feelings of frustration and pressure. On the other hand, some adolescents may be anxious to work toward forgiveness and these feelings must also be expressed. Again, as with most treatment activities, the process should encourage the expression of a variety of feelings so that no one attitude or ideation is presented as most valuable.

Who is the Victim?

The second step in this complicated treatment process is to emphasize the unfairness of the victim, needing to take care of the offender or the family. Revisitation of those treatment activities, which encouraged a sense of "crime" may be necessary at this point. For active or demonstrative groups, role playing may occur where one victim takes on the role of a legal professional, such as a judge or a prosecutor. The group should be reminded in this step of the treatment process that sexual contact is a crime, much the same as a bank robbery. The analogy of a bank robber being rescued by a bank teller may assist victims in understanding the absurdity of the victim taking care of the offender. Without emphasizing the criminal issue of sexual offending and, therefore, the inequality between the obligations of the "criminal" and the "innocent," this treatment activity will be very difficult.

Tell Me True

The next step in the treatment process is to assist victims in understanding the true meaning of forgiveness. Even though the criminal issue may have been previously emphasized, taking a step further and emphasizing that the true meaning of forgiveness is, in fact, the obligation of the offender will be most helpful to sexual victims. The forgiveness letter entitled, "A Process — Not A Product," should be presented to group members. Even though some of these concepts may be advanced for younger adolescents, time can be taken and issues can be explained. Therapists will always benefit if more advanced, older or more intellectually competent group members assist other group members who have difficulty understanding.

Atonement Equals Clarification

The true meaning of forgiveness should be explained as a process of atonement, whereby the sexual offender or the "sinner" pays atonement to those who have been sinned against. For those victims involved in the ideal treatment program where the offender will prepare a clarification, the task of avoiding forgiveness and waiting for clarification will enhance this process. If that is not possible, the clarification should be explained as a process for which the victim was **entitled**. Rather than look toward the process of forgiveness, the therapeutic approach should emphasize a clarification and a resolution.

The clarification process should be explained as a way in which the sexual offender accepts all guilt and responsibility for what has happened and puts forth effort to clearly define who, how, what, when, where and why the sexual abuse took place. Clarification is not an "apology letter," but a complicated process designed to assist the victim (see clarification treatment activities in this manual). Understanding the importance and the process of clarification will assist victims in being removed from responsibility for forgive the offender. The clarification was the perpetrator's obligation. If the victim does not receive a clarification, forgiveness is not a demand. If the child will be obtaining a clarification from the perpetrator, then the process of forgiveness or decisions about the process of forgiveness need to be postponed until the clarification has occurred. For victims whose perpetrator has died or who is unavailable, but the victim feels compelled to "forgive," the lack of clarification or the lack of the offender's ability or interest in paying atonement through clarification protects the victim from this deadly obligation.

Power to the Victim

Finally, each victim should be able to feel a sense of empowerment for making decisions about forgiveness. As the victim has become "culpable" and understood obligations, rights, responsibilities, about forgiveness, personal decisions about forgiveness will need to be made on a case-by-case basis. Therapists would benefit from spending significant time providing victims with knowledge of varying options.

This process should not be done quickly or haphazardly. Construction paper with cards describing options could be placed on the group room wall for several group sessions. Children could use writing paper and present options in some written form, either to a family member, to the offender directly, or to another significant individual outlining a list of options regarding forgiveness. Options should range from ''no decision whatsoever'' to ''forgiveness'' or to ''total rejection'' of even discussing the concept of forgiveness. Role playing may enhance this process with several group members acting out available options.

Following careful exposure and explanation of all possible options, each victim should make a decision that is symbolically represented in scrapbooks. Some victims may choose to ''seal in secrecy'' their decision, placing information in an envelope that is not available for general perusal of the scrapbook. Other victims may request that their decisions or their role play be either tape recorded or video taped for presentation at a later time to the group or to family members. This process of externalization will be particularly helpful for victims wishing to make specific decisions about the issue of forgiveness. And, other victims may decide to avoid deciding, which should be viewed with the same support and encouragement since the victim has become culpable and is now in a position to make the most appropriate decision.

TRAUMA ASSESSMENT PERSPECTIVE:

This treatment activity primarily pertains to the Relationship Perspective of the Sexual Victim Trauma Assessment. When pressure is placed upon victims to forgive the offender, there is usually traumatization and disruption in the identification of the victim and the offender. For younger children, the bottom of the triangle or the left hand side of the triangle may show these tendencies toward trauma.

This treatment activity could also pertain to the Situational Perspective and post-disclosure issues. Victims may be placed in a position to forgive the offender, rather than face trial, prosecution, abandonment or lack of visitation. Religiosity is obviously an issue in the third section of the Situational Perspective dealing with the entire environment or the "holistic" view of the victim's world.

"Forgiveness — Process or Product?"

January, 1983

Dear Victim:

If you are like most victims who have been sexually abused, you are asking many questions of yourself. We have all heard the old favorites from sex offenders, family members, ministers, and clergy, "forgive and forget," "let bygones be bygones," "let's bury the hatchet and start over." These statements seem to encourage victims to feel as though it is their responsibility to take action regarding resolution and forgiveness. This seems strange, since victims are innocent and not responsible for what has occurred. The question is then raised, "Who is responsible for resolving sexual abuse?" If the offender can ask for forgiveness, then the victim is responsible for "yes or no," refusal or acceptance. The "I'm sorry" subtly demands the victim give something back. The traditional meaning sounds as though forgiveness demands reciprocity from the victim. Just like the sexual abuse you endured, the offender is again asking you to carry the burden.

In this letter, I will share with you my answers to this dilemma. When I asked myself, as a Christian, should the victim, the innocent one, take on responsibility for forgiveness, I knew I had to find the answer. The questions shot right at the heart of my Christian faith. At first, I was confused, but as I studied, it all began to make sense. I hope these questions and answers help you as they have helped me.

In order to solve this very special problem of forgiveness between the victim and offender, I looked up the Greek word for forgiveness, repentance, and confession. Looking up the Greek word is a good way to find answers, because in translating, a lot of words get changed. A very special minister taught me that.

The Greek word for forgiveness is **APHIEMI**. This word primarily means to send forth, send away or remit. It has two conditions with no other limits, just like Christ's forgiveness. The conditions are repentance and confession, as shown in Matthew 18:15-17 and Luke 17:1-13. The noun form of the word forgive is **APHESIS**. It denotes a dismissal or release. Notice, in neither definition is the word "forget" used. "Forgetting" is not a part of forgiveness. For forgiveness to occur then, two things must happen, first, repentance and second, confession. Without these two components, there is no forgiveness. Also, please take care to note that neither of these two conditions are the burden of the victim. If the process belongs to the offender, then what is the offender's job or responsibility? Let's look at those two demands.

The first part is "repentance." The Greek word is **METANOEO**. This word means to perceive, afterwards. Then, **METEA** means after, which implies a change. **NOEO**, is to perceive; and **NOUS** is the mind; seat of moral reflection. So, if you put all of that together, you have repentance equals recognizing in your mind what you have done. Now, hang on to that thought and we will put all of this together soon.

The second part of forgiveness is the component of "confession." The Greek word for confession is **HOMOLOGEO**. This word means to speak the same thing, to admit, to declare openly by way of speaking out freely.

Now, if you put repentance and confession together, you have: "to speak out openly and freely of what one has recognized in your mind that you have done," and that is the essence of forgiveness. This means that if someone truly wants forgiveness, they must speak of what they recognize in their own mind they have done. This takes work on the part of the person asking for forgiveness, it does not mean work needs to be done on the part of the victim.

Apply that to your own life and to the relationship between you and your offender. If the offender wants forgiveness, the requirement is to speak openly and freely of what has been recognized in the mind, especially regarding what has been done to you, the victim. The **Forgiveness** the offender may receive from Christ, can happen in a matter of moments, but I am convinced that it takes a long time for offenders to recognize wholly what they have done to their victim. Let's face it, it took years for them to get to the point of becoming an offender. It will take many months for them to sort out all of the information in their minds in order to truly repent and confess.

This means that the burden is on the sexual offender to go through a "process." Offenders typically would rather have the "product" of forgiveness. They would rather have the act completed quickly of "I'm sorry, now, you forgive." If we understand the true meaning of forgiveness, it is the sexual offender who must move through a process and work toward the final product.

Hopefully, one day the offender will go through a therapeutic process, to sort out and understand what damage has been done by the offenders selfish actions. If this process occurs, then the offender may be given the opportunity to talk with you in a "clarification" session. It will then be your choice to examine and evaluate whether you believe **the process** has, in fact, taken place. It will be your judgment of the offender's repentance and confession that will give you the information needed to help you know whether or not you choose to accept the "process" completed by the offender. This is certainly not something that can be done in the beginning. It is something that needs to take place with careful contemplation on your part examining the offender's efforts at **the process.**

As you contemplate choosing whether or not to forgive, be sure and remember what we learned about forgiveness. Part of the definition of forgiveness is to release. I like that. You have the opportunity to be released from the power and the control the offender has had over you not only in the sexual abuse, but in your quandary about whether or not forgiveness should occur. The choice will be yours and because it is your choice, you have been given back your own power, you have been released.

If your offender does not want forgiveness this will happen. Resistance in understanding the damage and trauma will occur. Speaking about the "crimes," the pain, and the resulting suffering will be avoided. Therapy and change will be battlegrounds of conflict. Attack may be made with religion as a weapon "God has forgiven me, why don't you?" This kind of statement only indicates the offender's unwillingness to understand the true meaning of forgiveness and work toward the process. If the offender has truly repented, an eagerness to change will replace minimization and rationalization.

You see, the center of sin is capital "I." That inner self and selfish self that molested a child must change and this will take time. When people molest children, they are thinking of themselves and quickly, upon discovery, they want to be forgiven so that they will feel better. Offenders have practiced being selfish for many years and it will often take years to change. Therapy is a process of unlearning, relearning, and learning. This takes time, effort, and often pain on the part of the offender. This process, this pain, this effort, is, in fact, the true process toward repentance.

Remember, all of the people in this program care most about the victim. That's why this program is called "Restitution" therapy. We believe you as a victim are innocent and we demand restitution be paid to you in some form. You will learn that your rehabilitation is our goal. You are not responsible for the sexual abuse and you are not responsible for forgiveness. Your sexual offender is responsible for both of these things. The program is going to give your sexual offender an opportunity to go through this process. The choice will be up to the offender and whatever the offender chooses will not be your responsibility. You are a victim who was robbed of something precious and special. You need to be cuddled, nurtured, and protected, and we want to guarantee that happens. It is the offender who must do the work.

I hope this letter has answered some questions for you. It was fun to write and share this with you. There are some very special ministers who have helped me write this and have helped me put this letter in your hands. Your therapist can tell you about some of them if you want to talk with them further. Your therapists appreciate these ministers and appreciate the job they do. Hopefully, we can all work together in the months ahead.

Have a great day; you deserve one.

"ONE WHO WALKS WITH GOD"

#12

PURPLE FACES

OBJECTIVES:

1) Children will gain skills in relieving guilt and anxiety about discussing sexual issues.

2) Communication between parents and children will be enhanced.

3) Children will develop positive attitudes toward sexuality.

AGE GROUP:

10 and Under

SUPPLIES:

1) <u>A Very Touching Book</u> by Jan Hindman

2) Construction Paper

3) Writing materials

4) General Art Supplies

5) Purple Paper

6) Certificates

7) Camera

PROCESS:

This treatment activity involves a simple process of accentuating parents embarrassment about sexuality so that victims can become "helpers" of their parents. The general, overt goal is for children to help their parents while the subtle goal encourages communication between children and parents.

Purple Faces

The treatment process should begin with a discussion of grown-ups and their purple faces. Using A Very Touching Book, children can understand that often parents "get purple faces" when they discuss sexual matters. The message to children should not be critical of parents, but portray their inadequacy in a positive and humorous manner. Therapists may suggest to children that parents want to talk to their children and teach their children the right words for body parts, but that parents get "purple faces," which makes communication difficult. The group may process experiences children have had in the past or therapists may relate stories about their experience with purple faced parents.

After a great deal of humor and fun regarding parents' purple faces, children should concentrate on ways in which they can be helpful to their parents in relieving the "purple faces." It can be very effective for children to speculate how parents feel. This is an excellent example of empathy training if children can concentrate on the uncomfortable feelings of their parents. Lists of feelings that parents may experience should be prepared such as:

Embarrassed

Sweaty

Worried

Nervous

These feeling words could be presented on purple paper with grandiose decorations.

How Can We Help

The next step in the treatment process should encourage children to make a list of how they can be most helpful to their parents. The list, in actuality, should accentuate learning for children under the guise of teaching parents. Examples for the list would be:

"We should teach parents that their bodies are wonderful and special so that our moms and dads won't have purple faces."

"We should teach our moms and dads that using silly words for the wonderful, private parts of our bodies will make purple faces even more purple."

Big People and Little People

The process of making a list for helping parents should be done with great preparation, culminating with a process where children actually interact with their own parents. In ideal situations, parents could attend a group meeting and children could read from A Very Touching Book while parents exhibit the feeling cards that were previously prepared. Children could actively "watch for purple faces" and gain a great deal of empathy and skill in communication by helping parents deal with feelings of embarrassment and anxiety. When parents are not able to attend a group, therapists should decide whether it is advisable that children present their helpful list to parents in individual therapy. Each child's vulnerability in this area should be carefully evaluated before decisions are made since some victims may have uncooperative parents.

Finally, children should capture this activity's learning in their scrapbooks in a variety of different ways. Certificates could be awarded for children who helped their parents get rid of purple faces. Pictures of children interacting with their parents could be included or a variety of artwork could be done to emphasize the success of this treatment activity.

TRAUMA ASSESSMENT PERSPECTIVE:

This treatment activity pertains to the Developmental Perspective of the Sexual Victim Trauma Assessment. Younger children have the potential to develop sexual dysfunctions if a positive attitude about sexuality is not initiated during the early years of sexual development. Trauma seems to be especially significant for children who develop in families where restrictive and rigid attitudes prevade concerning sexual functions and sexuality, in general. Trauma Assessment information will dictate the extent of using this treatment activity.

#13

SANTA AND GOOD SECRETS

OBJECTIVES:

1) Children will gain skills in understanding appropriate secrets.

2) Children will be able to acknowledge existing support.

3) Children will be able to gain skills in learning empathy and expressing positive feelings toward others.

AGE GROUP:

12 and Under

SUPPLIES:

1) Boxes decorated in Christmas paper

2) Christmas Cards

3) Red Marking Pens

4) Ribbons

5) Scotch Tape/Staples/Glue

PROCESS:

Good Secrets

This is a simple treatment activity that can enhance children's positive feelings about themselves in conjunction with the Christmas holiday. This treatment activity should be prepared several weeks before the Christmas holiday. Anticipation should be instilled in children regarding Christmas gifts. Children should be able to anticipate receiving Christmas packages with "good secrets." Children should be able to clearly understand that packages and presents are examples of acceptable secrets. Reviewing the treatment activity comparing secrets to surprises (Treatment Activity #19) may be helpful. Most importantly, children should recognize that positive secrets at Christmas are acceptable since the secrets will be opened and the secret will be over.

Christmas Boxes of Secrets

After verbally processing the idea of Christmas and secrets, children should be able to decorate their Christmas box. Medium sized boxes should be decorated in a way allowing the lid to be opened and closed for several weeks. Children should decorate their boxes with their own style and imagination, but clearly, allowing the identification of each child to be visible from the outside of the box. To avoid disappointment, victims should also understand that the Christmas "present" they will be receiving through the group process will not be a toy or other desirable objects. Children should understand that they will be receiving secret "happy thoughts" in their boxes to be opened at Christmastime, rather than typical presents.

In the time period before Christmas, group members should have the opportunity to place "happy thoughts" in the boxes of other victims. This process will enhance teaching empathy and sensitivity to each child. Contemplation should be made assisting each child in preparing something positive for other group members through art work or Christmas cards. Therapists and other connected adults (parents when appropriate) can also make contributions to each victim's Christmas box. In the last therapy session before the Christmas holiday, therapists should bind the children's boxes with colored ribbon and allow children to take their boxes home to be opened during the actual holiday.

TRAUMA ASSESSMENT PERSPECTIVE:

This treatment activity could pertain to either the Developmental Perspective or the Situational Perspective of the Sexual Victim Trauma Assessment. Specific areas of trauma, either to the sexual attitudes of victims or in the thinking process of children, should be issues for specific "happy thoughts." Careful examination of potential trauma areas should occur so that those issues can be the focus of notes to children in their Christmas boxes.

#14

EASTER EGG HUNT FOR HAPPINESS

OBJECTIVES:

1) Children will be able to identify feelings of betrayal and abandonment.

2) Children will be able to resolve and control feelings of betrayal and abandonment.

3) Children will be able to break the cycle toward repeating the tendencies of betrayal to children in their future families.

4) Children will be able to improve self-esteem.

AGE GROUP:

Ages 12 and above

SUPPLIES:

1) Easter egg coloring kit

2) Eggs for each victim (not hard boiled)

3) Magic markers

4) Brightly colored paper towels

5) Camera

6) Construction paper

7) Writing materials

8) Blackboard

PROCESS:

How Does It Feel?

The first step in this process is to have group members identify feelings of abandonment, loneliness and betrayal within their families pertinent to each victim's unique situation. Therapist's attention to information found in the Relationship Perspective of the Trauma Assessment must occur and these trauma issues should emerge in the treatment activity. Identification of feelings should be represented on pieces of construction paper, a blackboard, or group members should make their own lists of these negative feelings regarding abandonment that is either real or imagined.

How Would I Like to Feel

The next step in the treatment process should be to look toward the future or complete the same process with victims portraying how they would like to have been treated in the sexual abuse situation. Again, lists or some tangible representation of "hopes" should be made from this fantasy or "wish" activity.

Handle with Care

The next step is to challenge group members to recognize the precarious nature of children and how easily feelings can be hurt. From this discussion, group members can be encouraged to decorate an Easter egg representing themselves. These eggs should not be hard boiled and obviously will need a great deal of care to avoid being broken. The comparison between protection of children and care for the "egg" must be made.

Finally, children should be challenged to care for their "egg" (a precious, beautiful, wonderful child that needs a great deal of protection) for the next two weeks. Victims should be encouraged to remember the painful feelings that were described in the first portion of this treatment activity, such as abandonment. Challenge group members to remember, as an example, that if their egg is left in the bedroom while they attend school, feelings of abandonment may occur. Children may need to obtain a "babysitter" for their egg or take their eggs with them to school so that feelings of abandonment for their "child" can be prevented. This assignment can be done in a humorous way, but also bringing the reality children's needs for protection to the surface.

Shell Shock?

A final step in the treatment process allows re-evaluation of the treatment activity two weeks from the first treatment date. If the eggs were broken, discussions could occur as to how that disaster relates to sexual abuse victims feelings. Additionally, victims should be able to discuss their feelings as a result of participating in an activity where they needed to respond like an empathic caretaker or parent.

Some tangible representation needs to be made in the scrapbook with the egg shells either being broken and dried or a picture of the child with their "intact" egg, that was properly nurtured and protected. Older victims may wish to project to the future how they will care for their own children. Many options exist such as having victims choose to write:

"An Open Letter to My Child." (Egg)

The focus of this option should be a promise to care for the child of the future, much the same as the victims have cared for their egg.

TRAUMA ASSESSMENT PERSPECTIVE:

This treatment activity primarily pertains to the Relationship Perspective of the Sexual Victim Trauma Assessment and negative feelings as a result of abandonment and betrayal within the incestuous family. Some emphasis in the Situational Perspective may also enhance this Trauma Assessment issue since victims tend to repeat cycles of abandonment in their future without appropriate knowledge and awareness of the protection needs of children.

#15

MOTHER'S DAY/FATHER'S DAY TRAUMA

OBJECTIVE:

1) Children will gain skills in understanding the multiplicity of feelings regarding the victim/parent relationship.

2) Children will gain skills in evaluating their own feelings regarding betrayal, abandonment, or support from their non-offending parents.

3) Victims will gain skills in breaking the cycle toward becoming a nonsupporting parent in the future.

AGES:

Age of six through adolescence

SUPPLIES:

1) Large pieces of construction paper

2) Pens

3) Crayons

4) Magic markers

5) Smaller pieces of construction paper

6) Brightly colored writing materials

7) Magazines

8) Decorations; such as stickers, paper doilies, or any other material that can be used to make greeting cards.

PROCESS:

Meaning of the Day

The first step in this treatment process requires a group discussion regarding the meaning or purpose of Mother's and Father's Day. The true meaning of honoring supportive and loving parents should be clarified. For older group members, trauma bonding toward a parent who is rejecting or abandoning the victim could be discussed, as long as equal discussion occurs concerning parenting that is supportive. A "balance" of views is important in this process step.

Possibilities, Possibilities

The group should then make at least 25 salutations for the "inside" of a Mother's or Father's Day card. This should be done as a group activity with one person writing group thought. Salutations should range from an extremely supportive and caring position, to an extremely blaming and abandoning position. All group members should go through the process of experiencing extremes, as well as those positions which tend to be neutral.

Examples for salutations could be:

"Thank you for believing me about my secret touching. I hope I grow up to be a father just like you."

"I'm sorry you don't believe me or love me on this Mother's Day. I hope that next year will be different."

"I remember lots of good things you have done for me as a dad, and I want to remember those more than I want to remember that you had a hard time believing me about my secret touching."

"It means so much to me that you believe me — Happy Mother's Day to a great mom."

"I feel like you hate me this Mother's Day. I hope it is different next year."

"Thank you for not only being a good dad all year long, but for helping me with my secret."

Balancing Act

It is very important that each group member experience and discuss a wide range of responses in order to create a balance. As an example, if those victims whose parents are minimally supportive recognize that other parents may be **extremely** attacking, the minimal support may seem to be more comforting. On the other hand, if victims have been abandoned, and many of the salutations suggest that abandonment is common, those victims may recognize they are not alone and they may experience a sense of "comraderie." For victims who have supportive parents, working through a variety of possible negative salutations will allow that victim to appreciate parental support, even more.

To The Drawing Board

After all the varying salutations have been presented, group members can then make their own Mother's or Father's Day cards. Some of these cards will obviously not be sent, but will be collected for the scrapbook. Some children may want to role play presenting their card to another group member if actual presentation to a mother or father is impossible. Several group sessions could be spent on this process with role playing. For example, demonstrating how children would **like** their parents to respond or how they might like to respond as a future parent will have many positive contributions to future recovery.

For younger children and for situations where the parent is involved in therapy as well, it can be a very effective treatment technique to have parents (in a separate group) read the possible salutations and contemplate which salutation their child may choose. The same process philosophy will apply to parents. If supportive parents are given the opportunity to read salutations where support does not exist, their support of their child may be reinforced and seem even more powerful. For parents who are neutral or who have provided minimal support, discussing appropriate parental salutations may encourage a more positive contribution to the victim. Hopefully, for those parents who are not supportive but are exposed to other salutations of support, changes may be made and the parent may become more helpful to the victim.

TRAUMA ASSESSMENT PERSPECTIVE:

This activity primarily deals with the Relationship Perspective of the Sexual Victim Trauma Assessment. The psychological identity of the perpetrator and the victim is either clear or confused and therefore, this assignment will relate to those issues found in the Trauma Assessment. Therapists should guarantee that salutations for specific groups reflect information found in group members' Relationship Perspective.

#16

THANKSGIVING FOR GOOD TOUCHING

OBJECTIVES:

1) Children will gain skills in understanding the positive aspects of affection, attention, and sexuality.

2) Children will understand specific issues related to trauma and relationships.

3) Children will understand the negative aspects of aggression and violence, as well as sexual abuse.

4) Children will be able to express emotions regarding sexual abuse trauma.

AGE:

Age six through adolescence.

SUPPLIES:

1) Thanksgiving decorations

2) Long table representing a Thanksgiving dinner table

3) Construction paper

4) Markers

5) Crayons

6) Thanksgiving stickers

(7) Possible potluck contributions from adolescent group members or snacks of some kind for younger victims.

8) If food is provided, eating utensils, napkins, etc.

9) <u>A Very Touching Book</u> by Jan Hindman

PROCESS:

Thanks for Thankful Thoughts

The group should begin with a discussion of the traditional meaning of Thanksgiving. The treatment process should include thoughts about thankfulness regarding sexual abuse. Anticipation should occur for participating in some kind of Thanksgiving "feast" (ranging from a full potluck dinner to simple snacks). If the luxury of a long table, table cloths, silverware, and edible treats are available, preparing a "thankful thought" before eating should be contemplated. If a representation of a meal cannot occur, then the group must simply work toward making "thankful thoughts" to take home for their own Thanksgiving dinner.

"Thankful thoughts" should represent hopes or positive wishes for the general protection of children concerning sexual abuse. <u>A Very Touching Book</u> could be used for emphasis of many issues relating to different kinds of touching problems. These thoughts should also cover such issues as disclosure and some thoughts should be reversed to reflect the avoidance of certain negative issues, such as violence, anger or abandonment surrounding sexual abuse. Examples of thankful thoughts are as follows: (Use humor!)

"I am thankful that turkeys don't know anything about secret touching."

"I am thankful that I have a wonderful, private, special body that is all my own."

"I am thankful that I gave up my secret and told about my touching trouble."

"I am thankful that this year we won't put gravy on the jello at Thanksgiving dinner."

"I am thankful that people believe me about secret touching."

"I am thankful that I get lots of good touching from my mom and dad."

"I am thankful that bad touching doesn't happen very often in my family."

"I am happy that I don't have to eat broccoli at Thanksgiving."

A wide range of issues should be reflected on large pieces of construction paper with thankful thoughts. The range of responses should be from extremely negative to delightfully positive. Each Sexual Victim's Trauma Assessment should be evaluated to guarantee all issues within the Relationship, Developmental and Situational Perspective have been reflected on the thankful thoughts cards.

Thankful Thoughts

Each child should be allowed to choose a "thankful thought" from the group responses. Younger children may wish to decorate their "thankful thoughts," while older victims may choose to expand on the thankful thought with either poetry, several written paragraphs, or by using another creative or artistic modality.

Participation in a meal/snack may occur at a Thanksgiving type of table whenever possible. Previous to partaking of the meal/snack, "thankful thoughts" should be read and applauded. Encouragement should be given toward the future Thanksgivings as well. Finally, any representation for capturing the "thankful thoughts" for the scrapbook should occur. For children who have been in treatment for more than one year, efforts should be made to encourage them to re-examine last Thanksgiving and to make comparisons of growth and progress. Newly established group members should project and consider next Thanksgiving.

TRAUMA ASSESSMENT PERSPECTIVE:

This activity pertains specifically to the Relationship Perspective of the Sexual Victim Trauma Assessment. Children who feel as though they have been clearly identified as the victim (exonerated from any guilt or blame) will find this activity fun and invigorating. Children who are confused about their status as a victim and overwhelmed by confusion about the offender's status will need this activity to assist them in looking toward the future. Some emphasis for this activity allows victims to recognize the potential for a positive change in the victim's future if current trauma exists.

This treatment activity also relates to the Developmental Perspective of the Sexual Victim Trauma Assessment as damage to sexual development can be repaired through positive body image and sexual self-esteem "thankful thoughts."

Finally, post-disclosure issues from the Situational Perspective of the Sexual Victim Trauma Assessment can be a focus for this activity. Therapists should guarantee that each child's distorted cognitions as a result of the sexual abuse are reflected in the "thankful thoughts" so that destructive coping skills can be alleviated.

#17

TRICKS OR TREAT

OBJECTIVES:

1) Children will gain skills in understanding the manipulative techniques of sexual offenders.

2) Children will gain skills in relieving guilt concerning sexual responsibility or sexual cooperation.

3) Children will gain skills in developing a sense of empowerment and control.

AGES :

Age 13 and Under

SUPPLIES:

1) Masks or Halloween costumes

2) Halloween decorations

3) Paper sacks

4) Role playing props with a door

PROCESS:

This treatment process could be used during the Halloween holiday time period or with a different name, during many times of the year. The title, "Trick or Treat," denotes that this treatment activity requires children to gain skills in recognizing sex offender manipulation, bribery and coercion, while also learning that victims have the power to say "no" to adults under certain situations.

Tricks or Treats?!!

If this treatment activity will be occurring during the Halloween period, some representation of the holiday could be made through decorations. Sacks for collecting "treats" through a trick or treating activity could be used as an example. Children may choose to role play trick or treating a house where another person (actor/sex offender) attempts to coerce or bribe children with a promise of treats. Treatment specialists must be aware of specific elements of bribery and coercion that pertains to victim's personal sexually abusive situations involving offender manipulation. These specific examples will need to be included in the treatment activity to be effective.

As the group watches the role play develop, advice may need to be given to the "child" who must decide whether what the offender is offering is a trick or a treat. As an example, the actor/victim could knock on the door and, when the actor/offender answers, a bribe could be presented that involves receiving a treat, but also may contain a "trick."

> "Yes, you can have this candy bar to put in your sack if you come into my house and let me take a picture of your private body."

> or

> "You can have this treat if you will be sure and take this treat home to your brother who wants some candy, but was too little to trick or treat."

Hopefully, children will be able to discern the difference between a helpful and hurtful request from the offender/actor.

The treatment activity could be finalized in traditional methods with some representation of the children's ability to understand tricks from treats being captured in the scrapbook. Pictures could be taken of "safe trick or treaters" or any other method could be used to capture the learning experience.

TRAUMA ASSESSMENT PERSPECTIVE:

This treatment activity primarily pertains to the Situational Perspective of the Sexual Victim Trauma Assessment. Issues relating to the sexually abusive "scene" emphasize offender bribery and coercion. This activity will not only teach children about prevention, but should assist children in re-examining their own trauma situation and recognize that children are often powerless to control offenders and avoid manipulation.

#18

VALENTINE'S DAY

OBJECTIVES:

1) Children will be able to identify feelings of trauma in relation-ships within their family.

2) Children will be able to express, share, and resolve negative feelings as a result of sexual abuse trauma.

3) Children will be able to recognize peer and group support.

4) Children will be able to gain skills in parenting and communica-tion for their future children.

AGES:

All ages

SUPPLIES:

1) Red construction paper

2) Blackboard

3) White construction paper

4) Red markers

5) Decorations for making of valentines

6) Envelopes

PROCESS:

Love, Love, Love

This treatment activity first requires understanding the term "love" and its positive and negative aspects within the incestuous family. Children should be able to identify the feelings they have regarding the word love and hopefully work toward a better understanding of the love they may or may not feel from individuals within their families. It is important to recognize that the ambivalence or multiplicity of feelings of love for victims regarding their perpetrators or non-offending parents is important to legitimize and affirm. A pervading message to children should be that positive feelings in the form of love do not change the fact that a crime was committed and that a child was sexually abused.

The treatment process begins with children participating in an activity to define the word — "love." Children should be able to recognize that love for such things as chocolate cake, roller coasters, Christmastime and people, exists. A long list should be prepared describing the different kinds of love that have nothing to do with **people.**

People Power

The next step should allow children to recognize and identify those **people** with whom they express the emotion of love. Tremendous sensitivity should be given to the important aspects in the Relationship Perspective of each child's Sexual Victim Trauma Assessment. Therapists should be advised that some children may be reluctant to express the love they feel toward their perpetrator. Encouragement should be given for recognizing that many children love the person who has offended them, yet some do not. If some victims express anger and outrage toward the perpetrator (total lack of love), those children should not be criticized, but should hopefully encourage other group members to feel comfortable expressing a variety of different feelings.

The next step should encourage children to discuss those individuals from whom they **feel** loved. This may be precarious if some children do not feel supported or loved by anyone. Therapists may need to expand the list to include aunts, uncles, grandmothers, etc. Love for each child should be recognized and emphasized. These three steps in the process will usually complete the first group session. Children should leave the first group session with a list of:

1) Non-human kinds of love

2) A list of those individuals whom the child loves

3) A list of individuals who love the child

Expressions of Love

In the next group session or the next process in an extended group session, should allow therapists to prepare presentations of Valentine salutations with a variety of love messages. These messages should range from salutations of betrayal of love to the full range of thanking individuals for their love in spite of the sexual abuse that has occurred. The following salutations are examples:

> I loved you a lot before the secret touching happened. Now, that love is gone.

> There are some things about you that I want to love, but the secret touching you did to me will never, ever be okay.

> Thank you for loving me and believing me when I told and gave up my secret.

All my love for you is "on hold" until I hear what you have
to say to me in clarification. Love is something that is earned,
not automatically given to people who hurt children.

Obviously, younger children will need more simplistic statements of love, but each salutation presented should have some issue of love as relating to the sexual abuse that occurred. Again, salutations should include a variety of issues, with a wide range of response, and most importantly should deal with problems that have emerged in each individual victim's household.

The last step to the process is to make valentines to either be presented directly to individuals or simply captured in the scrapbook. Some more sophisticated children may want to double the enhancement of this activity by making a valentine for themselves entitled,

"The One I Would Like To Receive"

from either an offender or family member. A wide range of opportunity exists for closing out this treatment activity.

TRAUMA ASSESSMENT PERSPECTIVE:

This treatment activity primarily pertains to the Relationship Perspective of the Sexual Victim Trauma Assessment. Victims who feel unloved, abandoned, or betrayed in love will benefit from this activity. The relationship triangle should be carefully examined for issues that need to be initiated by therapists to resolve relationship trauma for each victim.

#19

SECRETS AND SURPRISES

ACTIVITY OBJECTIVES:

1) Children will gain an understanding of appropriate and inappropriate secrets.

2) Children will be able to recognize the difference between secrets and surprises.

3) Children's ability to communicate will be enhanced.

4) Children will be able to protect themselves from future abuse due to this enhanced understanding of the difference between secrets and surprises.

AGES:

Children under age 8

SUPPLIES:

1) <u>A Very Touching Book</u> by Jan Hindman

2) Construction paper

3) Blackboard

4) Artwork supplies, such as:

Pens

Pencils

Papers

      Magazines

      Masks

      A wrapped present

      Easter egg basket

5) Treats, Certificates, Stickers, or other examples of positive affirmation for children

6) 3 x 5 Cards

PROCESS:

Secrets and Surprises

This treatment process is designed to assist children in recognizing appropriate and inappropriate secrets. The first step should assist children in understanding the word, "secret." The identification of the word should indicate that a SECRET is something that is very different from a SURPRISE. A secret involves something that doesn't necessarily have an end. Children should be taught to understand that a "surprise" usually has a closure resulting in other's knowledge. The treatment process should assist children in recognizing that the best secrets are really surprises. Lists, charts, discussions or activities should occur separating surprises from secrets especially concerning holidays and other issues related to secrets.

The next step in the treatment activity is to present examples of appropriate secrets or surprises. A wrapped box could be presented to the group with a discussion about opening the box and having the surprise "be over." Therapists may place something exciting inside the box, such as a treat, stickers, or <u>something positive written</u> about each child's ability to understand the difference between secrets and surprises. This step in the treatment process can also be enhanced by therapists putting on a costume and perhaps frightening group members to some degree indicating that Halloween is an example of an appropriate secret since everyone becomes surprised about "who is wearing the costume." Easter would be another example of an appropriate surprise and, if possible, therapists could hide Easter eggs in the treatment facility for children to find and display.

The End

The next step in the treatment process is to have children recognize that if secrets don't have an ending, they can be harmful. Using 3 x 5 cards, large pieces of construction paper or a chalkboard, children should list how secrets FEEL. Using A Very Touching Book, the four black and white pages regarding how children FEEL about secret touching could be emphasized.

> Secret touching may happen in the dark or in another secret place, and you may feel so, so alone...and too afraid to tell.

> Secret touching may happen with someone you love a lot! Someone whom you would feel bad about getting into trouble if you told the touching secret.

> Secret touching may happen with a trick... or a promise not to tell about the touching. You may be promised treats or fun or extra love. You may not feel like telling because you want the special things.

> Secret touching may happen with a person so... so... so... big and important that you feel too... too... too... little to tell.

In more general terms, children may simply wish to say "secrets hurt my stomach" or "secrets make me worry."

Secrets and Touching

The next step in the treatment process is to recognize that secrets usually hurt, especially secrets about touching. Elements revealed in each victim's Trauma Assessment should be included in the group process with children discussing the weight of their burden in keeping the secret. The philosophy of A Very Touching Book would encourage children to recognize that sexual contact between children and adults is ''breaking the rules'' and, therefore, ''the older or bigger person needs to keep the touching a secret.'' Children should finish this process by recognizing that there should never be a secret about touching and that the solution to secret touching is to ruin the secret and TELL, TELL, TELL, TELL, TELL, TELL.

This treatment activity could be represented in the scrapbook by using opposing pages. Some pages should represent acceptable and appropriate secrets or surprises while opposing pages should indicate not only the negative aspects of secret touching, but of solutions to touching secrets. These issues should be captured and placed in each victim's scrapbook.

TRAUMA ASSESSMENT PERSPECTIVE:

This treatment activity deals with the Developmental Perspective of the Sexual Victim Trauma Assessment, attempting to teach positive ideations toward human sexuality. Additionally, the Situational Perspective of the Trauma Assessment should pinpoint those children who have a potential to become secretive and withholding of information as a result of developing footprints or distorted cognitions for future coping skills.

#20

NIGHTMARES AND OTHER GOOD HORSES

ACTIVITY OBJECTIVES:

1) Children will gain skills in recognizing out- of-control phobic reactions and cognitive distortions.

2) Children will gain skills in eradicating tendencies toward sleep disorders.

3) Children will gain skills in being able to resolve conflicts regarding fear.

AGES:

All Ages

SUPPLIES:

1) Construction Paper

2) Magazines

3) Scissors

4) Crayons

5) Marking Pencils/Pens

6) Camera

PROCESS:

Sleep Stuff

This treatment activity should be specifically implemented for children who are diagnosed in the Sexual Victim Trauma Assessment as having the potential for sleep disorders. Although most children will discuss dreams or night terrors in a negative representation, there may be some children who can discuss positive ideations that occur in dreams. Nonetheless, all victims should participate in the activity of dream description, bringing out both positive and negative feelings about sleep.

Treatment specialists should pay close attention to the differences in representational systems. Some children will dream from a kinesthetic perspective, other children may have more potential to dream with pictures (visual representations) or with words and sounds (auditory representations). Close scrutiny of how children represent the world would be most effective before beginning this treatment activity.

The first phase of this treatment activity is to encourage children to present representations of their dreams to other victims. These representations can occur through the use of poems, verbal descriptions or collages. Creativity from treatment specialists would consider each victim's potential and skills. Some children may even choose to act out dreams in a play-like manner and this process should not be done quickly or haphazardly. For children with this competency, role playing dreams, assigning other group members to roles to portray characters in dreams can be very effective in the desensitization process.

New Dreams, New Safety

Children should capture their dreams (whether negative or positive) on some representation in tangible form before the next stage of treatment begins. For those children who have positive dreams, the second stage of this treatment activity should reinforce and solidify positive sleep patterns. For those children who have fears about dreams or who are traumatized by dreams, a reframing must occur.

As an example, if children fear a monster, a ghost, a critical parent or a perpetrator, the new dream can be created in the scrapbook where these characters are restrained by ropes, in cages, or otherwise under the control of safety rendering individuals. For children who seem to represent the world in visual terms, it is important to make a visual representation of the positive reframe of the dream. For kinesthetic children, more emphasis should be given to feelings, tactile representations and body memories, of both being traumatized and then being rescued. For children who seem to have auditory representational systems, using words to represent recovery and safety in dreams may be most appropriate. The purpose is to desensitize the dream through expression and then make positive reframes to provide a feeling of safety.

TRAUMA ASSESSMENT PERSPECTIVE:

This treatment activity pertains primarily to the Situational Perspective of the Sexual Victim Trauma Assessment. Distorted thinking, psychological safety or phobic reactions play an important part in the structure of night terrors. Other trauma issues may provide information in content of dreams, but the Situational Perspective of the Sexual Victim Trauma Assessment describes the formation of thinking patterns which formulate sleep disorders.

#21

CLARIFICATION — THE DESCRIPTION

OBJECTIVES:

1) Children will be able to "capture childhood," through emphasizing specific events and childhood issues.

2) Children will be able to appreciate the special, unique nature of personal qualities.

3) Children will be able to capture a sense of innocence through preparation of this component of the clarification.

AGE GROUPS:

All Ages

SUPPLIES:

1) Pencils/Pens/Other writing material

2) Lined paper

3) Construction paper

4) Childhood pictures, items or representations of the unique nature of each victim

PROCESS:

Ideally . . .

The resolution or clarification with the victim by the offender requires careful preparation. Evidence from the Trauma Assessment points to how the perpetrator can make an important contribution to victim recovery. Information gleaned in the Trauma Assessment regarding relationship difficulties, developmental problems and destructive coping skills can be undone and resolved by the perpetrator's clarification.

The purpose of the clarification process is to resolve, to clarify, to explain, and to empower the victim. The clarification is not an apology, it is not an attack on the perpetrator, nor is it a process of forgiveness. The clarification requires the perpetrator to put the sexual abuse in perspective so that the trauma, as a result of confusion, can be avoided.

Unfortunately, it is not an ideal world and not all victims have the opportunity to proceed through a clarification process with the offender. The ideal treatment program would require as much, however, a perfect world is not always available. The major components of the clarification process, therefore, should be created by therapists, by caretakers, or by proxy individuals accomplishing the same goals and providing the same information for the victim's resolution scrapbook.

The Lost Childhood

The next five treatment activities (#21 through #25) pertain to the clarification components that would be used for victims when the offender is not available. The first such component is the "Description," which has several purposes. The Description is very important to return the victim to childhood, providing a vehicle to recapture the precious, unique aspects of being a child. A more complicated issue, however, is provided with coordination of the "Description" with the "How" portion of the clarification process.

"Why Me?"

Historically, when sexual offenders were asked to explain to their victims, "Nothing about you caused me to do this," trauma was not resolved. It is important for victims to understand that they were not responsible for the sexual abuse. Unfortunately, the generic "nothing about you caused me to do this" provided no reason for the sexual offense. Victims became vulnerable. Innocence is important for sexual victims to capture, but innocence is different than vulnerability. Without tangible reasons for the abuse or for the choice of the abuse victim, feelings of vulnerability for victims were enhanced.

Additionally, it has become clear to sex offender therapists that it is very difficult to sexually abuse obnoxious, acting out or "brat" type of children. It would seem that sex offenders actually choose children with positive characteristics, but who are nonetheless vulnerable to exploitation. With these two issues in mind (returning the victim to childhood and providing victims with awareness of why they were chosen), the Description in the clarification process was developed.

The sexual offender should be required to describe specific attributes about each child, which were precious, unique, but that were also relating to how the offender was able to abuse the child. In other words, the unique qualities of the child should emerge in the Description, but those same qualities should be described later in the "How" portion of the clarification whereby the offender indicates that because of these **positive** qualities, the victim was chosen.

Special, Special Me

When the offender is not available, treatment specialists should create the same clarification components. Children should be able to be presented with an understanding of why they were chosen. Most importantly, these characteristics or qualities should be viewed in a very positive light. The unique nature of children must be captured and each specific child, whether three or 13, must be aware of their special childlike qualities. Even though the next phase of the clarification will indicate that the offender misused these precious qualities, the victim should nonetheless be able to peruse, to understand and to accept the positive qualities of childhood.

These representations would be ideally presented by the offender, but they can also be prepared by others. A description that would be appropriate for victims would have at least 10 to 15 "qualities" in each child. An example of one specific description of **a** quality would be as follows:

Good Attitude Suzie

"Suzie, one of the special things about you is that you were the kind of little girl who always had a good attitude and who always smiles. I remember at Christmastime, at Grandma Ida's house, when everyone had opened their presents, you always wanted to keep everyone happy. You would run around the living room and wrap the presents back up so that your brother, Brandon, and your sister, Missy, could open them all over again. You even wrapped one for Old Uncle Bert! You weren't interested in playing with your own toys or being selfish. You wanted everyone to be happy and for everyone to have the same smiles. You would wrap all the presents back up so that we could all have fun opening them again."

"I also remember another time when you had an especially good attitude. I remember when we were taking Franko, the cat, to Dr. Applegate because he was sick. Franko was sitting on your lap and you had on your yellow dress with green buttons. Franko wasn't feeling very well and he threw up allover your pretty dress. Even though it was yucky and awful, you kept smiling and petting Franko. You just kept giving Franko good touching and he appreciated that, even though he kept burping. That's one of the very special things about you, Suzie. No matter how yucky things are, no matter if everyone else is sad, you always smile and have a good attitude."

This special quality in Suzie is precious, but also clearly a tool used by the perpetrator in his abuse. The fact that Suzie puts forth tremendous effort to make others happy, is exactly the kind of characteristic preferred by offenders.

Treatment for sexual victims must examine the special, unique qualities of each child and these descriptions must be prepared for the scrapbook. For older children, writing their own Description "pieces" may be effective. For younger children, collateral information may need to be elicited from family members. These representations of special qualities of each victim should be presented with grandiose ceremony and placed in the victim's scrapbook.

TRAUMA ASSESSMENT PERSPECTIVE:

This treatment activity pertains to all areas of the Trauma Assessment, but perhaps most specifically to the cognitive distortions that may develop for children in adulthood. These distorted thinking patterns are commonly found in the Situational Perspective of the Sexual Victim Trauma Assessment. Most victims believe they are to blame for either the abuse or for disclosure upheaval, and most victims feel guilty. When these distortions exist, capturing the innocence of childhood will be most appropriate, as well as dispelling the beliefs of responsibility.

#22

CLARIFICATION — HOW

OBJECTIVES:

1) Children will gain skills in understanding their role as an innocent victim of sexual exploitation.

2) Children will gain skills in understanding how sexual abuse can occur within a family.

3) Children will gain skills in understanding offender manipulation.

4) Children will gain skills in feeling exonerated from guilt and responsibility.

AGES:

All Ages

SUPPLIES:

1) Pencils/Pens/Other writing material

2) Lined paper

3) Construction paper

4) General art supplies to decorate clarification components

PROCESS:

Tools of Trauma

In conjunction with the Description of the clarification process, this component relates to how the special qualities of the child were misused in order for the offender to be successful. Special care should be given to avoid having children feel that because of their positive qualities, they were sexually exploited. Ideally, offenders, after describing each of the special, unique qualities of the child in the Description, will then demonstrate how each of these qualities was misused in order for manipulation to occur. At the closure of each component, however, emphasis should be made that children who possess these qualities should be applauded and congratulated. These qualities should always be desired. Ideally, the offender will assist the child in understanding that these qualities are positive and that the only negative issue is that sexual offenders misuse these precious qualities in children. An example of this clarification component could be described in the following manner as it relates to the previous treatment activity describing the Description.

Suzie and Her Good Attitude

"Suzie, one of the ways I was able to do secret touching to you and keep it a big secret in our family was that I knew you tried so hard to have a good attitude. When I did secret touching, it was yucky for you. I made you do things you didn't want to do. I tricked you. It was very yucky. One of the ways I was able to do this was that I knew Suzie would always be smiling and always tried to have a good attitude even if things were yucky. Other kids are sometimes brats and don't care about happy things or keeping everyone else in the family happy like you do. Some little girls think only about themselves. I knew you were the kind of little girl who wanted things to be happy in the family. I knew you were someone who had a good attitude even if things were yucky. One of the ways that I could do secret touching to you was that I knewI could do yucky things and Suzie would keep her good attitude and not tell."

> "Suzie, I want you to know that being a happy kid and having a good attitude is wonderful. You should be proud of yourself and keep that good part forever and ever. There is nothing wrong with having a good attitude when things are yucky, there is only something wrong with people like me who trick little girls who have good attitudes."

Again, the ideal treatment approach would require each sexual offender to prepare corresponding "hows" for each component of the Description. Creative and proactive therapists, however, will complete this task if the offender is not available. Each victim should be able to understand how the abuse happened, and should be able to feel not only exonerated from guilt and responsibility, but should develop a sense of pride in the personal qualities that may have contributed to the offender's manipulation.

Guilt or Pride?

This concept may cause a conflict for professionals who wish to portray the victim as guiltless. This treatment approach never suggests that the victim is responsible for the personality qualities that attracted the offender, but it does encourage a sense of control for the victim and a proactive, positive rehabilitating attitude. Sexual victims should be able to understand that they possess qualities that are prized by most individuals, but that these qualities are the subject of manipulation for some individuals. The sense of empowerment can be profound for victims who are able to participate in this kind of process. There is a drastic difference in suggesting that victims are responsible for abuse as compared to suggesting that victims can understand why the abuse occurred.

TRAUMA ASSESSMENT PERSPECTIVE:

This treatment activity primarily pertains to the Situational Perspective of the Sexual Victim Trauma Assessment. "How" the victim feels responsible, guilty or to blame is typically found in the sexual abuse scene, which is intensely evaluated as the Situational Perspective of the Trauma Assessment.

#23

CLARIFICATION — TRAUMA ASSESSMENT

OBJECTIVES:

1) Victims will gain skills in desensitizing and externalizing sexual abuse trauma.

2) Children will gain skills in understanding intricate issues relating to their own trauma so that recovery can be enhanced.

3) Children will gain skills in participating in effective treatment planning to eradicate traumatic issues.

4) Children will gain skills in feeling a sense of control regarding their abuse.

5) Children will gain skills in recognizng their status as a victim for improving confidence and self-esteem.

AGES:

All Ages

SUPPLIES:

1) Pens/pencils/writing material

2) Lined paper

3) Construction paper

PROCESS:

You'll Never Know

The cry from many sexual victims is "no one cares, no one understands the pain." No matter how empathic or helpful either therapists or offenders tend to be in dealing with the pain of victims, it is clear that traumatization is a unique and personal process. No one will truly understand how each individual human being is hurt through sexual abuse.

In spite of this futility, efforts must be exerted for victims to proceed through a process of understanding the trauma. For younger children, this is especially pertinent since ongoing or developing cognitions will take place in the future making trauma even more profound and significant. Even though the true nature of each victim's pain may not be understood, the process toward externalizing that pain is an important treatment objective.

Again, the ideal program will allow the victim to externalize pain in a parallel fashion with the sexual offender. The sexual offender's treatment should focus on understanding the damage or trauma that has been caused to the victim. The victim should be anticipating a clarification where the offender will not only take responsibility for the trauma that has occurred, but will also describe, clarify and announce issues of suffering which will hopefully, and proactively, prevent outrage and frustration for the victim in adulthood who screams, "no one understands my pain."

If the sexual offender prepares the clarification component of the Sexual Victim Trauma Assessment, ideally it should mirror the professional's assessment. Sexual offenders should be able to describe a specific feeling that the victim has endured and then describe a story about that feeling or an etiology for how that feeling emerged. Each one of these statements should be separated according to the specific feeling involved. The following is an example of a clarification component describing only one feeling of trauma for a victim.

Suzie's Robbery

"Suzie, one of the ways I hurt you is that I robbed you of your mom. Little girls should grow up in families being safe and happy and, most important, being able to trust and talk with their moms. Little girls should be able to take their baths and put on pink Strawberry Shortcake Pajamas if they want. They should be able to have their moms help them get dressed and when they need a good night kiss, they should have their moms carry them in to their bedrooms with blue umbrellas on the yellow wall paper. Just before going to bed, little girls should be able to talk to their moms about anything they want. They should be able to trust their moms and ask their moms questions or tell their moms anything that is bothering them."

"I remember once when you were little, and you were in the Red Roof Market, by our house, you asked your mom, 'How do the store men get the stems in the apples?' Everyone laughed, but it was a really good question. You wondered about the apple stems and, like little girls are supposed to do, you asked your mom."

"But then, Suzie, I started tricking you and doing secret touching to you. I told you your mom wouldn't like you anymore if you told her what we were doing. I made it seem like you shouldn't talk to you mom or ask your mom any questions. I made you afraid to trust your mom. This was like robbing a little girl of her mom. This was not fair for me to do because little girls should have the right to trust their moms with lots of things. Even though your mom really wanted to help you, wanted to talk with you, and wanted to answer your questions, I hurt you by making you think you couldn't ask her. I robbed you of your mom by not letting you think that you could talk to her about secret touching or apple stems."

Ideally, the sexual offender would prepare many of these examples of the pain suffered by the victim with a "feeling" and corresponding childhood story. Even though the offender must always indicate to the victim that he/she will never truly understand the nature of the victim's pain, these scenarios will be helpful to the victim in preventing trauma in the future. Unfortunately, not all children have the luxury of having a clarification presented by the sexual offender and, therefore, a proactive therapist must become creative.

Each child needs to have their pain desensitized, clarified and resolved. Preparing the "Trauma Assessment" in encapsulating scenarios similar to the previously described example dealing with a specific pain will be most helpful for victims. At times, this can be done in the group process as victims share their feelings and become supportive of each other. Adolescents are often capable of preparing these trauma scenarios "by proxy" for other group members. For the younger patient, these preparations may be done without significance since younger children may be asymptomatic at the time of treatment and not understand trauma. It is also possible that through work with the non-offending parent, many of these Trauma Assessment scenarios can be represented, understood, and prepared for each victim's scrapbook. Even for the smallest of child, this tangible representation of the pain will be an important ingredient for survivorship.

TRAUMA ASSESSMENT PERSPECTIVE:

This portion of the Sexual Victim Trauma Assessment obviously pertains to all phases of the professional's Sexual Victim Trauma

Assessment. Perhaps, in no other area of treatment, is the formal Trauma Assessment necessary in order to guide either the sexual offender or other individuals to prepare the Trauma Assessment scenarios for each sexual victim's scrapbook. Issues pertaining to relationship damage, trauma to normal sexual development, as well as the development of cognitive distortions and phobic reactions will be directly addressed through this treatment activity.

#24

CLARIFICATION — WHAT HAPPENED

OBJECTIVES:

1) Children will gain skills in dealing with distorted cognitions regarding sexual abuse.

2) Children will be able to relieve guilt as a result of distorted cognitions.

3) Children will be desensitized to sexual abuse memories.

AGE GROUPS:

All Ages

SUPPLIES:

1) Pencils/pens/other writing material

2) Lined paper

3) Construction paper

PROCESS:

An additional component of the ideal clarification is a description of what actually took place during the sexual abuse. The Trauma Assessment of sexual victims usually reveals distorted cognitions and the potential for continued distortions of reality. A record, a clear understanding of what actually took place, will have a lasting value for the sexual victim.

Pain or Progress?

Unfortunately, this treatment activity tends to be the easiest to avoid for many therapists. Revealing the intricate details of sexual activity is usually not comfortable for human beings. Additionally, when the sexual contact has been exploitive and traumatizing, it is common to avoid this treatment component, hoping to protect both the victim and the therapist from unnecessary discomfort. In actuality, disclosure and confrontation with the facts of the abuse can be extremely helpful to sexual victims if it occurs within a "sanctuary of safety" as described in the therapeutic environment.

Research indicates that sexual victims will remember. Therapy should be "proactive" and construct the memory in a positive modality rather than being "reactive" and allowing the memory to change. This portion of the clarification, either presented by the sexual offender or described by therapists or other caretakers, is the best modality for creating a memory, which will be under control and which will have the best possibility for victim rehabilitation. Facing the reality of what occurred, will have a life long impact on preventing trauma for victims, which is the proactive approach.

The Corrected Memory

Some professionals fear that to remember will do nothing but retraumatize victims. This view is insensitive to the power of controlled memory and the power of proper framing. Somehow it is believed that if the victim is forced to relive the abuse, trauma will occur. Unfortunately, the victim will always relive the abuse. The only question is how will the abuse be framed and remembered?

The following examples provide the same "facts" of what occurred during the abusive scenario. One portrayal obviously is framed in a way to traumatize the child while the other scenario is sensitive to creating a positive memory in the future.

The Correct Memory

"Every time you came into the Sunday School class, I would get you to sit on my lap. You were a good little boy and you would always do what I wanted. I made sure that you always liked me and that you believed I was nice even though that wasn't necessarily true. I also made sure that I could put my hands between your legs and touch you on your penis with my hands. I pretended like I was reading a book or doing something else. My hands would be rubbing the front of you and touching you on your penis. Sometimes when we were standing up singing, I would make sure that the back of your head touched me between my legs. I did this lots of times when you came to Sunday School."

The Incorrect Memory

"I will always remember that you would come into the Sunday School class and sit on my lap. Sometimes my hands would find your penis because you were always sitting there and trying to get close to me. You seemed to like me and you always wanted to get close. There was nothing else to do. When we were singing in the choir, you would always make your head touch my private parts even though I wasn't doing anything but praising the Lord."

The facts may be the same in both scenarios, but obviously one description of what happened will be guilt-inducing for this child while the other will perhaps exonerate the child's status as a victim. If the offender is not available to provide these description of "what happened," a great deal of time must be spent by treatment specialists who need to create a positive, honest portrayal of what occurred with a reframe that will ensure the child's recovery.

TRAUMA ASSESSMENT PERSPECTIVE:

This treatment activity pertains to both the Situational Perspective which deals with distorted cognitions and phobic reactions, and to the Developmental Perspective of the Sexual Victim Trauma Assessment. Children who have distorted views of what occurred in the sexually abusive scene have the potential to have phobic reactions to sexual issues and, therefore, may be traumatized in normal sexual development. Completing a significant description for the clarification scrapbook of what actually took place will have the greatest potential to stop these traumatizing tendencies.

#25

CLARIFICATION — WHY DID THIS HAPPEN?

OBJECTIVES:

1) Children will gain skills in understanding sex offender denial systems.

2) Children will gain skills in relieving guilt and anxiety about sexual participation.

3) Children will gain skills in recognizing positive aspects of human sexuality.

4) Children will gain skills in appreciating the beauty of future consenting sexual decisions.

AGE GROUPS:

All Ages

SUPPLIES:

1) A Very Touching Book by Jan Hindman

2) Pens/pencils/writing material

3) Lined paper

4) Role-playing options

5) Thinking errors of offenders (Treatment Activity "Grooming or Criminal Thinking for Kids")

PROCESS:

Many treatment activities pertain to teaching victims why sexual offenders abuse. Some of those treatment activities are contained in this manual, but this treatment activity specifically pertains to the clarification process. Again, the ideal approach is to have the sexual offender prepare an explanation concerning why the sexual abuse occurred. This "ideal" presentation should have four basic components as follows:

Step 1:

The offender should describe a basic selfishness or criminal intent very similar to a robbery. ("I did this because I am the kind of person who takes things from people.")

Step 2:

The offender should explain why sexuality is a valuable commodity. The concepts described in A Very Touching Book are most pertinent to this issue. In this publication, sexual activity is portrayed as something positive, and something that is positively anticipated in adulthood. It should also be explained that adults appreciate this kind of touching and the "rules" indicate that adults should touch adults and that children should have the right to grow up and choose someone for touching on their own, in adulthood. This step is significantly important since Step #1, "I did this because I was selfish," is nonsensical unless a valuable commodity is presented in Step #2. Children may ask "Why did he/she take something that was awful?" If the victim learns in Step #2 why sex is valuable, the selfishness described in Step #1 is understandable.

Step 3:

In an ideal clarification, the offender should then discuss the character disorder that allows the offender to "break the rules." If the rules for sexual consent and for children being able to choose a partner on their own, in adulthood, are clear, a characterological disorder of the sexual offender must be described in order for comprehension to take place. In other words, if the rules are wonderful, something must be wrong with the sexual offender to break the rules. This "rule breaking" is the primary focus of the third step.

Step 4:

The final step for the sexual offender's presentation of "Why" should be a return to the issue of consent. Children should understand that they have not "picked" (or chosen) the offender. In Step #2, the sexual offender describes the beauty of consent and the beauty of anticipating adulthood where individuals choose a partner. The sexual offender must clearly close the clarification with statements indicating that the child has never chosen. By virtue of being children, consent is impossible and, therefore, a proactive approach can be implemented as the child looks toward the future and says,

"All my future choices will be wonderful since, as a child, I could not consent."

Ideally, the sexual offender would make this presentation. If that is not possible, then the group process or individual therapy with the help of a caretaker should present a reasonable facsimile to this presentation. Younger children will benefit from the logic in <u>A Very Touching Book</u>. They may choose to do role plays, puppet shows, or re-enactments of the abuse in other demonstrative forms.

For older children, adolescents may choose to study the thinking errors of sexual offenders, which will provide them with more information about sex offender thinking, explaining characterological disorders and the cognitive process of offenders, which allows the "rules to be broken." The most important goals of this activity should be to help the victim understand that not only was the abuse the offender's choice, but the victim's abuse has nothing to do with future sexual decisions.

TRAUMA ASSESSMENT PERSPECTIVE:

This treatment activity will have some impact on destroying cognitive distortions as a result of sexual abuse. However, the most prevalent portion of the Sexual Victim Trauma Assessment that this treatment activity addresses is the Sexual Developmental Perspective. Victims should leave this treatment activity feeling a rebirth of sexual decision making for the future. Feelings of humiliation, degradation, repulsion toward body functions and reactions should all be included in this clarification component so that significant trauma to normal sexual development for each child will be minimized.

#26

GROUP TREATMENT FOR
SEXUALLY ABUSED CHILDREN

OBJECTIVES:

1) Children will gain skills in identifying feelings regarding sexual abuse.

2) Children will gain skills in legitimizing feelings regarding sexual abuse.

3) Children will gain skills in learning prevention of sexual abuse.

4) Children will gain skills in appropriate preparation for puberty.

5) Children will gain skills in introspection.

AGE GROUP:

Latency Age Children

SUPPLIES:

1) Publication, Group Treatment for Sexually Abused Children by Joan Golden-Mandell and Linda Damon

2) Relating Supplies as Outlined in Publication

3) Handouts as Provided in Publication

PROCESS:

This publication provides specific treatment activities (complete with handouts for copying) to be used with latency age sexually abused children. The treatment manual provides an excellent modality for teaching children to introspect and discover their feelings about sexual abuse and work toward expression of those feelings. These treatment activities could occur over several weeks or months. Copyright privileges are available so that handouts can be presented to children for use in group activities and for inclusion in their scrapbooks.

But Beyond,

The primary methodology or focus of the treatment manual is to introspect and express feelings. These activities are excellent for this purpose, although "proactive" therapy will go beyond the expression of feelings and will capture those feelings in a tangible representation. The proactive approach will teach skills for management of feelings for the victim's future. The treatment activities in this manual are not specific to sexual victims, but therapists completing Sexual Victim Trauma Assessments can add specificity and uniqueness from individual treatment plans for use with these more general but valuable activities.

TRAUMA ASSESSMENT PERSPECTIVE:

This treatment activity primarily pertains to the Situational Perspective of the Sexual Victim Trauma Assessment where the development of distorted thinking creates tendencies for children to use coping skills that will be destructive in the future. The failure to express emotions or to understand feelings is often the precipitating factor in developing coping skills such as helplessness or abusability. It is also true that the inability to appropriately express feelings can encourage the development of abuse reactive responses as an outlet for emotions that cannot be expressed in more productive ways.

#27

WHEN DO WE
TALK ABOUT SECRET TOUCHING?

OBJECTIVES:

1) Children will be able to learn appropriate and inappropriate opportunities for discussing their sexual abuse situation.

2) Children will be able to open communication with their parents regarding sexual abuse so that secrecy in the incestuous family can be avoided.

AGE GROUP:

Age 10 and younger.

SUPPLIES:

1) Large pieces of construction paper

2) Wide tip felt magic markers

3) Elevated stage (optional)

4) Camera (optional)

5) 3 x 5 cards or smaller colored paper to capture for scrapbook.

PROCESS:

This activity is ideal for coordinating with parental attendance so that parents and children can attend sessions together. Children should be initially separated from their parents for the first part of the session. A parent group should be organized with discussions regarding parental frustrations related specifically to children's discussions about sexual abuse without appropriate boundaries. Professionals often encourage victims to feel enthusiastic about their disclosure while children often frustrate parents with open discussions about "giving up the secret" in uncomfortable situations. Parents should be encouraged to express their frustration if children are discussing the sexual abuse openly, which may be uncomfortable or embarrassing. Careful dialogue should occur, assisting parents in understanding the importance of the child's expression and description of what has happened, but parents should also be given support for feeling frustrated since boundaries for sexual abuse discussions have not yet been designated.

In a separate room, children should be preparing large pieces of construction paper with both positive and negative statements regarding disclosure opportunities. Use humor. At least 25 posters or cards should be printed in large letters, with such statements as:

> "It is okay to talk about **secret touching** in the grocery store."

> "It is okay to talk about secret touching, privately with mom, on the way home from group."

> "It is okay to talk about secret touching at the Thanksgiving dinner table sitting next to Aunt Harriet."

> "It is okay to talk about secret touching in court."

> "It is okay to talk about secret touching at mom's Tupperware party."

Teach the Teachers

Eventually parents will meet with children in a large group and participate in an "examination process." Parents should be encouraged to make mistakes so that their child can correct them, with the "stumbling, bumbling parent" eventually seeming to learn the appropriate response. Children should be enthusiastic and encouraged about quizzing their parents and finding out if their parents understand appropriate and inappropriate times to discuss "secret touching."

When parents and their specific children are joined, each child should be able to move to an elevated area or stage (if possible) with their parent, present a specific card, and quiz their parent. Parents should be taught to stumble, to forget or to make mistakes before the child finally teaches the parent when it is appropriate and inappropriate to talk about secret touching. If possible, a picture should be taken of parent and child, with the parent holding up the appropriate response. Collect these pictures for the victim's scrapbook.

TRAUMA ASSESSMENT PERSPECTIVE:

This activity pertains primarily to the Situational Perspective of the Sexual Victim Trauma Assessment where the potential for developing the coping skill of "secrecy" exists. This activity is designed to encourage communication between children and parents and to avoid developing coping skills of secrecy, guilt and blame often found in the relationship trauma.

#28

WHEN CHILDREN MOLEST CHILDREN

OBJECTIVES:

1) Children will gain skills in controlling "abusive" tendencies.

2) Children will gain skills in developing victim empathy.

3) Children will gain skills in developing problem solving techniques.

4) Children will gain skills in building self-esteem.

5) Children will gain skills in managing anger.

AGE GROUP:

Ages 4-12

SUPPLIES:

1) Publication, <u>When Children Molest Children: Group Treatment Strategies for Young Sexual Abusers</u> by Carolyn Cunningham and Kee McFarlane, Safer Society Press

2) Related Supplies as outlined in publication activities

PROCESS:

The Deadly Cycle

Sadly, there is a significant potential for sexual victims to become abusive in their futures. The "abuse reactive" child is common in treatment programs and provides particularly perplexing situations for therapists. Although it seems predictable that many children will become abusive, it is nonetheless a painful predicament for therapists who wish to support and nurture the "victim status" in children, but who also see abusive cycles developing, as well.

The publication, <u>When Children Molest Children</u>, is an innovative, structured curriculum for treating "abuse reactive children." This publication has many treatment activities complete with lists of objectives, supplies and process explanation. The activities in the publication could be used as an entire unit over several months. The problem solving subject matter is particularly effective and should be considered for use in many treatment programs as a component of treating the sexual victim who was also abuse reactive.

TRAUMA ASSESSMENT PERSPECTIVE:

Children tend to develop abuse reactive tendencies as a result of coping with their sexual abuse. These tendencies can be found in the Situational Perpsective of the Sexual Victim Trauma Assessment. The treatment activities found in this publication, however, would also pertain to sexual development as well as assisting in resolving many relationship issues.

#29

TELLING WHAT HAPPENED

OBJECTIVES:

1) Children will be able to gain skills in building trust.

2) Children will be able to gain skills in communication.

3) Children's self-esteem will be increased.

4) Children will be able to gain skills in being supportive of others.

AGE GROUP:

All Ages

SUPPLIES:

1) One Large Poster Board

2) 3x5 or 5x7 Cards

3) Magic Markers

4) Construction Paper

5) Envelopes and/or Boxes

6) Magazines

PROCESS:

Inside Out

Sexual abuse victims need to externalize their pain. This will occur through treatment modalities that move the sexual abuse pain that is internal and make it external. A common modality for treatment of sexual victims is to have children "tell what happened." Unfortunately, verbalizing about the abuse that occurred is very painful for victims and, in actuality, perhaps the least effective strategy. This treatment modality attempts to create a variety of ways beyond verbalization in which children can externalize their pain, share with others, and then capture the externalized pain for their scrapbooks.

Correct Memory

This treatment activity is especially important for young children. Great controversy exists regarding children's memory and the appropriate response to memory. What is clear is that children will have many affective or sensory memories even if the cognitive memory of the abuse does not exist. For younger children involved in this therapeutic process, it is extremely important to make a clear concrete and tangible memory of the abuse so that trauma bonding does not emerge as perceptions change and memory is re-evaluated. Choosing activities that will recreate the sexual abuse memory in a constructive and positive way, framing the child as the innocent victim and the perpetrator as responsible, will provide tremendous contribution to victim rehabilitation in adulthood.

For older children, many more options for remembering may exist, which will enhance the therapeutic process. Again, verbalizing the memory is perhaps least effective. Adolescents may choose tape recordings, role plays, skits, drawings, poetry, or activities such as sand trays for recreation of the abuse memory.

Preparation

The first step in this treatment process is for therapists to carefully examine those potentially traumatizing memories for each child. This will only occur through the Sexual Victim Trauma Assessment. Treatment planning should result in a prepared list of issues that need to emerge in order to provide a correct memory.

Choices, Choices, Choices

Next, victims should be presented with many options for creating the correct memory. Agonizing over the choice of options should be a helpful, exciting, grandiose, but nonetheless positive process.

. . .Maybe I will make a collage.

. . .Maybe I will do a puppet show on video.

. . .Maybe I will put "what happened" in a box.

Be Specific

Only the Trauma Assessment will reveal how the last step of this treatment activity will be completed. As an example, if the Developmental Perspective reveals that the victim sexually responded and feels tremendous guilt, this issue needs to be presented by the therapist so that normal body functions involving arousal occur in the memory. As an example, a "thought bubble" over the cartoon figure representing the victim may say,

> "Just because my body works, and these parts of my body feel good to touch, I was the victim and you were the criminal."

For victims who have been abused over long periods of time, therapeutic decisions must be made according to what limitations and inclusions will need to be made in order to provide an accurate memory presentation.

Capturing, Sharing and Scrapbooking

The capturing of memory may be an ongoing process or a specific time may be arranged. The **"process,"** with choices is important. The memory must not only be captured in a way chosen by the victim, but it must be presented and shared (with grand celebration) with another person or with a group before being finally captured for the scrapbook.

TRAUMA ASSESSMENT PERSPECTIVE:

This treatment activity primarily pertains to the Situational Perspective of the Sexual Victim Trauma Assessment. What occurred in the sexually abusive "scene" has the potential to develop amnesia, dissociation, memory confusion, and other distorted cognitions.

#30

WHO DO YOU TELL?

OBJECTIVES:

1) Children will gain skills in relieving anxiety about recurring abuse.

2) Children will gain skills in becoming more assertive.

3) Children will gain skills in recognizing appropriate and inappropriate resources for assistance in potentially abusive situations.

AGE GROUP:

8 and Under

SUPPLIES:

1) Access to Musical Instruments, such as symbols, guitar, piano, kazoos, etc.

2) Pictures or Representations of Individuals Who Can Assist Children in Sexual Abuse Reporting, such as Sheriff, Police, Counselor, Minister, Family Member, etc.

3) Various art supplies

PROCESS:

Tell

This is a very simple process designed to put words to songs to empower children and develop a sense of safety. First, children should be able to understand that giving up secrets and reporting sexual abuse is important. A prerequisite for this treatment activity, however, is that children should understand the difference between GOOD, BAD, and SECRET TOUCHING and should also understand that a solution to secret touching is to TELL. Treatment activities teaching children to say NO and to keep telling should be a prerequisite to this process.

Who Do You Tell

If children understand the appropriateness of telling, it is important to then explain appropriate resources for making reports. Therapists may wish to role play or dress in costumes representing individuals who could help children. Role playing with children giving up secrets, (even though role play scenarios are fictitious), could be followed by cheers, applause, and support from other children.

The next step in the treatment process puts words to songs that encourage an understanding of appropriate resources for reporting. An example might be:

Who do you tell

Who do you tell

Who do you tell

Hi Ho the Dairy Oh

Who do you tell

This song could be sung for a parents group with children dressed in costumes of helpful people or a video could be made with a "commercial" to be played for others, provided confidentiality of each child was respected. At a minimum, children should watch themselves on video singing a song about telling before finally capturing the treatment activity in scrapbooks to enhance the learning process.

TRAUMA ASSESSMENT PERSPECTIVE

This treatment activity pertains to the Situational Perspective of the Sexual Victim Trauma Assessment dealing with children's sense of powerlessness and their tendencies to become helpless. Additionally, victims may also have a potential to develop trauma bonds about "why didn't I tell" and caution should be exerted in this treatment activity so that children feel that telling is something that should happen, but, at times, is impossible. These tendencies for guilt to emerge about a lack of report will be found in the Situational Perspective, as well.

#31

NO MORE SECRETS FOR ME

OBJECTIVES:

1) Children will gain skills in recognizing they are not alone in their status as a victim of child sexual abuse.

2) Children will gain skills in understanding ways to protect themselves.

3) Children will gain skills in expressing feelings about sexual abuse.

4) Children will be able to resolve feelings about their own secrets.

AGE GROUP:

Children under Age 8

SUPPLIES:

1) Resource, No More Secrets for Me, Oralee Wachter

2) Construction Paper

3) Crayons

4) Magic Markers, other writing material

PROCESS:

This is a treatment activity that uses the resource, No More Secrets for Me. This is a publiction to read to children assisting them in understanding that they are not alone, and this book also teaches about prevention. The process should begin by examining the subject matter from the books' cover and discussing what the book "might" be about. Anticipation of the contents and message should occur before the book is read creating a better way to induce learning.

But What If...

After the book is read, either on video or to the group, children may wish to "trouble shoot," strategizing on how other possible outcomes for the child could have been disastrous. Specific issues regarding each victim's personal "secret keeping" need to emerge and be resolved. If children participate in an activity where more negative solutions are presented by therapists, the positive solution as outlined in the book will always be more powerful.

Finally, children should capture the learning from this resource in their scrapbooks. Children may choose to write fictitious letters to the characters in the book providing support or advice. Children may create artwork, lists or other tangible representations of the treatment activity.

TRAUMA ASSESSMENT PERSPECTIVE

This treatment activity pertains to the Situational Perspective of the Sexual Victim Trauma Assessment. Post-disclosure issues are important in this perspective and children need to not only understand these concepts to protect themselves in the future, but they also need to resolve these issues surrounding their own abuse.

#32

LITTLE ME (STEP II)

OBJECTIVES:

1) Children will be able to understand the incompetencies between children and adults.

2) Children will be able to recognize their inability to resist sexual offenses from adults.

3) Children will be able to capture the innocence of childhood.

4) Children's tendencies toward symbiosis will be alleviated.

AGE GROUP:

All Ages

SUPPLIES:

1) Glue

2) Scissors

3) Paper

4) Pencils

5) Birth Certificate Footprints (whenever possible)

6) Photographs from Childhood

8) Representations of Childhood Toys, Pets or Other Items

PROCESS:

This is a simple treatment process in design, but perhaps one of the most complicated in philosophy. As outlined in Chapter Six, several different options are presented to therapists in organizing each victim's scrapbook. Some plans choose an organizational process where two sections (step II and step III) counter balance the innocent, incompetent child with the child who is empowered. This treatment activity pertains to that choice of organization for the scrapbook although if other scrapbook options are chosen, some pages (perhaps not in sections) of the scrapbook need to represent the incompetent child. Treatment activity #33 provides the opposing representation. The competent, empowered child will balance with this portrayal of the innocent, competent child.

The Lost Childhood

This treatment activity must occur at the discretion and organization of the therapist and pertain to each specific child. Old photographs, as an example, could be used that demonstrate the innocence and incompetence of children if pictures represent, baggy clothes, missing teeth or rumpled hair. This process will enhance the innocence of children.

Victims should be able to either make footprints or handprints that represent the smallness of their bodies during the abuse or they may wish to secure their footprint from birth certificates. Pictures or drawings of the child's home or representation of pets from the time period of when the abuse took place may also be important for inclusion. At times, parents may cooperate and write stories about children that represent small, unique incidents or issues that are very important for children to understand. Whatever method is used, this step in the treatment activity could create a significant section in the victim's scrapbook where childhood is clear, presenting the child as incompetent, little, precious with the subtle message indicating, "unable to protect against adults."

TRAUMA ASSESSMENT PERSPECTIVE:

This treatment activity pertains to the Developmental Perspective and to the Situational Perspective of the Trauma Assessment. Obviously, the loss of childhood is a developmental issue, but certainly the loss of childhood evolves to create distorted cognitions for victims who have a tendency to believe they were responsible and guilty for the abuse.

#33

COMPETENT ME (STEP III)

OBJECTIVES:

1) Children will gain skills in improving self-esteem.

2) Children will gain skills in developing a sense of assertiveness and empowerment.

3) Children will change distorted cognitions that perpetuate guilt regarding the sexual abuse.

AGE GROUP:

All Ages

SUPPLIES:

1) Videos, cameras, tape recorders, etc. (optional)

2) Artwork paper/supplies for drawing

3) Lined paper/pen for letter writing

4) Representations of previous treatment activities

5) Certificates or other representations of accomplishments

PROCESS:

The Competent Child

This treatment process is the counter balance to treatment activity #32. If the scrapbook organization process chosen dictates a section for the incompetent "innocent" child, this treatment activity projects the opposite for counterbalance and for breaking the potential trauma bonds of helplessness. This treatment activity should portray the competent child and should document childhood examples of empowerment. Through working with parents or perhaps obtaining information from the Trauma Assessment, therapists may encourage children to write stories about themselves and their accomplishments. Pictures (either drawn or through use of cameras) of children in tall, powerful positions may be helpful. Treatment activities where the child demonstrates success should be captured. Letters from parents or from group members outlining victims' competencies or special qualities are other examples of how this activity can be accomplished and used to balance the incompetent, innocent child.

TRAUMA ASSESSMENT PERSPECTIVE:

This treatment activity pertains to the Situational Perspective of the Sexual Victim Trauma Assessment. Distorted cognitions are often manifested in tendencies toward helplessness and hopelessness. If only the empowerment of children is demonstrated, victims may eventually feel as though they have failed since "if I was so powerful, why did I let this happen?" On the other hand, if only the innocent, incompetent child is portrayed as indicated in step #32, children will develop tendencies toward hopelessness. The combination of these two treatment activities can be directly related to tendencies that emerge in the Situational Perspective of the Trauma Assessment and create dysfunctional "footprints" for the future.

#34

GROOMING

OBJECTIVES:

1) Children will gain skills in recognizing the concept involving "grooming."

2) Children will be able to gain skills in understanding the traumatization which takes place because of grooming.

3) Children will be able to gain skills in relieving guilt and anxiety pertaining to sexual abuse through understanding the process of grooming.

4) Children will be able to gain skills in protection as offender manipulations are presented.

AGE GROUP:

12 and Older

SUPPLIES:

1) Children's Drawings

2) Pencils and Papers

3) Writing Papers

4) Statement of Offenders Representing the Grooming Process

5) Children's Resources, such as books, toys or pictures

PROCESS:

Little People vs. Big People

Children who have been sexually abused often feel responsible for not reporting or for not resisting sexual advances. Because of this tendency, it is important victims that understand the process of grooming to relieve guilt. The first step to the treatment process teaches victims about the inequalities between children and adults.

This treatment step has many values. Victims should be made aware of how children are different than adults. This is a prelude to understanding the process of grooming, but it is also important for breaking the cycle of sexual abuse since victims need to understand the special nature of children for their future families. If the childhood of victims has been "robbed," they tend to be individuals, who in adulthood, have very little understanding about the unique nature of children.

Many suggestions could be made to accomplish this step. Children's books could be read to older children showing how children believe in fantasies, how children have much lower levels of understanding, as well as teaching how children do not think the same as adults. Demonstrating children's drawings, having older victims read story books or examine children's toys are other ways to accomplish this step in the treatment activity.

Verbal Manipulations

The next step is to teach what sex offenders say or how offenders verbally coerce children into secrecy. The following list of offender bribes, coercions and manipulations would be helpful in this process. These statements may be written on 3 x 5 cards and distributed in a group, or role playing using these statements could occur, or any other methodology could be implemented demonstrating the verbal manipulation of offenders.

Examples of Grooming

This is our special secret — I like you better than any other kid.

You can tell if you want to, but you don't have to.

If you don't cooperate, I'll tell your mom about what you did with me last time.

If you do this with me, I promise I'll leave your sister alone.

Mom will start drinking again if I ask her to start touching me again — she doesn't like to do it.

If you work very hard at this, it will help you be very popular.

Your parents paid me to do this and it's okay.

I have picked you out of all the kids — I like you best.

Your mother and I did this when she was little, too.

Your dad would cry if he knew we did this. It would hurt his feelings if you told.

You can have anything special you want — friends, jeans or presents if you will cooperate.

This will help you know about what men will try to do to you. You will be a lot better off learning about it from me because I will be gentle and not hurt you.

You know I would never do this to you if I didn't know you really wanted me to.

Do you have any idea what your mother would say about you touching me like this?

Grandma would have a heart attack if the family found out.

If you tell then...

>   you will go to a foster home.

>   I will go to jail.

>   your mother will go crazy.

Remember what mom said she would do if anybody ever did this to you girls again.

If you tell, mom will think it's her fault.

Because I love you so much, I won't tell your mom what you're doing.

Now Me

The last step is to have children relate to their personal situations involving grooming or coercion. Manipulations and coercions that were used should be explained in reference to the inequality of children. Victims should be able to clearly see themselves as unable to resist these grooming processes because of the differences in children and adults. As an example, children may wish to prepare drawings of themselves being represented as being very small and being confused about what the offender is saying. The offender could be drawn in a huge perspective with a loud voice and the entire visual representation suggests the child's total inability to respond in any other way than cooperation.

TRAUMA ASSESSMENT PERSPECTIVE:

This treatment activity pertains to the Situational Perspective of the Sexual Victim Trauma Assessment. Conversations, family issues, regarding pressure or manipulation are all found in the Situational Perspective and can cause trauma in children's future if resolution does not occur in a therapeutic program.

#35

HAPPY BODY IMAGE

OBJECTIVES:

1) Children will gain skills in adapting a more positive body image.

2) Children will gain skills in developing trust within the therapy process.

3) Children will improve self-esteem.

4) Children will become aware of support from professionals and agencies designated to protect children.

AGE GROUP:

10 and younger

SUPPLIES:

1) Roll of butcher paper

2) Marking pens

3) Crayons

4) Paints

5) Paint Brushes

6) Yarn

7) Scissors

8) Construction paper

9) A Very Touching Book by Jan Hindman

10) Camera

PROCESS:

Great Bodies

Children should be gathered in a circle and first **process** the treatment activity. Use <u>A Very Touching Book</u> for discussion regarding the human body being positive in its natural form. Discuss how "grandmas" or "grandpas" may look different than ten-year-olds, but that everyone has wonderful, special bodies. Encourage discussion toward positive ideations regarding the uniqueness of each human being.

Trust

Working one-by-one, have each child lay in the middle of the group, on butcher paper, while another child traces the body image. Discuss feelings and issues of trust and safety while one victim seeks permission to trace around the body of another victim. Allow each group member to participate in the drawing of **each** body so that the process is shared among group members (i.e., one child draws around the left arm while another child draws around the right foot).

Happy Body

Have each child "decorate" their personal body image on paper in any desirable way, perhaps using yarn to create hair, crayons, paints or markers, to create other body features. Children may choose to draw genitalia and they should be supported. Some children may also create representations of clothing on their new "bodies" and discussions about privacy of body parts can be encouraged. Close group activity with a photograph for the scrapbook making explanatory statements, such as "my body is special and wonderful."

And, Presenting . . .

If possible, **and with permission**, allow children's created body image to be displayed in a safe place, such as the waiting room or the hallway of the treatment center. Children should obviously have control over whether their new "bodies" are displayed. Make sure the child's name is displayed, as well. Whenever possible add an "autograph page" beside the paper creation of the child's positive body image. Encourage professionals in the office to write statements of encouragement and support, such as:

> "Good job, Michael."

> "I liked seeing your picture in the waiting room. You look terrific and happy."

Capture for scrapbook using several methods.

TRAUMA ASSESSMENT PERSPECTIVE:

This activity primarily pertains to the Developmental Perspective of the Sexual Victim Trauma Assessment. Positive body image is extremely important in the recovery of sexual victims. Losses in normal sexual development can be related to the lack of a positive sexual "sense of self."

#36

IT IS AGAINST THE LAW

OBJECTIVES:

1) Children will gain an understanding of the criminal aspects of sexual abuse.

2) Children will learn that in spite of emotional and psychological confusions about sexual abuse, the behavior is nonetheless against the law.

3) Children will recognize existing support from the legal system.

4) Children will learn how to break the cycle of abuse.

AGE GROUP:

All ages.

SUPPLIES:

1) Cameras or videos (optional)

2) Pictures of police station

3) Pictures of the courthouse

4) Autographed pictures of the prosecuting attorney, or any other law enforcement official

5) Copies of law books describing sexual abuse statutes

6) Quotes from publications regarding sexual abuse and criminal aspects of sexual abuse

7)   Play or actual law enforcement ''badges''

8)   Any other **legal** representation of opinions or attitudes regarding contact with children.

PROCESS:

It Is A Crime

The process of this activity encourages children of all ages to make tangible representations of the criminal aspects of sexual abuse for their scrapbooks. For older children, copies of law books, excerpts from publications or such items as newspaper articles about sexual criminals may be used. When possible, younger children should have their picture taken in front of the courthouse or law enforcement agency. Pictures can be taken of victim in the courtroom, on the witness stand, even though testimony may not have occurred. Some of these representations (i.e., pictures of the police station, courthouse, etc.) may be kept on hand and routinely presented to all victims.

The process of helping children collect these items is very effective and should be used whenever possible. It can also be valuable to have a law enforcement officer, an attorney, or the prosecuting attorney, visit a therapy group and discuss the legal aspects of sexual abuse. It is important that the technical and legal aspect of the law should be the focus of this treatment activity. Representations of a crime need to be in each child's scrapbook relating to each specific victim.

Respect should always be given to emotional responses that may differ among children. As an example, it is extremely important for all children completing this exercise to recognize that regardless of how they **feel** about the perpetrator, a crime was committed. Positive and negative attributes toward the offender may be recognized and affirmed during the treatment activity, but they must be clearly separated from the elements of the crime that was committed against the victims.

TRAUMA ASSESSMENT PERSPECTIVE:

This activity pertains primarily to the Relationship Perspective of the Sexual Victim Trauma Assessment. In evaluating the relationship between the offender and significant others, the criminal aspects of the sexual act must be emphasized since the court has a significant input on the bottom of the triangle relating to how others view the offender. Information from the Trauma Assessment should indicate the concentration or depth needed for this activity to be successful.

#37

DEAR ABBY AND ANN

OBJECTIVE:

1) Children will have the opportunity to understand and accept a wide variety of feelings toward perpetrators.

2) Children will be able to learn appropriate skills in dealing with a multiplicity of feelings regarding sexual abuse.

3) Children will gain skills in being more empathic toward peers.

4) Children will gain skills in social aptitude.

5) Children will gain skills in becoming more appropriate parents in the future.

6) Children will gain skills in understanding short and long term goals for recovery.

AGE GROUP:

Latency or Adolescent

SUPPLIES:

1) Typing paper

2) Xerox copy opportunities

3) 3 ring binder

4) Lined paper

5) Pencils/pens

6) Blackboard and/or easel

PROCESS:

Dear Abby from Me

The first step to completing this group activity is for professionals to recall significant issues found in the Relationship Perspective of the Trauma Assessment. Conflicts or traumatization that has occurred due to lack of support for the victim should be the focus of fictitious letters written by therapists to a "Dear Abby" or "Ann Landers" correspondence consultant. Letters should be written according to the age and sophistication level of group members. The "fictitious victim" writing the letter should be complaining and asking advice regarding situations that are similar to each victim's trauma. Children should receive a letter, but not necessarily the letter specific to their needs. Group discussion should occur regarding how to respond to these letters.

Feelings Forward, Then Needs and Goals

Using a blackboard or easel, the group should first attempt to identify the feelings of the letter writer. Secondly, the group should discuss what the victim needs immediately and what the victim would need in the future for a long term goal. The purpose of using short and long term goals is to provide **HOPE** to victims who may be in a position of futility at the present time but may need to look more toward the future. As an example, if a mother is not believing a child represented in a letter, the three step process may be:

1) Identify feelings:

Anger

Abandonment

Worry

Sadness

2) Short term:

"This victim needs to know that her feelings are acceptable, that her feelings may change, that she is not alone in her feelings, and that she has the support of many people even if her mother doesn't seem to care now."

3) "This victim needs to understand that it may take time for her mother to believe. It may also be important to recognize that she will be a different kind of mother for her children and, as time goes on, she will gain more and more support from many people."

It is important to have all group members write a response to each victim and put these responses in a notebook. This activity may take several sessions. The Dear Abby notebook should be "revisited" at a later time to assess progress and growth from group members. It may also be effective for some victims to take on the role of writing thank you letters to group members for their helpful responses. These letters should be captured for scrapbooks.

TRAUMA ASSESSMENT PERSPECTIVE:

This treatment activity pertains primarily to the Relationship Perspective and the confusion for the psychological identity of the "victim and the perpetrator." Some attention could be given to post-disclosure issues from the Situational Perspective, as well.

#38

SAYING ''NO'' — SENSE OF EMPOWERMENT

OBJECTIVES:

1) Children will gain skills in empowerment.

2) Children will improve self-esteem.

3) Children will learn to evaluate appropriate and inappropriate situations where they may refuse directions from adults and may choose noncompliance.

AGE GROUP:

All ages.

SUPPLIES:

1) Construction paper

2) Markers

3) Pens

4) Crayons

5) Paints and Brushes

6) Easels

7) Blackboards

8) Any supplies that can create visual representations of choices.

PROCESS:

Good No's

This activity begins by processing the issue of noncompliance. Depending on the age of children, a list should be made of appropriate and inappropriate examples for children to deny compliance with adults. For younger children, saying "no" to a chore list would be an example of inappropriate resistance. On the other hand, children should have a clear understanding that saying "no" to any touching that is confusing, uncomfortable or a secret, is a legitimate reason to resist compliance. For older victims, more complicated discussions regarding adolescents privileges and responsibilities need attention. Lists should be made using either an easel or a blackboard for adolescents while younger children may benefit from putting each "good 'no'" on large pieces of construction paper.

"You can't say No to being nice to your sister."

"You can say No to tricks about Touching."

And The Big People

This is also an excellent treatment activity to share with parents. If parents and children meet separately, the issue of appropriate and inappropriate compliance can be discussed in group therapy with parents while children are preparing the "situations" for contemplation on large cards. The groups can move together for the "quizzing" of parents, with parents being coached to make mistakes, which will require children to correct their parents. It is always effective if children can teach their parents an idea that parents are "covertly" wishing to teach children.

For younger children, it may also be appropriate to have some representations of the word "no" in scrapbooks. Making large letters by gluing macaroni to paper is an effective example. Any artwork activities that can create a positive, strong, assertive representation of the word "no" will be helpful, provided it is in the appropriate context.

For older children, the use of the word 'no' can be expanded into many different areas, such as saying "no" to sexual advances from peers, saying "no" to invitations to break rules or saying "no" to peer pressure. Adolescents could, as an example, make some kind of representation of the learning by preparing a

Ten Commandments of Saying No

or

My Yes and No List

TRAUMA ASSESSMENT PERSPECTIVE:

This treatment activity may deal with the Situational Perspective of the Sexual Victim Trauma Assessment if certain issues in the Trauma Assessment revealed a great deal of coercion or secrecy in the sexually abusive "scene." Assisting children in recognizing that they were powerless to say "no" is an important part of this process and should be emphasized for those children whose Trauma Assessment revealed this specific problem.

#39

ANGER MADNESS

OBJECTIVES:

1) Children will be able to identify a range of feelings including feelings of anger.

2) Children will be able to identify aggressive acts exhibited by themselves and others.

3) Children will be able to identify potential consequences to self and others for aggressive behavior.

4) Children will be able to identify thoughts that occur prior to aggressive acts.

5) Children will be able to gain skills in coping with anger.

AGE GROUP:

All Ages

SUPPLIES:

1) List of Feeling Words

2) List of Words that Express Anger

3) 3 x 5 Cards or Construction Paper

4) Paper Sacks for Masks

PROCESS

Anger Ranges

Sexually abused children have tremendous potential to become abusive reactive due to unresolved feelings of anger. Strong tendencies toward self-abusive behavior or abusive behavior exist for victims of sexual abuse. Victims tend to be in a trauma bond with extremes of feeling anger. Some victims seem to have absolutely no ability to be agnry at the perpetrator or to be angry at their situation. This places children in an "abusability" position for much of their future. On the other hand, some children find themselves out of control because of anger toward their situation, which is destructive, as well.

There are many, many varieties and ways this treatment activity can be accomplished. The first step for all ages of children is to discuss the issue of anger and process inappropriate ways of expressing anger. This portion of the treatment process could take several weeks or several hours. It is best to use the "inappropriate" emphasis first.

Silliness Seriousness

Children may wish to role play angry situations so that they look absurd and ridiculous. Ideally, these anger scenarios would be captured on video and children would watch them at a later time for full impact. Being demonstrative and absurd should be the focus of this therapeutic step.

Secondly, children should process and understand the negative aspects of inappropriate expressions of anger. For older children, failing in school, losing friends, being fired from a job are all role playing scenarios that could be presented. Victims should be able to recognize that if they are angry at the perpetrator, their parent or the system, usually they become the victim of their own anger.

This portion of the treatmnt activity should not be done haphazardly or quickly. Recognizing the impact of inappropriately expressed anger must occur before victims will be willing to make changes. If the treatment activity moves too quickly, there will be less motivation to learn alternative ways of expressing anger.

Good Anger

Finally, children should contemplate ways in which anger can be expressed in a positive way. Some situations could occur where children recognize the difference between aggression and anger. In this way, a natural emotion of being angry can be productive while the act of aggression can be avoided. As an example, if children learn that often the impact of inappropriate anger is trauma to their bodies, a natural alternative or response is to implement positive actions to the body, such as jogging, swimming or "good touching." Some adolescents who used music to express their anger or who may have discussed music as an impetus to anger may find alternative forms of music that is perhaps romantic, loving and soothing. Obviously, expressing anger through the use of punching bean bags, yelling loudly, making video tapes are all appropriate if they are completed in the group process and not rendering victims into destructive behaviors.

Finally, children should be able to capture the learning experience in three steps, for their scrapbooks. The inappropriateness of anger, the effect of anger and positive reframes of anger should be included in the three step process.

TRAUMA ASSESSMENT PERSPECTIVE:

This treatment activity pertains to the Situational Perspective of the Sexual Victim Trauma Assessment. Out of control behavior becomes a coping skill or a footprint that needs adjustment in therapy. Additionally, expressions of anger may have some influence in the Relationship Perspective of the Trauma Assessment.

#40

CRIMINAL THINKING FOR KIDS

OBJECTIVES:

1) Children will be able to identify the thinking patterns of sexual offenders.

2) Children will be able to relieve feelings of guilt regarding sexual abuse.

3) Children will gain skills in empowerment.

4) Children will gain skills in being able to break the cycle of sexual abuse.

AGE GROUP:

12 and Older

SUPPLIES:

1) Examples of Thinking Errors of Sexual Offenders

2) 5 x 7 Cards

3) Role Playing Facility

4) Video

5) Play Microphone

6) Optional Stage Props

7) Inside the Criminal Mind by Dr. Stanton Samenow

8) Construction Paper

9) Magic Markers

PROCESS:

Offenders and Their Thinkings

It is generally helpful for children to understand the thinking processes of sexual offenders. This relates to criminal thinking and the use of thinking errors. This can be a complicated process for adolescents who wish to be exposed to Stanton Samenow's book on criminal thinking or to sex offender thinking errors commonly used in offender treatment.

For older children, understanding thinking errors can be an important process. Going through examples of thinking errors and placing thinking errors on large pieces of construction paper which can lay on the floor during the group process can be helpful. Older children need to understand that manipulation, intimidation and distorted thinking was a very important part of sexual offending.

It is also important to note that adolescents may have a tendency to take on those same characteristics and discussing thinking errors or understanding how offenders use thinking errors can be of a benefit for adolescents who may have tendencies toward using manipulation themselves.

Tricks, No Treats

For younger children, using words like "tricks" can be helpful. Even younger children are capable of understanding how people can trick themselves into thinking different ways or they can trick others. For younger children, completing a role play activity presenting different scenarios of criminal thinking would be helpful. As an example, a moderator could interview a child and ask him or her to give the appropriate answer to a scenario as follows:

You are home alone with your five-year-old sister. You're supposed to babysit and take care of her, but she is kind of crabby. She drops the jam jar and breaks it. You are real mad at her and would like to hit her. What should you do?

Three options can be posed to the "actor":

A) Go ahead. She's only five, you're bigger and she can't hit you back.

B) Go ahead and hit her because even if she tells on you, no one will believe her because she is little.

C) Don't hit her. It was an accident and besides five-year-old kids make a lot more mistakes than 10-year-old kids like you.

A variety of scenarios could be presented to younger children with the rest of group members booing and hissing at inappropriate options while clapping and praising the right answer. For older children, scenarios involving general interviewing where the "actors" use thinking errors with significant proficiency can be humorous and fun. Whenever possible, video tape scenarios and play them back for group participation will enhance the treatment process.

TRAUMA ASSESSMENT PERSPECTIVE:

This treatment activity pertains to the Situational Perspective of the Sexual Victim Trauma Assessment. Understanding offender manipulation, coercion, bribery, etc., is very important for dispelling distorted cognitions in children. It is also important to recognize that children may have a tendency to develop these footprints or coping skills themselves and these tendencies would be discovered in the Situational Perspective.

#41

HELPER TOUCHES

OBJECTIVES:

1) Children will be able to understand the concepts of good, bad and secret touching.

2) Children will be able to understand the concepts of secrets as they relate to sexual abuse.

3) Children will be able to understand and demonstrate their understanding of genital touching between adults and children that is appropriate.

4) Children will relieve tendencies toward developing phobic or fearful reactions to non-abusive genital contact.

AGE GROUP:

Children Under Age 10

SUPPLIES:

1) A Very Touching Book by Jan Hindman

2) Construction Paper

3) Magic Markers

4) Crayons

5) Artwork to Create Scenarios of Visiting the Doctor, Bathing or Other Healthcare Activities

PROCESS:

Three Kinds of Touching

This is a very simple process and actually an addendum to the treatment activity teaching children GOOD, BAD, and SECRET TOUCHING. These concepts can be found in several resources, however, <u>A Very Touching Book</u> most clearly explains these three concepts. The treatment activity or process should begin with reviewing the concepts of the three kinds of touching and teaching children to not only identify the three types of touching, but to make representations of how those touchings relate to day-to-day activities, especially concerning touching #1 and touching #2.

The first kind of touching should be "presented as 'good touching'" and many activities can be implemented, teaching children the importance of affection and attention. Younger children should be able to make charts of people who provide them with affection and attention. Hopefully, the treatment modality of touching is a common component of therapy and, therefore, this kind of touching explanation should be easily expedited.

Touching #2 should be explained as "Bad Touching" and should relate to aggression and violence. The "badness" of aggression should be clearly attached to this type of touching so that children who feel badly about their sexual contact, can proceed through this proces removing the stigma of badness. Creative therapists will find ways to deal with aggression and violence in the group process by teaching children to be kind, to communicate and to appreciate others. Abusive tendencies for sexually traumatized children is common and this treatment component avoiding "bad touching" should not only be completed for this activity, but should be an ongoing process in victim therapy.

Secret Touching

Finally, the concept of secret touching should be explained as indicated in <u>A Very Touching Book</u>. For the purpose of this individual treatment activity, however, emphasis must be placed on teaching children to understand that some genital contact between children and adults is normal and natural. Creating touching phobias for children can be one of the most destructive treatment outcomes if children are simply taught,

"Don't let anyone ever touch your private parts."

Normally, adults need to touch their children's genitalia at times. Without education, there may be a feeling of betrayal for children who are given blanket statements to avoid all genital touching and, as an example, are taken to the doctor for a physical examination. Even though children may not resist the doctor's probes, the underlying message is one of discrepancy, which may make children more vulnerable in the future. If the "rules" are disregarded easily, without explanation to the child, then a sexual offender touching a child may fall into the same category of "disregard" as far as the child's perceptions are concerned.

<u>A Very Touching Book</u> may be used for this activity as three examples of non-abusive genital touching are given, which include a medical examination, a diaper changing activity, as well as a bathing scene. <u>A Very Touching Book</u> also initiates an activity where children "touch" the right answer to determine if the situation is appropriate or abusive. Therapists could present scenarios, either by using <u>A Very Touching Book</u> or by creating additional scenarios that could be read to children.

To create a demonstrative and active group process, children could run to "touch" a buzzer, a "right answer button," or some other representation of a "yes" or a "no." The activity should have a reasonably simple explanation created with action, noise and fun. Children could be encouraged to clap, whistle, ring bells, or participate in any other kind of demonstration which indicates success with the correct answer.

A final process of this treatment activity should suggest that even though this process is primarily for children under 10, coordination with adolescents in this issue could be very helpful. Adolescents could create scenarios of nonsexual abuse situations where genitalia was touched and perhaps participate in a group activity for younger children, quizzing and teaching the correct answer celebration.

TRAUMA ASSESSMENT PERSPECTIVE:

This treatment activity deals with the Developmental Perspective of the Sexual Victim Trauma Assessment. If children believe that all touching of the genitalia is wrong, they have potential to develop destructive attitudes about body image and they also have tendencies to manifest sexual dysfunctions if they develop sexual phobias or extreme negative feelings about genitalia and the touching of bodies. Through this treatment activity, children may become more comfortable with not only their bodies, but with normal healthcare and hygiene activities.

#42

GUIDED IMAGERY

OBJECTIVES:

1) Children will be able to recognize the importance of relieving stress.

2) Children will be able to learn skills in relaxation.

3) Children will be able to share details about sensory activation or "triggers" relating to sexual abuse.

AGE GROUP:

All Ages

SUPPLIES:

1) Paper

2) Coloring Materials

3) Tape Recorders (optional)

PROCESS:

Rest and Relaxation

This exercise can be facilitated in many different ways. There are resources involving guided imagery tapes, however, for the purposes of working with sexually abused children, therapists can create their own. The purpose of the activity is to teach children how to relieve stress and encourage relaxation, then capture images of sensory memory followed by a positive reframe.

The first step in this activity is to have children lie on the floor and either listen to a person's soothing voice or to a prepared tape. The tape or the instructions should encourage children to close their eyes and take part in activities of tensing and then relaxing each part of the body. This should begin with fingers and move toward all other parts of the body that are accessible to muscle tightening and relaxation.

Sensory Connections

The next step is to have children, in the relaxed position, think about what they see, hear, smell, taste or feel when they think about their sexual abuse. Those images can be shared verbally. Children should not move from the body positions. When all children have shared the images or the sensory activation through this exercise, the activity should be interrupted so that children can capture these issues on paper.

The next step will require children to return with the memory or the image of the trigger and attempt to make positive reframes. As an example, if the child remembered the smell of cigarette smoke, then the child should be given an opportunity to picture a strong wind moving into the scene and blowing the cigarette smoke away. This activity should close with children being able to again make a tangible recreation of the positive reframe for their scrapbooks.

TRAUMA ASSESSMENT PERSPECTIVE:

This treatment activity pertains to the Situational Perspective of the Trauma Assessment and the development of phobic reactions. "Triggers" exist for children and will continue to return them to the sexual abuse affective responses unless these "stimulators" are brought under control.

#43

SECRET FEELINGS AND THOUGHTS

OBJECTIVES:

1) Children will gain skills in recognizing they are not alone in sexual abuse trauma.

2) Children will gain skills in understanding sex offender manipulation and coercion.

3) Children will be able to understand specific issues surrounding male victimization.

4) Children will be able to learn ways to avoid traumatization through secrecy.

AGE GROUP:

10 and Older

SUPPLIES:

1) Resource, <u>Secret Feelings and Thoughts: A Book About Male Sexual Abuse</u> by Rosemarie Narimanian

2) Construction paper

3) Markers/Crayons

4) Video

5) Lined writing paper

PROCESS:

Yes, Males, Too

This recent publication is one of the few children's books available specifically concerning male victimization. The publication presents a story about male sexual abuse and the particular problems facing the male victim. The treatment process could follow guidelines as used with many other stories. First, victims should anticipate the contents of the story from examining the cover of the book and its title. The anticipation will always assist in enhancing the learning process.

Reading the book can be done in several ways with children sharing turns or listening to the therapist read sections. Video taping of the reading can always enhance the process as children can watch the video at a later time and review the material.

Capture the Moment

Processing the publication could occur with children making lists of the learning process or other products as writing letters to the characters in the book or to the author. Capturing the feelings of secrecy could also occur for victims under a variety of "secret situations." It is important for children to recognize that males are sexually abused, but for both males and females, the pressure of secrecy is perhaps the most important focus of this publication and treatment activity.

TRAUMA ASSESSMENT PERSPECTIVE:

This treatment activity primarily pertains to the Situational Perspective of the Trauma Assessment where secretive issues become the focus of significant trauma for victims, as well as confused thinking which denies the activity of the abuse from the male perspective.

#44

SUPER BODY

OBJECTIVES:

1) Children will be able to identify body parts.

2) Children will be able to learn the appropriate names for body parts.

3) Children's anxiety regarding genitalia will be alleviated.

4) Children will gain a positive attitude about genitalia.

AGES:

Ages 10 and Under.

SUPPLIES:

1) A Very Touching Book by Jan Hindman (optional)

2) Large pieces of construction paper

3) Magic markers, felt pens

4) Paints, crayons

5) Black board or large paper for writing a list

6) 8 1/2 x 11 inch paper

7) Written material for preparing an "official promise or pledge"

8) Butcher paper

PROCESS:

Name the Body Parts

The process of this treatment activity first elicits understanding and descriptions for names of body parts. This can be done most effectively by using a handout of "empty bodies" drawn for the children. For older children, drawing a body outline on butcher paper may be effective. The first drawings should be nondescript and have no identifying characteristics. This can be done on large pieces of construction paper or on plain, smaller pieces of 8 1/2 x 11 inch paper or on body size pieces of butcher paper.

Stumbling, Bumbling, Grown-Ups

The second step of this treatment activity requires making a humorous portrayal of the names that are typically used for body parts. Generally, children feel nervous and anxious about describing genitalia. In this activity it is most anxiety reducing if therapists can appear confused and ask silly questions such as "is the elbow a belly button." Children should be allowed to laugh at the therapist's confusion and make corrections.

The next step of the treatment activity inquires about the names children use for body parts, especially genitalia. Again, therapists should present even more confusion. It may also be appropriate for therapists to relate the names of body parts they learned as children.

> "My mom told me I had boobs, but I didn't know for sure because my friends called them 'knockers'."

The purpose of this step is to create an atmosphere of silliness and comraderie. Effort should be exerted to learn the correct words for the private parts of the body. Therapists must indicate, however, that before this process can occur, the silliness or wrong words need to be thrown away.

Giggle Gaggle

The "giggle gaggle" can be initiated as outlined in <u>A Very Touching Book</u>. With the help of therapists, children should provide the names for body parts they have learned from friends, parents, jokes, swear words or other unreliable sources. The process will require the children to present the "silly names" and then participate in the GIGGLE GAGGLE, which will giggle away the silly words so that the right words can be learned. In this way, children will not feel criticized or ridiculed if they have been using incorrect words. Therapists should allow children to provide the names of genitalia that are incorrect. If some children are uncomfortable or do not have inappropriate names, therapists should whisper names they learned as a child so these children will have a response. A long list of words, such as "weiner, butt, poo poos, pee pees, potties," should emerge on a chalkboard or butcher paper. This should be a humorous activity. This process should also delineate lists of male body parts as being separate from female body parts.

The giggle gaggle then requires therapists to go back through the list and point to each word s-l-o-w-l-y. Children should be instructed to laugh loudly, "giggling away" the silly words. This activity should be done with a great deal of loudness, clapping, yelling and enthusiasm.

The Right Stuff

The next step in this process allows children to learn the right words for body parts. This should also be done with great enthusiasm and positive structure. Genitalia names such as "breast, penis, vagina, vulva," etc., should be listed on the black board and repeated with "great dignity." Genitalia names should be marked on drawn bodies in very artistic and positive ways. For some children, they may wish to make their own list of the inappropriate words for these scrapbooks and, in some grand fashion, indicate the rejection of those words. This can be done through such efforts as making a list of silly words and then having children cut out a large "X" that can be super-imposed over the "silly word" list. Some children may find scribbling through the silly words or taking some other way to dispose of the silly words used for body parts to be effective. Finally, children should be able to create a positive body image with positive labeling of correct body parts.

I Promise

As children leave the group, a pledge or a promise may be created, or for older children, making out a "contract" may be appropriate. The pledge, promise, or contract indicates that not only will the children use the appropriate words, but that they will help their parents and friends with "giggle gaggles" to avoid using inappropriate words. The pledge, promise, or contract should resurface in the future for review. Finally, this activity should be captured by some method for the scrapbook.

TRAUMA ASSESSMENT PERSPECTIVE:

This treatment activity primarily relates to the Developmental Perspective of the Sexual Victim Trauma Assessment. This activity teaches children positive ideations about their bodies and human sexuality in order to prevent trauma to normal sexual development.

#45

GROUP FEELINGS POSTER

OBJECTIVES:

1) Children will be assisted in being able to express feelings about being sexually victimized.

2) Children will gain feelings of comraderie for group members.

3) Children will gain the ability to understand that vacillation or multiplicity of feelings is understandable and expected.

4) Children will be able to see positive outcomes of therapy.

AGE GROUP:

All Ages.

SUPPLIES:

1) Large sheets of butcher paper

2) 3 x 5 cards or 5 x 7 cards

3) Magic markers

4) A wide variety of art supplies for decorating words of feelings, such as glue, glitter, yarn, dried noodles, rice, or beans, ribbons, colorful wrapping paper, tape, or any significant fabric.

5) Camera

PROCESS:

Feelings and Feelings

Prior to the actual treatment session, therapists should prepare large pieces of paper stating:

"When kids are sexually abused, they feel"

(for older children)

or

"When children have secret touching they feel"

(for younger children)

A wide variety of feelings should also be written on smaller 3 x 5 or 5 x 7 cards:

1) Bewildered

2) Hurt

3) Angry

4) Afraid

5) Sad

6) Lonely

7) Lost

8) Forgotten

9) Sick

10) Furious

The first part of the group should concentrate on expression of feelings and encourage children to recognize that they may have many feelings or that their feelings about their sexual abuse may change from time to time. This activity can occur similar to a card game, while passing the feeling cards to each child who comments by accepting or rejecting each feeling. The process of touching the feeling cards, passing the feeling cards, and generally moving the cards from one child to another is important and valuable. There is a physical focus on the card then the "feeling" is passed.

Choosing a Feeling

The next process step should allow each child to choose a feeling or perhaps several feelings that best represent a current affective status. This process should not be done haphazardly and should be done with great explanation in order to desensitize feelings appropriately. Children should be encouraged to discuss the feeling and how they believe this feeling has occurred. When a choice has been made, each victim should be able to decorate a large piece of construction paper with the feeling they have represented in a word. For adolescents, this process may need to be "grandiose" with important decorations or perhaps role playing the feeling in anticipation of a group picture being taken.

Eventually, when all feeling cards have been represented for each victim in very artistic form, a group picture should be taken. Victim's pictures should be taken with their feeling card. The group picture should remain in the group room and subsequent pictures taken as hopefully, feelings change and process.

The last step of this activity should be to have each child speculate how this feeling may change as they move toward "graduation." Statements may be made, such as,

"During my next group poster, I hope I feel _____ ."

This proactive activity will allow children to look toward the future with positive outcome of therapy.

TRAUMA ASSESSMENT PERSPECTIVE:

This portion of the Trauma Assessment deals primarily with the Situational Perspective pertaining to distorted cognitions and the prevention of coping skills in the future, such as self blame or tendencies toward self-abuse. Expression of feelings may contribute to breaking the cycle so that these children do not develop tendencies toward secretiveness and communication avoidance.

#46

ALICE DOESN'T BABYSIT ANYMORE

OBJECTIVES:

1) Children will gain skills in recognizing potentially abusive situations with babysitters.

2) Children will gain skills in recognizing that females as well as males can sexually offend.

3) Children will gain skills in protection of future sexual abuse.

AGE GROUPS:

10 and Under

SUPPLIES:

1) <u>Alice Doesn't Babysit Anymore</u> by Kevin McGovern

2) Construction Paper

3) Writing Pens

4) Writing Paper

5) Various Art Supplies

PROCESS:

Beware Babysitter

The process of this treatment activity includes providing children with knowledge about sexual abuse occurring with not only babysitters, but with female offenders. Kevin McGovern's book, <u>Alice Doesn't Babysit Anymore</u>, presents a scenario where children are manipulated and coerced into sexual contact by a female babysitter. This story should be read to children and processed to assess the competence for children understanding the concepts. Most important in presenting this story is encouraging an understanding of offender manipulation.

As with many publications on child sexual abuse, this book can be read to group members and processed. Children can prepare lists of manipulative techniques used by the babysitter or lists discussing the "feelings" experienced by the children who were being abused. Children may want to discuss babysitting scenarios from the past that perhaps included conflicting situations or concerns.

Reading the book, <u>Alice Doesn't Babysit Anymore,</u> should not be the sole modality for this treatment activity. Reading of the book should initiate a process for the children creating tangible representations of what they have learned. These "learning" techniques should be done with a variety of modalities, using art work, photographs or representation of the book.

TRAUMA ASSESSMENT PERSPECTIVE:

This treatment activity pertains to the Situational Perspective of the Sexual Victim Trauma Assessment. "How" children are sexually abused, presents issues in the sexual abusive "scene" that have the potential to create distorted cognitions. This is especially true for those issues related to offender bribery or coercion that may render children feeling guilty and responsible.

#47

MY PLACE PUPPET

OBJECTIVES:

1) Children will improve self-esteem.

2) Children will improve attitude about mental health involvement.

3) Children will improve ability too communicate.

4) Children will be able to discuss and express internal feelings.

AGE GROUP:

Children Under 12

SUPPLIES:

1) Inexpensive Cloth Puppets

2) Cup Hangers

3) Yarn

4) Velcro or Some Other Way of Placing Names on Puppets

PROCESS:

My Place Too

This treatment activity is simply designed to improve the attitude children tend to have about therapeutic involvement, as well as improving children's ability to express feelings and communicate. As each child is introduced into the treatment center, a puppet should be provided with each child's name attached. Children should have access to their puppets during many therapy sessions. When children have access to a modality like a puppet, they will often be able to express feelings and emotions that were impossible to express under normal therapeutic circumstances.

As children enter therapy, their personal puppet hanging on the wall becomes a symbol of belonging to the treatment center. Feelings of importance may occur. Additionally, children will also have access to a modality for improving the success of treatment, which will enhance self-esteem and the therapeutic process, in general. When children leave the treatment process, they should be able to have their puppet included in their scrapbook.

TRAUMA ASSESSMENT PERSPECTIVE:

This treatment activity pertains to the Situational Perspective of the Sexual Victim Trauma Assessment. Children tend to develop negative coping skills and poor self-esteem. Additionally, post-disclosure issues can be painful for children as they feel punished by their therapeutic involvement. This treatment activity would hopefully change negative attitudes about post-disclosure issues.

#48

POSITIVE PACKAGES

OBJECTIVES:

1) Children will gain a positive attitude about treatment participation.

2) Children will gain skills in improving self- esteem.

3) Children will gain skills in providing positive support for others.

AGE GROUP:

All Ages

SUPPLIES:

1) White Letter Sized Envelopes

2) Stickers or other Decorations

3) Magic Markers

4) Any Other Art Supplies for Children to Personally Decorate their Packages

PROCESS:

Change the Focus

This is a group process that may be completed in a single group session for an existing group, but should also be an ongoing process as children are involved in therapy. Sexual victims often feel punished because of a demand for therapy attendance in addition to feeling alienated, uncomfortable and embarrassed. The treatment center is usually a threatening environment unless effort is put forth to change that attitude. Victims benefit more if they have a sense of belonging to the clinic or to the therapy process.

Additionally, sexual victims tend to have low self-esteem and they either become depressed and lethargic because of those attitudes or they tend to become hostile and aggressive toward others. By using this treatment technique, children can improve their self-image by receiving positive feedback from others and they can also gain skills in being positive rather than resorting to other more destructive methods of resolving low self-esteem conflicts.

My Piece of Pride

During a single session or as each victim joins the group, effort should be made to have children decorate an envelope or a package with personal identification items. The child's name should be placed on the package or the envelope for not only the victim to recognize, but for others to view. During the victim's first session, when the envelopes are decorated, it will be helpful to have children take a turn and participate in positive feedback. Other group members should use paper when writing is possible and write a positive compliment, a statement or word of encouragement to each specific group member. The messages should be placed in each group member's envelope as all group members have been in the position to receive positive "pieces." As the session closes, group members should be able to read the positive comments to other group members and return them to their private packages.

Therapists should have the ability to place the personal packages on the wall or in some kind of display before each group session. Previous messages should be removed by therapists so that each group member has an empty package before each therapy session. Therapists can use this "post office" modality to provide feedback to group members on an ongoing basis. This will be especially helpful as some children may be involved in particularly difficult times, such as court participation or separation from family and may need special words of encouragement.

Additionally, the personal packages can be used as a group activity by asking other group members to provide messages for the personal package of another victim who may be struggling. By using this technique, children can see their package displayed in an important position and various "mail" can be distributed to victims. Children can also have an avenue of receiving compliments and support from a variety of professionals on an ongoing basis, that will be rehabilitating and helpful.

TRAUMA ASSESSMENT PERSPECTIVE

This treatment activity pertains primarily to the Situational Perspective with the development of negative self-concepts through cognitive distortions. Post- disclosure issues found in the Situational Perspective are also important for this treatment activity since ongoing conflict with others may be quite perplexing to victims and they may need ongoing support.

#49

THE LET'S TALK ABOUT TOUCHING GAME

OBJECTIVES:

1) Children will be assisted in discussing their own sexual victimization.

2) Children will gain skills in preventing sexual abuse.

3) Children will gain skills in adapting effective problem solving techniques.

4) Children will gain skills in controlling abuse reactive tendencies.

AGE GROUP:

Ages 7 and Older

SUPPLIES:

1) Let's Talk About Touching Game by Toni Cavanaugh (Supplies included)

2) Artwork for Capturing Treatment Activities

3) Videos or Camera (optional)

PROCESS:

The Game Plan

This treatment activity involves using the therapeutic game, Let's Talk About Touching. This resource is designed for children who act out sexually or for victims who are at risk for acting out sexually. This is a simple game, which is played using the rules of "fish." Children are presented discussion cards with problems and solutions. The game encourages thinking and problem solving skills. It is recommended that this game be used in a group process and, if possible, parental involvement should also occur.

The Let's Talk About Touching Game could be played in intervals over the course of treatment. The game could also be used as a pre and post test allowing children to not only make improvements, but to see their own process or improvement over time. A proactive approach would complete this treatment activity by capturing representations of the progress children have made as demonstrated by the game or some other methodology. Children could have their pictures taken playing the game, either with a camera or video. They may also write an evaluation of the learning that occurred or find some other way to capture the activity for scrapbooks.

TRAUMA ASSESSMENT PERSPECTIVE

This treatment activity pertains to the Situational Perspective of the Sexual Victim Trauma Assessment. Victims of sexual abuse often adapt tendencies of rage, anger and abusive behavior toward others as a way to cope with the feelings of trauma. This valuable resource assists children in learning more appropriate coping skills.

#50

BEE ALERT

OBJECTIVES:

1) Children will gain skills in understanding how to protect themselves from further enticement and bribery relating to sexual abuse.

2) Children will understand ideas relating to the issue of sexual consent.

3) Children will gain skills in recognizing their rights as children as compared to the rights and power of adults.

4) Children will gain skills in recognizing their powerlessness in sexual abuse which will enhance their **"victims status"** and create ideations of innocence.

5) Children's sense of empowerment will be enhanced.

AGE GROUP:

All ages

SUPPLIES:

1) A "BEE" like object that can be thrown around the group room. A yellow nerf ball would be ideal, although a yellow balloon decorated as a bee would also suffice. If possible, a toy or mechanical representation of a bee would be even more valuable.

2) Paper with lines

3) Plain construction paper

4) Writing utensils, such as magic markers, crayons, or pens

5) Other art supplies that can capture feelings of bribery

PROCESS:

Caution

An overview of this treatment activity must occur before actual implementation. The therapeutic process should be understood by all therapists concerning its value, but also its potential to harm children if administered inappropriately. This treatment activity will discuss bribery and coercion used with children to enhance compliance with sexual abuse. Eventually, the process will encourage children to become alert to future abuse. The subtle value of this assignment is for children to recognize that they were innocent in their abuse and that the coercion and bribery was so strong, they had no alternative but to comply.

The danger of this kind of activity is in suggesting to victims where overt bribery and coercion did not occur, that they failed or that they were "guilty" since compliance that occurred without overt coercion was unnecessary. As an example, asking children,

"What did the offender say to you to make you keep the secret?,"

may imply that something **should** have been said and that, if no comments were made, the child obviously complied unnecessarily. Insensitivity to this issue could be traumatizing to children and cause difficulties in the future. Therefore, understanding these "potentials" is a prerequisite for this activity.

Overview

This treatment activity will occur in several steps. First, children will recognize their rights to protection even though they are younger, smaller and perhaps not able to overtly protect themselves. Secondly, generic coercion tactics used by sexual offenders will be processed and that list will describe covert or nonspecific coercion and bribery. The powerful position of the offender, the power of silence and the size of the offender, should all be described on a list and should seem as powerful and controlling as more overt coercions, such as threats or bribery. During this second step, children who have not had **covert** bribery should feel comfortable recognizing that bribery does not necessarily need to be obvious and overt.

The final step of this treatment activity allows each child to talk about his/her own experiences with coercion and place many shared group examples on paper for the scrapbook. It is important that the treatment activity not be specific for each victim until great effort has been made to protect children who have not personally experienced overt bribery.

Rights to Privacy

Further implementation of this treatment process requires therapists to be demonstrative about recognizing the rights of children. The issue of privacy should pervade this discussion. The purpose should be to help children of all ages recognize their rights to privacy regarding their bodies. A Very Touching Book may help in this regard or children may simply be placed in a position where they can recite the rights of children, to keep their bodies private, special, and unique. For younger children, such statements should be made concerning examples of rights to privacy in the bathroom, or at school. For adolescents or older children, the issue of consent in peer and adult situations will apply.

The next step in the treatment activity should elicit an understanding that bigger or older people coerce children into situations where children's rights are violated. It is important to frame this process in the "violation of rights" perspective. Children should be presented as "innocent" and worthy of protection, but due to the power of older or bigger people, they are coerced.

Bribery and Coercion

Along with coercive behavior, bribery should also be explained in this second step. Examples of coercion should be made on large pieces of construction paper. Many of these examples should be overt and specifically related to the Trauma Assessments of victims in the group. Most importantly, covert bribery should also be clearly represented. Statements for large pieces of construction paper could be made with the following examples:

> "She told me that she liked me very best and I didn't want to tell and get her into trouble because she was so nice." (overt)

> "He just scared me. He never said anything at all, he just made me feel afraid." (covert)

> "He told me that if I didn't do this and that if I told, I would be in trouble and everyone would be mad at me." (overt)

> "I just liked him, that's all. He was nice, and I felt bad, thinking about telling on him." (covert)

> "She was the boss, and I heard my mom and dad say, 'be sure and mind or you'll be in trouble'." (covert)

To complete step two, each group member should have a piece of construction paper with a coercive behavior written upon it. The "Bee" should be thrown around the room and caught by group members.

When the Bee is caught by a group member, they may read aloud their example of coercive behavior. Eventually, as each group member reads their card, new threats and examples of coercion and bribery can be discussed. Therapists should allow the construction paper cards to initiate responses to the assignment, but eventually as the Bee is thrown around the room, children should be making more spontaneous examples not listed on the cards. While this activity is taking place, therapists should record these statements for later.

Step three occurs with children being able to describe the types of coercion that were used in their own specific incidents. These situations can be role played for preteens or for younger children and can be used for more indepth discussions or other "process" treatment activities for older children. Some adolescents may choose to take several group sessions and write poems, find song lyrics or capture other information in society that describes a representation of the coercion they experienced in their abuse. Eventually, the treatment activity should move toward capturing the coercion that was used in each specific incident for each victim and then designing a process where victims can be alert to future exploitation or Bee Aware.

Future Partners

This treatment activity can be particularly helpful for preteen or adolescent victims who may be in the process of choosing partners or mates. Coercive or manipulative behavior may be discussed in the group process that pertains to sexual consent on dates or in other social situations. This treatment activity should culminate with victims being "aware" of not only their right to consent, but their ability to protect themselves in the future.

Finally, all coercive behaviors must be tabulated and documented and all group members should "Bee"come Aware. **Bee Aware** is the attitude closing this treatment activity. An excellent learning process can occur with older victims teaching younger children how to Bee Aware. Older victims may also participate in activities that project ideations toward making their future children "Bee Aware" of sexual abuse.

TRAUMA ASSESSMENT PERSPECTIVE

This treatment activity pertains to the Situational Perspective of the Sexual Victim Trauma Assessment as far as coercive events occurred in the sexual abuse "scene" causing many distorted cognitions. Children who develop coping skills by believing they are abusable, will benefit from this assignment.

This treatment activity also emphasizes the Developmental Perspective of the Sexual Victim Trauma Assessment where negative ideations may be developing regarding sexual consent and inappropriate sexual role models. This treatment activity will not only assist children in recognizing their helplessness in the sexually abusive scene (Situational Perspective), but will also enhance the possibility of repairing damage to normal sexual development.

#51

LETTERS TO THE EDITOR

OBJECTIVES:

1) Children will gain skills in eradicating cycles of helplessness and abusability.

2) Children will gain the ability to recognize a support system that exists within the community.

3) Children will be able to take a "pro-active" response to sexual abuse and improve individual self-esteem.

4) Children will be able to eradicate the tendency toward continuing the cycle of sexual abuse in their futures through community awareness and recognition of societal influences.

AGE GROUP:

Age 12 and up

SUPPLIES:

1) Previous letters to the editor from sexual victims if possible. (If not, letters should be prepared by therapists).

2) Pieces of paper indicating editor's address, etc.

3) Lined paper

4) Pens

5) Video camera (optional)

6) VCR (optional)

PROCESS:

Errors, Errors, Errors

The first step in this process should teach children about typical misconstrued, inappropriate attitudes that pervade society regarding sexual abuse. A variety of modalities can be used for this process. If therapists do not have letters from the editor from previous incidents, or if items cannot be found in the literature, a list of myths and misconceptions can be presented to children regarding erroneous ideas commonly held about sexual abuse. Demonstrative therapists will act out these erroneous ideations, either through role playing, skits or perhaps through simply presenting large pieces of construction paper with an inappropriate attitude expressed. These attitudes could be found in the <u>IMPACT MANUAL</u> (Hindman) or through other examples of information portraying erroneous attitudes and ideas. Examples of these thoughts are:

> "Only girls are sexually abused, this never happens to boys."

> "Sexual offenders are dirt bags who hate people."

> "Once sexual abuse has been reported, everything is fine."

> "Sexual abuse usually happens to older children, never to younger kids."

> "Sexual abuse happens in large cities, not in small towns."

> "Sexual abuse usually happens to people who are poor, under-educated, and don't go to church."

This part of the treatment activity should assist children in becoming somewhat angered and outraged at misconceptions commonly held by society. This elevated level of frustration should result in significant response from group members.

Why Should We?

The next step in the treatment process is to compile a list of "goals" for writing letters to the editor of the local newspaper. Even though anger was purposely elicited, children should be helped to understand that outrage and anger will usually bring the opposite outcome. Victims need to see the purpose in writing letters as to educate others, not necessarily to criticize or attack. When appropriate goals are prepared, children will be much better equipped to write letters of information and education while accomplishing the same goal.

Examples of Goals:

We want to teach people that girls aren't the only ones sexually abused.

We want to help people understand how much it hurts when people blame kids.

We want people to be aware that sexual offenders are everywhere and some of them are nice in other ways, while some are just rotten.

After clearly defining and outlining goals, children should write letters to the editor. This should be an activity with significant professional input — avoiding the issue of trauma bonding. The letters should be informative, but also avoiding the tendencies of the raging child or the pleading, begging child.

Privacy of victims should always be protected. The treatment center may need to address letters to the editor with victims names being changed. Obviously, if these letters are accepted by the editor of the local newspaper, clippings should be made and captured for the scrapbook.

TRAUMA ASSESSMENT PERSPECTIVE:

This treatment activity pertains to the Situational Perspective of the Sexual Victim Trauma Assessment. Tendency toward developing coping skills of helplessness and abusability are profound for victims and this activity teaches children to become more assertive and in control of their situations. This treatment activity also can pertain to the Relationship Perspective since many children feel as though their perpetrator was viewed in positive terms by the community, preventing children from accepting their status as "the victim." The category of "significant others" in the Sexual Victim Trauma Assessment is very important to consider when conducting this treatment activity.

#52

TOUCHING, TOUCHING, TOUCHING

OBJECTIVES:

1) Children will gain skills in understanding different kinds of touching.

2) Children will be able to recognize appropriate affection that may be emotionally stimulating, but is not abusive.

3) Children will be able to recognize the impact of aggression and violence.

4) Children will be able to understand the difference between sexual abuse and normal health care activities that include genital touching.

5) Children will be able to resist tendencies to become abusive.

AGE GROUP:

Children under age 10

SUPPLIES:

1) Handouts or pictures illustrating positive and negative representations of touching

2) Pieces of construction paper

3) Large letters, paints, or markers to make large letters

4) A Very Touching Book by Jan Hindman

5) Crayons, magic markers, felt pens for drawing

6) Paints

7) Glue

8) Scotch tape

9) Staples

10) Video (VCR) or camera (optional)

PROCESS:

Good, Bad and Secret

The beginning of this treatment activity should not be done in a haphazard manner. Simply learning the three kinds of touching, "good, bad and secret," is not sufficient. Children need to work through a process of conceptualizing "badness" as being related to aggression and violence. Most children who have been sexually abused feel "badly." Therefore, a discussion of "bad touching" should occur and the word "badness" should be separated from sexual contact and sexual abuse. Sexually abused children who apply the term, "bad" to their own abuse often take on feelings of badness and move into adult sexuality with an impression that sex is bad. They also have tendencies to beocme abusive because of these "bad" connotations.

Negativism concerning sexual contact between children and adults should be directly related to the **violation of consent** on the part of the child and not related to the actual sexual behavior that occurs. Badness, the criminal element, should be related to consent, not to sex. This philosophy is outlined and explained in the publication, <u>A Very Touching Book</u>.

It is very important, therefore, for the treatment activity to generate a grand presentation of the first kind of touching, which is "good touching." Children should be given an opportunity to see a "#1" and the words "good" displayed on large cards. A great deal of attention and affection should occur in the group process and whenever possible the activity should be video taped or pictures could be taken to capture the element of positive attention and affection.

Good Touching Givers

Lists could be made for each child regarding those individuals who provide them with good touching. Therapeutic groups for sexual victims should always have a very strong component of appropriate touching that is not secretive as outlined in treatment modalities (Chapter 4). Therapists should gain skills in being able to demonstrate affection to children that is not of a secretive nature and that usually takes place in the presence of others and in combination with conversation. Non-sexual, non-committal, non-secretive touching is an extremely important modality for treatment of sexual victims.

Appropriate touching should begin each session or serve as a greeting to all children. Touching should be used to commemorate events or award praise. Touching should be routinely initiated to provide consolation or support for emotional stress exhibited in group. Finally, positive touching should be used to close each therapy session. Touching is appropriate under these conditions if it occurs in the open area, if it includes a variety of individuals and if "talking about touching" occurs in concert with the physical contact. Statements should be encouraged such as:

> "Boy, you deserve some good touching after sharing that,"
> or "Great little boys like you should never leave without
> good touching from at least three great kids in the room."

Bad Touching

The second kind of touching should be presented as "bad touching." Therapists should be demonstrative in the activity and role play an aura of BADNESS without initially providing information to children regarding the meaning of the concept. Anticipation in defining badness should occur. It is important for children to anticipate the sense of badness as it relates to sexual abuse, but then to have that cognitive process interrupted by the recognition that "bad touching" applies to another concept — that of aggression and violence. Tremendous relief may occur for victims who participate in this treatment step. Victims often fear they have been "bad" because of the sexual abuse. Attaching the words "bad touching" to other kinds of contact through this process will be reassuring and helpful to the victim. Badness must be attached to something else, other than what definition the victim has previously perceived.

Again, this treatment step should not be done haphazardly. Some children may wish to role play aggressive and violent behavior. Plays or puppet shows could occur with added discussions of how physical harm hurts and, therefore, is quite obviously, "bad." Children may need to have their pictures taken representing bad touching or they may need to make images in their scrapbooks concerning this negative touching. It is also very important for younger children to create lists of individuals who have provided bad touching in the past. These complicated and carefully prepared lists and descriptions of both good and bad "touchers" will allow the third kind of touching to be expressed in more comfortable ways.

Issue of Consent

The third kind of touching should be presented as SECRET TOUCH-ING. The issue of consent is **most** important in explaining the concept. Using A Very Touching Book, children can learn that certain rights exist for children regarding keeping their body parts private and protected. Sexuality in the future must be presented as positive and as an attainable goal. The issue of a child's rights to privacy should be presented and sexual genitalia should be presented in a positive way in order to enhance a child's interest in protection of this valuable commodity. (Other treatment activities may need to preface this activity for clarity).

Children should next be presented with the ideation that, if an older or bigger person touches their genitalia, the older or bigger person is making a **mistake** and needs to keep the activity "secret." In presenting the concept of secret touching, therapists should be quite demonstrative regarding the rights of children. Posters and banners could be used and "parades" could be organized throughout the therapeutic facility. The issue of secrets could be presented in a very demonstrative fashion with therapists discussing secrets that are exciting, fun and acceptable, but also drawing attention to the fact that secrets should **never** occur concerning touching between adults and children.

Finally, effort should be made to capture a portrayal of who has provided each victim with secret touching. If previous effort encouraged children to feel comfortable creating representations of those individuals who provided good and bad touching, this portion of the assignment will seem routine and productive. These portrayals should be captured for scrapbooks for educational reasons and also for the purpose of desensitizing the sexual abuse.

TRAUMA ASSESSMENT PERSPECTIVE:

This treatment activity pertains to the Developmental Perspective of the Sexual Victim Trauma Assessment. Therapists will be wise to consider each victim's Trauma Assessment and pay attention to what appears to have been lost, or has the potential to have been lost, in normal sexual development. As the discussion of "good, bad, and secret touching" occurs, those specific trauma issues relating to trauma in the child's sexual development will be addressed.

#53

FOR FEELINGS

OBJECTIVES:

1) Children will gain skills in recognizing levels of coercion that occurred during their own sexual abuse.

2) Children will be given the opportunity to externalize painful and potentially destructive internal feelings regarding their sexual abuse.

3) Children will be able to gain skills in breaking the cycle of sexual abuse so that incest is not repeated in their future families.

4) Children will be able to create a positive framework for feelings that were once associated with sexual abuse.

AGE GROUP:

All ages

SUPPLIES:

1) Blackboard/chalkboard

2) Large pieces of construction paper

3) List of feeling words (attached)

4) My Feelings publication by Marcia Morgan

5) Camera

6) Miscellaneous art supplies

7) Puppets/dolls

PROCESS:

Identify, Express and Reframe

There are many exercises relating to the feelings of sexually abused children. Treatment activities processing feelings could encompass an entire year of therapy for victims of sexual abuse. Encouraging victims to identify feelings is not enough, however. Being able to identify, express and reframe feelings relating to the abuse is the proactive approach to this common treatment activity.

The first step in the treatment process should encourage participation in activities that identify a wide variety of feelings. For older children, the attached list can be helpful. The same list can be used for young children, although obviously some complicated feeling words need to be omitted or redefined. This step in the treatment activity can be enhanced if the feelings are not only discussed, but perhaps re-enacted in skits or role playing. Puppets can also be used to express feelings. With younger children, puppets can become a way to re-enact feelings without taking children through the process of internalization of their pain.

Any and Many, It's Okay

Regardless of age, the second step in this treatment activity should teach children that all feelings are legitimate. A reverse kind of approach can be most helpful. For younger children, skits or role plays can occur with "villain" characters being critical of a child's feelings. In the skit, the child who is being criticized for expressing a feeling should be "rescued" by other group members with affirmation of children's rights to have **any** or **many** feelings. This will be particularly important if issues in the Sexual Victim Trauma Assessment reveal specific needs in this area. (Situational Perspective).

For older children, this step in the treatment activity can occur with a process discussion of legitimizing any feeling victims may have concerning their abuse. This is particularly important for both age groups who have victims wishing to express positive feelings toward perpetrators. This step in the treatment process should culminate with children recognizing that all feelings are legitimate and acceptable.

Yes and No, Good and Bad

The next step in the treatment process would include activities that demonstrate positive and negative reactions or responses to feelings. Adolescents, as an example, should be able to discuss how feelings are often manifested in other ways. Using the construction paper, scenarios can be presented, such as:

"When I get mad at my mother, sometimes I kick my cat."

"When my friends hurt my feelings, sometimes I hurt the feelings of my little brother."

"Sometimes I feel yukky inside and then I act yukky on the outside."

For younger children, this step in the process needs to be more direct than simple. Some children may want to role play the cards, hide the cards, destroy the cards, or keep the cards secret. This activity should teach children how resisting expression feelings or by keeping feelings inside can create a potential for pain. It is also important to explain how feelings resurface during dreams if they are not handled appropriately when the child was awake. This step in the activity process should create an understanding that to suppress or to fight feelings, without having appropriate ways to channel feelings, can cause problems with out-of-control responses or expression of feelings.

After feelings have been identified, legitimized, and recognized as being potentially destructive, avenues for expressing feelings should be examined and implemented. Children of all ages should be able to do "trouble shooting activities" where solutions are found to certain feeling situations. Children should be taught that being angry is acceptable as an example, provided healthy outlets exist for the expression of anger. Role playing, skits, puppet shows or perhaps writing short stories could be implemented in this step of the treatment activity. Obviously, being involved in the therapeutic process is one example of a healthy outlet for emotions and feelings.

Positive Frame

The final step in this treatment activity is to reframe a positive counterpart to each of these emotions or responses concerning the abuse. As victims have been able to identify feelings relating to their abuse, they also have the potential to be "triggered" back to the abusive scenario as they move through the future experiencing these emotions. The stimulus or the "trigger" will always occur in the victim's life. Therefore, it is important to reframe the same stimulus and resulting emotions in a more positive and helpful way.

This is particularly important for use in the resolution scrapbook. Opposing pages work best for this activity in most situations. As an example, during the first part of this treatment activity process, a child may have identified a feeling of helplessness regarding the abuse. The child may have been able to draw a picture that represented helplessness, the child may have created a poem or another representation that elicits the feeling of helplessness relating to the abuse. The first steps in this treatment process should have identified the feeling, affirmed the legitimacy of the feeling and externalized the feeling on paper. This next process takes the same abuse "feeling" and creates a reframe for helplessness. Using this specific example, it becomes clear that the opposing page in the scrapbook should be a reframe of strength and control — which is the opposite of helplessness.

Example:

> If the original identification and affirmation of the feeling created a scenario such as, "When I think about secret touching, I felt helpless and afraid." The opposing emotion and reframe would indicate the following: "When I think about my secret touching, I felt helpless, but I am not helpless any more. These are the things I do because I am not helpless." The child then will have pages and pages in the scrapbook accentuating power and control. These could be done in a variety of ways, some relating to sexual abuse and others not necessarily related to sexual exploitation. These representations could be generic activities, such as learning to ride a bike, assisting a sibling in a certain activity, or capturing any kind of positive body movement or physical accomplishment. The positive reframe is the opposite of the feeling of helplessness.

Treatment specialists should be aware that this treatment activity is **extremely important** for all victims regardless of age or capability. Being able to take these emotions and identify, affirm, legitimize and reframe could take several months in treatment. This is particularly important for all victims who tend to identify feelings, but also tend to accentuate those feelings in a destructive way. This reframing captures and redirects the negative tendencies.

TRAUMA ASSESSMENT PERSPECTIVE:

This treatment activity primarily relates to the Situational Perspective of the Sexual Victim Trauma Assessment, as children have the potential to develop deadly coping skills for the future as well as phobic reactions to certain emotions or "triggers." Specific Trauma Assessment information should be applied to each victim and the length of time involved in this treatment activity should directly relate to the extent of trauma suffered by children as indicated in the Situational Perspective of the Sexual Victim Trauma Assessment.

Some issues in both the Relationship Perspective and the Developmental Perspective may also pertain to this treatment activity. Feelings about relationships, as indicated in the Trauma Assessment may need to be resolved and reframed. Negative feelings toward body functions, body parts and sexual functioning also may need attention if indicated in the Developmental Perspective of the trauma assessment. This is a very important treatment activity and could be expanded to include all aspects of the Sexual Victim Trauma Assessment.

FEELING WORDS FOR VICTIMS

scared	panic	wild	powerful
lonely	bad	embarrassed	unfriendly
confused	miserable	discouraged	unwanted
down	sad	mad	desperate
mean	concerned	enraged	hateful
disappointed	brave	frustrated	jealous
nervous	guilty	disgusted	destructive
afraid	ashamed	humiliated	powerless
rejected	worried	terrified	shy
furious	sorry	upset	protective
ugly	unloved	weird	angry
hurt	uncomfortable	frightened	displeased
bored	helpless	intimidated	awkward
annoyed	distant	talkative	tricked
misunderstood	helpless	betrayed	tired
let down	self pity	indecisive	tense
cheated	sympathetic	ignored	desperate
nauseated	awkward	rejected	beaten
out of control	horrified	rebellious	stubborn
rage	sneaky	getting even	suicidal
abandoned	threatened	violent	

#54

MY BODY BELONGS TO ME

OBJECTIVES:

1) Children will gain skills in preventing sexual abuse in their futures.

2) Children will gain skills in identifying sexual parts and using proper vocabulary.

3) Children will gain a positive ideation about their bodies.

4) Children will improve skills in being able to communicate about sexuality.

AGE GROUP:

10 and Under

SUPPLIES:

1) Publication, <u>My Body Belongs to Me</u> by Kristen Baird

2) Writing paper and pens

3) Various art paper

4) Camera

5) Crayons, markers, etc.

PROCESS:

Me and My Body

This treatment activity involves the publication, <u>My Body Belongs to Me</u>. This is a very simple book teaching children appropriate names for body parts. The general perspective of the book is one of body ownership and pride in privacy. Reading this book to children is another way to enhance many treatment goals that are needed for children to prevent body contamination and issues such as sexual dysfunction.

The book could be read to children and the learning process could be captured in some art form for children's scrapbooks. Most importantly, children's individual pictures should be taken with captions repeating some of the messages in the publication. Children should choose a favorite page to represent themselves. Body movement as children participate in the treatment process, can enhance the value of the treatment activity, especially if those "controlled" body movements can be captured for each scrapbook.

TRAUMA ASSESSMENT PERSPECTIVE:

This treatment activity pertains to the Developmental Perspective of the Sexual Victim Trauma Assessment. Victims have tendencies to develop distorted views of their bodies and they have potential to disregard issues, such as privacy and body empowerment. Although this treatment activity is simple and basic, these goals need to be reviewed as children proceed through the therapeutic process. Although sexual dysfunction and destructive attitudes about sexuality may not be exhibited for young children, the potential for trauma to normal sexual development is significant and can be prevented through a variety of treatment activities, such as demonstrated in this process.

#55

INTIMATE IMAGES

OBJECTIVES:

1) Children will gain skills in being able to express feelings.

2) Children will be able to externalize, evaluate, and express emotions.

3) Children will be able to compare their individual responses to other group members and expand their own personal perspectives of self-image.

4) Children will be able to desensitize memories of their sexual abuse.

AGE GROUP:

All ages.

SUPPLIES:

1) Magazines or books that can be dismantled or cut

2) A variety of fabrics or fabric pieces

3) Glue/tape/staples

4) Paper

5) String for hanging

6) Display area

7) Magic markers

8) Camera

(Any other items that seem to be able to represent auditory, visual, or kinesthetic memories.)

PROCESS:

This activity will have three steps which will include victims thinking about themselves previous to their abuse, during their abuse and then picture themselves following their graduation from treatment. Through this process, children should see a past and a positive future. The first step is to have victims represent themselves with a flower, animal, bug, or bird that pertains to how they see themselves before the abuse.

For younger children who do not have the ability to respond to verbal structure, they may do best lying down on the floor with group leaders; holding hands and making a "wheel spoke." The heads of each group member should be pointed toward the center of the "wheel." All group members should close their eyes and while they are being touched with hands, should, (with the group leader's verbal instructions) picture an animal, a bird, or a flower that represents their abuse. These "pictures" should be shared with the group.

"When you think about your secret touching, what kind of animal, bird or flower do you think about?"

For older victims, lying on the floor without touching may be more appropriate, although if positive peer support has been established in the group, touching may be possible, and, therefore, the activity may be enhanced. The first "picture" should be each victim's representation of how they appeared previous to the occurrence of the sexual abuse. Enhance the process by having victims capture the representation in a tangible form through drawing, or other artwork.

Before, During and After

Each group member should then share the image they have of themselves during the abuse. In choosing an animal, bird, bug, or plant, they should be able to share with other group members how they see themselves while the sexual abuse occurred. If possible, this activity should be expanded so that group members may use pictures, drawings, fabrics, or make any representation of how they see themselves while the abuse was taking place. It is very important that this treatment activity focus on how each victim is represented within a specific time frame of "before, during and after." In some cases, victims may want to use construction paper to make these representations or may wish to use other forms of material, which are more tactile or auditory. An entire group session may be spent on each of these steps with group members making a representation of themselves as they felt, saw, or heard themselves while the abuse was taking place.

The next step in this process requires group members to repeat the same process, but to concentrate on themselves following the abuse. Therapists should be proactively involved in this activity so that children consider and perceive themselves as positive and deserving of disclosure. If victims express themselves in ways that suggest they were contaminated or degraded previous to their abuse, or wrong for reporting the abuse, these attitudes must be resolved so that a positive image emerges or at least an image of something that needed protection, such as a:

— fluffy kitten who fell in a puddle.

— beautiful daisy that was in a hail storm.

Eventually, each group member will emerge with a visual representation of themselves previous to the abuse, as well as during and after the abuse and share that artwork with other group members. These representations should be created and then shared with other group members with a great deal of support for individuality.

Proactive!

Finally, group members should participate in a proactive process that encourages positive future outcomes to therapy. Each group member should attempt to perceive themselves as being represented by an animal, bird, flower, or bug concerning how they will be or feel at their graduation from treatment. Under the proactive treatment focus, therapist should encourage a positive attitude about the completion of treatment, long before treatment has been completed. In this way, treatment will always be enhanced as its closure is anticipated in a positive way. This activity, therefore, is important for assuring cooperation in treatment and for affirming therapeutic progress.

Whenever possible, children should be encouraged to make a tangible representation of the three phases of this activity. Victims need to perceive themselves before, during, and after their sexual abuse and project toward their sexual abuse recovery. For adolescents, the word "recovery" is very important, while for younger children, the word "graduation" should be included in the artwork. Whenever possible, this "three phase" representation should be created and displayed. For some victims, a hanging mobile representing three sides could capture the changing phases. More visual children may choose three posters that are attached. Other victims who tend to be more kinesthetic may choose a three sided box, a tent, or another geometric form. In some instances, younger children may take an opportunity to present their three phases to parents in a play or a group sharing activity.

TRAUMA ASSESSMENT PERSPECTIVE:

This group activity deals primarily with the Situational Perspective and the development of distorted cognitions. Children who have been sexually abused tend to adapt feelings of contamination, depression, and helplessness. In many instances, they may become abusive to others or may see themselves as negative, so that recovery is impossible. This process allows children to re-evaluate themselves previous to the abuse, express feelings about their self-esteem or self-worth, and then move toward discontinuation of those distorted cognitions.

This group activity may also deal with the Relationship Perspective of the Sexual Victim Trauma Assessment. Some victims' trauma may be related to how others view the child as the guilty party. Issues pertaining to distorted views of offender/victim identity can be resolved through this treatment activity.

#56

QUIZ TIME: "NAME THAT BODY PART"

OBJECTIVES:

1) Children will gain skills in recognizing body parts.

2) Children will gain skills in creating positive ideations toward the human body.

3) Children will gain skills in recognizing positive aspects to sexual consent and human sexuality.

4) Children will develop skills in team work and comraderie.

AGE GROUP:

All ages

SUPPLIES:

1) Accommodations for two "teams" to be separated (use of chairs, desks, tables, etc.)

2) Video camera (VCR, if possible)

3) Large pieces of construction paper

4) Markers

5) Whistle, horn, or some kind of timer, which will make a loud noise

6) Prizes

PROCESS:

Two Teams

The process of this group activity should first divide the group into two equal teams. Sensitivity should be given toward children's abilities, not necessarily toward children's choices. This activity should overtly be a competition, but should covertly recognize the potential traumatization through competition among vulnerable children.

Previous to the group activities, questions should be prepared regarding naming the correct terms of body parts. (Many different issues regarding sexual abuse trauma and prevention could be integrated into this activity.) Obviously, for adolescents, the questions can be more complicated. Questions could be prepared with the following examples in mind:

> What is the name of the "not so private part" in the middle of our arms?

> What is the name of the very special, private, wonderful part of our body on our chests?

> What is the name of the "inside private part" for a girl's body?

> What is the name of the not so private part of our body in the middle of our leg?

As the game begins, each team should be given an opportunity to "huddle" and name their group. Therapists should suggest positive names of terms dealing with body parts, such as "super body team" or "the great body part team," but still allow creativity and preference on the part of children.

Control, Control

Rules should be established so that control can be guaranteed. Children should be allowed to express enthusiasm, clapping, and yelling when an appropriate answer is given. Encouragement should be given to control the group, however, so that order can be maintained. It is also significant, that through the establishment of some kind of order, children will be able to contemplate the answers to the questions in their own minds even though they may not be directly involved in questioning, which is process, process, process.

An important group rule designates that no **one** team member provides an answer. When a question is posed to one team, the timer should begin and the team should be able to huddle (Good Touching!) for contemplation of the answer. The answer should then be written on a piece of construction paper by a team member or, in the case of younger children, by a therapist. Both teams should be given the opportunity to answer the **same** question. In this way, if both team members are correct, positive reinforcement can occur for all children. Older children will be able to handle the situation of competition better than those who are young, but group format and composition may also determine the level of acceptable competition for specific group member's needs.

Some kind of scoring effort should occur. Group leaders should be sensitive to children's needs and plan accordingly. Rather than simply "winning" the competition, the group should gain some other prestigious position such as certificates for the scrapbook, earning stickers that are positive and designed with treatment goals in mind or perhaps some other kind of prize should be awarded, such as receiving a positive sexual abuse prevention book or other sexual abuse materials.

The ultimate opportunity exists in this assignment to have the treatment goals and objectives become even more emphasized and productive. If the "quiz show" can be videotaped, the entire process can be enhanced while the group is able to watch the video at a later time. Most importantly, there needs to be some representation of the quiz show questions, answers and competition award in each child's scrapbook.

Therapists should be advised that this kind of activity, dealing with the learning of body parts, can be expanded for adolescents to the point of discussing body functions, certain sexual behaviors or issues related to reproduction. Many of these topics are difficult and uncomfortable for adolescents to discuss under traditional circumstances. If the treatment activity centers around a "quiz show" type of education, however, volumes of positive learning can take place without using traditional methods of discussion and contemplation.

TRAUMA ASSESSMENT PERSPECTIVE:

This treatment activity primarily relates to the Developmental Perspective of the Sexual Victim Trauma Assessment. This treatment activity will enhance positive ideations toward human sexuality and the human body, as well as dispel negative attitudes of sexual functioning that may have emerged due to the sexual trauma.

#57

MY SECRET BOX

OBJECTIVES:

1) Children will be able to understand the elements of secrecy within the incestuous family.

2) Children will be able to gain control over distorted cognitions that relate to guilt or anxiety as a result of incestuous family secrets.

3) Children will be able to understand the importance of open communication so that the cycle of sexual abuse does not continue in their futures.

AGE GROUPS:

Ages 9 and older.

SUPPLIES:

1) Various shaped boxes: (Younger children will prefer larger boxes with lids. Children must be able to place items inside their box and remove them so that this activity can be either videotaped or captured in pictures. Adolescents may want very thin boxes [such as those used for hosiery or nylon stockings]. Adolescents may also want to include their thin "boxes" in their scrapbook.)

2) Magazines (to be cut)

3) Glue, paste, tape, staples

4) Magic markers or other writing materials

5) Camera or Videotape

PROCESS:

Family Secrets

This process will encourage children to understand family secretiveness. Most incestuous families appear to be represented one way on the outside, yet another representation often exists on the inside. This treatment activity encourages children to make the outside of their boxes appear to be a representation of their family, as others saw the home. Children may choose to make a collage on the front or the sides of their boxes specific to each family member. For more active therapy opportunities or for group processes that have an abundance of supplies, group members may choose to make a separate box for each family member. As an example, if the perpetrator appears to be very positive, helpful, and open to others, victims may choose to represent the offender in these terms while other views from different individuals may have been held for the same perpetrator. Inside the box, the reality of the perpetrator may be portrayed by the victim.

Handle with Care

Therapists should always anticipate a wide variety of emotions, reactions, and feelings. Victims who feel negative toward the perpetrator need support and encouragement, but they also need to recognize that other children may have positive ideations. This is always a precarious group activity since many victims (especially adolescents) may feel an obligation to express only negative ideations toward the sexual offenders. Helpful participation will encourage both the expression of positive and negative views. It is also common for many perpetrators to have both positive and negative attributes on the inside and outside of the box. It is especially important, however, that those children who feel some positive ideations toward the perpetrator may have an opportunity to express those views.

Whenever possible, therapists should use this activity as a way to represent feelings and attitudes within the scrapbook. If boxes cannot be used for this activity, children may be able to make construction paper representations of the outside of their family. Super-imposed construction paper, over the top that is cut down the center, can be opened, revealing the reality of their family. Whenever parents are involved in treatment, this activity can be enhanced by having children demonstrate their secret boxes to parents.

TRAUMA ASSESSMENT PERSPECTIVE:

This treatment activity pertains to the Relationship Perspective of the Sexual Victim Trauma Assessment, as well as the Situational Perspective. Most relationships within an incestuous family are secretive and have two opposite perspectives. In order to complete this assignment, children must be encouraged to discuss, evaluate, and describe the dysfunctional relationships that took place in the family. The Trauma Assessment will reveal those specific issues which need to be encouraged by the specialists.

The Situational Perspective of the Trauma Assessment will also reveal the tendency toward distorted cognitions. Therapists should be aware of those tendencies for each victim in treatment and make sure that those ideations are encouraged to emerge during this treatment activity.

#58

FACES OF FEELINGS

OBJECTIVES:

1) Children will be able to evaluate many different feelings regarding their sexual abuse.

2) Children will be able to gain comfort in expressing opposing feelings or a multitude of feelings regarding their sexual abuse.

3) Children will be able to recognize that they may change their feelings about family members, the offender, or about the sexual abuse disclosure.

AGE GROUP:

Below Age 12

SUPPLIES:

1) Large balloons

2) Yarn

3) Magic markers

4) Colored paper

5) Scissors

6) Glue

7) Mirror(s)

8) Camera

9) Any other supplies for creating facial features on balloons.

PROCESS:

See and Tell

Children should be gathered in circle where they can discuss and list a variety of feelings, such as happiness, anger, scared, etc., relating to their sexual abuse. Exaggerated facial expressions should be used while passing a mirror for children to see themselves. Have each child enter the circle and express an emotion while the group attempts to identify the emotion. Cheering and clapping with each presentation should occur when group members guess the feeling accurately.

Children should then move away from circle to an area where they can decorate a balloon. Have children make at least two or three different sides of the balloon with different facial responses (happy, sad, afraid, etc.). Return to the circle. Therapists should make many statements to entire group requiring each victim to choose an emotion to express:

"When I think about the person who did secret touching, I feel . . ."

"When I think about coming to group, I feel . . ."

Encourage many opposing feelings and provide support for children who feel differently about the same statement. Encourage individuality. Take pictures of different feelings expressed on different sides of the balloons. Create statements on construction paper to correspond with balloon expressions such as, "This is how I felt about giving up my secret," etc. Capture for scrapbook. Give support for opposing, changing or multiplicity of feelings for the offender, specific family members or post-disclosure issues. Create pages for the scrapbook with the variety of emotions expressed.

TRAUMA ASSESSMENT PERSPECTIVE:

This activity emphasizes the Situational Perspective of the Sexual Victim Trauma Assessment and the development of distorted cognitions. This activity can discourage the development of such coping skills as feelings of helplessness, guilt, symbiosis misdirected outrage, and abusive or self-abusive tendencies.

#59

WHO CARES — SOMEBODY!
(Children Under Age 10)

OBJECTIVES:

1) Children will gain knowledge regarding their support system.

2) Children's guilt will be alleviated through the realization that others care, and object to sexual abuse.

3) Children will gain skills in protecting themselves from future abuse.

AGE GROUP:

Age 10 and younger.

SUPPLIES:

1) Construction paper

2) Crayons, magic markers, or other writing materials

3) Pictures of professional or other representations of agency people or places (pictures of the police station, school counseling office, social work office, etc.)

4) Copies of a single sheet of paper with the statement:

This is a Person Who Cares About Me

PROCESS:

Who Cares?

The purpose of this treatment activity is to encourage younger children catalog, discuss, evaluate, and describe those individuals who care about sexual abuse. This activity should also encourage children to recognize their own support system and, break the cycle of abuse by teaching children to become supportive parents in the future.

For younger children, xeroxed sheets of paper, cataloging and describing <u>each</u> supportive person is an excellent technique. This emphasizes the support of each individual person especially if a large representation of the supportive person can be made. Representing single people on one sheet of paper allows children to experience vast support, rather than having children simply discuss those who care, or putting all of those caring individuals into a collage on a one page "list." Decorations can be made of each caring person to enhance the feelings of support.

In the System

Second, treatment specialists will benefit by cataloging individuals, agencies, or professionals who care about children, but who may not be directly related to children. This activity would include, as an example, pictures of the local police station or mental health clinic. Autographs can be obtained from many individuals who are not directly involved with the sexual abuse, but on the periphery of those agencies who respond to children, such as secretaries or accounting personnel. Those people who may not have been directly involved with group members, but who respond appropriately, should be included in the pages of these children's scrapbooks.

All representations of individuals who care for the children should be contained in pages of the scrapbook. Decorations, artwork, autographs, etc., should accompany and finalize this activity.

TRAUMA ASSESSMENT PERSPECTIVE:

This treatment activity pertains primarily to the Situational Perspective of the Sexual Victim Trauma Assessment. Children who emerge from sexual abuse scenarios often view themselves as not being supported, and they feel guilty for disclosing. Through this activity, those ''guilty'' cognitions can be resolved.

This treatment activity also pertains to the Relationship Perspective of the Sexual Victim Trauma Assessment. In examining the relationship ''triangle,'' many individuals under the ''significant other'' category were supportive of children, but were not necessarily acknowledged by the child. As an example, a church member, or an extended family member may have actually supported the child and the child's disclosure, but this information was not known to the child. In conducting a Sexual Victim Trauma Assessment and becoming aware of this support, treatment specialists can guide victims to understanding and accepting the care and support from others.

#60

WHO CARES? — SOMEBODY! (ADOLESCENCE)

OBJECTIVE:

1) Children will gain knowledge regarding their support system.

2) Children's guilt will be alleviated through the realization that others care and object to sexual abuse.

3) Children will gain skills in protecting themselves from future abuse.

4) Children will be able to project and reframe hope and encouragement toward a positive future.

AGE GROUP:

Age 10 and older.

SUPPLIES:

1) Construction paper

2) Crayons, magic markers, or other writing materials

3) Pictures of professional people or other representations of agency personnel or places (pictures of the police station, school counseling office, social work office, etc.)

4) Mimeographed copies of a single sheet of paper with the statement:

This is a Person Who Cares About Me

5) Plain pieces of white writing paper with lines

6) Writing materials

7) Envelopes

PROCESS:

This treatment activity for adolescents is very similar in goals and objectives to the same activity for younger children. Younger children need to recognize their support system and resolve distorted cognitions through recognition of support that was not previously conceived or understood. For adolescents, the potential exists to expand this treatment activity far beyond what is possible for younger children.

Project and Reframe

In this activity, adolescents will not only recognize their support and become aware of support that existed, (but was not known), but projecting and reframing nonexistent support needs to occur for the purpose of enhancing a future of sensitivity and empathy. This activity will be a "reframing" exercise or an enhancement of hopes or future goals. Adolescents will be encouraged to pretend, fantasize and project support that is currently impossible, but nonetheless important. Hero figures, rock stars, or other individuals not personally connected to each victim will be the focus of this activity.

After adolescents have proceeded through the same steps as younger children by collecting autographs or making individual pages of individuals who realistically support them, encouragement to contemplate a **desired** support list should be made. This activity would encourage adolescents to hope or to fantasize about support they might receive from such individuals as rock stars, television figures, or other "heroes." Adolescents should be encouraged to write letters to themselves from these important people.

Treatment specialists should join the activity and contemplate the kind of letter they would like to receive from perhaps, a movie star or popular role model regarding their ability to be a therapist. This allows the therapist to demonstrate the desired outcome by fantasizing that, as an example, "New Kids on the Block," wrote a letter of support for the therapist's ability to help victims.

Treatment specialists should then encourage adolescents to write their own "pretend" letters. For those children who do not have verbal or written competencies, treatment specialists may need to write the letters and have victims read these letters aloud in group. If the letters are written by professionals and children did not write their own letters, a process of "evaluating" the letter would be important. Each letter of support should be shared with other group members and included in the scrapbook.

TRAUMA ASSESSMENT PERSPECTIVE:

This treatment activity pertains primarily to the Situational Perspective of the Sexual Victim Trauma Assessment. Children who emerge from sexual abuse scenarios often view themselves as not being supported and feeling guilty for making a report. Through this activity, those distorted cognitions can be resolved.

This treatment activity also pertains to the Relationship Perspective of the Sexual Victim Trauma Assessment. In examining the relationship "triangle," many individuals under the "significant other" category were supportive of children but were not necessarily acknowledged by the child. In conducting a Sexual Victim Trauma Assessment, "necessary" letters become obvious.

Additionally, older children will be able to put forth effort to break the cycle of abuse by participating in an activity that suggests individuals who are not particularly involved with children (such as governors, police, Rambo, Bart Simpson, etc.), but who have a great deal of power in society, are supportive of the sexual victim. This process may enhance the older victim's level of confidence regarding disclosure.

#61

PROACTIVE PREVENTION

OBJECTIVE:

1) Children will recognize community support for victims of sexual abuse.

2) Children will be able to enhance self-esteem.

3) Children will be able to gain the ability to appreciate the right of sexual consent.

4) Children will be able to eradicate tendencies toward abusability and helplessness.

5) Children will gain skills in avoiding repetition of the cycle of sexual abuse with their future families.

AGE GROUP:

10 through adolescence

SUPPLIES:

1) Large pieces of construction paper

2) Markers

3) Cameras

4) Microphones connected to audio systems (if possible) (This activity can be "suggested or pretended" as children role-play interacting with the community member on a public address type of system.)

PROCESS:

Secrets Hurt!

The first step in this treatment activity is to have victims discuss secrets. Other assignments may be a prerequisite to this treatment activity where children are encouraged to recognize that secrets are painful and that secrets usually contribute to difficulties within the home of the child. Effort should be exerted to assist children in recognizing the pain of secrets, especially secrets about sexual abuse. Examples of hurtful secrets could be:

"Secrets make us feel stuffed up."

"Secrets make kids worry a lot."

"Secrets are too heavy for big kids or little kids."

The Other Side

The next step of the treatment process is to have children formulate ideas about the opposite of secret such as openness and honesty. These examples should initiate the understanding that through awareness, sexual abuse can be erradicated if secrets are destroyed. Therapists should not necessarily ask children to share personal experiences in a public forum concerning their sexual abuse, but concentrate more upon opening up the issue of sexual abuse prevention to people in the neighborhood, in the family, or in the community. For adolescents or older children, this kind of activity may encourage contact with different groups, such as the Kiwanis, Rotary or the Lions Club. For younger children, making a video of group members educating others with large posters explaining sexual abuse prevention may suffice. Phrases such as, "Shout it out, Get it Out," should pervade this activity.

Take Action

For groups who cannot or choose not to actually address the public, effort should be made to make posters or some kind of visual representation, such as a bumper sticker. The "proactive" approach of this treatment activity allows children to see their "cause" as reliable and important to everyone in the community. Obviously, it would be more productive if a community group would accept the task of designing bumper stickers which could be given to citizens by victims. Children who have been sexually abused often feel degraded and humiliated in their status as a victim. Any of these activities that become proactive in sexual abuse prevention will not only protect children in the future, but will enhance the victim's status.

In this kind of activity, it is always important to emphasize that exposure to the public must be classified in a positive avenue. Disclosure should be directed toward protecting other children and making citizens aware. Disclosure should not be personal and should not stigmatize the victim. Additionally, each individual child's contribution to public awareness should be captured for the scrapbook.

TRAUMA ASSESSMENT PERSPECTIVE:

This treatment activity pertains primarily to the Relationship Perspective regarding children's inability to see themselves as a victim and their perpetrators as guilty. Through eliciting society or community input, children will be able to readjust the destructive attitude in the "significant others" relationship triangle.

This treatment activity also pertains to the Situational Perspective of the Sexual Victim Trauma Assessment relating to the potential for developing cognitive distortions. Treatment specialists will be particularly aware of the potential for specific children to develop unique responses, and those issues should be a focus of this treatment activity.

#62

PRIDE AND PRIVACY

OBJECTIVES:

1) Children will gain an understanding of the importance of privacy.

2) Children will gain skills in understanding a sense of protection about their bodies and about sexuality.

3) Children will be able to protect themselves in a positive way, avoiding feelings of fear or repulsion to sexuality.

4) Children will develop a positive attitude about sexuality.

AGE GROUP:

Children under age 12

SUPPLIES:

1) <u>A Very Touching Book</u> by Jan Hindman

2) Crayons

3) Markers

4) Glue

5) Scissors

6) Individual small boxes for each child or individual envelopes that can fit in the scrapbook

PROCESS:

The philosophy behind this treatment activity recognizes that even though some children grow up appreciating the need for privacy, they do not necessarily have an understanding toward the positive reason for privacy. Children who have not been sexually abused, usually learn that their genitalia or their sexual body parts are not to be exposed, discussed or touched. The sense of privacy is clear to most children. However, there is rarely a sense of PRIDE about privacy.

"P.P." Pride and Privacy

In order to complete this treatment activity, the prerequisite of proceeding through the treatment activity entitled, "Why, Why, Why," should occur. In other words, children should be taught a logic for why they should avoid sexual touching when they are children. This treatment activity teaches children about future adult sexuality in a positive way. If that treatment activity is completed before this treatment activity, the PRIDE AND PRIVACY concept will be enhanced.

The first step in this process is to review the "Why, Why, Why" treatment activity and recognize that children have rights to protect their bodies because "**When they are older, they may choose someone to share their body with in the future.**" Children should see a logic or reason for protection beyond simply saying, "No," or telling.

Great Bodies = A Valuable Commodity

The second step of this treatment activity is to encourage children to discuss their body parts and make some visual or tangible representation of those body parts. Some children may want to have a school picture or a portrait mounted on a piece of paper. Victims may draw or write about the names of the body parts that children keep private. Obviously, nude pictures would be inappropriate. Some children may choose to draw themselves describing body parts while other children may simply wish to place the names of body parts on cards and decorate the cards. Taking a picture of the child with other representations of the body parts is effective.

The purpose of this step in the treatment activity is to have children make a tangible representation of body parts and sexuality. A "valuable commodity" needs to be processed concerning body parts. Tremendous pride should be enhanced as this activity is conducted. Creative therapists will find appropriate ways to create a tangible positive representation of the human body with artwork, cameras or other demonstrative activities.

The next step in the process requires children to place the tangible representations of "proud body parts" and sexual consent into something that represents privacy. Small boxes may be used, although envelopes that could fit inside scrapbooks may also be effective. Children should be able to place the positive "pride" representation inside the envelope, seal the envelope or box, and then decorate the outside of the envelope or box with art work that represents adulthood and future consent. Adolescents or older children may contemplate wishes about their future when consentual decisions will be made, such as where they would like to live or plans for their education. Younger children may draw future houses or may try to represent themselves as an adult in some other way. This part of the assignment should clearly indicate to children that privacy should be in concert with PRIDE and that sexual decisions will be postponed until later due to the beauty of intimacy and consent, not due to shameful issues which pervade typical sex education scenarios.

Consent

Finally, it is important to recognize that this treatment activity must enhance children's feelings of positive consent at a future date.

Children who have been sexually abused often tend to manifest symptoms of feeling abusable, contaminated, and without a future. The sense of both pride and privacy until future sexual decisions can be made is very important to victims in helping them avoid feelings of contamination. For adolescents, of course, it is feelings of worthlessness or contamination that usually encourage promiscuity. Victims completing this treatment activity should have a sense that all of their consensual decisions in the future will be productive, helpful, and positive.

TRAUMA ASSESSMENT PERSPECTIVE:

This treatment activity pertains primarily to the Developmental Perspective of the Sexual Victim Trauma Assessment. Damage to normal sexual development often occurs and can be eradicated through this treatment activity by creating a hopeful sexual future. Specific information about such things as sexual phobias, abusive sexual role training, and other sexual development issues should be used by therapists to develop treatment plans for each victim.

#63

PUBLIC SPEAKING

OBJECTIVE:

1) Children will gain skills in recognizing their own powerlessness in their sexual abuse.

2) Children will gain skills in being assertive and empowered.

3) Children's status as a "victim" will be improved and applauded.

4) Children will gain skills in survivorship.

5) Children will gain skills in verbal expression.

AGE GROUP:

All ages

SUPPLIES:

1) A Very Touching Book by Jan Hindman

2) Poster boards

3) Sexual abuse prevention literature

4) Brochures on sexual abuse information (including community resources)

5) Chalk board

6) Camera

7) Writing Material

PROCESS:

Big People's Secrets

The first step in this treatment process is to help children understand their previous inability to protect themselves from sexual abuse. The emphasis should suggest that "secrets" commonly pervade the subject of body parts and human sexuality. As an example, adolescents often know that parents rarely talk to their children about sexuality and some adolescents do not even consider their parents to be sexually functioning partners.

The concept of parents keeping their own sexuality from children can be a humorous activity. "Can you all close your eyes and imagine your conception?" is a great ice breaker for both male and female adolescents. The issue suggests that parents keep their sexuality from children and most children do not think of their parents as sexual. For younger children, emphasis can be made upon recognizing that when the sexual abuse took place, they were little, uninformed, helpless and in secrecy. "We just didn't know!"

"What If"

Therapists need to emphasize that victims are made vulnerable through the **lack of information.** The "what if" game could be used for each child, suggesting scenarios where children may have had different responses to sexual advances if someone had helped them. Role playing skits or any other activities that would enhance the understanding that if each child's situation had been different and more information had been provided, the sexual abuse may have been different. "If only," or "what if," are insertions needing to be processed. The result of this first step in the process should be to have children recognize that a **lack of information** about sexual abuse or "secret touching" made them even more vulnerable. These examples of "what if" information need to be made tangible on paper or posters.

We Must Teach!

The second step in the treatment process should encourage children to see a need for education. Younger children may wish to teach even younger children about the three kinds of touching, i.e., "good, bad, and secret" or teach others how to **TELL**,! if touching trouble occurs. Allowing 9-year-olds to teach 6-year-olds is very helpful. Older victims are encouraged to teach their peers in a "formal" or classroom style setting. Subjects should explain how to parent children in the future or adolescents may need to make a "wish list" of things they would like to teach others so that "secrets don't continue to hurt kids."

Stopping Secrets

Public speaking engagements for "STOPPING SECRETS" could be initiated as long as safety of the child's emotional situation and confidentiality are is respected. If all confidential and personal concerns have been secured, public speaking can be arranged.

It will be most appropriate if, during public speaking, children discuss generic issues regarding sexual abuse and secrets, rather than using a public forum to talk about their own situation. The public speaking efforts for younger children should encourage group comraderie. Rarely, should a child be asked to speak alone. A group of children, however, presenting information to the Kiwanis Club, a teachers' staff meeting, or a group of parents within the treatment program can be very effective. A group of younger children may want to sing a song, read a poem, or simply distribute information. For older children, group participation is usually beneficial with each child providing one piece of information. Therapists should make sure that each child within the group has an opportunity to express themselves in a way that is comfortable. This should be an educational forum designed to alert the public, with a secondary goal of teaching victims they are respected and protected in the community, rather than feeling shamed or contaminated.

TRAUMA ASSESSMENT PERSPECTIVE:

This treatment activity pertains to the Relationship Perspective of the Sexual Victim Trauma Assessment when victims are unclear about their status as a "victim" within the community ("significant others" category). This treatment activity also pertains to the Situational Perspective of the Trauma Assessment relating to the development of negative and destructive self-abusive coping skills in the victim's future.

#64

FLOAT AWAY FACES

OBJECTIVES:

1) Children will be able to express their inner feelings as masked by outer expressions.

2) Children will gain skills in recognizing defense mechanisms and coping skills that are destructive.

3) Children will gain ability to express natural feelings without hiding behind external facades.

AGE GROUP:

Age 10 through Adolescence.

SUPPLIES:

1) Helium filled balloons on strings

2) Magic markers or felt tip pens

3) Construction paper

4) Glue

5) Black board

6) 3 x 5 cards

7) Camera

PROCESS:

Inside and Outside

The purpose of this treatment activity is to assist children in evaluating and understanding facades or outside appearances used to mask inner feelings. The activity begins with a discussion of how children feel when they have been sexually abused. A black board or 3 x 5 cards could be used to describe feelings. These feelings can be processed best through use of a "sentence completion inventory," such as:

When I think about my secret touching, I feel _____.

> Mad
>
> Sad
>
> Upset
>
> Worried
>
> Lonesome
>
> Betrayed
>
> Frustrated

Next, discussion should occur regarding how children tend to experience one feeling but use other ways to express those emotions. The original list of feelings should be revisited and the process should encourage an understanding that when a feeling emerges, a similar behavior often follows.

> When I feel bad, sometimes I act bad.
>
> When I feel afraid, sometimes I act tough.

Victims should be encouraged to role play or demonstrate a variety of feelings regarding these emotions. An excellent way to initiate this discussion is to have therapists act out an emotion while another person suggests an "inner" thought or feeling. In this way, children can observe the process of acting in a certain manner while portraying another internal emotion that is different.

Example:

Group member or therapist "stomps" into the center of the circle with an angry expression. Speculation could be made about how the actor feels **inside** when the actor looks angry on the **outside**.

Masks

Eventually, each victim should be able to discuss their own "masks" or ways in which they tend to hide their inner feelings. Children should choose a piece of construction paper that is the same color as a specific balloon. Children should decide upon a feeling they have and decorate a face representing that feeling for their scrapbook. For adolescents or older children, they may choose a poem, a statement, or another description of how they feel on the inside.

Eventually, group members should be able to demonstrate external feeling or how they expressed themselves externally by decorating a balloon of the same color as their inner feelings. These balloons should be decorated and the emotion should be shared with other children. To close the group activity, group members should be able to release their helium filled balloons into the air and vow to discontinue the facade of using the outer emotion when, in actuality, the inner emotion is felt. For the scrapbook to coincide with the construction paper expressing the true feelings of each group member, pictures should be taken of the balloon being released.

TRAUMA ASSESSMENT PERSPECTIVE:

This treatment activity pertains to the Situational Perspective of the Sexual Victim Trauma Assessment. Victims tend to develop coping skills in order to avoid dealing with the reality of their pain. These tendencies will be discovered within the Situational Perspective of the Trauma Assessment. Treatment specialists should be aware of these tendencies and emphasize their discovery and accentuation during this treatment activity.

#65

NEWSLETTER

OBJECTIVES:

1) Children will gain skills in expressing feelings about sexual abuse.

2) Children will gain skills in preventing sexual abuse in the future.

3) Children will gain skills in recognizing public support for sexual victims.

4) Children will gain skills in becoming more assertive.

AGE GROUP:

Age 12 and Older

SUPPLIES:

1) Xerox Copying abilities for newsletter type of printing

2) A variety of artwork

3) Collection of items from children's personal expressions, such as poems, letters or songs

4) Mailing equipment or opportunities (optional)

PROCESS:

Process, not the Product

This treatment activity is designed to have children gain comfort in expressing their feelings about sexual abuse in the form of a newsletter. Older children benefit from accepting the task of "educating" other individuals in the community for the purpose of preventing sexual abuse. The "product" will be the newsletter that could be distributed to parents involved in the treatment program, to faculty members of the local school, or to community organizations. The process of preparing the newsletter will allow children to express feelings and emotions.

Items used in the newsletter will vary according to the Trauma Assessments and those issues that need to be resolved. In the Relationship Perspective, as an example, a victim may have conflict with a nonbelieving parent. That victim may need to write a letter perhaps entitled, "If I had a Fairy God Mother." Some children may wish to write poetry, prepare a "public alert," write stories, or complete drawings of what happened to them. Rules of confidentiality should be an important consideration. Additionally, copies of newsletters could be placed in children's scrapbooks before closure.

TRAUMA ASSESSMENT PERSPECTIVE:

This treatment activity could pertain to all areas of the Trauma Assessment. As an example, relationship issues could be resolved, potential trauma to sexual development could be eased through public awareness and distorted cognitions and thinking dysfunction patterns from the Situational Perspective could be resolved.

#66

THE COURAGE TO HEAL

OBJECTIVES:

1) Children will gain skills in understanding the dynamics of sexual abuse trauma.

2) Children will be able to gain skills in expression of feelings.

3) Children will be able to enhance their support system.

4) Children will be able to gain skills in dealing with crisis.

5) Children will gain skills in resolving relationship issues.

6) Children will be able to gain skills in developing appropriate problem solving techniques relating to sexual abuse traumatization.

SUPPLIES:

1) Publication, <u>The Courage to Heal Workbook for Women and Men Survivors of Sexual Abuse</u> by Laura Davis.

2) Writing Material

PROCESS:

The publication, <u>The Courage to Heal</u>, as well as the accompanying workbook can be used for adolescents in many circumstances, provided sensitivity toward intellectual limitations are appreciated. Although the publication is primarily designed for use with adults, many of the treatment activities could be used for adolescents. The "workbook" is a structured treatment approach giving adolescents a sense of competency and accomplishment. Many treatment goals can be accomplished as victims proceed through the carefully designed treatment activities. Using the <u>Courage to Heal Workbook</u> can be an excellent way to enhance group therapy for adolescents as the workbook can be completed individually and/or supplement group process activities.

TRAUMA ASSESSMENT PERSPECTIVE:

This treatment activity pertains to all aspects of the Sexual Victim Trauma Assessment. Much of the workbook involves resolving relationship issues, changing distorted views about sexuality, as well as combatting destructive coping skills and thinking patterns.

#67

BODY CARD GAME

OBJECTIVES:

1) Children will be able to reduce anxiety about sexual issues.

2) Children will be able to gain a more positive body image.

3) Children will be able to improve communication skills.

4) Children will be able to develop group or peer comraderie.

AGE GROUP:

All Ages

SUPPLIES:

1) 3 x 5 or 5 x 7 Cards (age 13 and older)

2) Construction Paper (children under age 12)

3) Writing Materials

4) Playing Board for Moving from Start to Finish

5) Dice

6) Tokens Representing Each Child or Team

PROCESS:

Questions

This group activity primarily focuses on anxiety about sexuality, body image and embarrassment. The first step is to create "questions" that perplex children regarding their bodies and sexuality. These questions should be written on cards through the therapy process. Older children may use 3 x 5 cards for questions and may prepare complicated questions. Younger children will need guidance and perhaps questions should be placed on larger cards. For younger children, questions may need to be stimulated by therapist is a covert manner.

For younger children:

What is the right name for the wonderful part of our bodies on our chests?

For older children:

Can boys say no to sex, too?

These questions should be prepared in a tasteful manner and always with a positive attitude about sexuality. Many previously conducted therapy sessions could be reviewed in order to provide material for questions. Tastefully presented does not necessarily mean serious. Humor is a great ice breaker and can be extremely helpful for these exercises.

Caution

When the game is played, younger children may represent themselves and play individually since questions can be formulated and guided by therapists so right answers can be solicited from children and success can be ensured. For older children, there may be tendencies for children to "fail" the answer. Group therapy should not encourage competition and, therefore, it would be more productive if older children were in teams rather than singly facing each question.

Dice can be thrown and children can move around a board according to appropriately answered questions. If possible, some squares on the playing board could be designated for "touching trouble'' cards, which would require children to either move backwards or forewards according to consequences from right and wrong answers.

This activity should be a positive learning experience with children gaining the ability to become comfortable, to share information, and to create a positive image about sexuality.

TRAUMA ASSESSMENT PERSPECTIVE:

This treatment activity pertains to the Developmental Perspective of the Sexual Victim Trauma Assessment. Even though cards could be generated in a generic fashion, special attention should be paid to those children who have the potential to develop specific phobias, obsessive behaviors, or trauma to their arousal system. This is especially true for children who have had sexual responsiveness during the abuse and this activity would assist them in recognizing sexual stimulation as a normal body function.

#68

LETTERS TO MY OFFENDER

OBJECTIVES:

1) Children will gain skills in expressing a multitude of feelings toward the offender.

2) Children's sense of empowerment will be improved.

3) Children will be able to resolve relationship conflicts with the offender.

AGE GROUP:

All Ages

SUPPLIES:

1) Letter Writing Material

2) Large Pieces of Construction Paper for Younger Children

3) Regular Writing Tablets for Older Children

4) Envelopes

5) Magazines

6) Writing Material

7) Creative Artwork

PROCESS:

This treatment idea is commonly used in the treatment of sexual victims. Being able to express feelings toward the perpetrator seems to be important to children. In appreciation of new research, however, "trauma bonding" indicates that victims rarely have "one" feeling toward the perpetrator. It is also clear that feelings toward the perpetrator change for victims. This treatment activity accounts for the changing of trauma bonding, but also appreciates children's needs to express feelings and create different "reframes" of responses to the perpetrator.

Contact Concerns

Hopefully, most children are protected from sexual offenders while they are in treatment. Typically, sex offenders cannot have contact with their victims and, therefore, it is important to provide children with the opportunity of one-way communication. Children should understand that they did not commit a crime and, therefore, they do have the right to have contact or send a letter to the perpetrator (obviously, interagency coordination must occur regarding this issue).

Choices and Options

The next step is to present children with a wide variety of options for letters. Simply having children write their letters moves too quickly, does not account for children's inequality and inability to have a single feeling and is also not appreciative of moving trauma bonds in the future. Therapists could begin by presenting a variety of different sample letters. Some letters should be extremely critical and offensive to perpetrators while others should be neutral and some permeated with humility and pleading.

After children have perused these letters, they may wish to write several letters from different views. Younger children may benefit from "dictating" a letter. Again, the process is most important. If, as an example, a group of 10-year-old children are given pencils and paper and allowed to write their own letters, each child will only concentrate on their personal letter. If, however, each group member takes a turn entering the circle, pretending as though they are the "boss," dictating a letter to the "secretary" (who is a therapist), all group members will gain from each letter. Some children may have several letters, while some children may have one letter. All children should be given the right to decide, but that decision should not occur until many options have been made available.

Big Decisions

A final decision for this treatment activity concerns whether the letter should be sent. The Sexual Victim Trauma Assessment Relationship Perspective will indicate a "potential" for traumatization if the letters are sent or withheld. Therapists' discretion is extremely important. Finally, all letters should be captured for the scrapbook.

TRAUMA ASSESSMENT PERSPECTIVE:

This treatment activity primarily deals with the Relationship Perspective of the Sexual Victim Trauma Assessment. Adjustments could be made for this activity if post-disclosure issues are of concern and those issues should be included in the letters from children to their offenders.

69

WHO AM I?

OBJECTIVES:

1) Children will gain skills in improving self-image.

2) Children will gain skills in feeling accepted by others.

3) Children will gain skills in becoming introspective.

AGE GROUPS:

All Ages

SUPPLIES:

1) String or Fish Line

2) A Vast Array of Artwork, Including Construction Paper, Markers

3) Scissors

4) Glue

5) Coat Hangers

6) String

PROCESS:

Find the Goodness Within

This is a simple treatment activity designed for any age of victim with the purpose initiating an introspective process and self-awareness building. Basically, children should be involved in this process so they can learn about positive attributes within themselves. This awareness seems to be particularly difficult for sexual victims who traditionally struggle with such issues as self-esteem. Some victims may find it difficult to recognize personal positive attributes and treatment specialists should provide encouragement and support. The plan of this treatment activity is respectful to the idea that victims may find it easier to recognize positive attributes of other children before they are able to provide this recognition about themselves through introspection.

I Can See You

Breaking down the treatment process is important since self-esteem is usually a difficult issue and overtly receiving compliments should not be approached directly during the first part of this treatment activity. Children should be able to prepare lists, cards, or some type of representation of personal positive attributes of other children. In some cases, paper could be passed for other victims to participate in designating positive qualities within their colleagues. At times, using 3 x 5 cards with positive statements would be more helpful than verbalization for children who have a tendency toward dissociation or vagueness. Children can collect the cards from others.

Now I See Me

Once a list has been prepared so that each child recognizes approximately 10 positive qualities given by others, effort should be made to create a tangible, personal representation of those positive qualities. Making mobiles from coat hangers with representations of the positive qualities hanging from string or fishing line may be effective. There seems to be a positive response to children viewing positive qualities as being displayed or represented. A visual impression of the mobile can be particularly helpful to children who may have affective responses of "badness" even though the cognitive process of understanding positive qualities has taken place. The tangible representation of these positive qualities is important for children to touch, see, view and process.

For some children who are more advanced in the treatment process, making mobiles with practical assets and liabilities may be a very productive component of this treatment activity. For extremely traumatized children, accentuating the positive attributes by therapists or through the work of others may be especially important in the initial stages of treatment. For children who seem to be more balanced and more capable of recognizing the multiplicity of qualities in individuals, a representation of positive and not so positive personality characteristics may also be used.

TRAUMA ASSESSMENT PERSPECTIVE:

This treatment activity pertains to the Situational Perspective of the Sexual Victim Trauma Assessment where distorted cognitions, such as self-depreciation, hopelessness, abusability, etc., are manifested in children's thinking processes. Often, sex offenders statements, levels of coercion and bribery, or other elements found in the sexually abusive scene, or in the holistic environment of the child pertain to the development of poor self-image or self-blame. These issues should be investigated by therapists and included in the treatment activities.

#70

ONCE UPON A TIME

ACTIVITY OBJECTIVE:

1) Children will be able to resolve unconscious feelings regarding self-image through the use of stories and metaphor.

2) Children will be able to gain a sense of empowerment through the use of metaphor and stories.

3) Children will be able to improve self-concept through the use of metaphor and stories.

AGE GROUP:

All Ages

SUPPLIES:

1) Resource, <u>Once Upon a Time...Therapeutic Stories to Heal Abused Children</u>, by Nancy Davis

2) Construction Paper

3) Crayons/Writing Material

4) Variety of Objects and Art Supplies in Order to Create Representations of Story "Characters"

PROCESS:

Story Time

Nancy Davis' book, <u>Once Upon a Time</u>, is an excellent resource for using metaphor or story with sexually abused children. This resource guide has specific stories that can be tailored toward sexually abused children or children who are abuse reactive (becoming abusers themselves). This resource concentrates heavily on unconscious memory and feelings and creates metaphors or stories to deal with those unconscious thoughts.

Sexual victims can feel a sense of identification with themselves if stories can be tailored to fit each victim's needs as related to the Sexual Victim Trauma Assessment. This resource also allows adaptations of stories to fit specific children, which is an excellent opportunity for therapists to insert Trauma Assessment material or objectives. Children seem to be able to resolve a variety of conflicts and feelings (as will be identified in treatment planning through the Trauma Assessment) through listening to metaphors and stories that have solutions.

Special Needs

In appreciation of the special needs of sexually abused children and in appreciation of proactive therapy, it is recommended that metaphors and stories be used for children, but that the process of capturing these stories in each victim's scrapbook becomes an important addition not outlined in the publication. Tangible representations of the metaphors can not only be captured in artwork, but hopefully can be presented by children to other group members or parents and eventually placed in each child's scrapbook. These metaphors or stories are designed to stimulate the unconscious feelings that are in conflict and create a resolution. By making a tangible representation of these metaphors, there is even more opportunity that the unconscious will emerge and the effect of resolution will be even more powerful.

TRAUMA ASSESSMENT PERSPECTIVE:

This treatment activity primarily pertains to the Relationship Perspective of the Trauma Assessment where through the use of metaphors and stories, many conflicts can be resolved by fictitious characters that represent individuals in the relationship triangle. This treatment activity could also pertain to the Situational Perspective of the Trauma Assessment to resolve distorted cognitions. Through the use of metaphor, reality can be provided in the unconscious, which will hopefully assist the child in rejecting tendencies toward distorted cognitions and destructive coping patterns.

#71

SORT IT OUT

OBJECTIVES:

1) Children will recognize their ability to have both positive and negative feelings toward the perpetrator.

2) Children will be able to gain skills in stopping the tendency for trauma bonding through vacillation of emotions toward the perpetrator.

3) Children will be able to gain skills in resolving the multiplicity of feelings felt toward the perpetrator.

4) Children will be able to increase confidence in personal decision making.

AGE GROUP:

All Ages

SUPPLIES:

1) A Vast Array of Art Supplies, such as:

Construction Paper

Glue

Paste

Scissors

Magic Markers

2) Blackboard

3) Large Pieces of Poster Paper

4) Magazines

NOTE: This is a treatment activity that can be done in many ways depending upon supplies available. These supplies are optional and can be substituted for other items depending upon therapist's creativity or children's wants and needs.

PROCESS:

Typically, children are sexually abused by a perpetrator with whom they have a relationship. Only a small number of sexual abuse cases seem to involve a stranger. Because of this relationship, there is usually positive and negative feelings between the victim and the offender. This treatment activity requires therapists to find the best way possible, for each victim to find a balance between positive and negative feelings.

Lots of Stuff

The first step in the treatment process is to have children identify the multiplicity of feelings they may have about the perpetrator. This should be done in a rather scattered fashion. Words like "hate, mad, love, disappointed, good, bad, funny," etc., could be placed on cards or a chalkboard and used for process discussion. These feelings could relate to how the victim feels about the perpetrator or relate to qualities the victim designates to the perpetrator, both negative and positive.

In some instances, victims may not feel positive toward the perpetrator and these children should not feel as though they have failed this treatment assignment. Examining each victim's Trauma Assessment will prevent difficulty in this area. In this situation, a victim who has a specific negative feeling toward the perpetrator may assist other children or may choose to spend time discussing negative qualities. Sensitivity toward future changes in that attitude should occur, however, if victims are consistent and unchanging and if the group process has been objective, the victim's decision should be respected.

The Checks and Balance

After all possible feelings toward the perpetrator have been processed, victims should choose a modality to demonstrate their positive and negative perceptions of the person who sexually abused them. Some victims may choose a "debits and credits" approach on a balance sheet paper. Other victims may choose to make two collages with positive and negative attributes of the offender or positive and negative feelings the victim has toward the offender. If the opportunity exists, some groups may be able to stage role plays where the victim is interviewed and takes very specific stands, both positive or negative. Symbolically, the victim may then choose to change a costume, change position for the re-interview, and project the opposite opinion. Additional options might include choosing to make a deck of cards with a variety of liabilities and assets on the cards regarding the offender.

Many other modalities could be used for victims to gain control over the multiplicity of feelings they have toward the people who abuse them. Representations with a balance or with a sense of control should be made for the scrapbook. Some victims may choose opposing pages, while others may choose pictures of themselves completing another activity in the therapeutic process, such as the staged interview. Other children may choose to put the deck of cards they have made in the scrapbook.

TRAUMA ASSESSMENT PERSPECTIVE:

This treatment activity primarily pertains to the Relationship Perspective of the Sexual Victim Trauma Assessment. The Trauma Assessment should reveal the extent of multiplicity for feelings between the victim and the offender so that therapists can be guaranteed that those feelings will be revealed and worked into this balancing activity of "sorting out" feelings for the offender.

#72

PROMISE NOT TO TELL

OBJECTIVES:

1) Children will gain skills in resolving issues surrounding secrecy.

2) Children will gain skills in recognizing potentially abusive situations.

3) Children will gain skills in experiencing a sense of comraderie while improving self-esteem.

AGE GROUP:

10 and Under

SUPPLIES:

1) Book, <u>Promise Not to Tell</u> by Carolyn Polese

2) Writing paper

3) Pens

4) Construction paper

5) Crayons or drawing material

6) Video (optional)

PROCESS:

This treatment activity is simple, designed for victims with a story about a sexually abusive scenario. As with many prevention approaches, a character is faced with an uncomfortable situation where sexual abuse is either attempted or takes place. Eventually, the child tells and is "rescued." There are many other resources that would be effective for the same purpose as this publication. A treatment process concerning these types of resources should be outlined with the following steps.

What Could Happen

The first step is to process with children, by examining thinking options. The title, <u>Promise Not To Tell</u>, should be discussed and the content of the story should be contemplated. The learning experience is always enhanced if children are in a position to think about what the story may present in several different modalities. When this occurs and many scenarios are presented in children's minds, the value of learning is enhanced.

Positive Pauses

The story can be presented in one session or in several therapy involvements. Video can also be used for replay. Whenever possible, the group should pause for discussion. Some caution should be exerted. Prevention material that is frightening and foreboding usually traumatizes children. Therapists should insert positive statements, such as

> "I wonder if she really knows she has a great, wonderful body that needs to be protected."

The more positive the resource, the more likely it is for children to remember it and to accentuate it. Negative modalities are often forgotten or distorted.

Finally, some tangible response must be made. Children may choose to write a letter to the characters in the story providing much needed advice. Some children may wish to draw a picture and other children may choose to list those issues which were gained or learned from the activity on a form of artwork for the scrapbook.

TRAUMA ASSESSMENT PERSPECTIVE:

This treatment activity primarily pertains to the Situational Perspective where the sexual abuse "scene" is visited. Post-disclosure issues are also prevalent in this type of activity which are found in the Trauma Assessment Situational Perspective.

#73

WHY DO THEY DO IT?

OBJECTIVES:

1) Children will gain knowledge of why sexual offenders offend.

2) Children will gain a positive attitude about sexuality.

3) Children's feelings of guilt regarding sexual abuse responsibility will be resolved.

AGE GROUP:

7 and Older

SUPPLIES:

1) <u>A Very Touching Book</u> by Jan Hindman

2) Anatomically Correct Dolls (optional)

3) Anatomically Correct Drawings (optional)

4) Colored paper for creating "rules" lists

5) Magazines, media, examples of robberies

PROCESS:

The Valuable Commodity

This treatment process can be simple or complicated, taking either a half of group session or several months. This treatment activity is specifically related to treatment activity #8 relating to the logic of sexual abuse. The first step in this treatment activity is to provide children with an understanding of why human beings prize sexual touching. <u>A Very Touching Book</u> is excellent for this purpose. The anatomically correct dolls or drawings could be used. Sexuality must be portrayed in a very positive way and the genitalia or the private parts of human bodies must be portrayed as feeling different to touches for different reasons. Most importantly, the "rules" of touching must be emphasized.

The Right Rules

Children of all ages understand the word "rules." This treatment step should discuss and process how children are forced to follow rules. The breaking of rules should also be contemplated as an issue that may be desirable, but not appropriate.

> The rules say you can't take ice cream from the store unless you pay for it. The "wants" say, But, gee, I really like ice cream. The rules say no.

Group discussion should indicate that like ice cream, sexuality is something of value and people generally want to either be touched or have someone touch them. The rules, however, protect children and even though the touching of private body parts feels wonderful, the rules protect children and grown-ups are not supposed to break the rules.

The Robbery

The treatment activity should then focus on the criminal arena. Questions could be formulated concerning other crimes where something is taken.

> Question: "Why do people rob banks?"

> Answer: "Because they want money to buy toys and motorcycles."

The question then can be presented to children:

"Why do people touch children's private bodies?"

And the answer is:

"Because they like it and they want that good feeling."

This treatment activity process should avoid forcing children to evaluate pros and cons of their specific perpetrator. The important issue is that "people take things." Children must recognize that the robbery of sexual privacy is very similar to the robbery of a bank or an ice cream store.

The treatment activity should have parallel examples of crimes represented in a tangible form from magazines, newspaper clippings, or from the media. Treatment specialists who have conducted Trauma Assessments will be aware of personal traumatic issues, but this treatment activity should lean toward a more generic approach placing all sexual offenders (regardless of whether they have been abused as children, whether they were alcoholic, whether they had a difficult marriage, etc.) in the same category as people who break the rules. "Even though" lists could be prepared so that victims separate the person from the act of robbery.

TRAUMA ASSESSMENT PERSPECTIVE:

This treatment activity primarily pertains to the Relationship Perspective of the Sexual Victim Trauma Assessment. The identity of the victim and the offender is the critical issue. Again, specific traumatic issues for each victim should surface in this treatment activity in a subtle way since each child will have to make individual decisions about the offender. Presenting the offender in a very generic way in this treatment activity can be helpful in moving children toward making the appropriate decision.

#74

CERTIFICATES

OBJECTIVES:

1) Children will gain skills in recognizing public support.

2) Children will gain skills in building self-esteem.

3) Children learn more positive methods for evaluating abuse.

4) Children will recognize the unique nature of children.

AGE GROUPS:

All Ages

SUPPLIES:

1) Certificates that are Printed with Specific Headings

2) Generic Certificates

3) Stickers

4) Writing Pencils

5) Camera

PROCESS:

The Idea

This is a very simple treatment process or perhaps a treatment thought. In appreciation of general objectives, this treatment activity is basically designed to improve self-esteem and to teach children about support that exists in the community or in society, as well. An indirect value of this treatment activity is to teach the community or members of society to be more sensitive and empathic toward sexual victims.

Basically, this treatment activity requires therapists to be alert for opportunities when children of all ages can be awarded a "certificate." Although this treatment activity could be overworked, there are many aspects of therapy for sexually abused children that could be praised, appreciated and "certificated." Therapists should simply be alert to opportunities for providing children with honors.

Examples of certificates that could be presented are:

This certifies that you have passed the "good touching class."

This certifies that you are a "touching expert," knowing all about good, bad and secret touching.

This certifies that you are an expert in "kids rights."

Big and Little

To provide young children with certificates, complete with stickers, etc., will be a pleasant experience. For older children or for adolescents, a special announcement may need to be placed on each certificate in order to prevent adolescents from feeling that the activity is demeaning or disrespectful. Even though sexually abused adolescents have difficulty exonerating or rescuing the "child within" themselves, they will nonetheless have the potential to be offended if they are given certificates that should be presented to younger children. In order to combat this potentially difficult situation, certificates for adolescents should always indicate a statement about the purpose of the certificate pertaining to the loss of childhood. In this way, older victims can receive the same support as younger victims while their dignity will also be respected.

"If we would have known about your touching troubles when you were little, we could have given six-year-old Ryan this certificate to make him feel great."

And From Others

Finally, it is important to realize that exoneration or certification from public figures is not only helpful for victims, but, in many situations, is much easier to do than normally considered. The governor of a state, a legislator, or any other public figure may donate certificates or may sign generic certificates for children. This may not only be helpful to children receiving certificates, but may have an impact on the publics attitude, as well. Certificates signed by important people may be generic in nature, but may have the capacity to be tailored toward specific children's trauma both currently and in the future.

TRAUMA ASSESSMENT PERSPECTIVE:

This treatment activity primarily pertains to the Relationship Perspective of the Sexual Victim Trauma Assessment particularly to the bottom of the triangle and public support from the "significant other" category.

#75

KIDS RIGHTS

OBJECTIVES:

1) Children will gain skills in understanding issues surrounding sexual consent.

2) Children will relieve feelings of guilt and anxiety because of in sexual contact.

3) Children will gain positive ideations about future sexual activities and sexuality.

AGE GROUP:

All ages

SUPPLIES:

1) Parade type posters with sticks so that posters can be mounted.

2) Video

3) VCR player

4) Furniture for portrayal of television shows

5) A Very Touching Book by Jan Hindman

6) Kidsrights handouts that have been printed by treatment specialists

PROCESS:

This process begins by teaching children about rights concerning touching. A copy of "Children's Rights" could be prepared and given to children or a list of rights might be made for a wall sign or on a chalkboard. The three most important rights for children to understand are:

CHILDREN HAVE A RIGHT TO FEEL GREAT ABOUT THEIR BODIES.

CHILDREN HAVE A RIGHT TO CHOOSE SOMEONE TO SHARE THEIR BODY WITH, ON THEIR OWN, WHEN THEY GROW UP.

CHILDREN HAVE A RIGHT TO KEEP THEIR BODY PARTS PRIVATE AND VERY, VERY SPECIAL WHILE THEY ARE CHILDREN.

For Everyone

As with other treatment activities, this modality can appear to pertain to only smaller children. Reading A Very Touching Book or other prevention materials can enhance a sense of children's rights for younger victims. Older children, however, traditionally do not understand their own rights to privacy and will need to benefit from this logic and understanding. Sexual promiscuity, future abusability and poor decision making, plague older victims because they do not understand their rights to protection. For adolescents, this activity can be presented as a way to teach appropriate parenting in the future. Both male and female adolescents will accept this activity protocol if it is encased in their future as adults, rather than presenting this "childlike" treatment modalities as pertinent to adolescents at the time of treatment. The treatment activity, however, is as important for adolescents as for younger children.

This treatment process can be enhanced in a variety of ways. Reading A Very Touching Book, especially the pages considering the "Kids Rights Parade" can emphasize treatment goals. Children may want to create a variety of examples in demonstrating their understanding of kids rights. A parade is very effective for children, even if the parade takes place in the treatment center office, only for the benefit of clerical staff. Children need to have their picture taken holding posters of kid's rights and, of course, if possible, a video can be made of the "parade" and played back to children at another time to enhance the value of the treatment process.

Tune In to Kids Rights

For older children, a television show may be enacted with interviews conducted of very important people. Children may fantasize or wish for affirmation of children's rights from a variety of important individuals, such as rock stars, the President of the United States, or television figures. Victims can be asked, "Who is the most important person in the world that knows about kids' rights?" Children may wish to role play interviewing important figures (obviously fictitious) and these important figures will provide affirmation as to children's basic rights to privacy. All of these activities must be captured in children's scrapbooks for later reference and for treatment enhancement.

TRAUMA ASSESSMENT PERSPECTIVE:

This treatment activity primarily pertains to the Developmental Perspective of the Trauma Assessment concerning losses or damage to normal sexual development. Children participating in this activity should gain positive ideations toward human sexuality and toward protection of rights. Guilt and anxiety about sexual participation during the abuse should be alleviated through this treatment activity.

#76

I SEE SOMEBODY

OBJECTIVES:

1) Children will gain skills in developing group comraderie.

2) Children will gain skills in improving self-image.

3) Children will gain skills in combatting feelings of poor body image.

4) Children will gain skills in developing positive ways of communication.

AGE GROUPS:

Children 12 and Under

SUPPLIES:

1) Polaroid Camera (preferred)

2) Other Camera

3) Construction Paper

4) Markers

PROCESS:

This is a simple treatment activity designed to take pictures of children and not only improve victim's attitudes about body image, but to also develop skills in children to be complimentary and supportive of each other.

The process will be completed under the task of playing a card game. The "cards" are pictures of each child involved in the group process. Ideally, a polaroid camera will be available so that with ceremony and grandiosity, each child's picture can be taken. With proper preparation, children may wish to stand on a stage, a chair, or be involved with some other kind of "prop" so that the "picture taking process" is done with enthusiasm and ceremony. As the picture is taken, lists of positive attributes for each child should be discussed.

Pick A Card

Sitting in a circle children could then randomly choose a "card," which is actually a photograph of another group member. Holding the cards, children should play a game involving providing other group members with clues about the person in the picture. The identity of the person in the picture should be a secret known only to the child drawing the card and the assisting therapist. The clues should be positive and in order to guarantee the positive nature of the clues, therapists must work carefully with children. If the picture taking process has planted seeds of positive attributes then this activity will be much easier. For older children, preparing lists of positive attributes previous to the picture taking process may be even more effective.

As children hold the cards of their group members and provide clues to others, positive statements should be made and other group members should guess who is in the picture. If only positive statements are made, and if children are enthusiastic about keeping the identity of the person in the picture secret for a short period of time, this treatment activity can be particularly rewarding.

Caution should be exerted to ensure that clues are positive and that clues are not only related to physical attributes of children. Sexually abused victims often feel tremendous trauma due to poor body image or due to the fact that they believe their physical appearance caused the sexual offense. Internal qualities of children used for clues will be most effective for this treatment process, especially when internal qualities may be more difficult for group members to remember or to guess and, therefore, the guessing game can be prolonged, creating a source of excitement for participants.

TRAUMA ASSESSMENT PERSPECTIVE:

This treatment activity pertains to the Developmental Perspective of the Sexual Victim Trauma Assessment regarding poor body image and feelings of body contamination. Some elements within the Situational Perspective of the Trauma Assessment could also be emphasized if negative self-image has been verbalized to children by offenders, which will be revealed in the sexually abusive "scene." For children who seem to be developing tendencies toward either being abusive or being abusable, this treatment activity may interfere with that process and teach children to develop more positive personal coping skills.

#77

LIGHTS, CAMERA, ACTION

OBJECTIVES:

1) Children will be able to recognize trauma suffered upon disclosure through system intervention.

2) Children will gain skills in recognizing how system "players" may have exerted trauma that was unintentional.

3) Children will recognize and desensitize feelings of rejection, abandonment and betrayal.

4) Children will be able to gain skills in responding more appropriately to others in therapeutic endeavors.

5) Children will improve their ability to communicate.

SUPPLIES:

1) Video cameras

2) Space and modalities that would allow a skit or a play to be performed

3) Chairs

4) Stage

5) Curtain

6) Dress up clothes for specific roles, such as police, judge, prosecutor

7) VCR

8) Television

9) Cards or paper for writing script

PROCESS:

Train the Trainees

This treatment process should be presented as an activity for educating and training PROFESSIONALS in the community. The age group for this activity should be 12 years through adolescents. Older children seem to respond more appropriately to treatment activities that are for the benefit of others, rather than necessarily directly for themselves.

Ouch!

The first step in the treatment process is for the group to list and recall traumatic events that occur due to typical system intervention. Attention should be given to specific issues in the Situational Perspective of the Trauma Assessment (regarding post-disclosure issues) for each victim. Children should be able to discuss their personal situations where painful events occurred while they participated in interviews, disclosed in court, grand jury, etc. If children are unable to verbalize their own personal issues, additional lists and information should be prepared by therapists detailing general information known to traumatize children. Examples are:

''I felt like the policeman was mad at me.''

''Court made me feel so little.''

Plans should then be made to make a video production with two separate steps. The first step should encourage children to act out the traumatic event that occurred. It may be effective to have a moderator or a group member who will explain each scenario and then interview the "actor or actress." Painful feelings related to the inappropriate system response should be the topic of the interview. The moderator will then ask the participants to re-enact the situation in a positive way.

As an example, a common trauma scenario is an insensitive interview that may occur at the police station, social work office, or the school. The moderator should set the scene with a victim making a report and then being taken to the interview room. The role play should be video taped. From the list that was outlined in the first step of this process, a script should be given to the character of the inept, insensitive, clumsy interviewer. Statements should be made by this interviewer that cause trauma to the victim. The victim's (actor) response should lead the interviewer into even more insensitivity, fear and embarrassment. The role-play should end with the actor-victim being evaluated by the group as obviously traumatized.

To The Rescue

Next, the moderator of the role-play should explain the scene and what has occurred, bringing empathy from the group to the victim. The moderator should then re-enact the scene so that the stumbling, bumbling detective now interviews in a way that is helpful to the victim. Preparation for this scenario will be extremely important as the group strategizes a better response. A single group session or several sessions may be needed for each role-play scenario. As the investigator re-examines the victim in a helpful way, all group members should applaud, cheer, and give affirmation to the appropriate response from the "changed" investigator.

This process may be repeated with a courtroom scenario, interview with the judges, grand jury, or with lawyers. All issues in the Situational Perspective of the Trauma Assessment "post-disclosure" section should be carefully woven into the scenario role-plays.

Finally, the process should allow the group to view both the negative and positive role-plays on video and perhaps use these videos to actually train interagency team members involved in the system. Parent viewing of this video tape may also be effective since the role-play may criticize insensitivity to victims, and encourage parents to demonstrate empathy to children who have had these unfortunate experiences.

TRAUMA ASSESSMENT PERSPECTIVE:

This treatment activity pertains to the Situational Perspective of the Sexual Victim Trauma Assessment. Post disclosure issues can be extremely traumatic. Breaking the cycle of sexual abuse that occurs in the future for victims is also an important issue, and this treatment activity may teach sensitivity for victims' future children.

#78

HIGH FIVE FOR PROGRESS

ACTIVITY OBJECTIVES:

1) Children will be able to see a "process" to treatment.

2) Children will be able to identify goals and objectives for their specific treatment plans.

3) Children will be able to establish a positive identification of mental health intervention.

4) Children will be able to improve self-esteem and gain comfort in rehabilitation.

AGE GROUP:

All Ages

SUPPLIES:

1) Finger paints

2) Large sheet of butcher paper

3) Heavy magic markers

4) Buckets of soapy water

5) Paper towels

PROCESS:

Now Comes Control

This treatment activity should allow children to establish their own treatment goals and then work in a process where those goals are detailed and accentuated. Treatment that is generic, ongoing and directionless can traumatize victims who have spent a great deal of time feeling out of control. Treatment that is clearly defined helps victims feel in control.

The first step in the treatment process is to have children identify their own treatment goals and make a list of these goals for either their scrapbooks or for display in the group facility. Obviously, for younger children, the goals will be more simplistic, such as:

Learn about good touching.

Learn about secret touching.

Learn to not be so angry.

Learn to say "no" to any secret touching.

For adolescents, the goals should be more direct and sophisticated:

"I need to learn that I can have many different feelings about the person who abused me."

"I need to learn that I did the right thing by telling."

"I need to learn how to stop feeling depressed."

"I need to learn that none of what happened was my fault."

As these goals are listed for each child, they should be decorated and perhaps placed in a position to be viewed by other group members and/or parents.

High Five For Progress

The next step in the treatment process is to construct a scale entitled, "High Five for Progress." The scale should appear like a ruler with numbers from one to five. There should be a great deal of space between each number with many marker lines. A short scale will be less effective than a long scale that covers an entire wall. A piece of butcher paper is effective so children can use finger paints to indicate a hand print for where they see themselves at the time this assignment and periodically thereafter in the treatment process.

Hand prints need to be dated. Concentrating on goals from the individual papers and viewing graduation on number "5" should help children see how they are progressing toward recovery. This is especially positive for younger children who may want to make a grandiose process out of putting their hand prints on a certain part of the poster at each session. It is also helpful for adolescents to see tiny handprints of other children.

Keep Moving

The attainment of treatment goals will be greatly enhanced if the first time this assignment is done, children see themselves as doing well, but needing to accomplish specific tasks further along on the chart. This chart should remain in the group room or should be put away and then later displayed at different intervals. It is important that children have a visual representation of themselves moving up the chart as they re-examine their specific lists of individual goals at each group.

Therapists need to constantly remind children of their earlier needs and accentuate each accomplishment. These goals will routinely be accomplished, however, the value of the accomplishment is lessened if children do not recognize the small steps toward attainment of the goals.

Finally, a smaller drawing of the High Five for Progress chart could be made for each child's scrapbook with a final finger paint hand print on the number 5. Another tactic would require taking a victim's picture standing underneath the large chart with a statement, "purple hand prints and High Five ," "I DID IT!"

TRAUMA ASSESSMENT PERSPECTIVE:

This treatment activity could pertain to the Relationship Perspective of the Trauma Assessment if treatment goals require resolution and clarification of relationships within the incestuous family. From the Developmental Perspective, if children have tendencies toward developing negative attitudes about sexuality, those goals could also be established and accomplished. Children have tendencies to develop coping skills of lethargy, apathy, and hopelessness as examples of issues pertaining to the situational perspective.

#79

PALE MOON

OBJECTIVES:

1) Children will be able to identify feelings of trauma regarding sexual abuse.

2) Children will be able to use the medium of music to express feelings.

3) Children will be able to relieve stress and anxiety through musical representations of trauma.

4) Children will learn auditory methods of self-expression.

AGE GROUP:

13 and Older

SUPPLIES:

1) Copy of "Pale Moon" Album by Sandy Abegg, Abegg Productions

2) Other taped albums primarily relating to childhood victimization.

3) Writing paper

4) Tape recorder or cassette player

5) Collection of Music or Poetry (various expressions of child abuse)

PROCESS:

Listen to the Pain of Silence

This treatment activity is primarily for adolescents who seem to have a particular interest in music and lyrics. From a sexual development perspective, it seems as though adolescents have tremendous needs for intimacy and closeness, but do not have the skills or ability to accomplish intimacy with the onset of puberty. Listening to music or other activities from an auditory modality (such as talking on the telephone) allows adolescents to be close and intimate without clumsiness or ineptitude. Using an album pertaining to child abuse, such as "Pale Moon," or any other representation of child abuse music is an excellent way to enhance "intimacy with trauma" for the purpose of resolution.

This treatment activity could be enhanced if adolescents are allowed to lie on the floor with their heads facing the center of a circle in the form of "spokes." Music should be played in sections with the presentations and discussion about the lyrics before listening. Using the title for discussion can help victims anticipate the message. A variety of feelings and emotions can be elicited, but the treatment process will be enhanced if those feelings are anticipated, discussed and then re-evaluated following the music presentation.

Other adolescents may choose to externalize the expression of feelings by writing letters to the song writer or singer, which may or may not be mailed. These letters, however, should be captured for the scrapbook. Additional treatment process could encourage victims to present to the group other forms of music that may not be related to child abuse, but tend to cause traumatization. As an example, Madonna's album, "Like a Virgin," may have had a particularly traumatizing effect for many female sexual victims. The recommended album, "Pale Moon," is an example of identification of feelings with victims. However, albums such as Madonna's are potentially traumatizing to victims and the balancing of these two examples can be helpful.

TRAUMA ASSESSMENT PERSPECTIVE

This treatment activity pertains to several issues in the Sexual Victim Trauma Assessment. First, the Relationship Perspective may be impaired and victims who are in trauma bonds may identify with lyrics of songs that relate to abandonment and rejection. Additionally, for male victims, as an example, traumatization to the Developmental Perspective could be identified in such songs as "Men Don't Cry," which would elicit sensitivity to male victims' pressure to be sexually aggressive and sexually accessible. Other developmental issues could also be addressed through music that involves "sexual taking" or sexual exploitation.

#80

NO, GO AND TELL

OBJECTIVES:

1) Children will gain skills in developing preventive techniques so that sexual abuse will not occur in the future.

2) Children will gain skills in developing a sense of empowerment.

3) Children will gain skills in resolving conflicts over their inabilities to tell.

4) Children's guilt and anxiety will be relieved concerning improper responses following sexual abuse disclosure.

AGE GROUP:

Children Under 8

SUPPLIES:

1) A Very Touching Book by Jan Hindman

2) T-Shirts with Printed Letters "NO, GO TELL" (optiional)

3) Video

4) Art Supplies

PROCESS:

Just Say No

Early prevention and treatment efforts suggested that children needed to "just say no" in order to be safe. This simplistic approach tended to traumatize children who did not tell and encouraged those children to feel as though they had failed. While children shout "say no," children who were not able to "say no" felt guilty and overwhelmed since "saying no" seems so easy on a Tuesday afternoon in a classroom of fourth graders.

Eventually, prevention approaches became more empathic to children's inabilities and added that children should "say no," but they should also "go and tell." This approach was somewhat effective in relieving children's frustration, but nonetheless continued to suggest that "saying no, going and telling" was an easy task. Additionally, this approach, although better, failed to respond to those children who told and were either rejected, abandoned or punished. Finally, the most acceptable approach indicated that children should:

"Say no, go tell, and keep telling."

This treatment activity purports these ideas provided cautions are exerted. First, the Trauma Assessment will reveal how children feel about their disclosures or their lack of disclosures. If children participating in the group process were unable to tell for long periods of time, then "saying no," "going and telling" needs to appear as an insurmountable task for children. For some children who were able to tell, this activity will reinforce their tenacity and assertiveness. For children who were not able to tell, but in this treatment process perceive children represented as young, small and unable to tell, they will feel exonerated for their lack of disclosure.

It Sounds So Easy?

It is important that children feel equipped to tell, but children's past inabilities to report need to be protected. With specific issues resolved surrounding Trauma Assessments, children can work through this treatment process making representations of the four steps:

''No''

''Go''

''Tell''

''Keep Telling''

In some situations, T-shirts can be made demonstrating children's learning process. Pages in the scrapbook can represent these four steps provided special consideration is made to individual Trauma Assessments and individual post-disclosure problems.

TRAUMA ASSESSMENT PERSPECTIVE

This treatment activity pertains to the Situational Perspective of the Sexual Victim Trauma Assessment dealing with post-disclosure issues. Relationship issues could also pertain to this activity if the power of the relationship with the perpetrator was the reason for lack of disclosure.

#81

DEBITS AND CREDITS

OBJECTIVES:

1) Children will be able to gain skills in identifying losses or trauma relating to sexual abuse.

2) Children will be able to identify the feelings of trauma as a result of system intervention.

3) Children will be able to identify positive contributions from others.

AGE GROUPS:

All ages

SUPPLIES:

1) Plain paper (8 1/2 x 11)

2) Blackboard or large butcher paper

3) Red and black markers

4) Rulers for lining paper or blackboard

5) Individual balance sheet (accounting format)

PROCESS:

Can I Take It Back?

This treatment process attempts to balance feelings of trauma that have occurred in post-disclosure situations. Many children feel overwhelmed by what has happened to them after reporting the abuse and they may not be aware of positive intervention or support that occurred but was unknown. The purpose of this activity is to create a balance so that children recognize the positive aspects of intervention even though the negative trauma from disclosure may seem overwhelming.

The Balance Sheet

For older children, a list of DEBITS AND CREDITS is a productive way to complete this assignment. A list can be prepared on a blackboard or large piece of paper with the losses being written in red, similar to a financial statement. A case scenario can be presented to use for the lists. The positive things that have occurred in the case presentation should be written in black. Negative issues or losses should be written in red. The "balance sheet" or the final tally should indicate that there are many more positive aspects than negative. Therapists need to break down positive issues for severely traumatized children so that the positive list is longer and appears more powerful. Negative items should be grouped to have the black list seem shorter.

Eventually, victims should move toward making their own debits and credits tally sheet as the assignment becomes more personal. These lists should be captured for the scrapbook. Information from the Trauma Assessments must be known to therapists and processed on each victim's debit and credit list.

For younger children, the concept of debit and credit may be too sophisticated. Some representation of positive and negative issues should be made on younger children's lists by perhaps using a "smiling face" or a "sad face" delineating good and bad outcomes. It is very important that children of all ages participate in this exercise and that therapists initiate a long list of support or positive ideations concerning disclosure. Children should leave this assignment with an overwhelming feeling that although trauma has occurred during post-disclosure, the general response is nonetheless more positive than negative.

TRAUMA ASSESSMENT PERSPECTIVE:

This treatment activity pertains to primarily the Situational Perspective and the Relationship Perspective of the Sexual Victim Trauma Assessment. Identifying areas of trauma is important for the "debit" or negative portion of the list. Additionally, the positive influences within the triangle of the Relationship Perspective needs to be accentuated, especially concerning for support that is unknown to victims.

#82

I'M OKAY

OBJECTIVES:

1) Children will alleviate fears of body contamination and disease.

2) Children will gain skills in recognizing and learning about public health issues.

3) Children will alleviate fears of disease.

4) Children will develop a more positive body image.

AGE GROUPS:

All Ages

SUPPLIES:

1) Access to Medical Facility or Public Health Department

2) Certificates or Correspondence from Medical Professional

3) Transportation

4) Funding for Medical Testing

PROCESS:

Unfolding and Unnecessary Trauma

This is a simple process, but one that has tremendous impact for children who have been sexually abused. Sexual abuse victims have the potential for developing trauma as a result of not knowing whether they have been contaminated or whether they have sexually transmitted diseases. In children's future, they will become aware of such things as Gonorrhea, Syphilis, and AIDS. For children who have not been tested, many fears will abound in their futures. This traumatization will usually be a slow process, as children become cognizant of these diseases, often long after treatment has been completed. Children will begin to wonder about themselves and trauma often develops due to the lack of information about their medical condition.

This treatment process simply encourages testing of all victims and a documentation of their health. In many instances, children are examined and tested, but the results of those tests are not made known to victims. Trauma unfolds in the child's future through the lack of information. If each child is tested and if the results of the test indicating "no contamination" are placed on a certificate or in correspondence from a medical person, trauma can be averted. This is a proactive treatment activity that looks to the child's future and recognizes that without information documenting health, victims are likely to develop trauma because of unnecessary concern and worries.

TRAUMA ASSESSMENT PERSPECTIVE:

This treatment activity pertains to the Developmental Perspective of the Sexual Victim Trauma Assessment. Healthy sexual attitudes can be severely influenced by the ongoing process of developing beliefs of contamination and poor body image.

#83

"QUIZ TIME: TOUCHING"

OBJECTIVES:

1) Children will gain skills in understanding the aspects of tenderness, affection, and appropriate touching.

2) Children will gain skills in understanding negative aspects of aggression and violence.

3) Children will be given the opportunity to avoid attaching negative attitudes to normal sexual touching.

4) Children will be able to understand the issue of sexual consent as it relates to sexual abuse, rather than to generalize all sexual touching as being negative.

5) Children will gain a positive understanding of future sexuality.

AGE GROUP:

All ages

SUPPLIES:

1) Accommodations for two "teams" that can be separated (use of chairs, desks, tables, etc.)

2) Video camera (VCR, if possible)

3) Large pieces of construction paper

4) Markers

5) Whistle, horn, or some kind of timer, which will make a loud noise

6) Prizes

7) <u>A Very Touching Book</u> by Jan Hindman

PROCESS:

Team Up

The process of this group activity should divide the group into two equal teams. Sensitivity should be given toward children's abilities, not necessarily toward children's choices. This activity should be a competition, but should also be sensitive to the potential traumatization of competition for vulnerable children.

Questions should be prepared previous to the group session regarding the different kinds of touching. <u>A Very Touching Book</u> could be used to explain "good, bad, and secret" touches. Questions will obviously vary according to the different age of victims and according to what children have accomplished in previous treatment sessions. As groups are prepared for adolescents or older children, the issue of sexual consent is profound and complicated. The following are examples of the kinds of questions that could be used with varying age groups.

YOUNGER CHILDREN

What do we call the kind of touching when we get pinched and it hurts?

What do we call the kind of touching that is hugging, kissing, "safe" and feels nice?

What is the kind of touching when an older or bigger person tries to touch a child's private parts?

For older children or adolescents, the questions would not only include the aforementioned topics, but would also present issues relating to "consent" or to problem solving concerns about touching.

Is it good, bad, or secret touching if someone threatens to hit you if you don't give them your lunch money?

What kind of touching is it if someone wants to hug, kiss, and hold you and you don't want them to do it?

Obviously, some of these questions will need more than a one word answer. Since questions will vary, it is recommended that specific answers be clear in the minds of the therapist previous to the treatment activity so that children can be successful in answering the question. For a more complicated issue, therapists should present multiple choice questions with one answer being most appropriate. Multiple choice answers could be developed with the following kind of structure.

SAMPLE QUESTION

What if someone wants to hug and kiss you, but you don't want them to do it?

A) It is good touching no matter if you want it or not.

B) It is good touching if you wanted it, but you don't, so it's wrong.

C) It's really not good to force someone into this kind of touching, but you should go along with it anyway so you will be popular and you won't make people upset.

Children should form teams and both teams should answer each question as a team. Some kind of scoring should occur for the right answers. Therapists should be sensitive to children's needs and plan accordingly so that even wrong answers have a positive outcome. Rather than simply winning the competition, the group should gain other commodities such as certificates for their scrapbooks, stickers, or perhaps some other kind of prize such as an award or a sexual abuse prevention book.

Capture the Creativity

If the "quiz show" can be videotaped, the entire process will be enhanced as the group is able to watch the video at a later time. Most importantly, there needs to be some representation of the "quiz show" questions, answers and competition in each child's scrapbook.

As indicated in other treatment activities, the quiz show format could be expanded to many different areas of victim recovery. If this format is successful, many goals and objectives can be accomplished through the use of this modality. Creative therapists will use this method in dealing with many different treatment concerns, especially when Sexual Victim Trauma Assessments have been completed and specific needs for unique problems emerge.

TRAUMA ASSESSMENT PERSPECTIVE:

This specific treatment activity (with the general treatment modality of "quiz shows") pertains primarily to the Developmental Perspective of the Sexual Victim Trauma Assessment. Children will gain a positive understanding of human sexuality and sexual consent. This will be a positive and helpful portrayal of prevention of not only of sexual abuse, but of sexual exploitation that could occur in these children's future. This treatment modality, however, could be used for many issues needing resolution.

#84

SAFE SECRET SHARING

OBJECTIVES:

1) Children will be able to gain skills in building trust.

2) Children will be able to gain skills in communication.

3) Children's self-esteem will be increased.

4) Children will be able to gain skills in being supportive of others.

5) Children will be able to avoid tendencies toward dissociation and secrecy.

AGE GROUP:

All Ages

SUPPLIES:

1) Large Poster Board

2) 3x5 or 5x7 Cards

3) Magic Markers

4) Construction Paper

5) Envelopes and/or Boxes

6) Magazines

7) Puppets, toys, dolls

8) Recording equipment

PROCESS:

The concept of secrets has a significant impact in the treatment of sexually abused victims. Children who give up their secrets usually have a better opportunity to rehabilitate. Using the therapeutic environment to process the "safe secret sharing" is a productive endeavor.

Safety Rules

The first step in safe secret sharing is to review issues surrounding confidentiality. This is especially important for adolescents or older children. A poster board could be made explaining rules of confidentiality. It would be most helpful if the confidentiality list was positive and helpful, rather than from a dictatorial view. Instead of "no talking outside of the clinic," a positive reframe should occur and state "our secrets are safe with each other in the clinic." For younger children, very simple rules could be established, such as "the only time to talk about our secrets is in group."

A second treatment step requires preparation and contemplation. Sexual victims tend to be most traumatized through verbal expressions of secret issues. "Safe secrets" are not typically shared verbally, since most children were instructed not to share information about their abuse. Therefore, this step in the treatment activity requires significant desensitization through comprehensive contemplation regarding a wide variety of options for sharing secrets. If children spend significant time anticipating which modalities they will use for sharing secrets, "IF" they will share secrets becomes an automatic assumption.

Safe Sharing

Victims should be presented with a wide variety of modalities for sharing secrets, such as perusing magazines and finding a representation of a secret that will be shared at a later time. Putting these items in an envelope, as an example, and then waiting for a stated time period before sharing the information about the secret, could be a method for approaching "safe sharing of secrets." Some children may choose drawing a picture or writing a poem that needs interpretation for sharing the secret.

Other secret sharing modalities might include making tape recordings, presenting "whisper" puppet shows, which will later be magnified into appropriate sound levels, or placing items in a box or in an envelope to be kept secret, but shared at a later time.

What If?

Depending upon information revealed in specific Trauma Assessments, therapists should accentuate this treatment activity. For some children who seem to be particularly traumatized or who appear to be withholding information, an intermittent therapeutic process step could occur. Rather than moving toward sharing secrets, it may be beneficial to spend time discussing, processing, and desensitizing what children anticipate will happen should they give up secrets. Making lists, tape recordings or processing these fears may need to occur before children can take the final step in sharing secrets.

Finally, some activity should occur emphasizing the exchange of secrets. This treatment activity may be a prelude to treatment activity #57. However, if treatment plans dictate that minimal trauma seems to have occurred because of withholding secrets, this treatment activity may suffice. It is not necessarily important in this treatment activity to discuss sexual abuse secrets, especially for extremely traumatized children. Sharing of secrets should be related to feelings, past behaviors, worries, or fears. Some secrets may include sexual abuse issues, but treatment activity #57 will pertain to that issue.

TRAUMA ASSESSMENT PERSPECTIVE:

This treatment activity pertains primarily to the Situational Perspective of the Sexual Victim Trauma Assessment since victims have significant tendency to develop coping skills surrounding secrecy. Internalizing tendencies for victims contributes to poor self-image and other self-destructive coping skills.

#85

TRIGGERS AND REFRAMING

OBJECTIVES:

1) Children will gain skills in identifying sensory activation that has the potential to create phobic reactions in the future.

2) Children will be able to desensitize themselves from the potential of sensory activated phobias.

3) Children will create positive frames for "survival" and control of phobic reactions.

AGE GROUPS:

All ages

SUPPLIES:

1) Construction paper

2) Magic markers

3) Writing materials

4) Magazines for cutting

5) Cameras

6) Items specifically related to abuse, which may include:

   Pictures of households

   Fabric from bedspreads

   Visual, kinesthetic or auditory objects

7) Art supplies of unlimited variety and quality

PROCESS:

1, 2, 3

This treatment process is perhaps one of the most important treatment modalities for sexual victims. It is likely that this treatment activity could take many weeks to complete and may need to occur on an ongoing basis. This treatment process has three steps, with the first step requiring recognition of the "triggers" or the sensory activation that is likely to return the victim to the same affective responses that occurred during the sexual abuse.

The second step requires a **desensitization** process where the "triggers" will become familiar and underneath the victim's control. This process will occur as triggers are represented in the scrapbook or other tangible modalities. The third step in the treatment process is to create positive reframes of those items so that when victims are "triggered" back to those feelings, they will have a new way of surviving the emotional impact of those experiences.

The Trauma Assessment will usually pinpoint triggers or items that need to be desensitized and reframed. Therapists should know the kinds of things that need to be captured, but should not necessarily be directive. Having children recapture their sensory experiences relating to their abuse can be an effective activity even though therapists may already be aware of the potential phobias.

Sensory I.D.

The identification of the triggers can emerge through such activities as having children lie on the floor of a group room and discuss sensory activation that occurred during the abuse. As an example, with eyes closed, victims could be asked.

"What do you see when you think about your sexual abuse or secret touching?"

Additional questions could be asked concerning smells, touches, tactile responses or auditory imprints. A list must then be made for children concerning their personal "triggers." This is a complicated process and should not be done haphazardly. Some victims may not be aware of their sensory triggers and will need assistance.

Questions can be posed concerning events or thoughts that require children to remember the abuse. This baseline sensory information must be determined in order to pinpoint the triggers. If children do not understand what is causing the activation, therapists may need to carefully intervene for each child. As an example, some children may be vague and say, "I think about (or **feel** about) my secret touching in the night." The trigger may be the onset of nighttime, smells relating to the bedroom, specific television shows, or other unknown items. The list could be prepared with at least ten different sensory activation responses for each victim even though **exact** sensory information may not be clear.

Desensitization

The second step in the process should encourage victims to collect representations of the triggers. This can take place by using magazines, photographs, drawings, or sometimes the actual item. As an example, if the bedspread that was involved in the abuse was "pink" and reminds the victim of sexual trauma, bedspreads that are pink should be used for desensitization. Perhaps, a piece of the actual bedspread would be appropriate or pictures of pink bedspreads. The desensitization of the pink bedspread needs to be powerful. This step should initially be painful as the trauma "bleeds" out.

Positive Frame of Safety

The final step of the treatment activity is to make a positive "reframe" of the color pink and bedspreads. Some victims may want to have pages in the scrapbook with positive representation of pink items, i.e., pigs, bubble gum, or strawberry ice cream. Additionally, positive reframes may concentrate on the issue of bedspreads, with representations of appropriate uses for bedspreads being described with perhaps soft, cuddling children and kittens.

This treatment activity cannot be stressed enough. Sexual victims will always remember the abuse and they will always be triggered. Effective treatment requires a positive representation of those triggers to occur. As each victim is triggered or placed in a position to remember, the positive reframe will take the place of the traumatic memory and basically, the victim will be "triggered" to safety.

TRAUMA ASSESSMENT PERSPECTIVE:

This very important treatment activity pertains primarily to the Situational Perspective of the Trauma Assessment with the development of phobic reactions and distorted cognitions.

#86

HUMAN SEXUALITY FOR PARENTS AND CHILDREN IN TROUBLED FAMILIES

OBJECTIVES:

1) Children will be able to improve communication with parents regarding sexuality.

2) Children will be able to gain knowledge about sexuality.

3) Children will be able to make decisions about attitudes and values regarding sexuality.

4) Children will be able to make appropriate decisions that avoid stereotypic responses to sexuality.

AGE GROUP:

Age 10 and Older

SUPPLIES:

1) Publication, <u>Human Sexuality Curriculum for Parents and Children in Troubled Families</u> by Toni Cavanaugh-Johnson, Ph.D.

2) Related Supplies and Materials as Outlined in Curriculum Guide

PROCESS:

The publication, <u>Human Sexuality Curriculum for Parents and Children in Troubled Families</u>, provides a creative curriculum for teaching human sexuality with both parents and "abuse reactive" children. The curriculum has nine modules ranging from discussing myths, misconceptions and stereotypic responses to communicating about sexuality, as well as providing basic information on sexual abuse, sexual functioning, pregnancy and values clarification. The modules are divided into specific levels, designed for use with both children and parents. The overall message of the curriculum is to create a more positive attitude regarding sexuality and to improve communication between children and adults.

The curriculum should not be a substitute for treatment since the approach is generic and not necessarily designed to deal with specific issues relating to each victim's Trauma Assessment. The curriculum is, however, an excellent way to prohibit trauma from emerging in sexual victims, especially in the area of sexual dysfunction. The curriculum could be used in its entirety or sections of the curriculum could be used to augment specific treatment planning for sexual victims.

TRAUMA ASSESSMENT PERSPECTIVE:

The curriculum, <u>Human Sexuality Curriculum for Parents and Children in Troubled Families</u>, pertains primarily to the developmental perspective of the Sexual Victim Trauma Assessment. Creating positive ideas about sexuality will prevent severe trauma to normal sexual development. This treatment approach, however, as outlined in the curriculum, can dispel many myths and erroneous information that could contribute to the development of distorted cognitions and phobic reactions as found in the Situational Perspective of the Sexual Victim Trauma Assessment.

#87

MY FEELINGS

OBJECTIVES:

1) Children will be able to identify and express feelings.

2) Children will be able to recognize how the internal process of identifying feelings can provide protection in the future.

3) Children will be able to adapt a sense of empowerment and protection.

AGE GROUPS:

Age 8 and Under

SUPPLIES:

1) My Feelings colorbook by Marcia Morgan

2) Color crayons

3) Paints

4) Magic markers

5) Camera

6) Scissors

7) Scotch tape

PROCESS:

This is a basic treatment activity that requires involvement with Marcia Morgan's coloring book, My Feelings. This treatment activity can take place over several group sessions, with each page in the color book being presented, colored, and then placed in the victim's scrapbook. The ideas and the concepts of the treatment activity are explained in the coloring book. It is important in this treatment activity for victims to recognize that internal feelings are not only legitimate, but that feelings can be used to detect potential abuse.

TRAUMA ASSESSMENT PERSPECTIVE:

This treatment modality pertains to the Situational portion of the Sexual Victim Trauma Assessment where victims develop negative feelings and distorted cognitions about their situation. Victims tend to use these emotions to develop destructive cycles of coping.

#88

REAL MEN, REAL WOMEN

OBJECTIVES:

1) Children will recognize prevalent sexual role training in American society.

2) Children will recognize the destructive nature of traditional role training.

3) Children will be able to identify the need to resist sexual role training that is destructive.

4) Children will develop positive sexual self-images.

AGE GROUPS:

12 and older

SUPPLIES:

1) Magazines for cutting

2) Glue

3) Construction paper

4) Magic markers

5) Writing materials

6) Camera

7) Media influences - music, advertising, books, etc.

PROCESS:

Real, Real Men

The first step in this treatment process is to have victims identify pervading sexist role training in American society. Through the use of either rock music, magazines, television scripts, etc., a profile of males (real men) should emerge that suggests pure sexist influences where real men are portrayed as strong, demanding, sexual and unemotional. A very narrow-minded and dogmatic portrayal of the male role in America should be presented. Victims should be able to discuss a humorous portrayal of "real men."

Example:

"Men never cry."

"Real men don't eat quiche."

"Real men were born wearing Levi's"

Real, Real Women

The same should be true for the representation of the female role in America. Humor and absurdity should persist as females are portrayed as emotional, ineffective and always concerned about their appearance. Again, a very dogmatic and inappropriate portrayal should emerge. This can be done in a variety of ways with victims preparing lists, a collage, or other art forms.

Example:

"Real women care more about their fingernails than they care about mathematics."

"Real women are sexy, but not sexual."

"Real women are fluffy and can't change tires."

Let's Share

Discussion should then occur regarding how ideally both men and women need to share male and female qualities. It is especially important for adolescents to recognize that a positive quality in males may be sensitivity and emotion, which is traditionally a female tendency. For mixed groups, it is very powerful for adolescent males to understand that female adolescents tend to appreciate males who can express emotions and feelings which is contrary to the "real men" role.

It is also important in this discussion to have males express an interest in females who have characteristics of males. Eventually, the roles should seem to merge and victims should be able to prepare an "ideal" portrayal of a male and female. This can occur through making a list, a collage, writing letters, or a story about themselves and their future. Being directive with adolescents and encouraging them to take on both male and female characteristics is a proactive approach to positive role development in the future.

"The ideal male for my future will have . . ."

"Women, I find most attractive, can do these things . . ."

TRAUMA ASSESSMENT PERSPECTIVE;

This activity deals primarily with the Developmental Perspective of the Trauma Assessment. Male/female role training can have an extremely destructive effect on victims unless eradicated and re-evaluated. Victims tend to repeat the same cycles of abuse due to role training within their household and this activity will be helpful in eradicating those tendencies if they are sexist and destructive.

#89

MY DAY IN COURT

OBJECTIVES:

1) Children will gain understanding of positive support through the legal system.

2) Children will reduce fears and anxiety in anticipation of the court process.

3) Children will gain skills in being sympathetic and empathic toward others.

AGE GROUP:

Age 12 and under

SUPPLIES:

1) Publication, <u>My Day at the Courthouse</u> by Nan Chamberlain

2) Furniture to be arranged so a court role-play can be simulated

3) Possible transportation to the courthouse

4) Possible photographs of the local courthouse

5) Camera

6) Poster, construction paper, blackboard

PROCESS:

This publication, <u>My Day at the Courthouse</u> by Nan Chamberlain, is a small inexpensive, cartoon book about children testifying in court. Treatment specialist should examine the book to find ways to illustrate certain concepts to children since not all children will have a personal copy.

When the presentation of the publication has been completed through reading, artwork, etc., the treatment activity should allow children to make lists of fears and anxieties about the legal process. These lists could be made on a blackboard, on paper, or on poster. Children should be able to understand that the court process may be frightening because it is unknown but that, after feelings are addressed, fear can be resolved through awareness and education about the court process. The lists of feelings and anxieties should be made permanent for each child's scrapbook.

Role Play

Role playing of a court process could occur in some groups. It would be especially important for some victims to "testify," but it is also important for other victims to adapt the role of judge, jury, prosecutor, or attorney. Each one of these roles should be defined and children should gain a sense of comfort as the roles are represented by their friends.

Under Control

Eventually, children should become desensitized to the court process either through role playing in group or through an actual visit to the courthouse. Therapists may need to consider avoiding contamination of pending legal cases through their treatment activity. Allowing a variety of testimonies from a variety of children will be most effective and will avoid problems. It is also helpful for children to learn to be empathic and supportive of other group members as the role playing or court visitation occurs.

This activity can be enhanced if the role playing or actual involvement in the courthouse is recorded on camera or on videotape. For those children who will be actually testifying, the process of watching themselves in practice testimony can be desensitizing and helpful.

TRAUMA ASSESSMENT PERSPECTIVE:

This treatment activity pertains to the Relationship Perspective of the Sexual Victim Trauma Assessment where the identification of the perpetrator and the victim is blurred. This treatment activity also pertains to the Situational Perspective of the Trauma Assessment where victims suffer from post-disclosure trauma.

#90

LETTERS FROM MYSELF

OBJECTIVES:

1) Children will be able to express oppositional feelings in regards to self-assessment.

2) Children will gain skills in stopping the motion of trauma bonding.

3) Children will be able to make a more accurate assessment of assets and liabilities.

AGE GROUP:

All Ages

SUPPLIES:

1) Pencils/Pens

2) Writing Paper

3) Construction Paper (for younger children)

4) Magic Markers

5) Envelopes

6) Crayons or Other Decorating Markers

7) Magazines

8) Scissors

PROCESS:

This treatment activity attempts to encourage expression of oppositional feelings within children that typically contributes to movement in trauma bonding. Feelings of self-hate, depreciation, humiliation and depression encourage feelings of hopelessness and, in fact, allow the "pleading, begging child" to emerge in the perpetual motion of trauma bonding. Additionally, feelings of stress, anger, frustration often contribute to implementation of the "raging child," which compliments the "pleading child" and also creates perpetual motion in the trauma bond.

Trauma Bonding

Therapists should recognize that the seeds for trauma bonding are planted in early childhood. By the time younger victims are adults or adolescents, they may be in constant, perpetual motion with their pain due to oppositional forces that have been internalized. This treatment activity is extremely important for allowing victims to recognize these conflicts and then work toward a balance.

Get It Out

This treatment activity should begin with encouraging victims to understand oppositional feelings and to participate in self-assessment. Role playing or other demonstrative activities could occur so that children understand that most individuals are commonly faced with feelings of self-depreciation and internal regret. Obviously, some sexual victims will have a tendency to emphasize self-criticism, but if the treatment process not only allows this activity, but encourages self-depreciation in a demonstrative way, desensitization may occur.

Children may wish to write letters to themselves emphasizing negative points. For younger children, assistance may be needed, but some activity such as making collages with negative pictures found in magazines may suffice. This treatment step should recognize that self-criticism is normal, especially when self-appreciation occurs.

Now, the Good Stuff

The second step in this process is to teach victims to be as demonstrative and verbal in the opposing position, self-appreciation. Many therapeutic endeavors fail in this treatment step if the previous option was not used. In other words, children who feel guilty, responsible and humiliated are not likely to initially accept positive statements about themselves. If, however, with grandiose preparation and demonstration, victims were allowed to express negative feelings, a greater opportunity to feel comfortable in expressing positive feelings will automatically occur. The process should be "equalizing."

Children may wish to write themselves letters proclaiming positive ideations and assets. Decorations could be made on the outside of envelopes indicating even more positive representations. The treatment process should allow children to have both representations equally balanced before moving toward the last phase of this treatment process.

Both, for the Balance

The ideal portrayal in breaking the trauma bond involving the "raging child" and the "pleading child" is to have an acceptance of both feelings in addition to control and moderation. Adolescents may choose to write poetry or letters accepting both facets of themselves in verbal form. Some children may choose to make a picture of themself drawing one hand with feelings of negativism and the other hand with more positive ideations. Other children may simply choose to have their picture taken holding both envelopes or collages. The trauma bonding stops with balance and the final step in this treatment activity should be to create a tangible representation of the child in balance and in control.

TRAUMA ASSESSMENT PERSPECTIVE

This treatment activity pertains to both the Relationship and Situational Perspectives. Trauma bonding can occur with people because the identification of the victim and the offender is blurred or the trauma bond can develop because of distorted thinking patterns which will be revealed in the Situational Perspective of the Trauma Assessment.

#91

LETTERS TO MYSELF

OBJECTIVES:

1) Children will gain skills in resolving feelings about abandonment and rejection.

2) Children will gain an understanding of existing support.

3) Children will resolve issues within the relationship triangle.

4) Children will be able to move from status as a "victim" toward "survivorship."

AGE GROUP:

All Ages

SUPPLIES:

1) Writing Materials

2) Pens/Pencils

PROCESS:

As children move toward the completion of treatment, their scrapbooks should also be moving toward completion. Proactive treatment approaches will look toward the future and confiscate all possible positive contributions that will imprint children in future years, long after the therapeutic involvement has terminated.

Relationship Trauma

Revisiting the relationship triangle, therapists should become aware of support for children that is known or unknown. As children are completing the final stages of their treatment, they will be aware of their scrapbooks moving toward fruition. Whether children are very young or in late adolescence, this treatment activity should assist children in making lists of desired contributions for their scrapbook.

For those children who asked for the impossible (i.e., a letter from a mother who is imprisoned in another state and who has emotionally abandoned the child), a proxy letter should be offered. It is also important to realize that many children will not be aware of their needs in the future and, therefore, therapists should elicit requests from children through sensitive questioning. As an example, if a young man has an elderly grandmother who seems to be reasonably supportive in a subtle way, proactive intervention would recognize that his grandmother will, more than likely, not be alive when this victim is in need of her affirmation. Even though the young man may not be seeking her letter, therapists must elicit that request in appreciation of his future needs.

Children should write letters designed or directed by therapists requesting individual letters. This letter should be created by children in a positive way. Younger children could write a letter similar to this example:

> Dear Aunt Suzie,
>
> I'm almost finished with therapy. They say I did great. Would you like to write about that, too?
>
> Love,
>
> Billy

Therapists should write a cover letter giving clear directions to individuals who have been solicited. Letters should first affirm the status of the child as a victim, but then speak of survivorship. Letters should be positive and helpful. Many individuals will resist writing letters if they have no direction or samples. Therapists would benefit from sending a very simple example of what would be helpful to the child.

It is also important to protect children from extreme vulnerability. Victims should not be requesting letters from individuals who are likely to resist. The Trauma Assessment should provide pertinent information so that children will not be disappointed.

It is also important to recognize that many inconsequential people nonetheless make an important contribution to children's recovery. Janitors, clerical staff, or even unknown, but important figures, such as the state governor, the branch manager of child protection agency, etc., can present letters to children with a powerful impact and very little effort.

TRAUMA ASSESSMENT PERSPECTIVE:

This treatment activity pertains to both the Relationship Perspective and the Situational Perspective. Resolution of relationships can often occur when individuals who were either not supportive of the child or when the support was unknown to the child can make important contributions to the scrapbook. This treatment activity could also pertain to the Situational Perspective and post-disclosure issues that can be resolved through scrapbook contributions.

#92

BE SAFE...BE AWARE

ACTIVITY OBJECTIVES:

1) Children will be able to gain skills in protecting themselves from future abuse.

2) Children will be able to understand their status as a "victim" relieving guilt regarding participation in sexual contact.

3) Children may be relieved from feelings of helplessness and hopelessness as relating to their sexual abuse.

AGE GROUP:

10 and Under

SUPPLIES:

1) Board Game "Be Safe...Be Aware" by Kevin McGovern

2) 3 x 5 Cards

3) Construction paper

4) Markers/pens/pencils

5) Camera

6) Certificates

PROCESS:

This treatment activity allows children to accomplish treatment objectives while they are participating in a board game. The game, Be Safe...Be Aware, provides an understanding of protection of children and helps children understand different kinds of touching. The board game is generic, however, and needs to be enhanced with questions inserted into the "cards" of the game that relate specifically to victims needs. This is not to suggest that the cards should not be used, however, issues in the Relationship, Developmental, and Situational Perspectives of each victim's Trauma Assessment could be written on "prepared" cards and used in place of the game cards which are included in the Be Safe...Be Aware game. In this way, children will relate to their own trauma issues while playing the game and more rehabilitation can occur.

As with all treatment activities, some tangible representation of success must be created to capture the success of the game. Children may wish to have a picture taken of themselves holding up the board, the box, or other items. Children could receive certificates for completing the "Be Safe . . .Be Aware" game. Not only should the game be played, but children should capture what was learned in the game for their scrapbooks.

TRAUMA ASSESSMENT PERSPECTIVE:

This treatment activity could deal with any section of the Trauma Assessment. Those issues that are painful for children in the Relationship realm, Developmental or Situational Perspective could all be used for preparing the cards used for playing the board game.

#93

TELLING OR TATTLING

OBJECTIVES:

1) Children will gain skills in understanding the importance of reporting abuse.

2) Children will gain skills in recognizing their support system for reporting sexual abuse.

3) Children will gain skills in problem solving.

4) Children will gain skills in protecting themselves from future abuse.

AGE GROUP:

Children 12 and Under

SUPPLIES:

1) Construction Paper

2) Magic Markers

3) Various Art Supplies

PROCESS:

Tattling or Telling

This treatment activity confronts the confusion children have concerning the difference between "tattling" and reporting sexual abuse. Although the treatment activity may be simple, this conflict can be significant for children who have been involved in sexual abuse where a great deal of coercion has occurred. This treatment activity is specifically important for children who have been sexually abused by children, as well.

The first step in the treatment process is to have children understand the concepts of tattling and telling. Scenarios should be presented by therapists describing situations where children are tattling. The difference between telling and tattling should be that tattling occurs when children have the ability to solve problems on their own. Demonstrating this concepts will be most effective if children are able to view a demonstration.

Problem Solving

An example of a demonstration could occur with perhaps two children eating lunch together and one child spills his milk. Rather than helping her brother with paper towels and napkins, Amanda runs and tells her mother about her clumsy brother. Children should be able to recognize that Amanda had other options and that it would have been more helpful if she had assisted her brother rather than tattling.

A wide variety of trouble shooting techniques could be explained to children. This portion of the treatment activity could be expanded to such issues as anger management, improving communication or gaining skills in communication and empathy. Children should be able to gain a sense of empowerment and control as they learn better ways to deal with their problems than "tattling."

The next step in the treatment process must teach children that telling about sexual abuse should always occur. Again, role playing activities may be most helpful, especially those that involve children attempting to sexually offend other children. Children should be encouraged to tell adults (and keep telling) any information about sexual contact.

The treatment activity could close with children either making lists or acting out scenarios where they clearly demonstrate their understanding of the difference between tattling and telling. This treatment activity can be enhanced if children are able to share their success with parents. This is also a treatment activity that could earn a "certificate" for understanding the concept.

TRAUMA ASSESSMENT PERSPECTIVE:

This treatment activity pertains to the Situational Perspective of the Sexual Victim Trauma Assessment where children have the potential to develop inappropriate coping skills. Learning problem solving techniques will be helpful to victims and feelings typical for children who did not report abuse (such as guilt and responsibility) can also be alleviated through this treatment activity.

#94

BIG "D" OF DENIAL

OBJECTIVES:

1) Children will be able to express feelings regarding abandonment and rejection.

2) Children will be able to gain skills in understanding how sexual offenders manipulate.

3) Children will be able to gain skills in becoming active community members concerning sexual abuse.

4) Children will be able to resolve relationships that have initiated traumatic responses.

AGE GROUPS:

Children age 12 and older

SUPPLIES:

1) Offender denial resources

2) Paper

3) Large paper or blackboard

4) Markers (large and small)

5) Index cards

6) Printing material capacity

PROCESS:

Denial Definition

The first step in this treatment process is to initiate an understanding of the treatment activities' purpose. The definition of the word "denial" should be processed, helping victims understand that tremendous resistance exists in accepting the reality of sexual abuse from offenders, from the community and from families. It is important for victims to learn about denial since the result of denial is that many victims feel abandoned, guilty and neglected. The words DENIAL can be written on a blackboard and other examples of denial not connected to sexual abuse may begin the discussion, such as "denial" surrounding studying for a test or "denial" concerning a chore list that requires cleaning a room. Typical denials used by everyone should be the focus of this large list.

Community Denial

The next step is to process an understanding of denial about sexual abuse in three separate areas. The first kind of denial can emerge from the community. Index cards could be prepared by group members with statements from community members in denial. Examples of those statements could be:

> "Of course, I care about sexual abuse of children, but that happens in big places, or in New York City, not in my hometown."

> "I know children lie about trucks and cookies, so they must be lying about sexual abuse, too. I can't believe it would really happen."

> "Sexual offenders may exist, but they're probably drug dealers or criminals, not the kind of people who live in my neighborhood."

Children involved in this treatment process should become outraged at community denial, but should also become educated. Many victims feel as though they have been singled out and that their abandonment or trauma is unique. This assignment will help children recognize that denial not only takes place in their own families or situations, but is prevalent throughout the United States and in most communities.

Family Denial

The next step should teach recognition of denial in families. Again, index cards could be presented or a list could be prepared on a blackboard. Role playing also can be an effective way to "listen in" on a conversation between family members accentuating and describing denial systems in families. Therapists would benefit from taking great care to include on the index cards, examples of actual issues of family denial that have existed and emerged in the specific Trauma Assessment of group members. Whenever possible, the role-plays should be video taped and previewed later.

Offender Denial

Finally, sex offender denial should be presented. Children should be flooded and bombarded with many examples of offender denial. Lists or 3 x 5 cards should contain such statements as:

"I did so many good things for him. What does it matter?"

"It was only sex education. I didn't hurt her at all."

"I was abused as a child and that's why this happened."

"She wanted it."

"I just wanted to be close to him. It really didn't hurt anyone."

"I was drunk when this happened."

"He kept coming into my room, and I could tell that he wanted to have sex with me."

If children are bombarded with fifty different examples of denial used by offenders, their own personal scenarios of offender denial may seem less significant. If, as an example, the victim's offender only used one or two forms of denial, a sense of relief may occur if the victim recognizes the possibility of fifty types of denial.

Now, to Home

The next step in this treatment process is to personalize the trauma of denial felt by all victims. Victims may need to make a chart of their families, communities, and offender's denial systems or make some other representation such as drawings, letters, or collages of denial for the scrapbook. This process should be done carefully and slowly as victims may tend to hurry to avoid the pain.

Finally, children need to take part in a very positive kind of activity where they prepare a list of how they would like to change circumstances relating to denial. This is a positive reframe of denial. As an example concerning community denial, the group may want to make a "public alert" list and actually contemplate publicizing the list in a newspaper or for distribution to school faculties. These presentations could be a proactive step to breaking community denial. Efforts may be made to print this public alert on paper that could be distributed at PTA meetings, the Mental Health Clinic or churches. The local newspaper may, in fact, want to publish a public alert written by a group of sexual victims.

The positive reframe of the offender's or family's denial can occur in a variety of ways. Some children may want to write a "wish list" of what they would like their family to know about sexual abuse. As another example, letters to family members that may or may not be delivered, is an effective way of combatting the trauma through denial. It will not suffice to simply have the issue of denial understood, a positive reframe or proactive intervention changing denial, is important.

TRAUMA ASSESSMENT PERSPECTIVE:

This treatment activity primarily pertains to the Relationship Perspective and the Situational Perspective of the Sexual Victim Trauma Assessment. Statements or conversations found in the situational scene of sexual abuse will be important. Relationship trauma will also be important to understand for each unique victim in order for this assignment to be successful.

95

CIRCLES OF DISTRESS

OBJECTIVES:

1) Children will be able to understand a variety of coping skills that have developed as a result of sexual abuse.

2) Children will be able to recognize the negative impact of these coping skills on daily functioning.

3) Children will be able to recognize how some coping skills have a tendency to produce aggressive or angry responses while other coping skills tend to move toward depression or anxiety.

4) Children will understand trauma bonding.

AGE GROUPS:

Adolescents

SUPPLIES:

1) Construction paper

2) Plastic or heavy paper in order to make "hands" (similar to a clock)

3) Felt pens/magic markers

4) Blackboard

5) 3 x 5 Cards

PROCESS:

This treatment activity is designed to assist adolescents in recognizing the "perpetual motion" of trauma bonding. This is a sophisticated treatment activity, but one that is extremely powerful and productive. The general objective is to teach adolescents to recognize coping skills or tendencies they have developed from sexual abuse that tend to direct them out of depression or negativism while other coping skills tend to move in the opposite direction toward internal struggles and depression. Without completing a Situational Perspective of the Sexual Victim Trauma Assessment, and understanding victims' specific coping skills, this treatment activity will be difficult.

Footprints

The first step in the treatment process is to prepare a list on a blackboard or large piece of construction paper of different kinds of coping skills used by individuals who are victims of abuse. The list should encase some of these ideas.

> Helplessness
>
> Avoiding help from anyone
>
> Abusive behavior toward others
>
> Self-abuse
>
> Secrecy
>
> Obsessive Privacy
>
> Amnesia
>
> Dissociation
>
> Cleansing Coping
>
> Symbiosis*
>
> *These examples are presented and described in Just Before Dawn

To enhance this activity, therapists may wish to put these coping skills on 3 x 5 cards with a brief explanation of each coping skill in order to encourage understanding and discussion. Group members may read these out loud and discuss.

Movement Trauma

The next step in the treatment process is to have each adolescent draw a circle of perpetual motion. Next, they should be able to list inside the circle, those coping skills which are primarily used in each adolescent's "circle of trauma" or distress. Some lists can be more specific, depending on the adolescent.

As an example, tendencies toward self-abuse may be specifically described as sexual promiscuity or drug use. Adolescents should learn from this activity that some of these tendencies or coping skills tend to pull the adolescent out of the bottom of the circle, but nonetheless other coping skills tend to keep the adolescent in MOVEMENT by pulling on the other side of the circle of distress. Adolescents should be able to understand that even though tendencies on the left side of the circle tend to pull them out of the depression, they also tend to bring them down the other side having other coping mechanisms that return them to the negative part of the circle. Adolescents may choose to make a "hand" similar to hands on a clock and use the circle during each group to communicate to others the feelings that foster the perpetual motion of distress.

Stop the Motion

Finally, adolescents should be able to discover that being at the top of the circle in a solid, "nonmotion" position pinpoints recovery. Adolescents may choose to super-impose a drawing or some representation of themselves at the top of the circle. Tendencies toward using these coping skills will always exist, however, awareness of the cycle or movement of these feelings will be helpful for adolescents in recovering from sexual abuse trauma.

The circles of distress need to be captured for the scrapbooks. Some group members may want to divide and sepate the opposing issues for the "motion" and use opposites for balancing pages in the scrapbook.

Examples:

"These are the things I remember about my offender that make me feel angry."

Opposing Page

"These are the things I remember about my offender that are good (but that have nothing to do with the crime committed against me)."

TRAUMA ASSESSMENT PERSPECTIVE:

This treatment activity pertains primarily to the Situational Perspective of the Sexual Victim Trauma Assessment. Coping skills that are developed must be understood by treatment specialists and presented into the discussion, in order for this assignment to be successful.

#96

SYSTEM PERPETRATION

OBJECTIVES:

1) Children will gain skills in understanding traumatization that occurs through the "system" response to sexual abuse.

2) Children will gain skills in understanding appropriate and inappropriate responses to discovery of sexual abuse.

3) Children will gain skills in breaking the cycle of sexual offending.

4) Children will gain skills in adapting behavior so that future, potential victims, will not be traumatized.

SUPPLIES:

1) Letter from "Cindy"

2) Role Playing Activities

3) Writing Pens/Pencils, Etc.

4) Writing Paper

AGE GROUP:

Victims Age 12 and Older

PROCESS:

This treatment process attempts to allow victims the opportunity to express frustration and anger about system intervention that was traumatic, but to also teach appropriate system intervention for each victim's future. As the research indicates, sexual victims have the potential to have their own children sexually abused in the future. Proactive therapy will not only allow victims to express frustration about system intervention, but will encourage victims to learn appropriate intervention for their future.

The first step is to desensitize and discuss feelings of trauma that occur for victims once discovery is made. Therapists may wish to expand upon this idea and discuss reasons for secrecy. Eventually, children should be able to describe how the disclosure was interpreted from the victim's perspective. Children who were exonerated and supported need to be encouraged to share that support with other group members who were less favorably treated.

Dear Cindy

Perusal of the poem by "Cindy" may assist victims who were treated favorably, to appreciate the support they received. For victims who were treated unfairly, a sense of comraderie with "Cindy" may provide victims with support and exoneration.

A final step in this treatment activity is to teach the therapeutic group to become proactive. Through the use of group discussion, contemplations could be made regarding how the group can impact system intervention in a more positive way in the future. Letters to Law Enforcement, the Prosecutor, case workers, or therapists may be prepared and either verbalized and resolved in the group process or actually sent to these professionals. Role playing activities may occur for children in a demonstrative group process that allows situations to emerge entitled, "The Way I Would Like It To Be." Whatever proactive technique is used, the emphasis should be constructive and positive, rather than blaming and attacking.

TRAUMA ASSESSMENT PERSPECTIVE:

This treatment activity pertains to the post-disclosure issues of the Sexual Victim Trauma Assessment. Some attention could be made toward the Relationship Perspective which will contribute to how disclosure of sexual abuse is perceived and either discouraged or supported.

Cindy's Poem

...a child's view of incest

I asked you for help and you told me you would
if I told you the things my Dad did to me.
It was really hard for me to say all those things,
but you told me to trust you—
then you made me repeat them to fourteen different strangers.
I asked you for privacy and you send two policemen
to my school, in front of everyone,
to "go downtown" for a talk
in their black and white car—
like I was the one being trusted.
I asked you to believe me,
and you said that you did
then you connected me to a lie detector,
and took me to court where lawyers
put me on trial like I was a liar.
I can't help it if I can't remember times or dates
or explain why I couldn't tell my Mom.
Your questions got me confused—
my confusion got you suspicious.
I asked you for help
and you gave me a doctor
with cold metal gadgets and cold hands
who spread my legs and stared, just like my father.
He said I looked fine—
good news for me, you said, bad news for my "case."

I asked you for confidentiality
and you let the newspapers get my story.
I asked for protection, you gave me a social worker
who patted my head and called me "Honey"
(mostly because she could never remember my name).
She sent me to live with strangers
in another place, with a different school.
I lost my part in the school play and the science fair
while he and the others all got to stay home.
Do you know what it's like to live
where there's a lock on the refrigerator,
where you have to ask permission to use the shampoo,
and where you can't use the phone to call your friends?
You get used to hearing, "Hi, I'm you're new social worker,
this is your new foster sister, dorm mother, group home."
You tiptoe around like a perpetual guest
and don't even get to see your own puppy grow up.
Do you know what it's like to have more social workers
than friends?
Do you know what it feels like
to be the one that everyone blames for all the trouble?
Even when they were speaking to me,
and they talked about was lawyers, shrinks, fees,
and whether or not they'll lose the mortgage.
Do you know what it is like when your sisters hate you
and your brother calls you a liar?
It's my word against my own father's.

I'm twelve years old
and he's the manager of a bank.
You say you believe me—
who cares, if nobody else does.
I asked you for help
and you forced my Mom to choose between us—
She chose him, of course.
She was scared and had a lot to lose.
I had a lot to lose too, the difference was,
you never told me how much.
I asked you to put an end to the abuse—
you put an end to my whole family.
You took away my nights of hell
and gave me days of hell instead.
You've exchanged my private nightmare
for a very public one.

--Feelings by Cindy, age 12

Put into words by Kee MacFarlane, 1970.

Reprinted with permission.

#97

IF I WERE A PARENT?

OBJECTIVES:

1) Children will be able to recognize issues surrounding trauma in relationships.

2) Children will feel a sense of comraderie in discussing feelings and trauma that have occurred in incestuous families.

3) Children will be able to break the cycle of abuse for their future parenting situations.

AGE GROUPS:

10 and older

SUPPLIES:

1) 5 x 7 index cards

2) Pens

3) Pencils

4) Writing paper

5) Some artistic items for decoration of a letter

PROCESS:

This treatment activity is presented to older children as either teaching them to be parents or teaching them to become "helper therapists" to younger children within the treatment clinic. Adolescents sometimes resent direct intervention from adults as a normal part of sexual development. They may accept, however, a treatment intervention that suggests an appreciation of their maturity (whether real or in the process of developing). Framing treatment activities as helping other therapists working with young children, or as preparing the adolescent for being a parent is much more effective.

Dear Mommie and Daddy

Index cards should be prepared with perplexing situations or questions concerning parent/child relationship conflict. These situations should be related to information that is gleaned from group members' Sexual Victim Trauma Assessments. These ideas can relate to relationships or to sexual attitudes. Examples for statements on cards are:

> Your fourth grade daughter comes home after school and says to you, (in front of your very best friend), "What's a period?"

> Your four-year-old son begins crying when you pick him up at daycare. He tells you that one of his teachers "keeps touching my pee pee."

> Your son who has been sexually abused by your husband asks you if it's okay to love his daddy.

> Your nephew tells you that what hurts him most about the sexual abuse that happened, is that his mother (your favorite sister) doesn't believe him.

Specific information from each Trauma Assessment should emerge on the cards presenting scenarios. Children should pass these cards in group and discuss each scenario. Advice should be given and, in some cases, therapists can arrange for, role playing or a skit. It is important to recognize that the **process** of the activity is very important. In other words, if a child asks a question about caring for a sexual offender, the answer should not be given simply, "it's okay." The feelings of ambivalence and confusion for the child should be discussed, the answer should be presented, and perhaps even arguments should be interjected by therapists creating healthy conflict and discovery. The **answer** to the dilemma is not as important as the process in reaching the **answer**.

Finally, children should be able to close this activity by placing some representation of the process and learning in their scrapbooks. Some children may choose to write letters to their parents thanking them for an appropriate responses in the past or write letters that may never be delivered to parents or individuals, either demanding an appropriate response or describing the trauma they have experienced through a parent's inappropriate response. This is a reframing exercise that should allow children the opportunity to describe the trauma they may have experienced, but also look toward the future of resolution. Writing an open letter to the victim's future children may also be helpful in this treatment activity. The purpose is to capture the feelings of trauma experienced by the child through inappropriate parenting and then move toward a future of change.

TRAUMA ASSESSMENT PERSPECTIVE:

This portion of the Sexual Victim Trauma Assessment pertains primarily to the Relationship Perspective. Although some disclosure trauma issues concerning the Situational Perspective will be important, this activity primarily deals with relationships and the trauma from family members' inappropriate responses.

#98

PERIOD

OBJECTIVES:

1) Children will be able to gain a positive attitude about human sexuality.

2) Children will be able to learn appropriate information about functioning of the female reproductive system.

3) Children will gain a positive attitude about medical intervention regarding female hygiene.

4) Children will be able to recognize moods and emotional responses associated with menstruation and hopefully be able to control these emotions through awareness.

AGE GROUP:

10 through Adolescence

SUPPLIES:

1) Publication Period by Louan Lopez and Joni Quackenbush

2) Construction paper

3) Magic markers

4) Xerox copying material or capacity

5) Camera

6) 3 x 5 cards

7) Certificates

PROCESS:

This treatment activity relies on the use of the publication, <u>Period</u>. This is an excellent book designed to teach females about their bodies, especially concerning menstruation and reproduction. The publication could be used for many group sessions or activities.

A variety of processes could be used with group members reading a page and passing the book around the group circle. Another treatment process could include activities where therapists cut the pages out of the book and hand them to group members for perusal and examination. In some instances, publishers will grant permission to copy specific pages of books to use for group discussion. The group process should not only provide accurate information to group members, but group members should make lists of those issues that are learned through the publication. These "learning logs" can be written on 3 x 5 cards or on construction paper.

Therapists will be advised to not move through the publication too quickly, but to focus on certain chapters individually and encourage group members to make a tangible representation of what was learned in each chapter. Eventually, a camera should be involved to take a picture of each group member for their scrapbook with some written testimony about positive descriptions of normal body functions.

Example:

"This is a picture of the outside of my body that works perfectly on the inside."

This group activity may also be enhanced if some kind of quiz or test is given. The test should be constructed by therapists so that the answers are easily understood and attainable. The test could be captured for the scrapbook and certificates of successful completion of the test could be given.

TRAUMA ASSESSMENT PERSPECTIVE

This treatment activity pertains to the Developmental Perspective of the Sexual Victim Trauma Assessment. Trauma to normal sexual development often occurs for victims and negative attitudes toward human sexuality in adulthood is the result. This publication and treatment activity is a positive representation of normal body functioning and reproduction.

#99

THE DONAHUE SHOW —
A PANEL OF OFFENDERS

OBJECTIVES:

1) Children will gain skills in developing a sense of empowerment and assertiveness.

2) Children will gain skills in being able to understand sexual offender etiology and thinking.

3) Children will be able to understand and recognize existing support.

4) Children's fears regarding sexual offenders will be desensitized.

AGE GROUP:

9 through Adolescence

SUPPLIES:

1) A panel of sexual offenders or actors

2) Video camera and VCR player (optional)

3) Writing Paper

4) 3 x 5 Cards

5) Poster Paper

6) Sticks for Mounting Posters

7) Donahue Costume (optional)

PROCESS:

This treatment activity allows sexual victims to either role play interviewing sexual offenders or actually participate in an experience where actual sexual offenders are available for interview. The purpose of this treatment activity is to assist children in feeling a sense of empowerment and in reducing their vulnerability to offenders. It is the process before the activity that has the most productive outcome.

Since this treatment activity has the potential to be emotionally powerful, the opposite of the desired response should be enhanced. Therapists should elicit from children feelings of apprehension, fear and anxiety that was similar to their sexual abuse situations. Trauma Assessment perusal and documentation will be particularly helpful. Specific children need to discuss these fears that occurred during their own personal abuse. Feelings that children express should be exonerated, but not necessarily over-emphasized since the next step will ask children to anticipate being in contact with sexual offenders.

The second step of the process will be completed with children making a decision to confront sexual abusers. Previous to contemplation of this decision should be efforts directing children to over-emphasize their vulnerability to the point of absurdity. Statements could be made as follows:

"I guess we'll all just have to hide from people who do secret touching."

"Do you think anybody is safe, even at the grocery store?"

"How do we know that a person who does secret touching isn't in our soda pop cans?"

Hopefully, through the use of humor and absurdity, children will begin to discuss the issue of out-of-control focus. Therapists can teach children to understand that the majority of people do not sexually offend children and, therefore, safety is more prevalent than vulnerability. Victims should learn the dangers in being constantly fearful of offenders.

The curiosity of children must be aroused in order for them to request contact with offenders. Questions need to be posed,

"I wonder why these people do this."

"If we had a Fairy God Mother, what would we ask people who do secret touching?"

"What would you like most to say to somebody who does secret touching?"

Children must develop a sense of empowerment and assertiveness as they demonstrate their projected responses to sexual offenders should an opportunity arise. Therapists can eventually make suggestions about children confronting offenders, but then the issue should be retracted, reminding children of their earlier feelings of apprehension. This technique will encourage children to convince therapists that they are perfectly capable of being in contact with sexual offenders and that, in fact, they have many questions that need answered. If therapists can be reasonably resistive, children may take it upon themselves to convince therapists of their competency, which is positive demonstration in assertiveness training for victims.

Finally, when victims have convinced therapists that they are interested in confronting offenders, a great deal of work needs to be done preparing questions for sexual offenders. Once questions have been prepared with guidance from therapists, the next process should encourage children to outline their fears regarding the confrontation. Certainly, this activity should not take place if victims are fearful. This is a delicate treatment activity and children should **never** be forced to participate if they are anxious or fearful. Generally, children feel as though they can participate in this activity and being asked to postulate their fears is most often accomplished with indignation and neutrality. Nonetheless, if children prepare on pieces of construction paper, "25 of the worst things that could happen" and those 25 cards are on the wall of the room where the offender panel takes place, it is very likely that none of those events will occur and even if one event does happen, but 24 other possibilities do not occur, victims have a sense of accomplishment.

Finally, if sexual offenders are not available, this entire process can be completed with offender "actors" who could be therapists or other sensitive individuals who would participate in the preparation process, as well. Again, it is the process in anticipating the activity, relieving fears, gaining assertiveness to postulate questions that is the value to this treatment activity. The actual contact with offenders or actors is secondary to the preparation process.

TRAUMA ASSESSMENT PERSPECTIVE:

This treatment activity primarily pertains to the Relationship Perspective of the Sexual Victim Trauma Assessment. Relationship conflict between the victim and the offender can be re-enacted and role played for resolution. Additionally, some issues surrounding post-disclosure traumatization may occur or issues relating to footprints of helplessness pertaining to the Situational Perspective can be resolved.

#100

SURVIVORSHIP — THANK YOU

OBJECTIVES:

1) Children will gain skills in recognizing existing support system.

2) Children will gain skills in developing a positive attitude toward interagency system.

3) Children will gain skills in developing a sense of survivorship.

4) Children's sense of abusability and "victim status" will be alleviated.

5) Children will gain a positive attitude toward mental health intervention.

AGE GROUPS:

All Ages

SUPPLIES:

1) Completed scrapbook of each victim

2) Thank you notes

3) Writing material

PROCESS:

This is a very basic, but important treatment process to be implemented previous to the "graduation" of each sexual victim. A sense of survivorship, balanced with a clear status of the "victim" (innocent child) is important to emphasize and exemplify the progress made in treatment as the scrapbook is implemented. Previous to graduation, however, the scrapbook should be perused by the victim for the purpose of responding to those individuals who have made important contributions. This treatment approach may receive criticism from some professionals who wish to have the victim status clear and wish to place the child in a position of "no requirements for reciprocity." The process of trauma bonding, however, would suggest that a balance is preferred and a sense of "survivorship" will be encouraged in victims who first receive testimonials and total support from professionals and others, but who, at the closure of their treatment reciprocate in an empowering manner.

Thank You for Survivorship

It is recommended that previous to the "graduation" ceremony for the victim, children should be able to peruse their scrapbooks and list those individuals who made appropriate contributions. Thank you notes should be prepared and through this process, children will move from the status of being a victim to an empowering position of survivorship. Children must feel a sense of reciprocity if the presentation can be made in a productive and positive way. The message should not be:

> "I must be grateful for everyone who has contributed to my scrapbook."

Rather, a powerful and empowering approach should suggest equality and the "right to reciprocate":

> "I feel so great thanking these people, they have the right to receive my thank you."

Trauma Assessment Perspective

This treatment activity pertains primarily to the Relationship Perspective and the Situational Perspective of the Sexual Victim Trauma

Assessment. Contributions from professional people assist children in recognizing support from "significant others" involved in the relationship triangle. Additionally, feelings of abusability, helplessness and inadequacy are often coping skills developed by victims and discovered in the Situational Perspective of the Trauma Assessment. This final treatment activity should encapsulate and emphasize victims' existing support and should encourage the belief in additional support for victims as they move toward the status of survivorship.

#101

GRADUATION

OBJECTIVES:

1) Children will gain a positive sense of treatment closure.

2) Children will gain a positive feeling toward mental health intervention.

3) Children will be able to recognize a support system.

4) Children will be able to improve self-esteem.

AGE GROUP:

All Ages

SUPPLIES:

1) Ribbons

2) Graduation Certificates

3) Gifts

4) Flowers

5) Any Other Representations of a "Ceremony"

PROCESS:

Sexual victims need to have a positive closure for treatment in order to create a positive attitude about mental health intervention and in order to enhance the entire treatment process. When children simply leave treatment, without a grandiose celebration, all issues accomplished in the treatment process are less powerful.

Each therapeutic environment will have different limitations and resources. The ultimate opportunity would allow children to send out invitations to their graduation and then actually participate in a ceremony, with the ceremony being attended by those significant individuals in the relationship perspective. Ideally, agency people could participate such as representatives from a Prosecuting Attorney, Law Enforcement, Child Protection, or any other individuals who participate in either the child's specific case or who are in a general position on an interagency child abuse team.

Ideally, speeches would be given, awards would be presented, children would dress formally, and autographs of congratulations would be signed in the last pages of each child's scrapbooks. For other agencies or for therapists with less resources, some limitations might occur, but striving toward the ultimate is very important.

However, it is important to realize that professional participation in positive aspects of sexual abuse treatment for victims is not only helpful for children, but it is also helpful for professionals to see the "product" of treatment under positive conditions as demonstrated through a graduation ceremony.

TRAUMA ASSESSMENT PERSPECTIVE:

This treatment activity primarily pertains to the Relationship Perspective of the Trauma Assessment at least as far as invitations and participants would be concerned. Some issues within the Situational Perspective preventing distorted views about guilt and responsibility would also be pertinent to this activity.

RESOURCES

Polese, Carolyn. <u>Promise Not To Tell</u>, New York, NY: Human Sciences Press, Inc.

Davis, Laura. <u>The Courage To Heal Workbook: For Women and Men Surviors of Child Sexual Abuse</u>, New York: Harper & Row Publishers.

Baird, Kristin. <u>My Body Belongs To Me</u>, Circle Pines, MN: American Guidance Service, Inc.

Chamberlin, Nan. <u>My Day At The Courhouse: A Book For A Child Who Will Be Witness In Court</u>, West Linn, OR.

Adams, Caren; Fay, Jennifer & Loreen-Martin, Jan. <u>No Is Not Enough: Helping Teenageers Aviod Sexual Assault</u>, San Luis Obispo, CA: Impact Publishers.

Hindman, Jan. <u>A Very Touching Book</u>, Ontario, OR: AlexAndria Associates.

McGovern, Kevin B. <u>Alice Doesn't Babysit Anymore</u>, Portland, OR: McGovern & Mulbacker Books.

Golden-Mandell, Joan and Damon, Linda. <u>Group Treatment for Sexually Abused CHildren</u>, New York: The Guilford Press.

Gardner-Loulan, JoAnn; Lopez, Bonnie & Quackenbush, Marcia. <u>Period</u>, Volanco, CA: Volcano Press.

Mayle, Peter. "<u>Where Did I Come From?</u>", New York, NY: Carol Publishing Group.

Mayle, Peter. "<u>What's Happening To Me?</u>," New York, NY: Carol Publishing Group.

Morgan, Marcia. <u>Safetouch</u>, Eugene, OR: Rape Crisis Network.

Morgan, Marcia. <u>My Feelings</u>, Eugene, OR: Migima Designs.

Adams, Caren and Fay, Jennifer. <u>No More Secrets</u>, San Luis Obisp., CA: Impact Publishers.

Cavanagh-Johnson, Toni. <u>Human Sexuality</u>, Los Angeles, CA: Children's Institute International.

Cavanagh-Johnson, Toni. <u>"Let's Talk About Touching"</u> Game, Los Angeles, CA: Children's Institute International.

Narimanian, Rosemary. <u>Secret Feelings and Thoughts</u>, Philadelphia, PA: Rosemary narimanian.

Hindman, Jan. <u>IMPACT: Sexual Exploitation Interventions for the Medical Professional</u>. Community Health Clinics, Nampa, ID and AlexAndria Associates, Ontario, OR.

Schoen, Mark. <u>Bellybuttons are Navels</u>, Buffalo, NY: Prometheus Books.

Gil, Eliana. <u>The Healing Power of Play: Working with Abused Children</u>, New York and London: The Guilford Press.

Samenow, Stanton. <u>Inside the Criminal Mind</u>, New York, NY: Times Books.

Davis, Nancy. <u>Once Upon a Time...Therapeutic Stories to Heal Abused Children</u>, Oxon Hill, MD.

Davis, Samuel M. & Schwartz, Mortimer D. <u>Children's Rights and the Law</u>, Massachusetts/Toronto: Lexington Books.

McGovern, Kevin B. <u>Be Safe . . .Be Aware Game</u>, Portland, OR: Alternatives to Sexual Abuse.

James, Beverly. <u>Treating Traumatized Children</u> , McMillan Publishing.

Hindman, Jan. <u>Just Before Dawn</u>, Boise, ID: Northwest Printing.

Hechler, David. <u>The Battle and the Backlash: The Child Sexual Abuse War</u>, Lexington, MA: Lexington Books.